Everyday People ...At work & play..FAMILY *foibles...kerfuffles and lifelong scars....*

A collection of short stories. Looking at Life & People, striving for and against each. Fiction dons the cloak of truth......exposing. Treachery, deceit, invasion and abandonment from most unlikely sources.

Some suggestive language & patois snippets !!!

Amusing satire by Jamaican Raconteur and

Author :   Colleen G. Lowe

Published by: Lignum-Vitae Investments, a dba of Import-Export Solutions, Inc. P O Box 831896, Miami-Dade Fl. 33283-1896 Email: Muteelegance@gmail.com

For volume purchases or distribution arrangements. Kindly contact Publisher at above address. Printed in the United States of America. First printing January 2020. Reformatted to Times New Roman 11 point for easier reading and re-edited. Fourth edition printing June 2022

Read excerpts and buy online at: Theglenwoodcollection.com.

Also sold on Amazon/Kindle. Search: Colleen G. Lowe

Delivery confirmation & USPS tracking data: 305-794-4820

ISBN-13: 978-0999122969 ISBN-10: 0999122967

Guaranteed uncompromized CLEAN.....Press to your Palm

Dedications..

....my mother Fredricka who gave me the gift of life. God grant her eternal rest.....

....my grandmother Louise, who loved and mothered me. Proving at times, love is a hurting thing......

....my father Henry, taught me wisdom to live life by. I still miss someone....

....the Darby's ,Tom and Rhoda. Sheltered our family from ravage of hurricane Charlie, sparing three lives. Friday August 17th, 1951

....the "Bunchie–genuine as sunrise". Loved me without parameters as only a woman can.....

.....every woman who unselfishly gave of herself, sustaining life and civilization. You are indeed God's gift to mankind....

Contents..

Autographs and Observations:

Everyday People at work and play. Fourth edition, revised and reformatted for EasyRead 11pt.-Fourth printing 06-2022. Peace, love and positive vibes in earth runnings.......Colleen Glonc Lowe

Foreword

Nostalgia is a feature of some people's present day existence, as they compare now and then with sublime expectations for future. 1968, Welsh folk singer Mary Hopkins' titled hit song. "Those were the days." Chorus line states. *"We'd fight and never lose. We'd live the life we choose. For we were young and sure to have our way."* In essence this reinforces youth's dominance, pursuing that which sates their appetite. If only because it is nature of youth to have their way by fight rather than truce. Let me hasten to assuage sensibilities, lest seed of discord be sown. Fight did not entail combat, resulting in injury and magisterial appearance. This was roiling ocean's floor bringing plankton to surface. Providing nourishment on which relationships thrived. There were less broken homes, children had benefit of dual parental guidance, so woefully lacking today. One youthful fixation I recall, was getting it on. Island life has natural tolerance for promiscuity, in pursuit of which some societies might not encourage. Yet rife in cross sections of such societies. Undeniable fact is, this pastime is prevalent within citadels of these societies. Life mirrors that of plebes as applies to intimacy escapades. When the feeling moves me let me groove you, kind of expectation. As in things of this nature, it takes two. If she is reluctant, there might be need to coax and persuade. This having failed, foreplay gets elevated and soon there's jostling and wrestling. Times this employed strategy of One wearing down other, at which time, towel's thrown in. She grudgingly concedes and lowers the drawbridge, he enters and is gratified. When new day dawns, she fixes him a working man's breakfast. A wife rationalized denying husband's frequent intimacy overtures, as ensuring she is not taken for granted. Rolling over and spreading her wings, devalues her virtue. Reminded there are fields wide open where he can happily graze. She stridently retorts. That's valid reason hating some women. Whose only life purpose is to break up happy marriages. I hasten to assure, this pursuit of will is not male dominated scenario. Oh no, it's not. Times, female initiates similar misguided pursuit in abject futility. Given there are obvious anatomical differences. Just about time this song was popular, I rented room from a couple. Two female boarders shared third bedroom. Still of night was often broken, by her swearing at, prodding him to pursue intimacy. We all know, unlike her, male needs a rising to occasion before he can participate. He being unwilling to be goaded. Does she not understand she's flogging a dead horse? How is this going to work to her satisfaction any time soon? Reinforcing truth of adage, regarding woman scorned. One night, he repaired to the car. She smashed every glass on it. Front, rear, side and headlights. After a year collecting rain, health team attached citation as mosquito breeding pond. It was sold to scrap yard dealer. Yet through all this aftermath, there was civility and camaraderie as expected of married couples. No talk about anyone put in dog's house, or calling for police intervention. Why? Because those were the days my friend, we thought they'd never end. Then came era of women's lib, which should have been accompanied by men's lib. Men do not want to be seen as disadvantaged and crying out for help. So when she says. No. That's what it means. Dude tries persuading, she hollers rape, he's off to hoosegow. Used to be, wife could not be raped by husband, in eyes of law. At least that's how it was in enclaves of Third World paradise. If question arose, it was explained as mere foreplay. Enjoyed by both in privacy of home. Unless of course, there was blood letting or visible bruising. The law intervenes, wife refuses to support prosecution. Bails her man from jail, they hug and kiss right there. Then go home and make love, each being remorseful for recent misdeed, passions rekindled.

First World has penchant incarcerating it's citizens. Prisons are a billion dollar industry with untold profits. Returns seem picayune, but when services are added for millions of heads. Therein lies difference in wealth creation. Pages ahead, Jean reprimands employee over unauthorized Gestetner^{tm} machine use. Bright electronic devices savants asks. What was that? Duplicating machine by British inventor, David Gestetner, standard office equipment then. Stenciled message, typed or hand written was attached to inked platen, turned by hand to print message on paper. Arm fatigue was relieved by newer, motorized models. Telephone switchboards, size of a jukebox. Had capped cords, which when plugged into sockets, made connections. A cable machine used addresses similar to web addresses. Telex machine was companion to, in most cases.

1971, I opened a business, having to go to nearest "Cable and Wireless" office, sending cablegrams to England. Office phoned when response came, customers went and collected. For fee, cable office would collect outgoing messages and bring responses, by courier on bicycle. One office machine surviving that era and upgraded, is postage franking machine. Brass balancing scale with weight denominations are kept in archives. Watch pawn sites, see someone walk in and ask an outrageous price. Someone expressed mental confusion to me recently, regarding touted jobs boom. Citing termination from her job of seventeen years. Agreed, there's misleading data in reports highlighting jobs created, whilst omitting jobs lost. This, from industrial modernization and automation. Let's look at electricity distribution. Cadre of meter readers, door collectors and disconnect technicians. Lost their jobs to smart meters, supported by beacon tower or pole mounted gadgetry. Technology infrastructure requires maintenance by skilled technicians. Those made redundant, could not be trained to grasp support technology of new apparatus. Hence, two hundred $25 per hour, ground pounding, gate rappers. Often running gauntlet of fierce dogs, and losing the sprint. Lost jobs they held for up to twenty years and more. For them, it was comfortable no brainer task with good benefits. Taking them to retirement, pensions and 401 IRAs. After schooling children, paying off mortgage, college loans and vacation tab. Their grandchildren are genii stepping into these new jobs. At salaries eclipsing that $25 an hour, they thought. Made them exclusive in job market of minimum wage earners and $14 an hour ceiling. That's how progress creates career opportunities for some, making others redundant. It applies to occupations at every level. Heyday of Sears Roebuck, entire floor was occupied by accounting staff. IBM computer in box space, made them redundant. If One cannot change with times, One gets cast aside. Those days my friend, we thought would never end, do end sooner or later. Look ahead, ask yourself. If tomorrow comes, how will it be different from today and how will I fit in? Am I ready to observe and not participate?

Threaten the Lychee Tree-1

My Lychee tree was ten years in the ground, before it began fruiting, sparsely but promising. Following year it bloomed aplenty and shed in similar vein. Yet giving more fruits than year previous. It neither bloomed or fruited following year, but came 2016 it did so abundantly. Branches bent, hung low under weight of coming harvest. Neighbours admired and asked to buy fruits. Told them, bide good time when fruits are ripe and ready. One sure sign of perfection stage was, birds visiting in flocks. As some of us would, they set up nests and hatched lings in this grove of abundance. Tweets and twitters filled the air, as did incessant chirps of happy lings. Often, exuberance of celebrating with a pirouette. Balance was lost, undeveloped wings flapped in desperation. Gravity and nature rewards waiting cat with a meal. Watching this life's pantomime unfold, gives glimpse of actors and chorus performers. In never ending stream before our eyes, that we most times fail to recognize. You know folks, if you took time from hectic pursuit of things that makes life worth living. Adopt a melancholy laid back look at nature's unscripted charades. Unexplored facets of existence, would reward you with hidden joys, so simple and fulfilling. My neighbour began reaping fruits. Passersby came with shekels to buy. Having long ago embraced supporting phrase. *"Best things in life are free."* Gave my harvest to neighbours, expressing surprise and gratitude. Having only Lychee tree in our small community, thought it made for good camaraderie, treating friends and neighbours. My attention was drawn to those four, being all from same family. Between them they were carting away more than fair share of fruits. Whistle blower went on to say. ***"The old guy, sometimes sells Avocado and honey from his truck under the overpass. I'll take you a bet, later on, his stock will include your free Lychee."*** Just goes to show nature of people. We are most of us, self centred and selfish. Focussed on us, we and ours. Sweating under summer heat as I raked leaves and twigs, tinge of remorse crept in.

"Maybe I shoulda sold fruits and be rewarded for all this grunt work." Quickly dismissed thought. Needing exercise, if for no other reason, trying to reduce my gut handles. End of crop was start of hurricane season, fierce storm came through. Taking down half my Lychee and Black Mango trees. All my Otaheiti Apple, Soursop, June Plum and Cashew trees. But, Lychee vegetated surprisingly quick, leading me to expect another bounty crop next season. Alas, this is third season that came and went without it fruiting. My neighbour also expressed surprise, said maybe it needs to be fertilized. Told him I sought farm store experts advice, who recommended 10-10-10 fertilizer. Maybe, it needs threatening, as in the old country, I said. He looked at me all agog. ***"Threaten! What the hell you talking about. How does One threaten a tree?"*** I introduced him to island lore, which brings you in loop also

11

and began. **"Back in the old country, a tree that would not produce or in expected abundance. Friend would come over, gab on this and that. Soon he would ask."** *"Whapp'n, your Ackee tree* (or any tree) *not bearing yet? My own laden, you can see it from Parade."* **"I don't know what happen to it. I throw fowl coob droppings at the root. Collect cow pat and horse dung. Melvin say, must drive piece of rusty iron in the heart, that will cure curse. Friend thinks a bit, then opines".** *"If me was like you, I would give it one more season and if it don't bear. Chop down it backside and plant something else. Shady spot can't full empty belly."* **"I would agree and…. You right. One more season without fruit, it goes into kiln and turn charcoal. Without fail, tree would bear fruit like token in and out season."** He looks at me, still with a dubious mocking snicker, then gets the answer.

"Well, back in old country, you threaten the tree in English or patois it understands. But this is Miami where mostly Spanish is spoken. So you can't threaten this Lychee tree in Jamaican lingo. You have to do the threat in Spanish. Root stock and supporting variables are Spanish derived. So, there my good friend." He ends with a mocking guffaw and continues. *"I heard stories about you island guys, when y'all gulp down that kick ass rum chased with Red Stripe. Bong gets lit and passed around. It's a wonder One of you didn't get into his car and drive to Miami. Drive back and tell his buddies. See? I told you it could be done."* Now he's really yukking it up, but I'm okay with that. Every friend deserves a good laugh, even at his friend's expense. That's what friends are for. If not. Then what's use having friends? Laugh at strangers and they'll probably despatch you to your creator and happy hunting grounds. Now, hear this. Oriental farmers in Miami-Dade Redlands. Employ similar scare tactics, using firecrackers and incendiary devices. It would seem, people of different ethnicity and global origin. Adapt and pursue lore, common to enhancing existence. Others, unfamiliar with, would castigate and ridicule, as inconsequential nonsense. Don't knock what you've never tried.

We wear the Chains we forge-2

From Charles Dickens', "The Cricket On The Hearth" *"We wear the chains we forge in life."* Willy Collins is his father's oldest son, but there's nothing to distinguish either apart. A long time ago, folks pointed to one of five and said. *"That's One of Willy Collins' boy being crazy. He best mind his pappy doesn't come and whoop his behine right there."* In later years, next generation, same folks pointed to one of four and said. *"Lord have mercy, that's One of Willy Collins' crazy assed kids playing the fool again. Them two girls be okay, but them boys needs medicine. Ceptin' the first One though. His mama wears a good head. Got reins on him like a rented plow mule."* Elder Collins' made home years earlier, in neighbourhood that lost lustre with time. Was now referred to as a Hood. Those of kind mind or cliche oriented, preferred "Inner City." Family life was stable, children were educated to acceptable levels. Now had jobs, made them self sufficient. As is customary, they took dislike to the old neighbourhood, dreaded visiting parents. When great housing bubble burst, siblings merged resources. Bought bank repoed property for sixpence and a song. Each gave skill and talent, soon had house restored beyond original grandeur. Mom and pop Collins moved in and all was well. Grandchildren could now visit. Not hear expressions, grating sensitive, suburban ears and horror of horrors. Have them echoed, in or out of context. Children can be like that, hearing strange word first time. Blurt innocently when parson drops in for tea, seeking fund raising committee's support. Before restoration was complete. Siblings had full time chore, saying, *"Not for sale."* to prospective buyers. They sat in council, decided seeking more properties. Each again lending skills, there was fortune to be made. Resignations were writ and handed in by a few. Others clung to County jobs, perks, 401 matched investments and pensions due at retirement. Suffice it to say, things did not go as expected in new venture. What with myriad of people getting similar brainwave. Bidding to acquire same properties. We know, nothing fuels price rise more than demand. But in time, ship jumpers got a hand from others on deck and storm was weathered. Willy Collins stayed in his childhood home and community. Fathered six children he acknowledged, there were three others. Between terrace, lane and street of same number going East to West. And similarly, avenue, court, place going North South. His children lived with their mothers, except last boy. He lived with his father, and daily changing roster of acting stepmothers. However, sandwiched close to each in their neighbourhood. It would not be a stretch, saying they grew together. This last born son was Willy's clone in every respect. Brash and ready to kick and stomp. Boy be playing street soccer, gets winded. Takes and kotches his bony rump on patrol car's fender. Officer Dillon shouts at him. *"Boy, take your overweight behine off State's property. Don't think because you grow up this area and I knew your daddy when he was a minnow. Will stop me slapping you silly, if and when you play fool."* Boy retorted to Trooper. **"All them things you said before, is only reason you don't get hurt."** Game pals ended play, hurriedly walked away that minute. Not wanting to be guilted by association. Willy always told close friends and coworkers, only last boy for sure was his. Others, were called by lottery. He was resolute not seeking paternity tests to find truth. Rudy Daniels told him. **"Dude, that's only sure way you find out who's who and what's what. It's a simple cheek swab, no needle or radiation."** Willy made statement that makes Clarence look smart. We know, intellect is not his strong point. Come to think of it, it's not even his weak point. It's just darned non-existent. Willy said. *"There's thing you guys don't know about DNA testing. If you are minority in this country. No matter which lab you do the test, they send it to government's DNA bank. It's kind of like a sperm bank for minorities and poe ass niggers. Jews, whites and those close to privilege are not included. Government runs your DNA through their unsolved crimes. Next thing, youse is off to do life sentence. That's if youse lucky and not stuck a crime over in Texas. There, they waste no time fry you like bacon* *for breakfast. Did you know, more than three quarters US prison population, are blacks and other minorities? I'm telling you, guys. You better off, sending a kid to school for eighteen years. Rather than do life sentence. Or worse, gets fried for something you didn't do."* Once there was to do on street where he lived and someone called cops. Seeing two patrol units arriving in response. Willy hastened to mid street, hands held high, signalling police to stop. When they did, he hollered.*"Everything's under control, we can handle this on our own. Don't want you killing another young nigger. Because he blinked and you feared for your life."* Cop told him on PA system. **"Sir, step aside this minute. This is your final warning."** In obedience, he said out loud. *"Y'all see? Mother....er said, final warning. When that was first and only warning."* His verbal taunts were ignored.

Parents had issue with mail carrier at their house. Mailbox was enclosed in fast growing, creeping plant. Note left in box, asked homeowner to have vegetation cleared, asap. Failing which, mail would be held at post office for pick up. Told of this, Willy took sick time. Awaited mail carrier's arrival at parent's home. His father asked, where were clippers he brought to trim the bush. Willy told his dad. *"Don't worry pops, got this more than I got anything else."* Dad began saying something and was silenced by Willy who averred. *"Dad, trust me on this."* Moment of truth eventually arrived. Mail carrier slowed, glanced at mailbox, was bent on cruising by. Willy hailed and ran up to his truck. *"Listen up letter man. I know you think you important like other dude on television. Well, I don't care who you are or think you are. My parents don't drive, even if they did. They not gonna go post office for pension checks, just because you say they should. What you call bush, is exotic vines. Have exotic aromatic flowers. All you gotta do, is open box and chuck mail in. Don't try to make out like you mayor or governor."* Mailman told Willy. **"Step back from the vehicle, please."** As he began moving away, Willy shouted. *"Hey!! You know who you dealing with? I will make your neck smaller than* *your pinky, and eyeballs hang loose on your jaws."* Willy's parents were upset. His mom chided. **"What for you come here and act crazy like that? We simply asked you to bring clippers from the shed and clip the bush. Why you got to make federal case of every thing? Don't worry yourself, we will take care of it."** Two days later, bushes were trimmed by landscaper, working at nearby apartment complex. Asked cost, crew member said, it's gratis. There's always solution to issues, without need for confrontation.

Next item Willy brought to discussion board was, his son's education and future. Told the lad to focus on two subjects only, if he wanted success in life. Days of nine to five hustle, was over and done with. Laddy needs only be good at ball and book. Any ball, football, basketball, baseball. *"If you're super good with a ball, wads o money rolls in on zeroes."* Role of book was to make him knowledgeable, managing his wealth. Not get ripped off by greedy managers and agents. It can't be right he taking bruises, and accept being used. In that pursuit he took lad to be enrolled at Ivy League prep school. *"There's reason why white kids and them top cat Hispanics attend that school."* He emphasized, pounding fists on table. Date was set for lad's interview and evaluation. Willy would be advised of outcome. On receipt of result, which was not as expected. He called school's office and tongue lashed person answering. Overstepped boundaries, saying. This and like places, practicing discrimination against black people, should be demolished by fire. Having called from workplace, investigation began by human resources and police. Two days later, Willy called school, from his cellphone, saying. In receipt of their letter regarding his son's failure at acceptance. He's requesting meeting with principal for possible review in lad's favour. Pal, Rudy Daniels in slack jawed awe, asked. **"Dude, what were you thinking? Those place record calls, same as our company. I'll bet you that dam machine or whatever. Can voice match and identify caller. Shoulda did quit while you was behind. I'm telling you as a friend. Give me your bail money, just in case."** Everyone laughed but there was nothing funny about the situation. All went quiet and it was taken, everyone's fear had been without merit. Supervisor arrived at Willy's job site, accompanied by Fleet technician. He was taken aback, not having called in problems with work truck. Supervisor drove Willy to work headquarters, while technician drove his work truck. Willy tried probing without success. Yard manager, his supervisor, union steward and Local's president. Human resources personnel and two men whose affiliation remains unknown. Sat at conference in the training lounge. Broke for lunch and resumed, staying until well past Willy's 15:00 hours shift ended. If he was not being fired, he was at least earning overtime. Next day, meeting reconvened at corporate offices. To this day, Willy. Characteristically verbose on any matter arising. Has not said one word, concerning these unusual events. What he did talk about. Was his girlfriend, having absconded with credit cards, which he reported as lost. *"So, MasterCard gonna either eat that or lock her ass up. If they come asking for her, I give her up faster than whale gave up Jonah. Bitch deserves doing time."* Willy exults, laughs loud and hearty. Not to worry though, he has a new girlfriend. Invites friends to meet and greet at her birthday party. Rudy Daniels and wife arrives, as do many others including yours truly. Not anyone could foresee what was going to happen, unless they had gift of being psychic. We four stood in circle talking about something of mutual interest. Joined by Rudy and his wife, who greets us and goes off to another woman who hails her. Willy hugs Rudy and greets him loud, says close to his ear. *"Hey Rudy, my Bro who's always got my back. I tell you man. I might not say it, but appreciate big time, man. Hey, take a peek and tell me what you think before I make intro. See, the One I told you about? Big milk jugs and tight ass. Go on, take close look and come back."* Rudy goes in the room, returns and says. **"She ain't there Bro, must have stepped out. There's just two of your daughters and friends, yucking and yacking."** Willy's face got knitted and twisted as he pounced on Rudy. *"What the f... you trying to say, Rudy? Come right out, say it mother* *f….er. Don't hide behind snide remarks or dumb jokes. I told you. Woman with huge boobs. She in a see through blouse, light blue jacket and skin fit jeans. She looks like my f…ing daughters or their teenage friends? Why you come to my house, start that kind of ignorant…."* Now, he can't find words expressing himself. Rudy calls out. **"Simone, come on. Now hon, we leaving on the double."** Turning to Willy, he says. **"You, mental, deep. Don't even think doing crap. I've got mine right here."** Pats his hip at waist level. **"So just let your evening end on happy note for you and your guests."** Willy went in the room, found his woman coming from bathroom and hugged her. Desmond, self styled guru from Trinidad said to me. *"It ain't nobody's business, but what true is true. I is see milk that girl mouth corner. No matter how big she breast. We know she nurse big Willy if he want. But she can't reach them to nurse she self. If you got friends, you have to laugh at youself sometimes. If food and liquor mot very come soon, I be leaving this place. Get curry and dahl roti over Guyanese roadhouse."* I ask for clarification. **"Did you say roadhouse as in, Roadhouse Grille?"** *"No, you to clean ears when you bathe. I is say, roach house."* **"If you know the place roach infested. How can you eat there?"** I ask, he replies. *"You is forget when we underground in boondocks. Only roach coach save we from starve. You never complain. What's more, to some people, roast roach be delicacy. Ever hear bout cockroach cocktails? You need start live before you get old and dead. I is gone. Monday, if life does spare."* Cockroach cocktails?

Now we look at essential Willy Collins and see him progress to self destruction. Second son he says, was his homecoming. After serving in US armed forces at age thirty-four. Young man now college sophomore, I will put his age at twenty. From that we can assume Willy to be mid fifties. His chosen career rewards him well, his habit became an addiction. He spends average, hundred dollars daily on lotteries and scratch off games. When jackpots grows to hundreds of millions. He stops at convenience gas station stores, buys twenty dollars

Quick-Pick tickets. It amuses to watch him negotiate traffic at 137 and 152 intersection, having three gas stations. Lore of workplace dictates. Once you wet feet at HR. It's only matter of time, before you sink and drown. First, comes random, computer generated drug tests. That never fails to include some people and exclude others, always. How does one employee gets random tested, five of five sessions in a year? They ask the wind, waits in vain for a whisper. Willy saw and swallowed a bait, got reeled in for dishonesty. Once again he was in a room. With supervision, management, union and HR personnel. It seemed he was going down like Titanic. But, he hollered magic lifeline, "discrimination." You know, like the racial profiling thing? He was baited because he's black. Why weren't any white guys similarly baited? Management responded. If there was indeed baiting, it was there for all and anyone. Others ignored, Willy went for it and should stand consequence. He got off with suspension. This had staunchest allies in awed disbelief. Circumstantial facts brought to light, showed overwhelming culpability. But, everyone was happy for Willy. Hope he took this as omen, wake up alarm. Willy reacted by resigning from the union, no longer a dues paying member. Ridiculed Local's president as incompetent, obese, management's brown noser. Whose drawers must have been squeezing his nuts like a vice. Causing him to accept HR's suspending Willy, without slightest whimper. Whether or not employee pays dues. Union has to argue on his or her behalf, if and when need arises. We know there is **arguing,** and there's *arguing.* Ever ask yourself why, with all available evidence, cigarette smoking kills. So many people continue to indulge this pastime or habit? Because they are addicted, and not strong enough to break free from. Was not long, ere Willy was caught with hands stuck in cookie jar. Asked his defence, went on an abusive tirade. Similar to that engaged in with the prep school. Resulting in unprecedented scene of an employee being escorted off site by corporate security. He has in-demand skill, finds ready employment with contractors. But not with prevailing benefits and perquisites as his former job did. Money is scarce, Willy could not shake his addiction.

Not that he even contemplated doing so. On holiday during break from college. Willy and Sophomore Kid went rumbling. Kid had no way paying forward for tuition and incidentals. Willy told him, he should be grateful having been carried thus far. It was now his turn to fend for himself. A position with which I give total and unconditional support. Find available grants, loans, on or off campus work. There are opportunities out there if he gets up off his fanny and seek them out. They are not going to walk up to his door and knock. Why so resolute in my position? I'll tell you why. What if Willy had dropped dead from an ailment? What if he had been sent up the river for arson threat? See what I'm saying? Be glad you've got someone to help row your canoe, but if he falls overboard and drowns. Don't allow yourself to drift into oblivion and be demised. Get going. This lad, like so many others. Never allowed his mind to drift ahead and ask all important. What if? Accustomed to being literally spoon fed, complacency set in. Was jolted into reality when daddy said, he could no longer be there to prop him up. As things go, it is not a far fetched expectation. Sophomore Kid would rally to encourage and support Willy in whatever way he could. But then, question arises. Was he brought up to be endowed with that kind of unselfish mindset? The song did say, they live what they learn and eventually water will always find it's own level.

A Love Story in Ward 3347-3

Henry was seventeen when uncle Manfred pulled string. Got him a job at railway ticket office. What's "pulling string?" It has to do with puppetry, where person reacts to inducement from another. In instance, practice of cronyism or nepotism. Simon Figueroa sat in a battery powered wheelchair, having lost both legs and an arm. First time meeting, he asked. *"Boy, why you want begin you working days in Dumps?"* Henry interacted with passengers at window, each called destination. First, second class or freight. Freight callers were given ticket to get goods weighed, brought back to window. He took and gave monies to Simon, telling him destination and class. He gave Henry, stamped ticket and change, which he gave to passenger, called. **"Next"** Seeing queue grow, and knowing the train was scheduled to leave soon. Henry got creative and told Simon. **"Two first class to Bristol, two second class to Anchovy."** Felt good seeing his genius at work until he said. **"First class to Catadupa and freight to Anchovy."** Simon looked up, and. *"Say what, son? Repeat what you just said. Make sure you listen to youself."* He confidently echoed, Simon asked. *"So now! If passenger going Catadupa first class. Who the hell going with freight to Anchovy?"* Henry said, they were two different persons. Oh how he snorted like a mule. Dribbled onto his shirt and into a handkerchief. *"You see is one hand them leave me with. How you expect me to serve two people same time? Who the hell made you king to rule over me?"* Shy, now timid. Henry, said he was sorry. Only tried expediting queue, so train did not leave passengers. Simon said, train been running before Henry came. Will run after he leaves, without stranding passenger. There were commercial freight and passenger freight, as obtains in airline industry. All freight went in freight car, passengers claimed at destination. Baggage deemed "excess" was not allowed on passenger cars, hence it was carried as paid freight. Youthful exuberance seeks solutions where no problem exists, it seems. So it was, Henry asked uncle Manfred. Why did railway not employ, able bodied person to ticket office. He too, snorted. Called Henry a dam fool. *"If whole man in there, what them would want you for? Drink milk bwoy, don't count cows and try give them shoes. Them will bruck them backside."*

Walter Pinnock was in charge of freight depot. His assistant was Dickie Bligh, young man mid twenties. He hobnobbed with new boy Henry, borrowing sixpence for lunch. Curious, Henry asked. What was "Tare Weight" painted on freight cars sides. Gross and nett, he knew. Dickie said, that's weight of empty car. Which had to be logged on station manifests. Henry was now more confused than minutes previous, yet did not enquire further. See how a question multiplies ignorance? Perplexity is such a burden and knowledge so exhilarating. Dickie said he had a girlfriend, asked if Henry did. Talked incessantly about his beauty queen, eventually introduced her at prize giving. She was very attractive and rounded as a lass. But giggled without reason and puppy touched. Looking at her intently, Henry saw undeveloped childhood in her face. Desmond would say, nursery milk at her mouth corner. Kind of like fruit exposed to sun that takes a hue as if ripe. Yet has ways being ready to be plucked. Henry asked, Dickie said, Jean was fourteen. Her dad accused her mother having secret affair. Both got into customary fight and he murdered her, when Queen Jean was one year old. Maternal grandparents raised her to about ten, at which age she began taking shape of early puberty. Home was in notoriously poor, almost lawless area. Grampus and Nana knew it would not be long, hooligans and coots would beat path to their door. So it was, the little girl came to live with Mrs. Bligh. Dickie Bligh watched her grow and decided, one fine day she would be his. From Grampus' and Nana's perspective, might not have been best that could happen. It certainly wasn't worst. Henry asked. **"Fourteen, Dickie?"** *"Not really."* He replied. *"Because, next year April she turn fifteen."* Henry did not point out, then was July of her fourteenth year. Not to mention, Dickie was almost twice her age. Henry confided, his chiding was driven by jealousy. Hungered to embrace her in his corner, keeping her safe from Dickie's and everyone's clutches. Self justified this, thinking. Jean was closer to his age than Dickie's. Getting back to rail yard stint. Henry went back to school, his heart wandered wherever Jean roamed. Infatuation faded with years. Henry is now late forties, operating a business that takes him to the docks. There are twin brothers with opposite characteristics. One is reserved and quiet, speaks in a hush. Other is brash, boastful and energetic. Trait that brings him under scrutiny with mixed comments. Operating "Karilift," container straddler stacking machine. Wharfingers agreed, he produces more, but unsafely so. Speed at which he rolls equipment around corners and wharf's front apron. There's fear of accident with terrible consequences. Despite meetings with stevedore's unions, no behavioural change is seen. Something about brothers fascinated Henry. Uncanny resemblance to someone, he knew he knew. Mulling it over, now cocksure.* He said to Brash one day, whilst both waited in canteen queue. **"You daddy Dickie, still at railway?"** *"Yeah man."* He said, not looking back, then went on. *"Him driving bauxite train now. We born to drive big things, cause we have muscles to handle big machines. Bet you soon see me way up there in one of those."* Alluding to gantry cranes that worked container ships. Henry went on. **"So, Jean is your mother?"** He spun round, faced Henry. Waved his arms animatedly and cocked his head around asking. *"You know my people, boss? Who you be?"* One hungry man in waiting, shouted. **"Step up or step out, so grub line can make progress."** Henry did not go that berth daily, young man worked shifts. It was more than month after canteen contact, they ran into each other again. Brash gushed how his parents knew Henry and were anxious for both to reconnect. So it was, after close to thirty years, three reunited. They both appeared quite different, years had not been kind to them. Maybe they thought same of Henry. You know how, "Eyes of the beholder" works. Dickie's face drawn, cheeks sucked in, cheekbones stood up like ridges. Jean had lost youthful glow, eyes did not reflect her smile. A little woman poised girl, say nine or ten gawked at Henry. He bent and asked her name. *"Rosemary."* She beamed, added. *"Me like you, Mr. Man."* Dickie said, sotto voce. *"Rosemarie like every man she see."* Henry could not help stare at her. Took him back to first time meeting Jean. There was happy in her eyes, she had pre-puberty stance and image. Identical to how Jean must have looked. Causing grandparents to hurry her out of Dodge to safety with Bligh family. Here we should break narrative and return to expound on the Dumps. I know you're not satisfied, how it was mentioned in passing and skipped over.**"The Dumps"** Was akin to "The Weeds." Area of dark, secret dives where skulduggery are born and thrives. Just off the waterfront, was all male domain. Where felons sprinted for cover, after crimes on persons. Knowing, chase would be aborted, not daring further pursuit. Nobody saw anything or knew anyone. No matter who was asking. Simon averred repeatedly, it was no place a young man begin his working life. About a mile square, area was bounded West by city's largest cemetery. Gully that drained into the shoreline. North was rail yard and station. East was city's only brewery and soda bottling plant. South was warehouse campus, white buildings where rum was stored for aging. A foreshore road separated these from cardboard and zinc hovels, built on silt and garbage spits, washed down in heavy rainfall. Inside the Dumps were, railway yard and station. Decommissioned gas works. Abattoir, City morgue and sewage treatment plant, sharing borders in that order. Referred to as "Slaughterhouse" "Dead house" and "Shit house" by citizens. Outside Dumps, was hubbub of daily commercial activity. Market district where rural farmers brought and sold crops. Wholesalers, retailers and light industries, teemed with people on the move. **"Red Stripe"** Brewery stood like gem among pebbles. If One was in right place at given time, One could see unbelievable sights, such as. Railway yard was enclosed by high chain link fence. Folks having business at the morgue, more so those from rural areas. Being unfamiliar with twists and turns of getting there. And having been forewarned, getting lost by a wrong turn. Could lead to harm or demise. Were encouraged to take easy route for fee, through large gaps in both fences. Often repaired by rail personnel, this was just as often undone by toll collectors on either side. Trespassers walked at will, dodging shunted cars on tracks they thought safe. Engines whistled, rumbling on tracks, seemingly headed away from. Until it was switched and headed their way. Of course, city undertakers went about their business by road to and from. Rural folks parked vehicles by fence. Walked across tracks, wooden boxes atop heads, to and from the morgue. This was daily ritual and taken as quite normal. Folks paid their toll without question, having been told of vehicles' tires found flat. On return of those who resisted collection efforts.

Unbelievable.......Whilst we are in detour, let's do *cocksure. It's a term coming down from old folks, having origin in the Bible. Cock was scratching to unearth tidbits for his brood and keep in harmonious graces with Hen. When Peter denied Christ, Cock knew it was a lie and crowed to reinforce truth. As told by the good book, thrice did Peter deny and twice did Cock crow loudly, reinforcing Peter's lie. Hence, person being certain, is cocksure of an event. Similar comment used is. "Sure as the man who farted and shat his beeber instead."

Here was Henry, awed at how identical Rosemarie and Jean of years ago were. Dickie spat to his left, then said. *"Six bwoys me had to make before me get her. God knows me wasn't going stop, until him give me her. Me did make up my mind. Keep going to well until my bucket come up with a pearl. And see? You couldn't ask for better."* This as he pointed at Rosemarie and spat again. Must have seen Henry look askance, quickly explained. *"Mouth giving me trouble, me teething again like baby."* There followed an exchange, only adults would understand. Jean said. *"Him know why him mouth giving worries. All him have to do is give up bad habits."* To which Dickie quickly rejoined. *"Don't pay her mind, me not eating under nobody table."* No One dared disturb the awkward silence that prevailed. Blighs lived next door to Gabbidons, who had two sons. Wesley, older was in high school. Patrick, younger, went to same prep school as Rosemarie. Usually co-ed, both children often did homework at Gabbidon's house. Birthdays came and were celebrated. Soon, Rosemarie at thirteen, was off to begin high school. Like her mother, she was fully developed beyond puberty. Kitten of cat they say. This had Dickie on pins and needles. Confronting boys, threatening to castrate those he saw making eyes at her. This brought angry parents to his gates. In one instance, station's sergeant of police. In effort to quell confrontations and resulting injuries. Jean suggested to Dickie, home school solution, until she reached age to face world of men. Asked her thoughts, regarding Rosemarie's early blooming and appeal. She said. *"What is to be will be.*

Ocean always rush to shore, washing over dykes and groynes." Henry quickly found out. Dickie's jealous obsession also included his wife, and men with whom she interacted. Said to him once, with toothless grin that was a scowl. *"Me don't feel patient when me walk up, see my wife and my friend laughing and talking. Yet them dry up as me come in."* Truth is, Jean behaved as he said, without rhyme or known reason. This time she was relating incident at work, reprimanding employee on unauthorized use of a Gestetner machine. So again, Henry and Blighs drifted apart. His not wanting to bear false accusations. If this was a movie, here's where the word "entracte" would appear on screen. Goading you to snack counter and now is your time to do likewise, because saga is only just beginning. Facebook sent a friend suggestion from Rosemarie Gabbidon. Mutual friend was Errol Passalaguie. Profile photo had Henry confused. It could not be Jean, but then he thought it could be. People, moreso women. Tend to use earlier photographs for profile pictures. But again, confusion reigns. Why would her surname be Gabbidon? Eventually, he solved self inflicted confusion, mulled possibility. Could it be?*"Rosemarie probably must have married her childhood neighbour."* She smiled, hugged Henry as her facial muscles obeyed her brain and twitched. Sure sign of inner turmoil. War of nerves, One might say. *"I'm so happy to see you, how much you'll never know. Did you know, every time I hugged and called you "Uncle." I had a crush on you and did not want to let you go? It was during my silly season. So much shit happened in my silly season. I know I would have had fond memories if you were part of it."* Henry stared at her as she ended her monologue. Quite befuddled, he said. **"Rosemarie, I am only seven years younger than your daddy. What were you thinking? Don't take yourself too serious. It's been said, thoughts at times takes wings. Sounds like yours were taking on turbo engines."** She dropped one tear, then another and yet another. She stared vacantly into vast nothingness of indecipherable mental realm and continued. *"Believe me, despite void of years between us it would…."* Here, she paused. Inhaled deep, held her breath and exhaled with a whoosh. *"Mom died last year from cancer. At first they said it was cervical, caught early. Things my mom should have shared with me, she never did. I tore my hair out and screamed, when I bloodied my clothes at nine years old in school. After clinic, children staring and whispering. That was when mom told me it was menses. Natural coming of age for girls, hers happened at ten. First time she took sick, she thought she'd gone into menopause. Two years later she began spotting. That's when she went to doctor. They told her it was caught early and cured. Last year she felt ill again, with stomach cramps and pain when peeing. That was it. She passed away, and you would not believe what my father did. He used to bring his sweetheart to the house, help mom take care of herself. She thought he had finally changed, after years of whoring. Would you believe, a woman has three daughters for him? Not one, not two but three. They all live in African place. You know one of those places where country's name change with every coup? Sweetheart's name is, Beverly Willis. Mom died, thinking she was the dedicated nursemaid. When mom died she was there, busy with arrangements and everything. She must have left cemetery and doubled back to church where she and my dad got married. Was literally that fast, I'm not telling you no lie."* Her eyes reflected haggardness of mind and spirit. Henry asked. **"You feel hungry? I am famished. Hear my gut rumbling?"** Trying distraction from misery and......She answered. *"Yes, I do. Thanks for asking. You're a real gentleman."* Still pushing funny to keep spectre of doom and gloom remote, he said. **"Good, so let's see now. Where can I find a patty and coco bread shop? We can all get two sky juice and we sip and eat as we chat."** She softly asked. *"They sell sky juice in America? Me never know that."* He laughed out loud and told her. **"Rosemarie, I am pulling your legs. Come on, let's go have a decent meal. You would really go with a man to be treated with patty, coco bread and sky juice?"** She said.*"Well, if that's all him can afford. What you expect me to say? No, thanks. I want lobster and steak?"* **"I hear**

you, but it's been years since we've seen each other." She smiled and asked. *"Why is only my legs you pulling? I won't stop you pulling anywhere else you want to, you know."* **"Come on Rosie, you a naughty child."** He said as he hugged her and they walked to the truck. She began a tale of her brothers, although Henry only knew twins. *"Dave and Raymond are here in the US. He's in Tampa and Dave works in Elizabeth. Any place there are ships, you will find those two. Kirk and Shawn came and joined the army."* She pauses and thinks before continuing. *"I don't know if is army or one of other groups. I just say army, because they all fight war with aim to kill people. No matter what they called. Army train them as mechanic and electrician. Not ordinary electrician. Ones that climb poles and such. Kirk went to Iraq and came home happy. War sweet him, he went back to Afghanistan and came home half crippled. He married a white woman. She very nice to everybody, but her family don't seem to like black people. We don't do Christmas or turkey time, unless is just him and his wife. She's really very nice white woman, I like her. Shawn now, he worked with electric company on the island after you pass Miami and go over the sea. He did not like the place. Because all his money went to pay rent and his boat. So he took a job with Arab company in Arab country. Says pay is more than good but he still complain. Because he can't do anything with a girlfriend unless they married. Says they have to hide, and if caught. Rulers pray first and chop off you head after. You don't know Shawn but I can tell you, he just loves exaggerate. Conrad and Paul still in Jamaica working with Sandals and other big hotel in St. Mary. What the man from England did buy and then build it up big and beautiful. I can't remember the name, matter how me try. It on my tongue tip."* She sucks hard on the straw, swallows and bolts upper body upright. Burps with a hand over mouth saying. *"Excuse me, please. I wonder if that's what they call, gas? Know from when that lump been there just sitting in my…….?"* Again, she erupts and says immediately after. *"Pardon me, sir. Gee, what a relief. You know something*

I've found out? I don't know if anyone else has. But there are times in your life when, you don't know you're suffering until….." Another soft eruption, after which she goes on. "*As I was saying, you never know you're suffering until you experience relief. That ever happens to you?*" She ends. Henry replies. **"I would think it fair to say, if One can suffer and not be aware. Then the malady was not severe or so deeply internal. To point it is not yet symptomatic."** She thought for a while then said. "*Could be that, or One has suffered so much. One's whole being just becomes inured to suffering and mind blanks it out.*" She hurries last word and softly burps again, then says. "*Excuse me. God! Hope that's last time this afternoon I ask to be excused.*" Henry said. **"I've been told, One should not ask to be excused for doing that over which they have no control. Such as, naturally occurring body functions, sneezing, belching or farting. Now if I step on your feet or carelessly bump you. Then should I ask to be excused for being clumsy, that could have been avoided."** Rosemarie threw her head back, covered her face with napkin. Laughed until she spasmed in hiccups.When she finally stopped, he saw her eyes had teared from joy. Resting a hand on his, she confided in a whisper."*You'd never believe, how many times I have farted among friends and not say a word. Then we sit there looking at each other, wondering.*"*Which Bitch did that?*" After which, her laugh was on again. Eventually, composing herself, she said. "*I needed that. A dam good laugh. Now, if I could top that off with a dam good……Let me not forget I am a lady. Next thing you think this lady is a tramp.*" They were quiet more than a minute. During which, he watched her eyes and face play out unknown thoughts going through her head. Henry asked. **"So, where is your daddy now?"** "*My dad?! My dad, my dad, my dad.*" She repeats contemplatively, then continues. "*Life has been very good to him and for him since mom died. I have to say, Mrs. Willis has been very good to him and good for him. Brought him to her home in Georgia, where they lived for awhile. Now they spend most their time in Costa Rica. I want to say*

Peru but am not sure which is, of many places they go. He says, lots Americans move there after retiring. Cost of living is comparably lower than in the USA. But they have not retired. He got treatment, bounced right back, healthier than before. Now they run chain of gift shops for tourists down there. From what he says when he calls, he's living dream he never dreamed of. Sometimes I think I judged him harshly, for keeping his whores with mom. Having outside children, but then. Who am I to judge anyone? I still see him as cur, for way he treated mom. I am only child who knows, he never married mom. After having her first child at sixteen. Everybody thinks she's married, because her name is Bligh. Grandma says that came from adoption, not marriage. When my dad began working trains, he had this brown skin woman down country. Her mother from Africa place, her father is Cuban. She ran away, lived with my dad in the country. He kept mom like rabbit in cage, breeding her when he came home. When African found her daughter with three girls, she took them and sailed away to England. After that my dad still hooked up with other women, wining and dining them like they were celebrities. While mom stayed in her cage and breed, taking care of her children. Not once being taken to a movie. A simple thing like a shilling movie, my dad has never taken my mom. And to top it all, she seemed so dam grateful. Makes me want to puke. For what is she grateful? There are things in my life I have never told neither of them. They hid their life and so did I. Parents are supposed to share life experiences with adult children, so they don't make similar mistakes and missteps. My mistakes began early, way too early. I didn't want to, during. Saw no point doing so, after. But I have to tell someone. You know, kind of things you only tell someone. After they take you on highest plateau of love making and you feel so gratefully satisfied .You would murder your mother if they asked you to. Or spill your gut of your deepest, darkest secrets? That's feeling I am talking about. Tell me a little about yourself. Did you ever have children? Were you married? Are you now, as we are sitting here?"

He told her. **"Yes, yes and yes. I got married in 1973. Had three children with that wife before we divorced. Married again in 2004 and we are not going to have children. She has two, and feeding five mouths are enough."** Rosemarie says. *"You married before I was even born and yet here we are, exchanging life's experiences."* She ended with that far away stare at nothing. **"How old are you?"** He asked. *"I am old enough!"* She retorted, with a tad of impatience and glint of anger in her eyes. *"What's with this woman?"* He rued as she began. *"I am asking you for fifty dollars, to do my car tag. It's forty-six or close. Do not say, no and disappoint. I am not asking for a loan. There will not be promissory note, written, verbal or understood. There are many I could get it from, but refuse to be beholden to some men. So just smile and be nice to Rosie. Happy you are chosen, above others. Tell me something. I am only asking, because I trust you to not lie. Did you ever have designs on my mother? Don't bother to ask why I ask. Dad thinks you and Mr. Moncrieffe had hots for her. You, I understand. Moncrieffe was an old man whose hands shook so bad, he would stuff them in his pockets. Even then, his pockets danced like puppets. Poor man."* **"Where are the papers for your car, you left them home?"** *"No, I am certain they're here in my pocketbook somewhere. Why?"* **"I could stop at an agency where the guy will take a credit card. On the job, I did them favours. They'll do same for me."** Henry told her. They were in and out less than ten minutes. He gave Rosie her decal and fifty dollars. She stared askance, he told her. **"Keep it in your bag, well hidden out of sight. One day when the rain pours, it will come in handy as your rain cloak or sun parasol."** She echoed. *"Parasol. Haven't heard that word a long time. Everyone says, umbrella."* He tells her. **"Parasols are sturdier built for unusual weather. You never see one flipped out, as often happens with some umbrellas."** They got to her home, she watched him put decal on. Next, he cut diagonal slices through. In answer to her alarmed question, told her. That was, so no One would steal it. A quite frequent occurrence in apartment parking lots. They hugged goodbyes, she asked. *"Are you going to leave me out here in harm's way? Be a gentleman, see me safely inside my apartment."* Then she giggled, went on. *"Matter of fact you should come in and look under beds, behind doors and inside closets before walking away."* They kissed inside the doorway, long and deep. She told him. *"I can feel your muscles tensing for a dash. What wifey don't know won't hurt her."* He kissed her again and despite her attempts to restrain. Told her firmly, he had to go. Looking at her, all he saw was a little girl whom he stooped to and asked her name. It was hard to see her any other way, but. They spoke on phone fairly often and texted by WhatsApp. Her car would not start, he stopped and did a quick look at it. Not having a ticket for that address, meant he was taking big risk. Vehicle being GPS tracked, but chances were made to be taken. Battery terminals had more frosting than birthday cake. She could not be sick another day, supervisor would not fall for it. Women knew, women only had first day cramps, that cleared up by day two. With a man, she could be sick for three days without reason. Her six year battery had four years to go. She got new one for less than thirty dollars exchange. Which she adamantly insisted on paying for. She had to go Publix for eggs…. Henry would go put air in tires and come back. He filled tank with gas and tires with air. Came back for and took her home. None the wiser? Tightly embraced and slowly moving to music, she said. *"Know what I'm trying to figure out? Are you good at what you do or am I so horny, it feels that way? Let's do it again, then I will really know."* Unaware, raising a dead subject he whispered. **"I need to reload the pencil, it's all out of lead. Maybe by tomorrow, today is all done."** She whispered back. *"You can't go back for air, fill the tank while I'm not looking? I'll go bathroom, you can surprise me when I come out."* **"You knew?"** He asked. She guffawed and said. *"If there's one thing I know about cars, it's the gas gauge. It's a habit when I get into a vehicle, whether it's mine or being driven. This girl won't be caught high and dry by dandy Randy."* When storms are ablowing, it's bonanza for some who are looking forward to storm duty.

Henry balked grossing eight grand plus in a pay period. Yet taking home less than half or barely. He'd rather take home three plus, from grossing five plus. Easier to swallow, he gets rest, feels more rejuvenated than overtime hogs. Dragging tired feet, whose legs are about to buckle. Sagging eyelids about to close. When next storm blew, it was not devastating as predicted. Historically they rarely are, but company prepares for worst and are happy with reprieve. So it was, Rosemarie and Henry had eighteen hours of freedom. During which, she talked like bubbling tar cauldron. He listened, attentively and silent, after being cautioned to not interrupt.

"I went into first form September, before turning thirteen in November. Patrick and I started at Miss Parson's nursery school when we were toddlers. His mother worked nights, so when she picked us up at nursery. Patrick's older brother Wesley, watched us till my parents came for and took me home. Growing up, going same school, it was easy for us to study and work together. Wesley used to tease his brother and say we should get married. Because I was pretty and we knew each other from babies. Patrick and myself usually laugh it off. That year I went into first form, Wesley was leaving sixth form and awaiting A level results. Although Patrick and I were first formers, our school's curriculum were different. I was at all girl's, he was at all boy's school. So we could not study and help each other as we did at coed prep school. I was introduced to science and math subjects that had me going circles. Wesley said I could come over, he would help. Dad said I should only go when aunt Phyllis was there. Mom said, that was a problem. Aunt Phyllis slept evenings before work. Did not want us disturbing her rest. Dad did not want me going over there with either uncle George, Wesley or Patrick being there. Mom said I could go to the French lady for lessons, but my dad said they did not have the money. See that? Very first time I went, for Wesley to explain math equation problem. He opened the door with one hand, rubbed my nipple with palm of other hand. I stupidly laughed, told him to not do it. I was mad as hell but

because I laughed, he rubbed other one. Said, my breasts are calling out to him. Knew if I told dad. I would have to grow rest of my life. Visiting him in prison as he waited on hangman's noose, because of me. Told Wesley, I would ask his parents to talk to him, if he ever did it again. He asked, if I was going to ask his parents to help me with homework. Was my dad psychic? I don't know. He just ups and says. "Don't go over that yard, with free swinging pendulums like that, distracting the professor. Keep on your bra, matter of fact. Just as how you come from school." Mom told him, bras were uncomfortable in worst way. Hence her getting rid of hers, moment she walked through the door. "What is there for you to get your britches all knotted? Don't make our daughter, a Dinah Dumbkin." Mom told him. He told her. "You watching the Pony, forget about Stallion in the barn." How can I tell you this and not feel like shit? I'll tell you anyway. Get it out in open. After a while, I began to not mind it. He helped with grades and way he coached, I really learned. I mean, he didn't do my work for me. He showed shortcuts to tough problems and ways to simplify and quick test for accuracy. Soon he wanted to know, when my menses would end. He'd look at, and gently massage my breasts. Then predict with fair accuracy, when my menses would start." Henry asked. **"Where was Patrick in all of this?"** She stared him silently, before carrying on. *"He was busy bee, doing football practice. Archery lessons, to qualify for the team. Schools challenge, debating practice. When he had a free day, he practiced practicing. Now I wonder, if Wesley threatened or coerced him to be away, when he knew I was coming over. There were times I stopped going over, managing on my own. Until new form, brought new dimension to same subject. When I asked if he would help. He agreed, whilst adding another level to his actions. Thus, fingering began. I was getting a thrill, participated willingly. One day he told me, wash my vagina and don't dry. I began crying. Told him I would not have sex with him. I was going home. By then he had my top, underwear and book bag tucked in his hamper. I cried out loud and he promised he* *was not going to rape me. Said he was going to do something for me. I would so love, I would beg him to do it over and over again. He knelt by the bedside. I did not see him making to, or take his pants off. I watched him come halfway up and kiss droplets caught on hair strands. He kept licking and going hmmmm. How does that feel? I closed my eyes and laid back. After a few minutes he spread my thighs, I sprang up frightened. He gently eased me down, began stroking my vagina with his tongue. I closed my eyes again, my body shivered with a tingling. I don't know why it did, but it did. At first I felt him penetrating my vagina and thought it was finger thing but quickly realized, it was his tongue."* Henry mentally mused. *"Been there done that."* Recalled initial sessions with Miss Candy. Only difference, he was eleven plus. Rosemarie was probably fourteen some. Herstory continues. *"He would do me, then hurry me home before girlfriend Debra came. He joined the army. My dad said he was a big thing, in control of things. Next, there was a function at army base. His parents and mine all went. He was with Debra, I stayed home and cried."* "Cried? Were you in love with him, or thought you were?" *"I don't know why I cried. He said we should start having sex. I told him, no way. Unless he stopped being with Debra. He promised he would. Said I would have to begin using birth control. I told him I was afraid getting sick, he should use condoms instead. He said he didn't care using them, but would for me, if I got them. I saved my allowance, got his brand at a pharmacy. Came to cashier, older woman. She rang up the gum then began, grandmotherly browbeating me. Looked at condoms and looked at me twice, eyes wide astare. Sensing a tongue lashing not far behind, third time she did it. I walked away and left everything at the register. Wesley told me. Give him the money, he would get them. Can you believe that shit!? It's not Wesley's fault, it's really my fault. So let me not go down that road. But still, he was taking advantage of me. I know you're a man, but, say yes. He was! For freakin' crying out loud!"* Henry agreed he took advantage of her, held her hostage. Because of his being able to help her attain scholastic goals. Rosemarie continues, after long, silent pause. *"Wesley said he could get condoms for free at his job, but they were coarse or some such excuse. He did oral sex one day and intercourse next day. When he did oral sex, he worked himself and spewed on a towel on the floor. As my sweet sixteenth birthday party was being planned. He said, Saturday, after party I should come over. He had something special for my birthday. Told him, no. I would not come, because he and Debra came to my party. Smooching and hugging as if it was going out of style. He said he didn't know why she kept hanging around, but he does not pay her any attention. I came and stood inside the door as he talked on the phone, unaware I was there. I knew it was Debra. When he hung up I told him. I wanted to know what we were going to do, before I agree. He said, if I enjoyed his doing tongue on me. Think how much more I would enjoy, doing tongue on him. I tell you now, before he ended the sentence. I already dented my sofa cushions at my house and fallen asleep. When I awoke, told me. I could get by without math. That phase of my life was at an end. Can you believe that vertical mound of manure?"* She asked Henry as he thought. *"What I can't believe, is you taking all that crap from a man and you not ugly duckling with low self esteem."* Breaking silence, she went on. *"Truth be told. I was completely turned off from men. In a way it served me well, for a time. Threw all my energies pursuing my degree. Qualified top of my banking and finance class, focusing on investments. Patrick and I knocked heads, soon became boyfriend girlfriend. Can you imagine that? Wesley married his Debra and they had four children. He left the army and took management job with a big security company. Before that he did time with money truck people. Why you look at me like that? You know the people that go and take business money to bank and so on?"* **"I know what you meant, but way you said it, I kinda equated it with a food truck."** She made for retort, changed her mind and continued. *"Patrick and I were two strange creatures. Don't know if he loved me. But always felt we were obligated to be together.*

Because of us being peas in pod from nursery school and so on. Was a beautiful concept to be pursued with fairy tale ending. Thing is, I could not love Patrick as I willed myself to. And after a while, told myself it was no good if I had to make effort. It should come natural as green grass without fertilizer. Knowing escapades, Wesley and I went through. Brought on intense guilt, like as cheating on Patrick. His brother knew. I knew. And when I thought about everything. What was his role in all of this? The fool on the hill? I told me, I could not do that. On other hand, he was so naively trusting. Times I thought, I would best come clean. How could that help? I had no idea. I would soil me beyond all hopes of being cleansed. For one, it would pit brother against brother. His parents, my parents and don't forget. I knew, I willingly allowed myself to be taken. Even enjoyed it until told I had to graduate to......Thought fills me with revulsion. Patrick and I each attained our goals, career wise that is. Well, not really, as it turned out. By time I qualified for my masters, I was beyond studying for anything else. My head was empty, I experienced a kind of hollowness. Here but not here, like candle without a wick. A tall wax cylinder that cannot, will not glow. Closed my eyes to escape reality. When I did open them, all I saw was daunting Alp of snow. My student loan. Patrick began working at private hospital in a resort city. Spurning civil service job. Said, government facilities were understaffed. Because of skilled manpower exodus and shortage. Under equipped, being underfunded and. Foregoing would lead to his being overworked and underpaid. We both had feet on solid ground, making good money. After saying, no, many times without telling reason. I said, yes. Let's get married and start a family. Not so fast with a family. He reined me in after we were married. His life's ambition had not yet been realized. His ultimate goal was to qualify and practice as cardiologist. Responsibility of family and raising children, would stand in our way. Our way? I asked him. You mean, your way. Well now, he could not pursue his studies and certification. Unless he came to America and joined a ranked hospital group. So, I followed my husband. Eight months after, he began working with Cedars Health. I was able to land very good position with a bank. Happy having chosen Spanish as second language in high school, instead of French. God always has plans for us, of which we are not aware until later it's made clear. After four years and some, Patrick finds he cannot qualify for MD licence in America. Best he can get, is certified anaesthesiologist. He's mad as hell because, goal of being a cardiologist has slipped away. I shouldn't say, slipped away. He needed to redo an aspect of training for certification, before allowed to take an exam. I'm putting it in simple form, as I got it. But, all was not lost, his goal required renewed efforts. Between us, he quit, plain and simple. Apart from ego shock to his fragile mental foundation. I thought we were doing much better than others in our peer group. I think, now I am certain. Our not having children was a huge relief financially. Although I wanted to replace myself, experiencing joy of motherhood. But, if it was not to be, then amen, so let it be. He sees and knows all. What we takes as disappointment, is sometimes really a blessing in disguise. Maybe. If you or anyone thought, climbing that so called ladder of success was difficult. I am here to tell you all, climbing is easiest part. Real test comes when you try staying on the ladder. Patrick said it was not his error, but his patient came out. Or was coming out of anaesthesia too soon and he was penalized. Placed on kind of probation, pending examination and re-certification. I am using my own words, as I did not ingest the medical mumbo jumbo he recited. It's insulting, when anyone speaks to you in language, they know you are not familiar with. It's like showing off, but maybe he's under stress and unaware of. What's a wife for, if not to make excuses for her husband? In essence, what I told you is what it was. I said to him, I am certain, notwithstanding. He must have been relieved the patient came out early, instead of not coming out period. He scoffed and implied. Maybe they would have been better prepared for latter event instead of other. Asked to explain, he uttered not another syllable. I am no Seer with crystal ball, but I saw a man. Who, having had setback attaining ultimate goal. Was not as dedicated to where he found himself. With compromised earnings, frustration not getting his cardiology goal. Man became irritable, arrogant and irrational. We lived together apart, then housing debacle. I knew and told him. We could live comfortably decent on his reduced income and mine. But he had to show, he's living larger with less than when he made more. Our house was as they say, upside down from the first punch. New language I learned, coming to America. Next body blow, government took control and shut down the bank. Feds say top guy was lending too much of deposits, to his various enterprises. Not stealing or scamming, just going against regulations. I was subpoenaed to be deponed by one office. And subpoena to be deposed by another tribunal. Can't figure out different words, processes were basically same. End of it all, grilled and examined. Found to have adhered, acted strictly within guidelines. Downsized and working with educational trust for now. Degree and qualification means much to qualify for position. But not for decent salary and perks as others. I keep up appearances as befits position and scrimps to not starve, after paying my rent and insurance. Gave up cable and internet last year. Kept my weight, so I wouldn't have to shop new clothes. Learned how to slowly descend the ladder and not fall to pieces. Honestly, I don't know what Patrick got himself into. There was talk about medicare fraud and possibility his having some involvement. He told me he's going to look at a project my dad and Mrs. Willis wants him to look at. Said it was kind of partnership and he'd be in it with them. Not having or given much to go on. Surmised it must have to do with his skills in the medical profession. Maybe where they are at, standards are not as stringent and licensing can be easier done than said. Seven months went by without a word from him. Tried calling my dad, but person I spoke with at their Georgia residence. Will not give me direct contact number to them. Said she will send a message to my dad and he will call. Haven't heard a peep from him or my husband. So, I say to hell with them. Debra came last summer with two of her brood on their way to Orlando fun park. Swore me to secrecy, said my husband is in Arab land. Shawn got him something good over there. Because, as a doctor over there he is next to a God. I don't know how true that is. Debra won't say how or where she got her information. Honestly, if I can have a friend to lean on. Don't give rat's ass about them or their secret existence. You know something? I am so very glad I did not bare my soul to anyone. Not to my parents, siblings and most of all not to Patrick. I will tell you though, that shit obnoxious to carry around all your life. No matter how you try, it can't be purged. Because it's part of your existence and stays with you to the grave. With you I have found reason to soar as never before, having shed my mental shackles." I know it's late my doing the math, but curiosity gnaws at me. 1973 when Henry got married, Rosemarie was not yet born. I am going to put her birth year no higher than 1975, which makes him thirty years or thereabout her senior. Now, before you go tsk, tsking, remember. He was prey, and Rosemarie, hunter.

Round about when he began working at the rail yard. Pansy was his girlfriend. In recent years, their paths crossed and dormant flames reignited. Derrick was her unconfirmed cousin whom she later married and both migrated to the US. Now he was in hospice care, succumbing to AIDS induced tuberculosis and opportunistic infections. On his way to a weekend retreat in the Cape. He and Rosemarie paid Derrick a visit. That man was dying with a burden he could not shed. I don't think he even tried. Both walked in the room, Henry made introductions and right away Derrick said to Rosemarie. *"Don't make him fool you, him have woman all over the place. Did try take my girlfriend from me one time long time. Tell me bout. Push, Derrick push and then drive and leave me standing. But in the end him never get her. Because is me she married. You is nice lady, so I have to tell you. That way him don't get chance to try fool you."* With a smirk he addressed Henry. *"You can bex* (vex) *till you bus,* (burst) *me done dead already and you can't tell me fi, push."*

With that realization sinking in, he began to cry. Henry gave him, care items brought and said goodbye. Never knew until after Derrick's passing, He had been identified to facility staff as his only brother. If you have ever shopped for. Do know, incontinent items don't come cheap. Henry was irked, Derrick couldn't bring himself to cleanse his mind of ill founded rancour. And be grateful for a brother's generosity. Of course, given such an introduction. Curiosity set in and Rosemarie asked to be told story of. Henry told her he would do better, gave her an entire trilogy, compliments of publisher. If you're similarly curious, please buy **"The Lucky bastard" Books 1-3,** and be sated. Sir Walter Scott wrote a poem that tells the story of Lord Marmion. *A Tale of Flodden Field* A quote from, reads. *"Oh, what a tangled web we weave. When at first we practice to deceive."* This has never been more apt than in twists and turns of following tale.

What's in a name? Raymond Vaughn is presently separated from wife, Shantrell. He's trying to get next to Rosemarie, who's married. Does not have clue, where her husband is. Rosemarie has never liked him, says his behaviour cheapens a woman. Concedes she might be. Yet does not want to be seen as, or so treated. Back in old country, he and Shantrell were sweethearts in their teens. Lisa and a ni.... from the streets-Blessid Union of Souls thing. To which her parents strongly objected. Unknown to anyone but themselves, they got married secretly. When this came to light, there was nothing parents could do but accept, with lump in throats. The Papa, he lost a temper. Oh, how he huffed and puffed. Newlyweds went into business, which like their marriage, was shrouded in secrecy. Living with glaring opulence, they were talk of the town. Shantrell came to the US and qualified for career in medical field. Whilst her husband backed and forthed, taking care of homegrown enterprise. Raymond ran into trouble with US immigration and customs, cause and extent unknown. Raymond Vaughn disappeared and in his place, Raymond Baugh came into being. Shantrell fell in love again. Divorced Vaughn and married Baugh. As expected, she filed residence papers on husband's behalf. As sometimes happens, their marriage fell apart by way of mutual infidelity. While both were stuck in different places. This is quite a doozy deed. Each contemplates divorce so they can cement relationships with lovers in abeyance. Back in home country, authorities having failed to contact owners of vast real estate holding. Lying in path of municipal development. Acquired holdings under purposed laws and deposited fair value funds to deeded owners' credit. Remember now folks, Mr. Vaughn cannot resurface to claim legacy. He's also thinking, if he divorces Mrs. Baugh and Mr. Vaughn having been presumed dead. The former Mrs. Vaughn can, will take hold of that money for her sole enrichment. Reality of which, he cannot embrace. You ask, how Henry came by this storied tale? Rosemarie says, she once had unexpected visitor. She agreed to see, after security checked and cleared. Woman identified herself as Raymond's wife. Assured Rosemarie, absence of animosity but wanting to talk to her, woman to woman. They spent part of that Saturday in Barnes and Noble's cafe. Discussing things as they're said to be. Why? Because, Mrs. Baugh now feared. Vaughn/Baugh was intent on killing her. She wanted to confide in another woman, should anything happen to her. Why would he want to kill her? Rosemarie asks. *"You both have each other's secret. Either of you squeal and both go down."* Mrs. Baugh volunteers, if she could get her hands on the real estate money. She would be able to breathe easier. How so, she is not saying and Rosie tells her she should. It's already established, first husband is missing without trace. Hence this is candy from a baby. Wish she could be so lucky.**"Oh no."** Counsels Mrs. Baugh. **"You need to watch those FBI shows on television. That money is cheese on rat trap. That I guarantee, US government watches 24/7/365 and 366 when it comes around. First move anyone makes on that money, they come down on that person like how they implode old buildings. Back home I could access that money without an eyelid flutter by our government. Even if Sam not watching it, once they see large sums of money moving in or out. They start**

checking to see if it's coming from terrorist related sources, to finance bombings and stuff like that. In this country, government makes it their duty to know more than we know they know. *"So, what is your advice?"* Rosemarie asks Henry. He hugs her and softly sings. *"Let's fall in love, why shouldn't we fall in love, our hearts are*.....She kissed his lips into silence. When the moon glows in the night sky. Henry stands by a window in an empty room, stares at brilliant shadows of trees. Animated by gentle breezes, their dance silhouetted against a wall. Then can be seen, moths and other winged life. Flitting and darting in endless choreography, before dawn heralds new day. Thus engrossed, Henry was briefly startled when Rosemarie gently hugged him from behind. Unawares she had been roused when he quietly slipped out of bed. His having failed to return, she came in search. They went back to bed but did not sleep. There was something she had to tell and would put it off no longer. She had been going to doctor for treatment over past eighteen months. For what she suspected was a cancerous growth, which her doctor would not confirm. Kept telling her it was being monitored and under control. She would be going into hospital at month's end for three days to have tests done. By coincidence, when new day dawned. Henry also began not feeling well, but drove to Miami-Dade and took her home. Told her he had to go, something was not sitting well with him. We are constantly reminded on our life's journey, we should always expect the unexpected. But do we ever? That night discomfort became unbearable, 911 emergency response was summoned. Henry was taken to nearby Baptist hospital's emergency room with diagnosed heart issues. Later confirmed to be brain aneurysm leading to a stroke. The marvel of medical science continues to astound. Threading through groin artery, doctors went to and snatched a clot from the brain and life goes on as before.Weeks after discharge, Henry had to undergo intense therapy sessions, temporarily losing touch with Rosemarie. She confessed to having wavered between, him being a near and dear friend. And possibility he had abandoned her because of her health situation. If only she knew, he was in hospital, she would have been there for him. She shows him a device with a tube inserted. In ignorance, he would call it a catheter. It gives constant dose of medicine to heal her condition and return her to robust health. Rosemarie tells him, she knows she's going to die soon. Yet, she will not cry, way my "brother" did. She had long ago taken hereditary traits into consideration. Told herself she would die at an early age, just like her mother did before her. Being younger twin of a mother with similar life development milestones. Why then would she outlive her mom by any extended period? Henry told her, because medical science unearths new cures and treatments by the minute. His father had three strokes and died. If at that time science was available, where they could get to his head through his groin. He would possibly have lived longer than he did. She thought on that but insisted. When One got to chemotherapy, it was time to prepare for inevitable. As she understood, and said to Henry. Treatment being administered, was in preparation for surgery. Making for less tedious procedure and quicker recovery. She was again admitted to hospital in room **3347** for more tests, prior to surgery. The set of books Henry gave her, she had read twice. In pursuit of solace from suspected desertion. *"You know when your faith in humankind gets eroded and slowly gets restored to the point your garden blooms. And one day you look through your window, the garden shows signs of wilting as if caught in a drought. And then you begin to wonder if your garden and it's blooms, were a mirage. But here we are and I know it was only a cloud passing over the sun."* She softly ended whilst squeezing his hand and a tear fell. It was a moment he reflected on. People experiencing similar Oneness emotions together. Yet comes around to hating and at times eliminating by murder and other devises. We are strange creatures indeed. Now she wanted him to write a book about people, places. Events, sordid, happy and everything about everyone. *"Leave nothing out. I want Wesley and Patrick wherever they may be, to read and recognize their truth. My father must know how I felt about him and anguish of preteen years. I want* *them to choke on tears and saliva.. Look at me."* She whispered. *"I have never known love until I knew you. Make me a promise, you will do all you can to make me die happy. Knowing you were my true friend to the end. Do not make excuses for my culpability, or conceal conscious participation in my own misery. Emotional pleasures derived from misguided, physical bombardment. How does the mind tolerate such variances?"* Henry told her, she should not venture into self loathing. She was a vulnerable child and should not have been taken advantage of. But, look who's talking. He was there early a Wednesday morning, her surgery was to begin at 10:00 hours. He can't remember if they used term "head nurse" but that's who she was. Came to Rosemarie's bedside, just before she was wheeled out and said to Henry. **"Don't worry, your daughter will pull through just fine."** Why do people assume and arrive at conclusions without guidance? Holding hands with firm grip, to point beyond which he could not enter. Rosemarie propped on an elbow and beckoned he bow his head. Thought she was going to whisper. Felt her warm, wonderful, wet kiss, long and unending instead. Nurse gave Henry, second look. Asked silent question for which there would not be an answer. We don't want people, home at dinner table, saying to family. *"I honestly thought he was her dad, or male relative. Old man with grey hair. She's young woman, early forty."*

Her funeral was a beautiful affair, if it can be described as such. Henry met most of her kinfolks. Gabbidons were there, except for husband, Patrick. Siblings were there, except for Shawn. Her dad and Mrs. Willis, looking quite regal. Like Lord and Lady of colonial era plantation. Young woman in twenties, whispered quite audibly to male escort. *"My God! Look at those two. Who are they? Standing and holding hands like prunes on lollipop sticks.. How deep are their wrinkles. Don't they spend money at spas and such places?"* He elbow nudged her, glanced over his shoulder to assess damage. Seeing Henry was only another wrinkled coot, he shrugged disclaimer. *"Hey, I'm not responsible for what she says."* Their day will come, if only they live that long. Wesley's family were there. He could not wait to ask how well Henry knew his sister-in-law. At the repast, he jostled for position next to Henry and quite unabashedly asked. *"So, did Rosemarie tell you family secrets or where their stolen treasures are hidden?"* **"No, she didn't. If there are such to be told, she probably did to company she engaged to write her life story."** Henry told him. He visibly panicked and laughed. *"Are you serious about what you just said!? She's writing her life's story!? Who's writing it!?"* **"I don't know, she did not tell me company's name or anything much. She mentioned it in passing once, never again. Maybe she wasn't serious, it was only an idea whose time never came. Then again, maybe it did. One never knows. Do they now?"** Henry ended. He thought for a moment then said with ridicule. *"Write her life story? Where would she get money from to do that? Did she tell you she lost her big time job at the bank?"* **"Yes, she did. When it comes to writing and publishing. I will admit not knowing much about how it's done. But I would think, if One had manuscript or story. Which a publishing company thinks could make them money. They would probably front initial production cost. Just as record producers front songs, and some become runaway hits. Singers don't usually put up money, as far as I know. But then again, I don't know much about these things."** Henry teased Wesley. Again, he went into a thought process, then shouted. *"Listen up, y'all. Rosie done gone and commissioned a company to publish her life's story. So watch out now, lots of skeletal bones gonna be tumbling out of closets."* He ended with a hearty laugh, trying to cover nervous tremour that made his voice rumble. Son of a Bitch. Wanting a sixteen year old to play chorus on his bonophone. To reciprocate his playing her skin flute, from she was a thirteen year old minor. Gad what a Cad. One thing she begged Henry promise he would see to, which he could not. She wanted "Gabbidon" expunged from, and to be known as her maiden name on programmes and in eulogy. Said she did not want to die and be remembered as a Gabbidon. Those who made preparations discounted this wish and cast it aside. It seemed bound to fail in any event, as death certificate did record her name as a married woman. Stands to reason, she could not be otherwise solemnized. Could have written "RIP Rosemarie Bligh Gabbidon." That too would be redundant fiction. As Henry stood gazing at her still form in the casket, two things came to mind. She lies there with minute particles of his DNA in her mouth. Taking a smidgen of him with her to the promised land. Henry thinks she sensed she might not have survived surgery. Hence that long, lingering, slathering kiss. Other event brought to mind, was seeing her at close to same age as Linda Creed. When she passed away, April 10th, 1986 from breast cancer. And Jill Ireland who also died of breast cancer May 18th, 1990 aged 54. She told everyone who would listen, that she did not want to die. To quote her. *"We all die one day, but I am not in the mood to do it yet."* She was fifteen years younger than her second husband, Charles Bronson. With whom she co-starred in numerous movies. He went on to survive her by thirteen years. Indication of how vicious a disease cancer really is. These are women I admired from afar without knowing them. Linda, because of her unequalled song writing and music producing talents. Jill for that unspoilt, hapless maiden innocence she portrayed. It is always hard to lose someone you treasure, for whatever reason. Be it disease, accident, old age or murder.

Rosemarie's playlist: There was a rainy day that defeated their plans to go out, so she decided to do laundry instead. Came back to hear Henry listening to Martin Denny's "Quiet Village" on his phone. *"What is that you're listening to? That's some kind of jungle safari you got going there. They are quite different, but this song reminds me of another quaint song I like, but haven't heard in a while. Don't know the name, but I call it the cow bell tune."* Holding a finger aloft, Henry asked for time then began playing Hugh Masekela's "Grazing in the grass" From then, he sent her songs he figured she'd like and she always did. Each visit to her bedside, he shared at least ten songs with her. Her phone has close to two hundred tunes, played on YouTube and shared to her by Henry.To name a few. Soft summer breeze-Eddie Heywood. The disadvantages of you-Brass Ring. Hill Street Blues Theme. Happy Organ-Dave Baby Cortez. You gotta have heart-Peggy Lee. Wheels, Tracy's Theme, Sail along silvery moon, Look for a star-Billy Vaughn. Theme from A Summer Place, Theme from The Apartment-Percy Faith. Patricia-Perez Prado. Bongo Rock-Preston Epps. The Syncopated Clock, The Typewriter-Leroy Anderson. Java, Cotton Candy -Al Hirt. Strangers on the Shore-Acker Bilk. Similau, Skokiaan-Bert Kaempfert. Summertime-Sam Cooke. Summer Samba-Walter Wanderley. Games People Play-Duane Allman and King Curtis Ousley. Oh what a beautiful morning-Ray Conniff met Billy Butterfield. Maria Elena-Los Indios Tabajaros. Love is Blue-Paul Mauriat. Mercy mercy mercy-Cannonball Adderly Quintet. Nadia's Theme-Henry Mancini. Knights in White Satin-The Moody Blues. Sail Away-Enya. Love's Theme-Barry White. Moon River-Henry Mancini Orchestra and Chorus from "Breakfast at Tiffany's". Moon River-Jerry Butler. Theme from The Apartment-Byron Lee & The Dragonaires featuring Leslie Butler on organ. Harbour Lights-Platters. I walk with God, The Drinking Song-Mario Lanza. It's me again Margaret, Ahab the Arab, I'm my own Grandpa-Ray Stevens. Don't you know, Not one minute more, Softly my love-Della Reese. No other love-Jo Stafford. Porgy, My baby just cares for me, Love me or leave me, Ain't got no, I got life-Nina Simone Here's something not common in the music industry. "Softly my love" and "No other love" are different songs by different singers, but using same soundtrack. Give both a listen, see what the shouting is about. Tip of an extensive playlist you should browse. Twice every year on her birthday and transition. Henry takes a bouquet to Rosemarie's vase. It saddens him that tokens of remembrance from family members are glaringly absent. It is understood, all good things come to an end and soon the memory fades. But surely for first year up to say five. Someone could reflect and recall her birthday. Patrick might have been quarantined by circumstances, not having attended the funeral. If I were he, I would ask someone to put a bloom in my honour on my wife's historic date. There are a lot that's unknown. You think he knew of shenanigans between his brother and Rosemarie? If yes. When did this come to his attention. After their marriage? Couldn't have been before. If so. What then would his motive be for marrying her, knowing as he did? So you're walking among graves at a cemetery. Three, four rows over, a woman talks to her dear departed and clams up as you approach. She doesn't want you to hear what she's saying to her loved One. Truth is, you're the only One who can hear what she's saying. Dear One was most likely eviscerated after death, ending any chance of their awakening from undetected coma. She knows that, we all know it. Yet go through similar escapade when we find graves of our dearly departed. I asked someone about this charade, which in acknowledging. She said, this ritual brings visitor an inner peace. When the mind believes, it brings contentment to the heart. It's part of life's games we play without knowing why. So you ask as she did. Do I talk to my dear departeds? Oh yes, I do. I greet, ask how they're doing and so on. Then, she asked a question, I never saw coming. *"What would you say or do. If beloved's voice from below ground returned your greeting and engaged you in conversation?"* Hmmmm.

Sex Deviants among sexes-4

Annette Pilgrim and Florence Dawkins were neighbours and close friends, up to graduating high school. Career paths took them different ways. Annette became chartered accountant and forensic auditor. Flo was a qualified nurse midwife, with sights becoming Gynaecologist. Parents were friends with Robertsons, whose son became eminent law professor at the university. Sisters qualified, set up successful joint practice in Paediatrics and Obstetrics/Gynaecology. Siblings three, were esteemed beacon of what's possible. When children of rural, black parents, having very limited cash resources. Can yet by dint of determined focus, attain unexpected excellence. Pride of having achieved, brings angst of being prevailed upon. To chair every organization and committee, for every purpose. One does not balk giving motivational speech at One's Alma Mater, or young people's endeavour at church. When service clubs, charitable and civic entities bombard, with requests for money and time, honour can overwhelm. Fame and infamy doth exact an equal burden upon them that are bearers of. Annette met Delroy Forbes, dated seven years before they thought getting married. Her mid thirties. He was mid forties divorcee, who previously worked at a large forge. Intent on setting up own machine shop. When this became reality, he proudly boasted. Having rare, Swiss computerized lathes on his shop floor. In era when computers were only mentioned in context, making his wife's position redundant. Told friends, she would not have married him, until he made a man of himself. He said, he waited until her age fell off the calendar. Leaving her very little, if any other option. Goes to show how two people can gaze at the sky. One sees moon whilst other sees sun. Unbiased passerby, asked to mediate. Will confuse and astound others. After conceding inability, by virtue of being a stranger in these parts. See how we unwittingly compound our miseries at times? Leave well alone. Nurse midwife Florence Dawkins, striving studiously to qualify as Gynaecologist. Married lettered Bajan Tyrone Devonish, who claimed certification in psychology and psychiatry. Before and after their wedding, friends discussed with fervour. Whether or not this was as they say, kosher. He did study medicine at Cave Hill and Mona, they reasoned. Hence the psychiatry designation was possible. But where and when did he find time pursuing psychology studies, had everyone flummoxed. Nevertheless he set up practice in a prestigious office building. After a while, hushed whispers went silent. Now we know, silence does not mean forgotten or accepted. It's mere dormancy awaiting event at which time. Someone will fist pound a wall and aver. *"I knew it, I knew it, I knew it!"* That's who we are, love the negative. We live for the day we can revel in friend's social misfortune or fall from grace.

By appearances, Annette's life was bed of roses. Ah, thorns created misery beyond endurance. Her company, acquired by investor group. Was in first retrenchment phase, on massive, unprecedented scale. Today, political correctness in vogue. We say, reorganizing, restructuring or downsizing, instead of passe "R" word. See how time changes words we apply to same event? Company memo and staff meetings told of changes that would require some personnel to be retrained, or find employment elsewhere. Redundancy package insisted on by union was negotiated in good faith. Payroll department saw most significant changes, losing twenty-six of thirty-one. Mammoth task, calculating fortnightly wages and monthly salaries. Required sheaves of bank notes and hogsheads of coins. Next came envelope stuffing, and unending queues to the glass window. By employees whose pay were incorrect. Hours were short, amounts on pay slips not in envelopes. It was ongoing confusion in continuous rote from pay period to next. Now, computer calculated time tickets. Wages and salaries were sent to the bank. Staff got hour early release on paydays.This encouraged some to opt for checking accounts. Others stood with brows knitted in long queues. Progress can be like garbage disposal at times. In order to get one place clean, someplace else must be made correspondingly dirty. We can see how Annette's angst came about and rapidly escalates. Inputting data for processing, requires four to six letter codes known as "conversations." That's first obstacle she has to overcome in relatively short time. Keeping status in management status, she needs to be lettered. Position now requiring a degree. Her good fortune, going from leader to being led. Has been brought home to her by management. In that, most of those led by her, got lost on the way. Times of yore, company helped with tuition loans. Deserving cases got grants on merit. Now all that had been taken off the stove, swept out the kitchen door. Brought about by union demands, backed with strike threats. Company capitulated, taking back good citizens perquisites. Conscience and goodwill jettisoned, hardball was in the house. Caught mentally between rock and hard place, she discussed this with friend Florence. Who without minute's hesitance, recommended consultations at her husband's practice. Human resources had budget to treat limited substance abuse and similar remedial therapy. So it was without hesitation, Annette began therapy sessions with Tyrone. I realize you were never told before, now you'll deduce. Annette and Delroy had one child named Laurel. Close friends joked, Annette gave birth to, Delroy raised the child. I would think shared parenting would be recognized as a positive, but maybe not. At seven years old going on eight, Laurel told her dad, she could have her bath without his help. When he showed no sign respecting her wishes, she spoke to mom who brushed her concern aside. Grandma came to spend time whilst her house was being repaired. Took to helping Laurel with personal care. When grandma got ready going back to her house. Laurel asked to go live with her and mom agreed. For a time all was well and each faced their challenges. It is said, life without challenges is mere existence. But we know, sometimes these can beat us down like sledgehammer in strong hands on boundary peg.

Miss Rachel was spry woman over sixty years old, carried herself well. Maintained a strict diet and did physical exercise to enhance her figure, as she put it. ***"To give young girls a run for their money."*** She was most frequent and renowned entrant in newspaper's annual, Miss Grandmother's contest. Could be because, she worked eight to two at newspaper's office and four to eight at Tyrone's office. He worked seven to three with a behaviour treatment facility, before coming to shared practice at evenings. Miss Rachel was woman Friday who kept rooms tidy, set water jug on tray with tumblers. Greeted visitors and collected fees, before sending patients in to see Tyrone. In lull of some days, Miss Rachel and her boss exchanged laughs, but got serious on confession couch. Of course, this induced him to be generous in kind. She took comfort in ability to seduce him. Despite his being married to and living with much younger woman. Oh, it gets so much better or maybe worse. Depends how these things are viewed and by whom. You know, they say a woman can always tell when a man is slipping away. Feminine intuition. Thing about intuition is, you got to make sure it is evenly balanced with common sense. Failing which you can get misled, end up being a fool and much worse. Miss Rachel however, did not need common sense or intuition. To see she was being let down and not very easy. Once Annette began visiting for therapy sessions. Usually she stayed until last patient left. Handing over day's take, and tidied office for next session. Annette was always scheduled as last patient. Tyrone told Miss Rachel to take evening off, after checking her in. Most times arriving by taxi or favour of co-worker. Today, Delroy dropped his wife off. Miss Rachel asked if he was by any chance, passing a distant bus stop. Turned out he did pass the bus stop, took her straight home. That and ensuing evenings, unknown to Annette. Now watch how this deck of cards gets shuffled and everyone dealt a hand. Her supervisor called her in for off clock powwow. Yes folks. Annette is now working under supervisor, whereas previously she was a manager. He told her this was off record chat to which she should pay keen attention. Yes, the company pays for twelve sessions each interval. There's nothing to prevent her taking all sessions for all intervals. However, she should look at it from another angle. Which might not make it advisable for her to continue doing so. Human resources analysts could conclude, she is not being helped by therapy. Hence, whatever ails her, could require deeper intervention. In which case, she could also be deemed unstable. Possibly compromising workplace safety. She confided, her negative lateral demotion with reduced income and more work. Was at base of her discontent. To which he told her to suck it up like toast in yolk. Or find another job which freed her of anxieties and possible negative motivations. Heeding advice she cut therapy sessions, opting for Saturdays. They weren't absolute friends, but exchanged more than casual greetings when in office. Annette asked Miss Rachel if she knew anyone for whom she could vouch their honesty, doing day's work at her home. Running laundry machines, vacuuming and dusting, changing linen and so on. Miss Rachel told Annette. *"Me don't make habit to vouch for people mam. Because some people change like green lizard. When you think you know them, is that time them do something cause you mouth to drop. Me can only vouch for myself mam, if that would be okay with you.*" Annette was elated, solving her problem without effort. Told Miss Rachel, she would discuss with her husband and let her know shortly. First, she discussed with Tyrone. He couldn't believe family's good fortune. Vouching for Miss Rachel's honesty, recommended her without hesitation. Only then did Annette tell and discuss the matter with Delroy, her husband. Now Muhammad did not have to sneak going to mountain. It came to him well dressed and smiling on a Saturday. Can you imagine how they palavered and indulged? Romped in wild abandon with reason tossing soiled linen in washing machine. Oh what sweet blessings in disguise. In all of this subterfuge it is apparent. Only unscathed puritan is Florence. I suspected, with time slipping away, she is focused on life's ambition, Being qualified as Gynaecologist. Has no intention, distracted by the mundane. Such as possibility, husband having extra marital shenanigans. Now, I am figuring. Miss Rachel must have whispered, suspicion or knowledge of. Liaison between his wife and her therapist to Delroy. Women do this to not only plunge the dagger, but twist it in the opponent. As they try solidifying position, as first and only other woman. Talk about life's challenges, without which it's an existence. And there being times, former creates the latter. Profitability had peaked, now headed downhill rapidly at Delroy's machine shop. Paradoxically, this came at a time of enhanced business opportunities and engagements. Despite which, if income is not being realized, solutions creates problems. Awarded a lucrative off site contract, fabricating and maintaining bulk handling facility. Delroy secured added capital to acquire machinery and vehicles. Income rose steadily from off site location, but fell precipitously at base. This should have been foreseen and measures put in place to forestall. Income from more than half work done at base, went into workers' pockets. They brought private jobs, used house materials, equipment and electricity. Completing at below cost rates and pocketing the windfall. Yet demanded, agreed hourly rates for showing up. Annette advised her husband, sell the shop and pay off bank debts with funds realized. Concentrate skills and focus on that over which, he could have direct control. No way would he even consider that as an alternative plan. His was most modern machine shop. Pride of ownership made him wanting to keep that flag hoisted. Here is a trade secret of banks, unknown to John Public. Banks continuously analyze every aspect of businesses in which they have vested stake. To determine current and future performance and sustainable profitability. Annette appraised the business, revealing chasm of disparity. Between it's worth and how much it could fetch as a going concern. We have heard that familiar real estate cliche, location, location, location. Area having undergone dramatic social change over years. Would be hard put, finding anyone willing to invest working capital. When once frequent customers, had taken business elsewhere, after being preyed upon by miscreants. Some came, selling stolen items. Others, quickly half wiped vehicle's windshield, demanding payment on customer's return. Which when not met, resulted in threats and near confrontation. Them that braved all this and came. Did so because, they got hundred dollar job done for thirty and even then, demanded unpaid credit. Faced with reality of situation. Delroy approached bankers with graphs and work-income charts. Supporting plan to relocate the shop. Bring back clientele, enhance income and return the business to profit. Repaying advances in shorter time than allocated. Was surprised when told, matter-of-factly. Expectations were contrary to facts and reality. Business relocation would not solve recurrent issues, without physical boundaries to isolate clientele from production staff and areas. System of jobs, costing and full payment, before work began was of utmost necessity. Completed job, not having value, except to person commissioning same. It was not something that could be sold to another client, hence need for prepayment. Struggling with double reality of his failing business, and her lateral demotion. Delroy and Annette agreed with each other. Thirteen year old daughter's place should be with them, instead of maternal grandmother. She was apt to be seen as, forgotten Pilgrim. Having spent half her life with grandma. Now at threshold of teenage leading to adulthood, it was time parents took crucial years of her development in hand. Grandma being more likely to guide by lore, instead of modern science. She could visit grandma on holidays. Home sweet home must be with mom and dad. Can anyone imagine how surprised Annette was, when Laura told her. *"I am never coming back to live with you and your husband. After all he did to me, forcing me to flee to grandma's house."* **"Child! 'My husband' as you call him, is your father and…."** It was grandma who cut her daughter off, saying. *"Careful how you talking, you only giving devil reason to glee."* **"Laura!"** Annette called her daughter's name. **"What could your father have done, you could not have told me. And even now, you don't seem wanting to?"** Laura remained mute, it was grandma who took up response. *"I know Laura is your child. But, when I tell you she not leaving here, I mean it. Now, if you like you can go and get the police, but I guarantee you. When they come, and after Laura and I talk to them. They going leave her right where she is. Where you and your husband going, is another question you might ask, and don't want hear the answer."* In a jaw drop daze, Annette hugged her daughter who hugged her mom and said. *"I love you mom, I miss you."* Annette said same words to Laura as both shed a tear. Annette said to her mother. **"Thanks for caring, mom. I don't know where to begin. But here and now is as good a time and place as any. I will stay in touch."** Grandma too got in on the hugging, and One would say. Sufficient unto the day is evil thereof. Matthew 6:34 Annette had long ceased going to Tyrone for therapy of any kind, but remained friends. Miss Rachel no longer worked at Tyrone's office. Came two days to Annette's and Delroy's house. He too had given up slapping flesh with the old lady. Although she thought she could still hold her own, outdoing best of best. We know how most men are, always focusing on cradle or romper room. Never mattered what prowess Miss Rachel thought she had. For Delroy, her time had come and gone, novelty flat like ice melted cola. This is true of people in general. Rarely do we recognize and accept, we are spent and crumpled. Just like dollar bills, banks withdraws from circulation. Annette was in quandary, such as never before faced in life. Wanting to know if Tyrone would have sessions with Laura, in pursuit of truth. Which she would follow, with a physical by Florence to determine extent of. Figured she could keep this among friends, without making it public. When Tyrone told her, *"No"* to both proposals, she yelled at him. **"What the hell you mean by, No?! My mother tells me my child has been messed with by her father. You're telling me, do nothing? I tell you what I'll do. I'll go home and bash his friggin' head flat as a fritter."** She began hyperventilating and crying at once. Tyrone hugged and let her have her cry. All done, washed her face, came back, sat on the couch and stared at him in anticipation. He calmly began.*"Annette, you are this moment, caught in quicksand. Those you are calling on to help you, can get stuck with you if they are not careful. Do not struggle, do not fight. Just stay calm and still, let's look at options. Okay? Now, if I talk to, and Laura says anything. That's even remotely close to accusation of wrongdoing. I am duty bound to report this to child protection agencies. Patient client confidentiality and privilege, does not apply. Where possibility of crime exists. Florence, doing physical is bound to report her findings, for same reason I have to. Your mom might not be aware. But she is only One with one foot out and other in jail. Why? Because whatever Laura said to her, she should have said to One or both parents. At which time a parent, which would have been you, as mother. Would have taken child to Paediatrician or doctor. Who would do physical after being told of accusation. Then you know what would get bigger as it rolled downhill. All I can say to you is, talk to a lawyer and find out how best to proceed. Only person you are obligated to protect is your child, no One else. Bear that in mind, and no head bashing please. I beg you. Lord have mercy."* Annette went home and packed a suitcase, then made two phone calls. First to her husband, he was not available. Shop foreman, Mr. Wilkins was and elected taking a message, or she could call back. We are still light years away from cellphones, so don't start thinking. *"Why didn't she call him on his cell?"* She slowly and clearly told Mr. Wilkins, whom she knew was slightly hard of hearing. **"Tell Delroy Forbes, stay away from me and my daughter. Or else he will be a dead man, for what he done to her. In case he gets to me before I do. I left a letter with details for police to hang him upended. Thank you, Pop Will."** Next call was to taxi despatcher for a cab to her mom's house. Brought mom up to date on what had so far transpired and advice given. To an extent, grandma was in most precarious position of adults. Here she was, faulting her mother for not having said anything to her. Soon as she got wind of this dastard deed. Now she was shocked and dismayed when her mother told her. She had repeatedly told Laura to pack and get ready to go home, when end of summer holidays drew near. Child wept and begged grandma, to not send her back home, but would not tell reason why. Child only promised to tell grandma, if grandma swore to not tell her parents. Child wanted to do so of her own volition, when time was right. Of primary concern to her, was fear getting her father in trouble. She could never live with knowledge, this would be brought on by her. Told grandma she would run away, not be seen or heard from again. So grandma sat on and incubated a crime. Hoping it would not hatch a life sentence. Looking at entire drama. I can envisage Delroy on needles and pins, sweating in fear Laura will say something to grandma. Time passed and calm prevailed, he figured hurricane season was gone for good. Now, he wanted to bring dear Laura back home and be reunited. Possibly, take up where he left off. Her now older, he could up his game. Who knows what goes on in mind of such a man? It is worth recalling, this union started out with Delroy having a twelve year age advantage on Annette. She never heard from or about Delroy, going forward. Took no interest in shop, equipment or disposal of. Tyrone prompted her doing so, citing. This was Laura's legacy to inherit. Years later, her mother passed, Annette sold her house. Matrimonial property could not be disposed of. Because Delroy had not been declared dead. But, just leave things to a lawyer, moreso a crooked One. Ways will be found, over under and around any obstacle arising. Documents were attested, occupants paid monthly sum for years. During which they paid all municipal taxes. When a stipulated sum was realized, lawyer would then allow occupant or survivor to take permanent possession by undisturbed occupancy over extended period. Laura is now an adult woman and mother to her son. For this she is happy. Because, if she had a daughter and a man did to her, what her father did. She wouldn't threaten as her mom did. Would carry it through by whatever means available. These times, gender does not insulate any child from sexual predators. But, let her be happy in her beliefs. It's all a state of mind. Thing I cannot understand and will not ask is. How did Laura qualify to be employed as maintenance manager for an apartment complex? Supervising and at times filling in for situations arising. Where and how did she acquire this multi-skilled proficiency? I am certain there aren't many women so qualified in a male dominated field. But again, I will ask no question and hear no lie. So now we take a closer look into this chapter's heading. Sex deviants among sexes.

What is there in male buildup that causes him to seek sexual gratification from his own seed? We don't hear of mothers raping or in any way, pleasuring herself in deviant manner with her son. Methinks it's all etched in female embodiment we call maternal instinct. Which is most times non-existent in the male. Focussed on sexual pleasure as he is, when a child does comes forth. Pride gives a paternal self congratulation. Only then is paternal connection fostered for some. Others hit and run, never to be seen until sometimes the child becomes a jewel. Which he now tries to fit on his crown for all to see. For the female it is much deeper. She becomes bonded to unborn child from moment she is aware of it's presence in her womb. It stirs at times, filling her with anxiety of oh happy day. Hence her being able to see her child as part of her, with which she could never think of seeking any pleasure.

Except of nurturing and caring as dictated by her inherent maternal capacity. Look back for a minute on Paolo. **"People at Play" chapter 16**. In front of mixed gathering. He admires Polaroid photo of baby daughter's vagina. Gushing with unconscious delight to Eduardo. *"Fica."* Who broadly grins and replies. *"Ah! Fighetta."* Women, including his wife and child's mother, all laugh as their askewed faces reflect abject embarrassment and shame. It is not far fetched to see him at some point forward, being engrossed with touching, and who knows where it can go from there. Which all evidence suggests, was situation with Delroy. Left in his care, bath and change brought him pleasures he pursued until it got out of hand. Although nature and extent of misdeed has not been disclosed. It is unforgivable, irrespective of extent. Most male animals are similarly endowed with unexplained desire to copulate without regard for relativity. You will see a Ram kid coming of age and taking a shot at it's sister and mom. She horns him away but he keeps coming back. A Rooster struts with pride around his newly hatched chickens. Keeps an eye on them as they become pullets, he drops a wing and circles them. Climbs aboard, lifts their tail, gives a satisfied chuckle after dismounting. I am not talking about sex with underage children. This is despicable behaviour indulged in by both male and female. Again, male thing predominantly so than female. Or maybe it's an equal score, but male transgression readily makes news. Because they're either caught with their pants down. Or child will talk, sooner or later under intense interrogation at times. Boys rarely talk about encounter with adult female neighbour, teacher or whoever. Why? Because, like me, he enjoys and revels in the encounter. It's a crown he cannot wear. But must let friends and inner circle know of his achievement. Which, more than likely they are yet to accomplish. I didn't tell anyone anything about Miss Candy. I was sworn to secrecy or else, and dared not let my lips become unzipped. Young lad, coached from Acorn to Oak is as thrilled. As Lass going from bobby socks to stockings. Unforgettable experience that can only event, once in One's lifetime. **"The Lucky Bastard"-Book One**

Rest room challenges

Fast food eateries without fail, provide unfettered access to restroom facilities for all and sundry. Restaurants with menu prices that sifts unwashed plebes. Has policy, discouraging restroom use if you are not a customer. Panhandler Pete hies to bush or bus shed. Walked into a minimum $45 per tab place, cashier asked. *"Table for one, sir?"* Broke protocol, asked. **"Where's your bathroom?"** *"Oh! Sorry, it's closed for sanitizing. I can seat you and someone will take your order. Our restroom should be available before your meal is served. Okay?"* This young woman has a smile to calm any savage beast. Does the business pay for denture maintenance as part of her grooming package? Told her I just wanted to take a quick pee. She repeated, restroom was being cleaned, sans the grin. Barely made it to Publix, turned my finger into a dipstick. Washed and dried, bought $5 lottery tickets. Store made a profit and I could make a fortune. Lack of public restrooms is major problem, civic leaders refuse to address or even acknowledge. Some older men develop prostate issues which creates frequent need to urinate. One gets off the bus. Goes to the bathroom before going to the train. First one is out of order. Next stop, the place is locked. Security has a key, but tells you, facility is out of order. Then, he adds. *"Go across the street to the SubWay."* The door is locked and clerk says, someone's probably in there. If you're not ordering, occupant won't be coming out any time soon. You make one more stop and security guard tells you. *"They started digging for new apartment buildings and busted all the pipes. None of the bathrooms working since."* Tempted to ask him where does he go when nature calls. Train is on the way so you do a sprint. Government Centre brings relief. Every time you squeeze holding valve, a small drip escapes. Back in ye olde backward third world country, there were public restrooms all over the city. Manned around the clock, a fee was required, but not enforced. One such, a quad unit was located in the hospital district where rural folks came in droves. These were gender neutral restrooms and two were open when two were closed for cleaning every hour. Patrons were mostly women. Men found a corner, bus shed, lamp post or bush to tinkle. No One went to jail doing this, authorities had bigger problems on their hands. Here in our first world city, public urination gets you a stint in jail. All the more reason One would think, why effort should be made to provide public restrooms. Intermodal facility, designed to accommodate fifteen bus routes connecting with elevated trains, has one restroom. There's toilet, urinal and wash basin. Most often it is out of order and unavailable. City or County owned property. How did their building department review and pass plans, allowing this to go forward is a mystery soon made clear. One thing is for certain, this shortcoming will be difficult but not impossible to be corrected. Question is. Will this be done? Not a chance. Let's see how lack of public restrooms, and businesses refusal accommodating John Public. Plays out to John's relief in a theatrical format.

Matthew is an active eighty years old man, retired but still employed to keep ends meeting. Letter from his bank warned. Rainy day stash had not had activity for some time. It was being declared dormant, and subject to monthly fee. Girlfriend told him, her bank paid higher interest and did not charge monthly fee to service her account. Riding second bus, having to catch a third. Now wished he had put on a diaper as advised. Avoids doing so, because diapers gives bulkhead image and brings stares. Began "holding" and fretted. Jeans' colour would expose incontinence. Here's a contradictory fact. Whenever urge to go arises, be it one or two. Do not hurry. Faster you try to hurry, less control you're going to have on holding muscles. In words of Desiderata. *"Go placidly."* Also, fart is not always what you think it is. Easy does it, or there could be lumps. **"Surprise."** Is never pleasant. Matthew walks in the bank, scans the building furtively. A young eager Beaver comes from around the counter. Greets with big grin and palm held for a shake. Matthew begins. *"I would like to borrow your bathroom key, if you would just point me in the direc…."* Eager Beaver interrupts. **"Sir, we reserve use of facilities for our** customers and...." Matthew addresses Beaver, by shirt's name tag. *"Daniel! Any second now. I could unload right here where I stand. Do you want to close shop and wait for off-site janitors to...."* Daniel was already entering keypad code, opened the bathroom door for Matthew. He went in, took his leak and breathed a long sigh of relief. Opening the door, he saw Daniel and Morgan standing. Latter, with storm trooper's countenance. Seeing him about to chide, Matthew preempted and said. *"I am here to get information on a higher than average, interest yielding product a friend told me about."* "Oh!" Morgan declared, with a smile that said. *"That changes everything."* **"I am sorry, sir. Promotion ended recently. But, we do have new promotions from time to time, and would welcome your interest at that time."** Plucks and hands Matthew a business card. For a minute he thought he'd prod the Bull and. *"Pardon me, sir. For being rude. You were going to say, before I interrupted. Please go ahead."* It is said, One should embrace succor prevailing and quit whilst ahead. So did old man Matthew, laying curiosity to rest. See how that image conjured mentally by Daniel, expedited his action?

Mary had a little lamb-5

It all began before I was even born, but I came to know the pipe smoking old lady. Who lived in an elevated one room walk up, behind the main dwelling. As it came to me, the old lady whom everyone called "Granny." Worked as domestic helper with family, owners that lived in the big house. Being a "live-in" she lived in a one room stilt house. Every structure on this and surrounding plots, were built at ground level. For no obvious reason, this room was built on stilts. Accessed by a wooden, weathered staircase of about twelve treads. So, it was fairly high above ground. Rickety and patched, it was a bit unstable and unsafe. Square holes evidenced banisters no longer in place. Talk about a trap on springe for that old lady. Maybe, design was a future flood refuge. Granny was old. I should say, ageless. No One knew her age for sure. Events she sometimes reminisced on in precise detail. Led folks guessing her age at over a hundred. She was hale and hearty, walked without aid of a cane. Spoke with tremor in her voice when she regaled. Other than that she was never ill or went to doctor for any reason. To accentuate her existence, follow closely here. When she came to work for these folks, they had one daughter. For whom Granny was nursemaid from day one. When parents passed on they left the property to only child, Rebecca. She married and had one boy, Saul. Whom Granny also nursed into adulthood. He was a lazy, weed smoking, neer-do-well. Smug in knowledge, mom's house would pass to him sooner than later. Possibly because mom was in poor health. Can you imagine that? Rebecca's husband died young, in tuberculosis scourge. Granny's room and board were taken care of by Rebecca. Granny had to have "coppers" in threadbag to buy munchies and incidentals. In this pursuit she sat small children, no more than two at a time. Made it clear to mothers, she did not want riches. *"That there boat sailed, left me at seaside waving."* She needed to buy pipe tubacki and keep a bit of bread under her pillow. So that when Gabriel came, she would not go home empty handed. A child was brought for her to sit, by a mother who was not from the area. Folks speculated. Child was fathered by Saul who wanted deed kept secret. How else would this strange woman just turn up with a child asking Granny to sit? Mothers had to get infants at day's end. This mother never came back, that or any day for some time. Child was as black as solid Onyx. Folks dubbed her, "Tar baby" but chipped in with clothing and feed. Someone volunteered bringing the matter to attention of police and went to the station. Sergeant listened, then told do-gooder. *"Don't worry, the mother soon turn up. You know how bus run bad sometimes."* Response brought back to community, created unbridled amusement. It was clear, police did not want to put time and energy on the matter. Hence, disingenuous response. One more example of how those in authority, might respond to the privileged. As compared to disenfranchised plebs. A letter came one day for "Granny." Courtesy of postman, familiar with aliases in his district. She almost fainted from surprise, not ever having received a letter before in her life. Inside was infant's age paper (birth certificate) giving her name as Petrona Ivey. Female child of Miss Drop the baby and run. Everyone settled down, taking care of "Tar baby." Proving in truth, it did indeed take a village to raise a child. So it was that "Tar baby" grew, was sent to school and taken to church worship. On receipt of birth paper, Granny naturally showed it to neighbours. They being involved in care of this child, entitled them to peruse and comment. Everyone thought child's name was backward. Taking Ivey to be her christian name, misspelt. She was called Ivey Petrona. I was about thirteen years old, having first met Granny and Ivey. When I was about eight years old. It goes without being said, Ivey was a grown woman to me a child. My mother at first dragged me to church with her, but I was soon more eager than she was to visit the house of worship. Having just ran away from August Town after maturing stint with Miss Candy. I was precocious beyond my years. Bob, a quite handsome chap was church leadress' nephew. Which gave him access to gab and laugh freely with young female Christians. I tailed him like Pilot fish that swims with sharks to get scraps. We both had a crush on our Sunday school teacher but worshipped sister "Black Ivye's" arse. I must explain monicker's origin before proceeding further. There were two Iveys in church, so members gave monickers to identify each. We already know, Petrona Ivey was blacker than night. It was no stretch when she was called **"Black Ivy."** Other Ivy was a brown woman, almost mulatto with snout for a mouth. They could have simply called her **"Red Ivy"** but opted instead for **"Hog mouth Ivy."** Let me hasten to add. These names were not used maliciously, although never face to face. It was just used casually in conversation, like. *"Hog mouth Ivy wear one Irish linen frock Sunday night. Wonder who give her that?"* Another time it was. *"Anybody hear the news? Hog mouth Ivy getting married to brother Cyril, the old man with the big banjo."* "Big banjo" was an upright base. Tall as the old man and played with a stringed bow. Back to sister Black Ivey. I found myself mesmerized by her arse. Lusted and imagined gently stroking it from crest to fall. When she wore her navy blue uniform with accordion pleats. Bishop intoned. *"Let us pray."* Eyes closed, I mentally pictured her arse. Like a banked river flowing in a slowly widening channel, towards waterfall's edge. Tumbling over rocky ledge, water spreads. Creating small vertical waves before dissipating in pool below. That was exactly how dress' pleats came apart, widening to hem. Folks referred to hers as a "bench" behine. We always called out to her after service. Like two parrots, we sidled up and. *"Hi, sister Ivey."* Each after the other. Once, she hugged Bob after his "hi." Momentarily jealous, putting it down to he being nephew of…Then it was my turn to be hugged. Oh, how I encircled her girth with inner glee. Dribbled my hand down to brink of her arse. She let go of me and walked away, not making much or even being aware of my perverted intent. You think? Brother Bennett called me over and.*"What's with you bwoy. Want turn man before time?"* Totally nonplussed, I said not one word, he added. *"Have to keep eye on you. You bigger than you size and older than you age."* Y'all see what I'm talking about? Us young perverts weren't only Ones fantasizing sister Ivye's arse. How else would brother Bennett, standing afar off, yet happen to notice my move? Me? Oh, I was near fourteen. Back benches were for visitors and children, or members being punished. For transgressions shown leadress by holy ghost. Sunday night, I came to church during song service. There was sister Ivey standing in third pew, bashing her tambourine. I jostled in close beside her, began clapping and singing praises. As we prepared to sit, I smiled broadly and greeted. **"Hi, sister Ivy."** She smiled back but said nothing. Tambourine and Bible she put left, against wood siding of building. I sat to her right, expanding a thigh to make contact. Luxuriating in warmth of her thigh and leg from end of my short pant leg. What a rise. She stood again, we sang praises to the Lord. I stayed seated. When next she sat, tambourine was moved to her right. She was firmly against the siding. Then came whispers and stares seeking confirmation. *"Sister Ivy in family way."* That's to say, she was pregnant. Now y'all recall when a similar thing overcame my mother. She was called up by tribuna. Tried, read out of membership and excommunicated. **"The LuckyBastard"-Book One** Hence, sister Ivey's punishment was mild in comparison. In time she had a son who was christened at church **"Malcolm Ivey."** My mother and her neighbour debated this, until it came out. Ivy was indeed her surname, spelt Ivey. Shortly after, church became embroiled in a scandal of secretary caught in adultery. And leadress similarly with deaconess' husband. Oh, it was era of shaming and damning. But it all passed and folks died or dispersed. In my early twenties, church going girlfriend lived in same lane as sister Ivey. I would greet her with a wide grin, which she returned with a cautious leer in silence. After a while I let her be. Still admiring her arse. Happens their landlady, was church deaconess. Heard sounds of ecstasy coming from next door apartment. Which she mistook for visitation by the holy ghost. Being more steeped in this spiritual phenomena, she came to guide and assist. Caught by surprise and tying to restrict my flight, a tussle ensued. My shirt got ripped to bare and deaconess fell. Later years, aged mid forties.Successful entrepreneur with business, sourcing goods for municipal bus company. Making delivery to stores, young man comes to verify and sign. I stare at him. **"Malcolm Ivey."** I say, puts a hand forward, which he snail like moves to grasp. Then says in a low voiced drawl. *"You know me, boss?"* **"I know you from you born and christen at mother Brown church. Also you mother. Sister Petrona Ivey was member."** I motor mouthed my reply. He verified delivery and signed the book. We stood silent until I asked. **"So, how's you mother? Haven't seen her for…."** *"Mom's awright."* He replied and went on. *"I will tell her you ask for her. What you name again? You come here all the time? I just start work here. Maybe that's why I never see you before."* **"Tell her, sister Hinds' son, Lenny."** Couldn't help thinking, he was slightly retarded. Spoke so low, One had to lip read whilst listening keenly to get what he was saying. A simple word like okay, could take three seconds with this guy. It wasn't a slur like being drunk or, he just spoke with uncertainty. As if he was reading from slow moving teleprompter. Next visit, not seeing him I enquired. He came forward from stock counting chore. ***"Moms say to ask, how your mother do. She will glad to see you if you feel like you want come look for her. We live up at….Let me get piece of paper."*** He walks away just as snail like as he talks. Something is wrong with that boy. He comes back and hands me a paper with the address, says. ***"Me can't stay too long, me doing stock."*** I look at him as he slowly sidles away and thinks. *"Boy, they moved your ass because garage personnel finds it quite irritating to interact with you."* Mechanic assigned a one hour job, does not want to spend twenty minutes getting parts. Hope he recognizes he is not being an asset to this operation. I suspect he is where he's at by someone "pulling a string" for him. Anyhow, I have an address to which I am going, a Sunday afternoon. Cruising to the gate, tooted "Big Red's" horn. My 1972 Ford F250. Got out and rattled the gate whilst saying. **"Hold dog, stranger."** Front door opens. Slim built, white haired man walks briskly to the gate. I stare at him, he so looks like. I am certain he's. **"Mass Rupert, the postman."** I blurt, surprised. ***"Rupert Malcolm, in person. And who moight you be ole chap?"*** He asks as he shakes my hand. We walk towards the door, I begin. **"Me was a little bwoy who use to live…"** I pause as he opens the door and announces. ***"Oi say now, Pet. Are you visitor ready?"*** In that decidely British accent. A curtain gets parted and a lovely three year old toddler steps forward. Unmistakably, cat's kitten, who is right behind and comes with open arms for a hug. ***"Little Lenny, my God look at you all grown up. I would pass you on street and not know is you. How you mother? Come in, sit down. Oh! I forgot my manners. This is my husband, Rupert and my daughter Millicent, Malcolm's sister. He waited twenty eight long years to get her, but he has to blame his father for that."*** As they say, there followed an awkward silence. Rupert it was who broke hush. ***"Well now, Oi told you. Oi'd be going to make good our future. And all you had to do was wait till I got back, jest loike Oi done promised. You kept to your*** *promise and waited, so did Oi. And we all here having jolly good toime. Let's get us a point and laugh, as we do in the ole pub back in good ole Lundun. Oh, Oi fugot ole chap. Nut a point in the house and the pub not open till later. Let's have us a good chat and laugh about it eh. Sholl we now? Now I ask you, ole chap. Would you believe, before I left. Locked the door, took key to England. Told Pet here, let no intruder break and enter or else. Whot doos I comes back and finds? Why, the door been locked tighter than when I left it. My Pet here is One herself only."* Pet blushed and said. **"Stop it, Rupert. You only man I know, talk crazy when he drink or when he not drink."** Kept my visit to doctor's and bid both goodbye, with best wishes for future. Just couldn't believe this could happen. A woman waits more than a quarter century for a man to come back and marry her? What if he had met an accident? As I got into my truck, the thought hit me. *"Times have changed. Little Millicent gonna have a tough time in school, through no fault of her own."* Well, maybe not. Few years later, aged twelve or near. She was on stage at private school's concert, doing karaoke of Junior Reid's **"Worry dem a worry dem foreign mind."** A reggae hit with lyrics. *"Look how me black, look how me shine."* Needless to say, as Millicent sang and gesticulated at her frame, hands in motion. There was prolonged laughter and loud applause at her apparent self denigration. If One trolls online, there's quite a roster of deep ebony supermodels, claiming fame, fortune and revelling in. See? I guess her next karaoke rendition will be. *"I will survive"* Bless that child. She cannot be thin skinned, or as Peggy Lee sang. *"You gotta have heart, miles and miles and miles of heart."*

The Piper? Still amongst us-6

Mortimer Saguenay IIIrd was born in then British Guiana, of Canadian parents. Dad, Mortimer IInd and Mom, Dominique nee Devereaux. Mortimer I[st] was born in city of his name, Quebec, Canada. Where he oversaw huge logging and pulp mill operations. Industry being in their blood it was no surprise, Mortimer IIIrd got his head deep in British Guiana's fledgling bauxite mining operations. Conditions on site paralleled a prison working environment. Wages paid miners were paltry, conditions were dangerous and lacking basic safety standards. This was open secret to them that had power to regulate. Most people were at the time, unaware. Seeds of a social revolution had been sown. Which could be fertilized to quicker maturity, with wealth from bauxite-alumina export. Commonwealth Caribbean countries, Jamaica and Trinidad, reaped modest windfalls from bauxite and oil exploration. There was overt evidence, supporting inhumane exploitation of workers on mining outposts. Them that had power to make changes, feared or were reluctant doing so. Not wanting to take steps that could drastically curtail progress towards their agenda. To succeed, a revolution requires different forms of support. Principal of which is that of a people. Hence, them that suffered in fields, were unwittingly making contribution. Monuments would be raised in their honour at appropriate time. Sons and daughters would see symbols of parent's and foreparent's contribution. To the newly, prosperous nation, rising from shackles of colonialism. Designated exploration areas were larger than some nearby countries. Totally under control of one man who regarded himself as quasi governor. Local businesses were under his ownership, selling goods at inflated prices. You see folks, being in this remote outpost. Workers were overjoyed getting that which they had been accustomed to in the city. Even at inflated price it was worth the while. There were those who worked three shifts on fourteen days schedule, to amass worthwhile paycheck which was spent right there on base. Once a month, bus loads of women came. Consorting with miners, scavenging what they could from tightly clenched fists. Miners with unresolved disciplinary events against their names, were not allowed visits to "hospitality barracks." Until such events had been resolved either way. In their favour or exoneration by penalty. It goes without being said, Saguenay family were endowed with untold wealth and influence. In this vast undeveloped

South American country's region of third son's birth. As happens in such instances, full extent and quantum of, will always be a secret. Maybe it was coincidence and maybe not. Ships that loaded and took bauxite to Europe and North America. Were all owned by Saguenay Shipping of Canada. Name being painted in white, along ship's port and starboard mid-sides. This, in and of itself, brought great prestige and elevation of stature to Mortimer IIIrd and his circle. He took pride of place amongst government and other dignitaries. Including, then Minister of Trade and Industry. Who threw symbolic switch opening the plant in March 1961. British Guiana's production then was drop in proverbial bucket, compared to industry leader, Australia. Still, it brought ample foreign exchange to support national development and social infrastructure. An unexplained, contradictory schism between trading nations creates situation. Where vendor nation, not only decides price for goods sold other nation. But, also price paid other nations for their goods. This vexing situation led five countries to meet in Baghdad, Iraq. September 1960, and form OPEC. Organization of Petroleum Exporting Countries. Needless to say, this took them accustomed, dictating prices for commodities, by surprise. Putting them in position of new disadvantage. But not for long, as they always get their way. Right always wilt under sunshine of might. Still, as things went. One could say, caught with pants down, put them on guard. In 1975 when bauxite producing countries tried similar gimmick, forming International Bauxite Association. Steps were taken by countries with interests at stake, to ensure impotence and strangulation of this organization. See how with time, aircraft making industry. Possibly, largest source of aluminium demand. Successfully developed and switched to composite materials. But alas, we are getting ahead of our tale. It is said with some degree of truth. *"There is no honour among thieves."* Mortimer IIIrd knew and agreed, free hand he enjoyed. Was to free his hand, making asset diversion to the planned revolution. It was sacrifice expected of everyone, each in his own way. Peter was being allowed to rob Paul, provided he passed loot on to John. We know, the only greed revolutionaries embrace is their own. Unrest began in 1962 as an ethnic riot, which incubated a general strike in 1963. Few heads bounced in melee and British troops were deployed to quell situation. Just so you know, heads do not roll as claimed. They bounce, because of ears. With independence from Britain, May 1966 and name change to Guyana. Them that waited impatiently to launch aptly titled agenda. "People's Revolution." Found themselves ill equipped to challenge entrenched authority. Smuggled ordnance were inferior relics. Quite unsuited for engaging established authority with umbilical ties to a world power. Mortimer took his family and joined his smuggled wealth, in staid, sanguine, Barbados. Where a multi-purposed business was established on Pinfold Street. Times of Britain's colonial occupation in Caribbean region, certain countries with ample acreage. Were more conducive to agricultural production and ultimate export to motherland. As such, there was demand for labourers, mostly from India and peddlers from Hong Kong. Bermuda, Barbados, Bahamas and Cayman Islands, each with sparse acreages. Were summer havens for British middle class, who sometimes made retirement Eden in one of these countries. Whatever agri-industries were attempted in these small islands, soon proved to be mere trophy undertakings. Lacking profitability by absence of volume. In elite discussion circles, Barbados was called "Little England." It should be mentioned, only first male of each generation was christened Mortimer with ascending numerical suffix. Mortimer IIIrd sired four girls with a wife and literally hundreds of both sexes, with concubines and field workers on minefields. Men as a rule worked in mining and equipment maintenance. Women were assigned housekeeping, canteen and trading post concessions. It never mattered whether or not women were married. They needed only be young and comely in eyes of Mortimer IIIrd. Last Sunday of every month, clergy person from rotating denominations kept church and blessed newborns. Baskets passed around, collected offerings which were turned over to mine managers. Who then gave stipulated sum from that collected to attending clergy person. Encampment had it's own police and grievance settling tribunal to keep order and peace. Religion was not primary focus, there was a structure not unlike that of Jim Jones. A self proclaimed Messiah who in 1978, got hundreds of Guyanese and American citizens to participate in mass suicide. When people isolate themselves from civilization and adopt cult guidance, untimely demise is a given. In short time, Mortimer Saguenay's heritage came to an end. Virtue of Mortimer IIIrd not having male offspring to don crown of IVth. Well, he did. But not with his wife, only by concubines. One such, named Desmond Brathwaite, came to Jamaica and worked with Sprostons. Canadian company that was also agents for Saguenay Shipping of Canada. Had he not been son of a concubine, he would have had glory of being named Saguenay. Thomas and James Harrison were brothers from Liverpool, who founded and owned Harrison Lines. Kirk Lines were owned by Kirkconnells of Grand Cayman. Think how tall Desmond Saguenay would walk, among such titled nobility and wealthy Mariners. He would not be called upon to provide birth certificate for ancestral proof in marine circles. When ships had **S A G U E N A Y** name in man sized white letters on port or starboard sides, exposed coming or going. Rumour mill would make him, modern day Lord Nelson and Captain Morgan all in one. Oh man, I would need sand bags to keep me tethered to earth. That my friends was how I met and befriended a descendant of Mortimers. In 1956, American trucker, Malcolm McLean. Explored and began guarded transition, moving cargo in metal containers. This was less labour intensive than previous methods. Made faster vessels turn around, thereby enhancing profits. Author is proud to have served McLean's company, SeaLand Service Inc., Under contract to equipment repair and maintenance facility. Kingston Container Terminal, Jamaica. As containerization took over cargo movement, ships had to be retrofitted to carry containers. Those that could not be or not worth cost of doing so, were ran aground at scrap yards. It cannot be said with certainty, this was factor Saguenay line closing shop in Kingston. Desmond Brathwaite, managed Jamaican divisions of "Sproston's" and "Jamtrac" Former, industrial equipment and materials supplier. Chiefly to bauxite mining company "Alcan" They also sold and serviced, British motor vehicles made by Rootes Group. Latter, was agent for "Caterpillar" equipment. He was a hard character to do business with. Always demanding a lot and giving very little, if at all. Now in sunset years, Brathwaite rues what he considers, life's cruel joke played on him. His second child was male, which would have been Mortimer had he been also. Over breakfast of ackee and saltfish with boiled bananas and fried dumplings, he lamented. ***"You know, I was this close being born great and at last minute, was cheated."*** I ask myself. What is this guy talking about? What last minute cheat is he referring to? Tells him I am just grateful for life and thrills it brings. Greatness would probably make me unhappy, bearing in mind. *"Unhappy lies the head that wears a crown."* From Shakespeare's Henry IV[th.] As close as he was to being born great, is as far as he ten times was from. It is easy for us to create illusions of greatness, then blame others for having deprived us of what we never had. Before closing this chapter, let's make an incursion into it's theme. That of Pipers being in our midst, playing a melody that enchants. Whilst leading us blindly to misery and ultimate annihilation. It takes just one person with an idea who asks the question. Why not? Then the idea gets whispered by ear of someone else who agrees and plot begins. First, we have to recruit like minded and right about here, deception begins. The project has to be presented in manner that glorifies, benefits and minimizes or eliminates negatives. Let's stay with politicization of a people, as we are more familiar with that subject. It bombards us from every front in repetitious cycle. If we paused to examine the melody. We would hear distant rumble of an approaching tsunami, soon to engulf body and soul. Entranced as we allow ourselves to become, we pay no heed. Piper blares his horn and we shout chorus of fanatical glee. He pauses to savour and revels in satisfaction. There is no turning back. His ascendancy is assured, there is no way but up. It's been said by those who have studied recurring phenomena, of mass hysteria or fanaticism. It is an inherent human reaction to certain stimuli. Same as propels bees to make honey and ants to secure queen and eggs in a flood. Mindless of their own survival. Yet, fact of existence teaches. First rule known to every life form, is that of self preservation. Us humans are of higher intelligence. Aren't we? Or Are we? Methinks, it's unconscious drift across divide between sanity and insanity. That divide being like a spider's nylon. Strong yet devoid of permanent resilience. Human decimation lies in our ability making decisions, which unlike other lifeforms. Does not prioritize rule of self preservation.

Hold on, I'm Coming?-7

Back in ye olde country, an honest supervisory level civil servant. Can, observing prudent spending habits.Save enough to qualify for mortgage on an average dwelling, by their mid to late forties. That's just barely squeaking in before the gate closes. At which point, mortgage would be denied by most lending institutions.. Unless they take on added expense of life insurance, with bank or lending institution as beneficiary. I was astounded, coming to the USA. Finding, age was not deterrent getting mortgage. Then again, some people never bother going through hoops. Chasing miraged glory of home ownership. Prefer having landlord or landlady fix what's broken, paint when necessary and most important. Pay big ticket items, like municipal taxes and insurance. Let's look at Reuben Grandison and see how this works for him. He came to the city, aged thirteen. From deep rural hinterland to attend high school. Boarded with aged couple, the Deeks. Both of whom were civil service retirees, living alone together. True. Children, all adults having gone off to raise their families and pursue vocations. Reuben being a country boy, as folks were wont to say. They got him out of the country, but try as they might. Couldn't get country out of him. Less than a month after settling in. That boy transformed front yard from bog of weeds and grass. To laid out beds of Petunias, Gardenias and Geraniums where butterflies and bees flitted. Aged Ones looked at him in awe, unaware he had only just began. They now loved spending times outdoors. Quickly got weary from standing and hurried inside. Reuben wanted to make himself a skate, already had two ball bearings. Wherever he went he never bypassed a bit of wood. Brought it home and made small pile behind the kitchen. First holiday from school he went to nearby sawmill, asked for some sapwood. Brought pieces home, hacked them with a machete. Making lengths of planks and flat boards, suited for skate making. Made instead, a bench for two. Nailed it securely to big Guinep tree by a corner of front yard. Having been invited to sit, the Deeks expressed hesitancy. Based on assumed skill at his age and quality of materials used. That boy demonstrated sturdiness of his bench by jumping up and down. As is said, he jumped nine and left ten in the dust. Now convinced, Deeks timidly sat, tried out the bench and it became outdoor haven. When the roof sprung leaks. Reuben climbed the Black Mango tree in back of the house. Let himself down onto the roof by rope and hammered zinc nails back in place. Then secured nail heads with boiled tar and cement. That homestead became a model farm, providing vegetables for Deeks and neighbours. Old man Deeks encouraged Reuben to take civil service exam, upon leaving high school. He would put in a word to right people on his behalf. "Pull a string" as folks would say. Deeks liked his girlfriend and treated both as their children. Truth be told. Visitors would not honestly think otherwise, unless told. Reuben was less than twenty years old when he began counter service at Collector of Taxes' city office. Four years later he was transferred to Collector General's office. Served by promotion, all departments. Until his now pending retirement at age sixty-five.Not only had Deeks passed on but so had their older children. Those still alive were in declining health. Cared for by grandson to whom Reuben paid rent over the years. Reuben paid rent in that house for fifty-five long years. Was now on brink of being thrown out. Grandson was free spirited Rastafarian. Wanting to get instant wealth from selling the home. Wisely, gave Reuben first go at the prize. Denied a loan, Reuben decided to apply his knowledge of the system. Became a licensed customs broker. Was in stead with lords of mercantile community and his church, where he was elder. But, see here now. Folks have never successfully segued from civil service to a job in commerce or industry. Again, it's that. "You get them out of the civil service, but can't get the civil service out of them" mindset. In the civil service, it doesn't matter if you are counter clerk or armchair warrior with buzzer on your office's door jamb. There's a woman whose only job is to bring you a fresh towel daily and glass of water with chipped block ice at frequent intervals. Even if you haven't touched the first glass, it's a symbol of position. Ice has melted and cold is getting tepid. She takes it away and brings you a fresh glass of sparkling thirst quencher. Even at this level, Reuben works leisurely. Gets a kick seeing queue get longer and faces more dour. Stoked ego gives him feeling of godship. His minute of creation is when he rejects paperwork for flimsiest of reason and calls out *"Next."* We know, Reuben can't take this bullshit mindset into real working world. By time he works up to an office with eight cedar filing cabinets. One sixteen inch fan, wobbling as it oscillates. Mahogany six drawers 72" by 48" top desk and Captain's or Mountbatten swivel chair. He has at his say so, ability to roll or quiet thunder. Ignores door buzzer and only answers four line phone, if certain coloured buttons gets lit. He pacifies his bleeding ulcer with crisp water crackers and warm cow's milk. Then slowly pores through last month's gazettes of tariff and procedure revisions. He belatedly discovers, redounds favourably on importer's submission, which was rejected. Forcing payment of a higher duty rate. But then, there are no penalties for over collection oversight. If by chance he detested the agent for whatever reason. He smiles and revels inward. *"Serves the son-of-a-bitch-right."* You understand, he knows he has to change if he wants to be successful outside the civil service. He tells himself he can do it, but they really can't. Never has or will. Fifty-five years of bad habit has become addiction from which there's no escaping for most others. For Reuben, there is a chance, because. He's going into self employed arena with purpose to succeed. We think it should be easier to adapt, but old habits as said, sometimes die hard if at all. One facet of Reuben's former top dog persona that's not boding well for him at present. Arises from how he handled puppies in his kennel. He snapped, barked and growled at them, for missteps so mundane as to be invisible. Now in their queue, they loathe him. Both are aware he can yet reach behind the counter and get them disciplined. Still, One will not waste opportunity to exact revenge. As one clerk shared at the lunch table. *"Although we can't cut out a guy's balls, we can still get a squeeze going."* They were all expressing surprise, at how drastic a change he had undergone since retiring. *"In his younger years, he was Tortoise. Now in his old age, he's moving like Hare."* One fellow opined, whilst another chirped in. *"I heard that he and his wife are trying to buy a house."* Were they successful? I did not follow through.

After all that beating around the bush. I come to Kathleen's saga with Johnny Gerberson and the Jacksons. Who recently moved into their home after years of scrimping and knotting pennies. Newly built four bedrooms home in middle class Washington Gardens. Named honoring a founding father of Jamaica's political dynasty, Norman Washington Manley. One of whose son is renowned populist, Michael Norman Manley. House was designed and built with what was called small side, standard configuration then. Big side was three bedrooms, bathroom, living and dining areas. Kitchen and back porch with exit to washroom and clotheslines out back. Small side was carport, one bedroom, toilet and shower. Kitchenette with access to back porch, washroom and clotheslines. Jacksons parked their old oil dripping Hillman Minx Hooptie to one side of the double carport. Allowing Kathleen, lounge area and access to small side she rented. Silently grumbling on having to mop polish and Hoover shine the carport every week, convinced she should not have to. Coaxed by her Manfriend who paid the rent, she did say this to Mrs. Jackson with a disarming smile. Ignoring her attempt at camaraderie. Mrs. Jackson laughed whilst suggesting, she find somewhere that did not include chore. Cleaning a carport without having car. Wished Kathleen would give opportunity. Getting higher rent for facilities she now enjoyed at lenient cost. Well, that died natural death. I swear, people should examine proposals in their heads before going utterance stage. My rule of thumb always is. What if situation in reverse and someone said or did that to me. How would I, or should I take it. We have to dry run things against ourselves first, before taking it to market and holding up a sign. Biased in our favour as we are, if there's remote chance we'd be pissed. Take it as gospel, other person will be hog tied irate. I think I should say though, in her defence. Kathleen figured she had to get feedback for Manfriend, when asked response from landlady. Given he was paying the rent and her not wanting him to think she didn't care. You can see how easily a relationship might be strained by such misconception. Let's not forget. Manfriend could be seeking way out of this play by pay relationship and it's obligations. After initial euphoria of conquest, frequency of being sated and cloyed. Men begin scanning the field anew. Ask Self if game's thrill is worth covert attendance and price of admission. They're not talking marriage and family, neither is he in this rent paying role indefinitely. He's probably searching horizon for new islets of paradise jutting from the surf. Let's say, Kathleen acted without having options. Women have inherent survival fortitude, but times they are forced to fetch water in wicker baskets. To their credit, when occasions arise they somehow pull through by dint of strength, although reputedly weaker of sexes. Johnny Gerberson was an insurance salesman, aged mid twenties. Two years younger than Kathleen, he was seen as better match for. Than father figure Manfriend in late forties. Johnny wanted to sell a life policy and take her for "a drink." She declined without emphasis, emboldening him to keep trying. She was I should tell you, a very attractive young woman with poise and style that turn heads. Especially after modelling a famous liqueur on television. Hence, her donned shawl in public. Manfriend's "contribution" for glory of her presence in his stable, was significant. She resisted invitation for a "drink." Not knowing when Manfriend might drop in and find her awol. He had her on short tight leash, which she silently resented, whilst freed from monthly obligation of rent. Not to mention, delicacies in refrigerator and pantry, they often went shopping for. We would say, she grinned and bore it well. Weekend on horizon, opportunity was going to come knocking. Manfriend's first daughter was getting married in a rural area. Family would be gone for an extended weekend. Kathleen told Johnny he could come and discuss insurance proposal, defiantly warned him. ***"Don't bring any wild ideas about you and me. Or else there won't be anything for us to talk about."*** Now, I realize you're guessing glaring punchline to the story. Yet has no choice but soldiering on to the end. Most Sundays after church, she relaxed in bra and panties after making sure, curtains were fully drawn. Played records on the old Telefunken stereo, dad gifted her before he died. Immersed in music she lost track of time, now scurried for quick shower. Normally she would take out clothes before going to bathroom. Now she did it in reverse. In birthday suit, she rummaged through drawers, taking out and putting back outfits.*"God, it's after four. It's a good thing he's a man and never punctual."* She speechlessly rued, rummaging drawers. Thought was broken by rapping at the door. She didn't need to, but asked. ***"Who is it?"*** **"It's me, Johnny."** He replied. ***"Okay, coming."*** She answered. Johnny heard. ***"Okay, come in."*** With a big grin, that young man walked in. Kathleen stood upright, frozen in fright for seconds. Brain directed hands to cover pubic area. No, best cover breasts. No, best try covering both and losing skill to cover, she yelled at Johnny. ***"What the hell you stand there staring at?! Take you ass out mi house!"*** View the promised land and not get there. I think it's fair, saying. Johnny found himself mesmerized, taken as is said, aback. Knowing he should *"Excuse me, I am sorry."*Retreat fast, versus *"Woweeeee, lucky Johnnyyyyyy."* She was not going to sit with him, discussing anything, after he had stared at her fully nude figure. She shoulda kept control by locking the door, always. It's a barrier against unexpected access, whether by invitation or mishap. "You learn" Quoting Alanis Morissette

Day with mi Amigo-8

Wilhelm called Al, needed a hand urgently doing something before a storm came through. Al drove to, met him at his gate, shook hands and asked. **"How's it going, Will?"** He said. *"Same game same dame."* Al stared unasked question. Will made circle with left thumb and index. Poked right index through centre of, he repeated. *"Same game! Same dame."* Ending with right thumb pointed to the house. Al laughed and told Will. **"It's same old same old."** Will rebutted. *"Hey my friend, to each his own. For you is hole, for me is the game. Let's go in and be respectful. She fright when hears strange voices. Thinks they come for the new mattress."* Al went in and greeted Will's wife, Miriam. She hugged Al briefly, then let go. After Wilhelm said to her. *"Miriam, don't hug so long and choke the fella, he's here to help me do work. Jeez. What is with you and choking?"* Miriam dismissed him and his comments with hand wave. Asks Al. *"How you beautiful young daughter? She no more teenager. I know you buy her car she like. She have the boyfriend, or she yet have the husband? Tell her, too soon for the babies. Live the happy carefree years, then babies. Two or three, but no more never. I remember how she very quick learned the driving so good. Surprised when I take her out first time. She say you not give her lessons and I say to me, she not tell truth. But when you bring her in the huge truck. I say, she true. I don't know how so good first time. But I talk too much and you not get say anything."* Al told her. **"You're right, little girl is now young lady in college. Mt. Holyoke, Massachusetts and no, there's no husband or babies yet. She's doing well though. Comes the summer, she's off to Ghana on some kind of exchange programme and…"** Three teenaged children came and shook uncle Al's hand, giving rise another comment from Wilhelm. *"See?! Our children smart people, they don't hug and choke. What if they hug and choke, he do the same? Ah, carrrramba."* Miriam waves a hand, tells Al. *"Pay him no mind, the head it worries him sometimes. He should get transplant like they do heart and the kidney and the…who knows."* She walks off, muttering, both hands gesticulating. Wilhelm steers Al through carport to open backyard. He initiates dialogue to which Al responds as you will follow. *"Now my friend, see my boat. You remember? Shiny, slick on the water. But you never took invite to come sail her with me. Now she up for scrap. I tell that guy to cut the tree, because all leafs from it fall in my boat. If I don't clean it, it's all bad for my boat. He says, if I want the tree cut, I cut what's hang over my boat."* "So, why didn't you cut it or have it done?" *"Well, shade also good for boat, but leafs not so good."* "It appears in good shape to me. Why you say, it's scrap?" *"Ah, you smart Al. Because you not buying, you say in good shape. Not so if you buying, then that time you say only good for scrap. Just like guy who come, say poquito dinero for scrap boat."* "Why don't you wash and take it out to enjoy the ocean? You're retired, love the water and love fishing. I remember, you used to bring back fish galore and call me to come get." *"Yes, I remember too, but now not like then. One cop pull up on boat. He say, no light, no this no that, so ticket. Other cop comes, says fish too small, fish too big. Then he counts bottles and caps. From that is more ticket, but I tell you now. Engine is no good, engine kaput. This good engine fellow looks at it and says. Gasoline ethanol not good for small engines. Use only ethanol free, but by then you know engine f…ed already. So what's use he today saying, use this and don't use that? Must go television, tell everybody. Then that be good."* Commotion of male voices next door, speaking in Spanish and yapping, snarling dogs. Prompts Al to ask. **"Will, what's going on over your neighbour?"** *"Oh, is the f...ing season before selling season and again a f...ing season and...."* **"What? They breed dogs over there for sale?"** *"That's right my friend. It's big business he gots going over there. One small dog is $600 and maybe $1000 when it's cannot move. When start moving, so does the money. Come, come and see here. We got holes for spying sons-of-bitches, them mother f...ers. Dollar a minute like back Delancey Street. One with no shirt, lives there and two Bitch dog. Sideways two, they pimp. See how that One stroke and rub the Bull? Know what I think?"* **"No. What you think?"** *"I think, if Bull don't make quick move. One them three, make move for his self. You see? They all got front load way out there, waiting for turn."* **"Front load, what front load?"** *"You look at them bastards. Asking, what front load? See? They be all stand bend over to hide el pito grande. That guy in holgada pantalones, what they say, baggy sweatpants. He's one eager mother f...er to move in if other two take walk."* Al walks to front, roars out laughing and says. **"You are something else man. I don't see the front load you talking about. You're imagining things. Forget the dogs. What you want us to do here today. What's the plan of action?"** Wilhelm whispers. *"Listen, my friend. When there's no dog action. They stand like we, talk all day, erguido, be up. When begin the, ah, coach. They get too, the impulso. Then do crouch to hide. Maybe my friend, you not see front load. Because you old and forget what looks like. Not me. I see front load, I use front load and....."* **"Hey, man! Listen up. You ask me here to give you a hand and then insult me by saying I'm senile and....."** *"No, no, no, mi amigo. You get story all wrong, you don't listen when I speak. Miriam, Miriam."* He calls and not getting response, tells Al. *"You wait right here, I tell you something good."* Just then, Miriam appears at a window, asks what he wants. He tells her. *"Cerveza fria for Al and un aguacate."* Says to Al. *"You like grande aguacate? Mucho nice, I tell you."* Miriam brings two beers and two large Avacado Pears. Al takes pears, tells Wilhelm. **"You know I don't drink beer."** He pauses, thinks and tells Al. *"Oh, sorry my friend, forget. I invite you my house. Must give your beer. Good Jamaica beer, the Red Stripe. I promise, next time I have for you the Red Stripe and we enjoy and laugh."* Al told him. **"Will, mi nuh drink beer or alcoholic drink or beverage, period."** *"My friend goes into the slang to show he not happy. I mucho sorry."* Miriam shouts to her husband. *"He says, he's not drink beer or alcohol never. Nothing unhappy about that."* Now it's Will's turn to reply. *"See? I knew all very long choking had to mean something. I work with you many years and not know slang. You come my house, very few times and my wife knows slang. But, I don't care, I don't care. So now, we talk about boat? Yes? Come on, let's do boat. I have good strong tools. I do all the work and you do drive. I raise the boat, first this side, then I raise that side. Each time, I take wheels off and put in the truck. We go tire place for air."* He clasps both hands and mumbles incoherently, then says to Al. *"I pray only air need, nothing more. We come back, I put tires back on boat. You tie the truck to hook and pull it out to shed in front. I call the guy, he brings tow truck and takes it away. I very sad to see my boat go. Mi bambino, but bring dinero. You know what I mean? But now bambino grow and time leave home like all bambino do. You agree, my friend? Of course, you agree. You bambino all gone, only my Miriam she keep them. Feed them and I sell my boat because..... .forget I said anything. So, it's very good? I do all work and you do drive?*

Very good. I'll tell you something again. I very much scared, whole tree fall over my boat. Comes down with the hurrican and smash my boat. Then, it's really scrap. I maybe have to pay the guy to take it out of here. God's truth, that's why I want it out in hurry, and also dinero. Very important that is, the dinero. I hide from Miriam, half the money and say I only get…..." **"Will, Will, Will!** Al firmly interrupts, goes on to say. **"Don't tell me anything about your family affairs. Because, Miriam finds out you sink off a portion of the money. Your very first thought is going to be. I whispered in her ear when she was choking me. So don't let me in on any family secret, keep it to yourself. I always tell people, to not confide secrets in me. So that when it comes to fore. I am not in their suspicion pool."** Wilhelm yet goes on to reply, after mulling Al's rebuke. *"You correct my friend, but I only hide half of money. So she not call her side family, and give my money all willy willy."* Then asks Al. *"Why you so much laugh, I say something funny?"* Al tells him. **"The saying is, willy nilly."** Will retorts. *"What you talk about? I is Willy. Who the f… is Nilly?"* Al tells him. **"Come on, bring the tools and let's get going. I don't want to be here all day."** Business is good at the tire shop, a wait is in the cards. How long or short, proprietor cannot commit. Wilhelm decides to search for candelabra base bulbs at nearby Home Depot, but balks at Al's intent to go on foot. *"You know, my friend. Walking is very much dangerous. Drivers you see there will run you over and not stop to see how you doing. I never no more walk."* Al tells him. **"We need exercise, it's stone's throw."** Wilhelm counters. *"You know when you come back, there will be big dent in your truck and nobody takes fault, because you didn't see. Others see but won't tell. Never."* Al kept walking and Wilhelm kept griping. *"Losing a pint by minute, feel like waterfall down my butt. Ah, this* *feels so f….in' wonderful. The guy who made aircondition was f…in' genius."* Both are browsing aisles. Al, for weatherproof socket covers. Wilhelm, for bulbs. Store stop selling spiral bulbs candelabra base, got to go LED instead. Wilhelm wanders off, Al finds his covers and goes to a cashier's kiosk that turns out to be customer service desk. Clerk points farther West to checkout queues. Rose, another customer service clerk says. *"I'll do it, bring it here."* With a smile that's so effervescingly warm. Al tells her. **"You are so accommodating. I have to tell you how much I appreciate the gesture."** *"Oh, I try."* Rose retorts with that warm smile. **"I know what it is."** Al tells her. *"What?"* She asks. **"It's good parental upbringing and please give my regards when you get home."** Al ended. *"Oh, thank you very much. Promise I will, you're so very kind."* She beamed. Later Al rewarded her with a complimentary copy of "People at Play" For which she thanked him ever so profusely.Wilhelm goes on the attack and accuses. *"You hitting on that child? She's baby, for crying loud. I stand way back cause I didn't want anyone to know, I know you. Like 'em young too but there's a limit, and you be at my house…."* Al yelled at Wilhelm. **"Yack, yack yackity yack, hold your horses Jack! I was telling her how well brought up she is and regards to parents for an excellent job. It wasn't a baggy probe."** All was quiet for a while as Wilhelm stood slack jawed then calmly said. *"I know, I know. I just make joke so heat don't get to me. See my friend?"* **"Let's give this lady our hands with her thing."** Al said, walking towards a mature woman trying vainly to manoeuvre oversized package into her car. **"Excuse me Miss. Would you like a hand……?"**Al began and paused, staring at the woman. She stared back at him probably wondering what was…Al blurted. **"Sister McGann? It cannot be, and yet."** He stood staring at the woman who smiled as if enjoying the moment, then said. *"You knew Sister McGann, young man? She was my mother and were she alive, would be vying for title "World's oldest person." How did you know my mother?"* Al replied. **"When I was twelve years old, she was Sister at University hospital and trained me to give my grandfather injections. Her and the Matron used to call me "Barefoot Doctor."** She reached out a hand to greet and said during handshake. *"Young man, you are talking about 1950's, late 1950's before my mother accepted position at newly formed, National Health Service and went to England. She came home, professor emeritus in 1982 and passed away February 1998, aged 104 years old. All her faculties were intact. She went to market, did her gardening and lectured at hospital's school of nursing. It is such pleasure to meet you. Here's my number, call me and we'll get together for tea and lots of labrish. My sister Violet was born in England, before mom first came to Jamaica. She'll be thrilled to meet someone who knew our mom from so far back."* Al and Wilhelm stowed her merchandise, after getting rid of packaging at her request. Wilhelm cautioned. *"Scuse me Sister, maybe you want take them for exchange. Or you not like when you get home?"* She told him, that situation would not arise. As both men walked towards the tire shop, Wilhelm said to Al. *"Jeezaloo man! You one old mother…."* Al stopped dead in track and stared at Wilhelm, who said. *"Easy, my friend, another heat joke. Don't go for machete or bazookeh. You never do jokes? She's good looking lady, nice to hug close. I think she means, we come for tea, not just you. I always love tea. Okay, I stop now. You want go solo for tea and leave your friend. I see that now, but I okay."* Soon, Wilhelm opened up a dialogue thus. *"I don't get something. If her mom was Sister, why she at hospital instead of church? It was maybe catholic hospital* *with Fathers and Sisters only? It's very much confuse."* Al explained. **"This hospital had nothing to do with church, it was operated under British system. There was Matron, who is in charge of the hospital, and there's head nurse in charge of all nurses. Her title was Sister. You are thinking of "Sister" as in a Nun, but this was not the case."** That settled, both men walked to the tire shop as Wilhelm kept up a monologue on heat and it's effect on him. Shop proprietor decided to await Wilhelm's input. Tires had deteriorated, to extent, road worthiness was in doubt. New valves were required but there was no guarantee tires could maintain pressure for any length of time under weight. Attempt at road trip was certain to see failures, soon as they heated up. Wilhelm scolded. *"What's you talking about road trip and that? You doing road trip? No One doing road trip. This here is my very good friend. He not road trip."* Putting an arm around Al's neck, he went on. *"I take wheels my house and put them on the sleigh. My very good friend here."* He paused, again hug Al before continuing. *"He put the hook and tow it to the front. I call the guy, say it in front and he come and take it away. He the One do road trip, he got problema if the wheel go down. That is way of deal, can't be all smiles and happy. Not every deal can be steal. You agree, my friend?"* One more hug to Al as he posed the question, to which Al smiled an acknowledgement. Another disagreement was abrewing, when proprietor told Wilhelm cost of job and there would be no receipt. *"Whata you mean, no receipt? I pay money, I need receipt for next year tax and…"* Wilhelm quickly aborted pursuit, being simultaneously hit with two no options. Al said. **"Wilhelm, come on. I got places to go and people to antagonize."** Tire man told him. *"Take your job where you get receipt for Mickey Mouse repair."* Wilhelm stood stunned, gazed at both men in turn. Al said to tire man.

"He's only joking, talks that way when heat gets to him."
Push came to shove, tire man installed valves and seated tires.
Told Wilhelm, inflate them as he liked. Ended with comment
in Spanish and loud laugh. At sea, Al asked Wilhelm what's
funny part. *"Oh, the guy think he funny. Says, maybe wheel
go boom. I mucho caca in pantalones. Real funny guy you
know."* Suffice it to say, tire man put wheels inside a cage
and inflated them from outside. Wilhelm put them on his
trailer, it is assumed all's well that ended well. There being
no further mention by him of the boat, which was hauled
away as expected. Did he hide proceeds of sale from his wife
as he planned doing? For certain he stuck to his plan. Did Al
go for Tea? Most certainly did, and was enchanted beyond
expectations. Home was a library, gallery and conservatory
of Jamaican and English historical collectibles. Ever been in
a place where couldn't decide, what was most appealing?

An Intern and an Inmate-9

Our tale begins at rural farming community, Coleyville in
Manchester parish, where Mabel Fisher had eleven children.
She sent Monica, the eldest at fifteen to live with aunt Sylvia
in the city and finish school. Monica became guardian for her
two year old cousin, Barrington. Took him to school, looked
after him generally. While aunt worked live-in with Keene
family. She dropped out of school at sixteen and aunt got her
a job with family Bronstorph at Barton's Aerie, St. Andrew
parish. Secluded enclave of the heeled and wealthy, nestled in
lush woodlands and mist shrouded mountains overlooking
city Kingston. Brings to mind, oft recited English nursery
rhyme. Author unknown."The Grand Old Duke of York,"
who had ten thousand men. He marched them up to top of the
hill and then down again. When they were up they were up

and when they were down they were down. And when they were only half way up, they were neither up or down." This illustrates, servants were quasi family members by necessity. Could not have ties to spousal or common law relationships. Monica was nursemaid to infant girl. All was well until she got pregnant at seventeen. Now who would believe that aunt Sylvia, once worked with Bronstorphs. And by coincidence, also got pregnant and retired, before going to work with family Keene? Saying, Mabel was upset with Sylvia would be putting it mildly. She accused her sister, sending her eldest in a known Ant nest and alas, her future was now blighted. Mabel's sights were set on her eldest being financial help to her siblings. Which hope was now dashed, her having child of her own. Folks declared Monica, having "friends in high places." This, said with knowing eyes exclamation. Seeing how, her and infant daughter Sandra were always well "put together." Not seeming to be materially lacking, as expected. Barrington and younger cousin Sandra by five years, attended same school. The One giving mature support to other. There was an unexpected anomaly that had folks confused. Adage is, "People will talk" and both children provided more than fair share of reason for. Both were dark complexioned, instead of brown skinned, as their suspected sire. Yet, both had curled brown hair, confirming paternal suspicion. Amos, village's lawyer or mouthpiece settled the confusion, stating. Black people blood always stronger than mulatto, there shouldn't be confusion. End of story. Monica got sewing job at an 807 garment factory, quickly rose to coveted position of quality supervisor. Mabel farmed out her older children to relatives and brought two younger ones to live with her and Monica's three in the city. Her pastor donned matchmaker cap and brokered a marriage between her and father of his two. Although the young man was not of the congregation.

Barrington and Sandra were inseparable, as the saying goes. "Thick as thieves" Both were said to "have good heads." Meaning, they excelled scholastically. Boy went off kilter and soon got caught up with a wrong crowd. At age eighteen, already made two court appearances and probated to be of good behaviour. Sandra took to stepfather Milton, as Duck to water. He in turn, tried prying her from cousin Barrington's grasp. This brought open conflict and threat of gun play by probationer. Aged nineteen, he had a Honda 50cc's bike with which he picked up fourteen year old cousin at school daily. Went places before going home, late and later until dusk. Cops seized the bike for lack of insurance. It was common knowledge, Milton had hand in this. Silently applauded by frustrated relatives. Sandra exhibited seesaw obedience to her step-dad, Milton. Positive when cousin was out of her circle. Defiant with sass when he was in. Not yet fifteen, birth control pills fell from her school tote, alarming parents. She claimed necessity, soothing menstrual discomfort and dared anyone think otherwise. Told she would be taken for medical exam. Declared intent to run away rather than submit. Time moved on, cousin did eighteen months in prison for selling ganja. Paroled, bought a car, took cousin Sandra here and there. She revelled in spotlight, sauntering runway mode. Face aglow with winning smile, amid schoolmate's envious stares, as she strutted by. Slowly stepped in and cousin roared their chariot away, scattering gravel and dust. We won't fault her. Given choice, some teens would likely embrace such bop and exhilaration. Seems, more efforts made to isolate cousins, stronger their bond became. At sixteen she got holiday job with her Ophthalmologist and instantly knew. This is career she was destined to pursue as adult. Every break from school, no matter how short. There she was at practice. Girl Friday, observing and learning whatever she could. Something big is unfolding. Barrington is riding South, police patrol close behind. Driver lags back, so as not to left turn, simultaneous with biker. Who now keeps glancing back nervously. Cops pick up on that like sharks on blood. He jumps off his moving bike, sprints away whilst tossing something into nearby bushes. He is chased, caught and a gun retrieved from bushes. He starts babbling about not being the One who held up a business place. Promises to take cops to where loot is buried. Friends, this is better than comedy. He takes them to yard, where men gamble table games under expansive Lime tree. Players scatter, some are cornered. Cuffed back to back in circle, around light pole. Let's see them run. Willing, curious citizens brought tools, began digging as directed by cops, based on Barrington's guidance. This was totally unnecessary. Hen in quest of worms for her chickens, could accomplish this task. Can anyone imagine how gambler's eyes popped wide. To think they sat inches atop plastic bags of money. As they put up and lost the last dollar, went home miserable and broke. Two coffee burlap bags held rusted coins. Hamburger meat bags held soggy currency notes. Cousin was charged, possession of unlicensed firearm. Spent nearly two years in remand. Lawyer successfully mitigated charges without trial. There are men behind bars chomping at the bit, to get at Barrington for giving up their tide over loot. Good things are happening for our Sandra. Or are they? Now high school sixth former, trying hard to get CXC passes and launch into medical orbit. Her foci and ambitions are no longer in synch with cousin's. Has a boyfriend from good family background. His parents adore her and she is, comfortable as bug in rug. One could say, cousin's two year hiatus was godsend. Who knows? Monica probably had bruised knees from relentless praying. Boyfriend, Grandison had unshakable stigma that clung to him like moss on Oak, from elementary through high school. Coming from long line of Foggartys, he bore ancestral name with pride. Ignored elementary school children trading F for H. Mild aberration, which was ignored until. Times changed, thrusting homophobia into spotlight and Foggarty took on new meaning. Julius Caesar's demise, taught us to be wary of well wishers. They milked Sandra, of engagement details and diamond studded ring. Whispered facts and derided her attraction to "that faggotty fellow." Distressed by whispers that ended on approach, she sought counsel of the preacher. She was deeply in love, but cringed at thought of marriage. Taking Foggarty name, likewise her children. Preacherman told Sandra, times are changing. Old customs and rituals are being replaced by today's thinking. For instance, couples now write wedding vows. Instead of blindly reciting that of the church. Also, not only do some women keep nee name. Husbands are known to take wives names, which would naturally be that of their children. She came away with sense of relief, shortlived as it turned out. In habit dry running ideas by Milton, she asked his opinion. He told Sandra, doubted Grandison and parents would embrace the idea, quickly adding. He being in similar situation would not. Grandfather took pride showing off his grandchildren. How was he to explain this anomaly to wider family circle and close friends? Barrington, fresh from detention was more vicious and evil. Had frightening effect on cousin Sandra and others. To her credit, made efforts to alienate and disavow friendship. Young man was brash and confrontational with everyone, ready to enforce and have his way. Which was not unknown characteristic of his. Now with elevated stridency. **Death of a Bachelor?** Maybe it could be taken as that of a salesman. Brave, blustering Barrington. Masterminded and led gang on restaurant holdup at Trafalgar and Haughton, which went awry for participants. It was unforgettable night of personal sorrow. Convoy of police vehicles raced through four way, Waterloo Trafalgar intersection. Soon, came echoes of rapid gunfire exchange. The curious invaded and milled about the scene. A young man lay face down in foliage, gasping for breath. Cop, with triumphant grin. Used a booted foot to turn young man on his back, as he stared unseeing. If One is celebrated gangster or arch criminal. When One passes, there'll be outpouring of sorrow, ending with ostentatious funeral and repast. Small time hoodlums like Barrington, will be grieved by his circle and even then. They do so quietly without fanfare. Some go further and deny close association with, as cousin Sandra was moved to do. Told those who would listen, she was under severe duress. Happy to be freed from shackles of infamy. Now, proverbial Spanish machete or two edged sword comes into play. Whilst Barrington's demise was being kept under wraps. Sandra's acceptance letter as university student, going for Bachelor of Medicine degree. Was being snapped and shared with friends and family, near or far. Her mother, mulled preacher's idea and with Milton's lukewarm support. Sought path, broaching to Grandison and family. Quite unaware, Foggartys were questing path. Broaching their disquiet about Sandra's known alliance with late cousin. How this would tarnish their image, should the engagement develop into marriage and....? Not seeing possibility of an acceptable, face saving compromise. Decision was made, ending relationship and good riddance. Preacher tried brokering resumption of harmony, inviting parties to round table discussion. Foggartys, not being of his flock, declined the invite. Milton seeing his stepdaughter in tearful distress, hugged and dabbed at her eyes, saying. ***"Grandison is only Snapper, there's Kingfish in the sea. No mug done broken, no coffee spilled."*** There's unknown end to drama. Sandra was by accounts, engrossed in studies and folks' scrutiny ebbed. Until it was noised, she had joined United Nations, working in far flung Asia or Africa. Questions were asked but never answered. Did she ever complete her medical studies? What is nature of her work with the UN? Did she get married and start a family? No One outside her family circle knows answers. It is assumed she has kept in touch with them, but she has never returned to her country of birth since leaving. Is this then, what becomes of a broken hearted? Or? And our world keeps right on turning.

Felon's right to life-10

Whilst your mind is where it's at, let's look at item of news that was fodder for fierce debate recently. We three sat down to chow jerked chicken, jerked pork and oxtail with rice and peas, fried plantains and steamed vegetable at **Banana Hut.** You know, famous Jamaican restaurant at Town and Country plaza on South side SW 152nd Street and SW 137th Avenue intersection. If you didn't know where it was before, you do now. Mike is a Food Nazi, do not rile him. Raphael clasped hands, rapped his knuckles on the table, which I mistook for impatience. Asked if he was that hungry to eat a horse, as Al Pacino declared in Scarface. He said, hunger wasn't source of discontent. News item on television, past evening was, and asked our opinion. Cautioned to keep open minds. Suggests his was closed on the subject, as he hashed his thoughts. It's undeniably true, folks, if put to the test. When someone opens debate, asking others to keep an open mind. Theirs is closed, hoping others will concur. May have been Dateline or similar news item. Diruncey is convicted felon, having served time for gun related offence. Condition of release from prison is. He's prohibited from using or possessing a firearm. Failure to abide, earns him life sentence. No if, but or maybe. Everyone agrees. Diruncey, on way to barbershop for a haircut. Looks at someone, who takes instant offence. Did you know, simple eye contact can get someone riled? Midst his haircut, three men rushes in, gun drawn. Massues a surprised, frightened Diruncey from chair. Barbers and customers, equally alarmed. Look on helplessly as Diruncey is dragged into nearby alley. Gunfire erupts, one assailant is killed, one wounded and other flees unscathed. So does Diruncey, who now recognizes he's in deep, you know what. No One in barbershop saw anything, could not assist police in quest for facts. Cameras however recorded event and so. Diruncey, wearing cap to disguise half mowed pate, was soon rounded up and denied being on scene. Have not slightest idea what cops talking about. Faced with video snippets he comes clean. Assailant's gun failed, giving him chance to draw and fire his gun, he shouldn't be carrying. Cameras backed up his version of events, cops are satisfied he acted in self defence. Hence, he will not be charged with murder or shooting of other. He is however being taken into custody, for being in possession of firearm. Which, as a convicted felon he should not have been. Raphael's argument is. If Diruncey had not carried a gun, keeping with status as a felon, he would now be dead felon. In this instance therefore, he argues. Diruncey should not be charged for having taken steps to save his life. Everyone has right to life, even if they are convicted felon after serving time for original deed. It is not matter for debate. Laws will be enforced strictly, without any deviation, however arising. Can anyone see Diruncey not going to prison for rest of his life? I can't, neither can Ambrose. Saving grace for Diruncey, if can be so seen is. Instead dying in the alleyway. He gets lease on life as long as he will be allowed to. Which will likely be interminable. How so? You ask. Girlfriend called to wish happy birthday and asked how old was I. Told and expressed wish for more years in good health, to which she rejoined. *"You and me have nothing to worry about. Only the good die young. We will live like biblical men of old, till put out to be sunned."* Ti's good she included herself in my category. Prison is known to be quite a violent arena, with cohorts of others on the outside. Willing to put a shank between your ribs or to the heart. An only the strong survives environment, where them that are mighty makes rules. Sooner or later they lose potency. Are classified among the weak and finally, recently demised. Humans can be akin to infectious viruses. Every generation mutates more rabid, vicious and evil than previous.

Back in old country, 1980's was period of upheaval, brought about by criminal and political activities. One seemed to thrive on other without being defined. Seymour Littlejohn's family, ran small grocery store in their neighbourhood. He had been robbed numerous times, yet frustrated police who came to investigate. Being unwilling to identify perpetrators. Fearing they would come and harm his family. After each robbery, Millis Littlejohn went to police and made a report. They in turn would ask. *"Seymour ready to talk?"* She would tell them, yes he was. Of course upon their arrival. Seymour made excuses, not getting good look at. He had worked on and fine tuned a plan to infinity. First, he contacted former port coworker. Bought a new firearm with ample supply of rounds. Devout Sabbath keeper by religion, excused himself accompanying his wife to church. Went instead into heights nearby hills, practicing use of weapon. Attaining proficiency, he waited for moment of truth. Began wondering if someone knew he had acquired a gun. There having been lengthy lull in his being robbed. Life has that strange way playing tricks on people. When we want something to happen, it never does. Like when we are on time, bus is a minute early and we watch it fade in the distance. We arrive with time to spare, bus broke down and no showed. We are not to be winners. A Saturday night about 23:30 hours. Seymour prepared to close shop, serving who he hoped was last customer. Scapegoat, known political enforcer. Emerged from hiding and stepped into the shop from house side. Seymour raised both hands, telling intruder, take the money and not harm him. Pleaded earnestly for his life, near tears. As Scapegoat cleaned the till and went for an escape. Seymour shot him once in the head. Next, he took saltfish chopper and chopped Scapegoat's lower arm. Alarm made of gun play, cops came post haste. Seymour told tale, being held at gunpoint by Scapegoat. Whom, caught in concentration emptying till. Was attacked by Seymour with the machete. Scapegoat tried overpowering him despite his wound. Seymour disarmed and shot assailant with his own gun. On face of, it was believable without any detective work. It was common knowledge, Scapegoat had access to and had used a gun to subdue political opponents in the past. Seymour on other hand, was pious grocer with no criminal connections, but yet police probed. Something, as is said "smelt fishy" **Aftermath:** I have said it numerous times. Less said to police, better your chance eluding guilt. Sooner rather than later they'll get you. First, they ask one question, ten different ways and catch you lying. At that late hour, Littlejohns begged police to stay. Whilst they grabbed what essentials they could carry, to place of rest for that night. For sure they knew, they would be attacked and annihilated, once police left. Maybe blinded by thirst for revenge. Seymour did not take into consideration. Family fled by taxi to destination unknown. Night sky was soon illuminated by orange flames and blue black smoke, of family Littlejohn's shop and house on premises. Looted structures burned fiercely to ground. Onlookers swore there were explosions from burning shop, sounding much like ammunition being discharged. This scenario when added with other evidence, of what could not have happened as described by Seymour. He was arrested and charged with murder. Being in possession of illegal firearm and ammunition. Notwithstanding reasons for and police being aware. Numerous occasions on which he had been subjected to unmitigated criminal attacks. His weapon of defence was illegally obtained and held. Not having wherewithal to pledge bail, Seymour awaited trial in jail. Courts being backlogged as they always are, it would be a long dreary winter before he could make appearance. Much more to be tried. Less than a year after being incarcerated, his wife died. He wasn't allowed to attend her funeral.Youngest of two sons was recognized and attacked by Scapegoat's cohort. Fortunately, lad was able to miraculously evade volley of gunfire. Unlike his dad, identified attacker to police. Both daughters gave up their stall at Bend Down Plaza and fled to the USA, where they still are. Two years and some after that Saturday night, Seymour died in hospital of natural causes after taking ill, waiting in jail. **Similar event:** Bernard Thorpe made it known, he was selling his bike for a song. It being in need of minor repairs. Prospective buyers came and made promises returning. Wendell Simpson, tenant in same premises as Bernard. Arranged to steal and sell the bike for less. Knowing when Bernard went to work. Wendell hack sawed a lock, securing the bike behind their kitchen. What he did not know was, Bernard worked two shifts previous night at the flour mill. Was asleep inside his room, as fate would dictate. Unaware of need for stealth. Wendell freed the bike from harness, confidently pushed down narrow path. Making noises that alerted Bernard. Taking stock, he saw and shouted at Wendell, who ran up the street. Seeing an angry Bernard gain on him, machete in hand, he let the bike drop. Which is where Bernard should have stopped. Folks will aver, adrenalin took over, he kept chase alive. Having aborted the theft, there was no reasonable incentive for him to maintain chase, but he did. Police station was mere yards West, at the four roads, Again, as determined by hand of fate. A cop stood at street entrance, enjoying smokes, watching citizens go by. Wendell ran past him and onto station's compound. Seeing Bernard approach helter skelter, cop hollered at him to *"Drop the weapon! I said! Drop the weapon!!"* Then a shot was heard. Bernard and weapon both fell, he dead. Folks argued, cop could have shot Bernard in a foot. We know cops always aim for body mass and it's most times lethal. Cop was not concerned with facts or origin of dispute. He saw citizen being chased by another, armed with weapon. Said citizen refused orders to relinquish weapon, he acted as dictated by law. Now, it would be difficult to keep citing fate in this episode. Once again it played role. Person unknown, angered at Bernard's demise. Cornered and shot Wendell at his home. Said venue from which he lived and stole Bernard's bike. Once again, he sprinted to police station. Where he hollered assailant's name, then dropped dead. Cops did not go looking for named perpetrator. Quite certain, he too would soon run to them and call a name. It was regarded as, evil destroyeth evil. From which melee, innocent parties had best stay aloof. Although situations differ, One could say, like justice. Law is sometimes also blind and will decide Diruncey's fate. Once again I take it, your curiosity has been piqued by odd name of retail mecca, referenced previous page. Large open air, flea market type venue. Where household small appliances, goods, clothes and footwear were sold by vendors. Who most times bought wares in Miami and Curacao. There were no stalls. Goods were displayed on large tarpaulins, spread on ground. When rain threatened or police raided in search of contraband.

Tarpaulins with wares could be scooped up. Vendors safely retreated with their prize to resume activity when dust settled. By now you should get picture of female customers having to stand and bend low, inspecting items being sold. Unless they dressed as males did, employing stoop instead. Once satisfied, exchange of money and goods took place. Hence, name by persons unknown **"Bend down Plaza"** I'll say folks, life in a tropical paradise is it's own theatre. Don't worry, be happy.

On Vaginae and Penii-11

There exists among some women, this vaginal sacrosanctness. Dictating unworthiness of males having unfettered access, other than birth process. Worse yet, unthinkable privilege of copulation. On a visit to my aged aunt, not for first time. She could not identify with me, unaware her sister gave birth. She asked questions. I answered as she tried throttling her fading memory. On revealing, my father worked at the hospital. No, he wasn't a doctor, as she queried with gleeful anticipation. He was a porter. Which caused her to sneer in contempt. *"My sister had a child for a porter?"* After a pause to digest, she ended. *"That is why I will die a spinster rather than cast my pearl before Swine."* Her reaction, prompted by lack of status, rather than inherent male qualities.You do recall Phoebe, stridently reprimanding. *"She's your maid, your maid for crying out loud. You do not ever sleep with your maid. My God, how low can you go. What kind of man are you?"* Where did this baseless prejudice originate, that marginalizes sexual partners by social status or position? It's preposterous and reeks of discrimination. Which, sad to say, it's a female thing. Men as a rule, do not engage in splitting hairs. Matter of fact some are accused, willing to jump on anything that moves. Wenches or princesses, maids or mistresses are all fair game. Some are known to find succor in animals, adding dimension to term "animal lovers" You will never hear a sheep or goat bleat r-a-a-a-p-e. Or a cow mooing h-e-e-l-l-l-p. To their credit, animals will stand still for any abuse, except a knife at the jugular. Francine said cow wouldn't, but she doesn't know that for fact. She was only angry and frustrated at young men, thrusting broom handles up her tuckus. When we celebrated her twenty-fifth birthday. I asked a girlfriend, as we danced cheek to cheek. Howcum she'd not yet found mister right. Hoping, response would confirm me as choice. Come on people, we gots to fly a kite sometimes. How else will we know what's "Blowin' in the wind" She replied, he hasn't yet been born and by time he does. She will be old and no longer interested in male companionship. Tightening lips and brow in disgusted scowl, she declared. ***"A man? Pawing and probing my body with filthy fingers and that cesspipe between his thighs? Oh, heaven forbid."*** With that she shuddered as if in ague. I suggested there were young men, ambitious, educated and qualified to make good partners for equally gifted young women. She replied with scorn. ***"You don't understand. Not all women are sluts."*** This abhorrence to male companionship has been around for a long time. Evidenced by retired school principal who was my neighbour. Eminent Howard graduate, she had in retirement been lauded and recognized by inclusion on our state's annual honors list. We found mutual interest gabbing with each other and spent long intervals at our fence line. At first it didn't register, she always talked whilst reading newspaper. When it did, further realized she never turned pages. Mentioning this to my wife one day. I said, it surprised me, a person educated to her level. Would engage in reading a paper whilst in conversation with a person. Did she not see that as absence of proper breeding? My wife replied. ***"The lady is a life spinster and does not*** *want to see anything that would frighten her. You should be ashamed of yourself. Showing no respect for a woman who could be your grandmother. Standing in front of her with your pride bulge, chatting as if everything is hunky dory."* It never dawned on me, I was being all this and more. I rebutted, saying. Had the lady been discomfited by my mode of dress or sparsity of. She would have avoided coming to the fence and engaging in dialogue. To which my wife replied. Doing so was indeed, evidence of superior breeding. There was period from early 1970's to mid 1990's when my only yard attire were Wolsey briefs. Made in England and sold by the London Shop. Called it my "freedom for the stallion" era. I will admit there were numerous eyebrows raised. But nary a person made comments to my hearing. With exception of the policeman, who came asking me if I was home. And my lying I had left hours prior. Taking my wife to Miami for urgent medical care. Satisfied with his loss he then asked. *"So you is them gardener, whapp'n to you clothes? Is roadside you at you know."* Told him, having washed my only suit and hung it to dry, had no choice. I admit being one turnip that fell from market truck on way to the city. Cousin Harze taught that social graces were redundant. *"Eat till you gut full. Don't follow you Granny, leave food on plate as manners when hungry busting you shirt. Listen to this. Matthew, Mark, Luke, John, put down your fork and nyam with you hand."* Then he would erupt in raucous laughter that most times ended in a coughing spell. He was kind of man who would, as David Snr. Did. Tell grandson, his penis is a dick. Allow me to clarify where doubt might have arisen. People of either gender should, when they go in search of a life partner. Take utmost care as far as they possible can. And make effort to find someone with positive character traits to influence and nurture young minds. Woman should assess a man's ability to find gainful employment. In field that allows him to shelter and support his family, somewhat above basic standards. A mother who struggles and constantly deprives herself in order to raise her only child. Was recently told by said child, now in teen years. Mom contributed more to hardships experienced as a child. Because, mom should have known, she was marrying a worthless bum. Yet gave him honour being called a father. Mom, hearing this, once too often, broke silence and told child. ***"I pray you will make a perfect choice for your children when the time comes."*** We know people are sometimes fickle. Unpredictable as storm's eye at standstill. Another facet of life some women needs look at. Is penchant to denigrate men who work trades. Taking pride in them that are clad in tweed, with dribbler hanging from throats. There are masons, plumbers, welders, carpenters, locksmiths and myriad of skilled tradesmen. Who out earn corporate jacketed, in cubicle counterpart, by leaps and bounds. When they start a business as they sometimes do, proverbial sky is the limit. Jesus Diaz dropped out school at seventeen, began cutting neighbors' grass. Not yet forty, he has landscape maintenance business. Cadre of staff, vehicles fleet and foliage growing nursery on expanding acreage.

Grandparents beware-12

If you're a grandparent, there is something you might not be aware of. Because your son or daughter has always shown you love, caring and appreciation. I have to tell you, this is a thin line or worse yet, thin ice. On which you had best be careful traipsing through. First, placid pond where son-in-law or daughter-in-law embraces mother-in-law or father-in-law unconditionally, is not as seems on surface. There's always underlying tension among this group with efforts to disguise.

To begin with, some mothers thinks, no woman is good enough for her son. Doesn't know how to cook his favourite meal. Doesn't give her leeway when she visits marital home, far too frequent and hordes of malicious discontent. There's also dad, whose thoughts are same as those of doting mother. Regarding his princess of a daughter. He intimidates and gets that lad to cower at mention of his name. But, they get by in strained, at times restrained harmony. Brokered and nurtured by near, dear relatives. At church christening of Giselle's first child, after which, event moved on to festive phase. It is not known, question is still asked and unanswered among guests. Was Lesford Barnes aware of son-in-law's presence or not? He however took a long look at his grandchild, then said to infant's grandmother. *"That child is image of it's father. I know we raised Giselle to recognize and appreciate quality. She could have done better."* From corner armchair, Colin Harper chirped in. **"So could your wife. That! Everyone can see. But, who's complaining."** Folks attending, saw Lesford's head whip round in direction from whence came the retort. His face metamorphosed through varying stages of anger, before saying in soft, quiet voice belying his features. *"Get this boy out of here, before something bad happens."* Boy Colin, snickered and said. **"In case you forgot, sir. I am home. I have nowhere else to go."** You see folks, at his workplace. Colin was known as "The Bull." Because, he was ever ready to butt heads with supervision and management. Those who knew, expressed view he was kept on because. His extensive knowledge and expertise made him invaluable asset, of which he's aware. Should be mentioned, christening tremor was preceded by temblors, months before. It was ingenious of Lesford, telling those gathered. His daughter's child was somewhat unbecoming. No woman wants to be told, her child is less than most beautiful ever to grace our planet. Certainly, not by her own father, which she will never forget. Her mom will encourage, forget and forgive. *"You know your father is always shooting from the hip, totally unaware of target hit."* To which she will ask. **"But mom, how could he say such a thing, and in front of guests?"** In this instance, there will be silent, ongoing warfare. Which others will make effort to keep from, as is said. Going viral. That then is one facet of familial disenchantment. Which, thankfully is not rife as we might assume. Let's look at overt harmonic scenario. Family, in-laws and relatives enjoy somewhat positive relationship. Most grandparents dote on grandchildren, seemingly more than did their children. Those with wherewithal, promptly set up prepaid college fund. Pays for dance and music lessons as well as instruments to support. Sometimes it's unconscious, vicarious pursuit by grandma. Wanting to excel at piano, violin or guitar in her youth and denied opportunity. Would love to see little Annabelle in recital, excelling to grandma's pleasure. She forgets having repaired that violin, thrice in as many months, but she presses on. Parents enjoy this relief from financial burden. Welcoming grandparents interference, but be warned, not always as a rule. A son-in-law looks this gift horse in the mouth. Sees generosity as veiled suggestion, of earning or financial inadequacy on his part. Says to his wife. *"Marcia, tell your dad. If Nicholas wants violin. I will get him one and thanks all the same."* See how thin that ice can be? When grandpa tells his son. *"You are growing that boy to be a sissy."* Or grandma tells her daughter. *"I don't see why you're piercing that child's ears when she's so young. We never put you through such barbaric cruelty when we raised you. For God's sake Elizabeth, the child is twelve years old. She's trying, but poor child. She cannot walk in heels. What for does she needs to be wearing makeup and those bicycle* *sized hoops in her ears? That dress is way too short and neckline too low. It's a church function, for crying out loud. I am ashamed to tell you what she looks like, going out way you are sending her."* In other instance, child retorts to parent. Grandma asks. *"You gonna let that child talk to you like that and get away with it?"* That's exact same question, Jimmy asked Tommy. Who then turned and shot, bartender Spider dead. But grandma keeps stoking flames. *"You know, if you tried that with me you'd be picking up your teeth from the floor."* Grands, whether your child responds in chastisement or subtly reprimands. It is unwelcome intrusion, however well intentioned you think it is. Sometimes, your child, now parent, hides anger and quietly says. *"Times have changed, mom. I could never grow my children, way you grew me. Don't let me recall my childhood. I beg you, let bygones be bygones."* Physical punishment you are alluding to, your child will tell you. *"Those were dark ages, dad. Don't forget, this is America. Child abuse is serious crime. They will take the child from you and send you to prison for a long, long time. It might not be what's best for child in long run, but that's how it's done."* What you see as constructive criticism, your son or daughter sees as critique of their parenting skills. You are saying, they know how to have children. But haven't first clue on how to raise them properly. You do not have carte blanche to open up with your views on how your children should raise children. If your guidance is solicited, then by all means, share your thoughts with disclaimer. Admitting times are different and step softly. *"I don't know. Have you considered doing this? You could probably try that. Have you tried talking to him, her. Getting to source of issue?"* And finally. *"You know we have a good relationship. Would you mind if I talked to him her? I would not make it known you said anything to me.*

Kind of put it like, from my own observation." Anything other than, at times creates angst within your children's relationship with their spouse. When a husband says to his wife. *"You know my mom doesn't mean anything by that."* Situation gets intensified, because wife expects husband to see things through her eyes, put his mom on a leash. Same expectation when parties are reversed. In absence of, partners begin talking to friends and co-workers as Karen did. They in turn, whisper your affairs to others. Whoever and before you can stifle a sneeze, there goes the neighbourhood. Last thing any relationship needs, is advice of outsiders. This without fail, always brings escalation of ill will that easily becomes irreversible. Advice to grandparents. You raised children way you saw fit. Allow them to raise theirs and answer only if and when called. It would not hurt to ask permission, before making big purchases for kids. Birthday presents, holiday stocking stuffers are exempted and might be welcomed. Avoid push cart or battery wagon which demands parents' maintenance or assembly. Making time to help a child enjoy. Grates dad's nerves, when child badgers for his participation. His having pressing, unfinished matters to focus on.

The Panhandler-13

Leroy Sutherland had always been theme of discussion in his inner city neighbourhood. Only man suspected of being his father, denied paternity. His mother could not be definitive on the matter. Hers was sad existence, hanging out at village bar. She bummed rum and cigarettes from men who bummed sexual favors from her, quid pro quo. Came time she quickly lost lustre. No longer appealed to them that slaked and quenched at her oasis in better times. When she died, aged early thirties from respiratory issues. Ignorant folks spread word, she had been demised by chronic tuberculosis. Her only child was then young man. Raised by grandparents on paltry resources. Not allowing sustained attendance at nearby elementary school. Source of silent ridicule among group of codgers, one of whom mockingly said to others. *"That boy too big for his size. He be real busboy"* Now, I ask you, rational souls. What kind of statement is that? Came the retort. *"He eats like a horse and just as strong."* Another added. *"He certain there's no One's watching, he'll eat that horse too."* Truth is, this was vilification in jest. They all gave him sustenance by odd jobs and handouts. Let's say, they were at point of their existence.Yearning for a symbol of amusement. Anything, no matter how mundane. So long as it tickled their osteoarthritic funny bone. Others, concerned for his future. Encouraged and guided Leroy on a path, focused on positive goals. Young man, gigantic and clone of his father, caused some to lament. *"How could Derrick Gilpin have denied fathering that boy?"* Leroy dreamed, playing baseball and practiced arduously. His dream morphed into nightmare of war and he was off to Asia. Here's where the narrative gets clouded. By Leroy's account, he single handedly laid waste, hundreds of enemy combatants. Others told of his being out of conflict, safely washing pots and peeling potatoes. Now in his sixties, points with pride where his amputated leg used to be and relates skirmish with enemy forces. Others said it was sugar, meaning diabetes that made him amputee. Still big in frame but somewhat frail in strength. Generous folks lent a hand with his mobility needs. You see patrons, Leroy was part of his problem. Given his formidable stature. He had difficulty propelling his chair by hand, even a short distance. Seemed he had sufficient resources with VA, Medicare and Medicaid. His mobility plight was brought to attention of local politico. Weeks later, neighbors saw box truck backed up by Leroy's house. Curious, as neighbors always are. Gathering to see what was happening, they also passed word by grapevine. Shortly after, there was grand celebration in the square. Aspiring politician presented Leroy, a new motorized wheelchair with charging accessory and access ramp. Talk about "Just how lucky can a poor man be." Leroy was. We know there are people who are indescribably reprobate of mind and deed. Architects of scheme that caused Leroy to make a hard landing. Backing out of home a Sunday on his way to church. Someone should have coached him, wisdom of "Eyes on path" always. It's dictated by gravity. Bigger an object, harder it falls. And as Brer Snuff always reminded. "It's not the sudden drop that hurts. It's the sudden stop, after the drop." Leroy was banged up pretty bad. Cracked skull and fractured arm among other ills. It was unnecessary cruelty at it's worst. And you are still wondering how did Leroy take a tumble. I'll tell you now. Miscreants or solo of, stole Leroy's ramp during the night. Some said there was ready market at scrap metal dealer. Others voiced doubt on this, saying by ordinance. Vendors had to be licensed to so trade. Well, let's say a thief is not aware of this. Disappointed when he turns up with his loot. He's not going to bring it back to crime scene and say, sorry. Neighbors will mock and ridicule, but they also have heart. Miles and miles and miles of heart, ala Peggy Lee. They're disposed to be kind and caring. So it was, when Leroy came out of hospital. He was wheeled into house, up a new wooden ramp. Made possible by neighbours' goodwill contributions of material and skills. Prompting another celebration.**What's next?** You might ask. Garfield Ambrosely was neighbourhood hustler, neer-do-well and suspect in theft of Leroy's ramp. Reinforced when he insisted. Leroy join him in raising pints of Guinness to their health. One codger whispered to another. ***"That's it, bottle of***

pick me up. After busted arm and caved in skull? Pshaw."
Garfield was repeat felony offender.Having done time behind
bars more than once. Now overheard saying to Leroy, over
their Guinness happy minute. **"Hey Hoss. You could roll up
by the off ramp there. Put on your sad face and get them
suckers to pony up a fortune. Better than candy from a
baby, believe me. I ain't lying Bro. I'll even make you a
sign. What you waiting for?"** Leroy was heard to chuckle
heartily before replying. *"Well, you would also have to make
a face mask. I'm a proud citizen who served his country,
and I'm not gonna be seen dead or alive. Holding out arm
for alms. No way Jose."* Contemplating briefly, he went on.
*"You know, I always figured you for a lick 'o' sense, until
just now. Man! I lost a leg, not none of my senses. Ptui"*
Infuriated, he upended the bottle, spilling contents and rode
off. No One can truthfully say, how ensuing situation came
to be. Some said it was threat and strong arm. Others said it
was culpable complicity for share of income. Pre-Halloween,
found Garfield in Leroy's wheelchair at eastbound end of a
turnpike ramp. Where it intersected city's surface street in a
four lane split. Two going left, one straight ahead and other a
right turn. This after travelling, by bus to train to bus from
home. Wheelchair had makeshift white flag on short pole
stuck in back. Sign affixed to side, read. **HELP PLEEZ.
DESABLE VETNAM VET GOD BLEST** Despite
worthiness of mission, his presence began generating calls to
FHP by concerned motorist. Given his reckless disregard for
safety, darting tween vehicles and lanes. Retrieving coins
from kind hands. You are familiar with Psalm 118:22. *"Stone
the builder refuseth shall..."*-Gifted new wheelchair, Leroy
sold his push chair to Glasseye Simpson for fifteen dollars.
He was paid five with a promise of balance when next social
security credit came. Both seemed to have forgotten debt and

promise. Which Leroy abandoned when Simpson died shortly after. Now immobilized, at least during panhandling hours. He sought out Simpson's grandson, a known crackhead. Who told Leroy he could have chair for thirty dollars. He balked at this. Garfield paid ransom and all was well. I'm telling you, it's blessing these people don't get into corporate mainstream. Then again, maybe if we examine rapacious mantra of some businesses. Some of similar mindset did, to our detriment.

Lorenzo lied about name, age and other data. Got a contract delivering phone books seasonally. In vestibule of Coral Gables apartment building, he gingerly crept by sleeping dog. Did something to irritate the animal. Causing the large cat to hiss, growl and snarl, whilst attempting to charge. Caught off guard, hurled bags of yellow and white pages at the animal and beat a hasty retreat. Pre-camera everywhere era. No One knew how the cat was maimed. Lorenzo recalled the incident with unbridled amusement. He however eventually lost the contract. This type of business took hold of him and over the years he pursued this as vocation, providing for a family. Now almost fifty five years old, he owns an eighteen wheeler. Kept busy with many delivery contracts under his belt. He is building business to near future, when he will acquire another eighteen wheeler. Wife Melba, cautions. Hired driver will create high repair expenses, caused by reckless equipment operation. With her support, business is doing well. Added responsibility will leave them no leisure time. *"We have to enjoy life, Lorenzo, it's not all about the money."* She chides, bringing his vitriolic retort. **"Without money, there's no f…ing life. It's just misery like guy with a cup in hand."** Kerfuffle took a new twist when Melba said. *"What's wrong with you, are you f…ing moron or what? How many times I have to tell you. Don't use language like that whilst my* *children are around?"* Lorenzo laughs loud. **"You mixed up so many ways, it's not funny. Your children? So what am I, their f...in uncle or grandma? You using same language telling me to not use swear language. You better take a chill pill. Those one-a-day you swallowin' not doing no good."** Monday at rush hour, US27 in Hialeah. Lorenzo's semi, slow rolled a four way signal controlled intersection against a red light. Pushing three cars ahead of him.Young man had a stroke and spent time in hospital recovering. Long hours chasing delivery deadlines, fatigue and street diet. Will combine to break body sinews down. Doctors tell Lorenzo, recovery could be faster. If he allows himself to be distracted of certain issues. Question is. Can he? Mortgage and other loan installments are overdue. Not mentioning his newest mental craze. Accusing Melba of dressing to entice suitors. Which now brings Garfield into his circle. Fate has such a way, making friends or enemies of unsuspecting travelers. Going home from therapy. Melba waits for signal to change. Garfield rolls up to her window. She has ashtray of quarters, made redundant by SunPass. Doles them in pairs to Garfields she meets. In taking coins, he arrests her hand and stares her with an ogling grin. This does not escape Lorenzo's attention. **"Did that mother f...er just grab your hand and you sat there and let him?"** He yelled, as she hits a button, winding up the window. *"Come on, Lorenzo, it was act of gratitude."* Melba dismissed the incident. **"He better pray I never get back in my truck. I'll run his ass over in that chair."** To which Melba told her husband. *"That's why God won't let you get back on your feet, he doesn't like ugly. If you spit in the sky it falls in your face. Think kind thoughts and you will be rewarded with goodness."* Once they were hailed by a doctor who treated him. *"Happy to see you're improving. You're not half the man you used to be."* Oh, that got his goat. **"Hear that guy? Now he's ready to move in and take over. Talking about me but feasting his eyes all over you."** She sighs. ***"Relax your head, he's praising your weight loss."*** She's back at her former despatcher's job, which is where she met Lorenzo. Sprightly teenager out of high school. Ditching her bobby socks for stockings and along came Lorenzo. With his smile, soft spoken flattery and rippled brawny stature she so admired. Unaware those chiselled laugh lines and Al Pacino like, squinted eye corners. Were thirty three years, instead of twenty-two as he lied. Presidents age visibly after years in office. So does an average self employed, hard working man. Responsibility and competition goals, takes rapid, silent toll on body and brain. Melba, as most young women do. Took care staying that way, was successful at it. A vivacious maturing woman, carrying herself with flair and pizzazz. Focus, now on victim, Lorenzo. Fully cognizant he might spend his life staring at fruit that hangs from the vine. Knowing, even if she did as Eve, and gave of the fruit. He dared not find will to partake. That's cruel and very unusual punishment. Could, would drive weak men to suicide. Once upon a time, FHP officer was seen interacting with Garfield. After which he went missing for two weeks, give or take. As Thanksgiving neared, he was back on his beat. Again went awol briefly. Now he's back again, maybe taking advantage of ongoing pre-holiday traffic. From observation, I'll tell you this. Living by panhandling is not all reward without sweat. Let's for a minute, discount obvious vehicular perils. When it's 90+ degrees and feels like 100+ in the shade, that's brutal open air existence. When it rains he can roll under the overpass. Swelter in surface tarmac heat, and from concrete overhead. I think I've solved mystery regarding choice of location. He has to be close to a plaza with businesses that allows bathroom access. Which is either a Publix or better fast food joint. Other business places find ways to restrict access. "Can't find keys". "Facility out of order, occupied (indefinitely) or being cleaned." It's daily ritual of the homeless who are sent out in lime green tees with decals and advertisements front and back. Standing at intersections and weaving through vehicles when signals allow. Waving to motorists and soliciting. I look at them and thank God for mercies. Although not having wealth, I have been spared their fate. As our daily existence goes on, there's certainty one day.**Good things will end:** Motorists arriving on scene, said it was a chase. FHP, denied it was. Driver careened in and out of traffic at high speed for no obvious reason. Headed southbound, suddenly decided to exit and doing so, swiped a vehicle. Spun halfway out of control, regained and headed down exit ramp. Seeing all four lanes blocked with vehicles, awaiting signal change. Headed for only open outlet. Verdant swale where Garfield sat in heat drunk daze, resting between trips twixt vehicles. Alerted by clash of metal, as out of control vehicle tore into sides of stationary units hurtling towards him. Mayhem and confusion developed in a flash. Rescue vehicles' sirens pealed in the far and middle distance. Ejected driver laid motionless on westbound lane. Vehicle rested hard against round supporting column on it's side. Fumes billowed and fluids flowed. Folks rushed to do what good they could. A woman took one look at the mangled wheelchair, and sign with imprinted tread marks. Began wailing hysterically. ***"Oh, my God! The cripple. Oh, my God, the cripple. Oh, my God. He's under one of these cars, dying or already dead. Oh, my God. Poor man!"*** Now we all know, occupant of that chair was as able bodied as he was born. Law enforcement and emergency crews arriving on scene, were not so aware. Immediately sought to find and rescue this man. If only they could. Chair showed no evidence of body trauma. There was no nearby waterway. Where a body could have been flung by violent impact. Sobered speculation began as to his whereabouts. Cynics quickly concluded. Disability was ruse bilking many unsuspecting motorists. Coworker related to Melba. Strange encounter she had with disappeared panhandler. Confirmed she knew the fellow. Recited the hand holding incident that infuriated Lorenzo. Much to her surprise, coworker told of similar, recent experience and Garfield mouthing to her, *"I love you."* She snatched her hand away, confessed being this close. Pushing him and chair over. onto the ground. Needless to say, Leroy ranted and raved. How could he get another chair, he pondered. Scribes soon advised, all he had to do was report it stolen and voila. Politico would come to the rescue. What with midterms just a year away. Did he?..Lorenzo sold his truck and after paying down the loan, is still indebted to the bank for shortcoming. Sadly, family's home was lost to foreclosure and there's daily struggle to survive. In-laws and grandparents assist with children's welfare and a heart frowns as a face smiles. This is midnight side of brilliant sunshine, self employment brings. Had Lorenzo been on company's payroll, insurance would have paid for hospitalization and recuperative treatments. There would have been lifetime disability payments and spectre of doom and gloom would not have been so overwhelming. We also know, majority self employed. Contribute minimum, if they ever do.To mandated statutory social benefit plans. Comes a time, help is needed most and realization rings true. Nothing in, means very little out. We often wish we had done differently. But if we could we would we should, always means it's too late. Does it not? So as we work and play. Can we learn from others' mistakes? If not, for what then is our life's purpose and meaning?

Parents want to know-14

Rory Dickson, like all Dickson males was heavyset, strong as a lad and later as a man. In school he defended the weak for a price. We could call him, the school bully who was loved and feared. Those being set up on, simply became friends with Rory. Tormentors let them be. Boys rewarded with marbles and rare tokens. Girls helped with homework and often did it for him. When there was a cricket game, Rory was umpire, deciding when he was out. Usually when he got heat, sweat exhausted or arm weary. Awarded a place to high school, he excelled at track and field, was dismal academically. Late freshman going to sophomore year. He was One of a group, known to smoke weed down the gully. In secret, they assured themselves. All schoolboys wore khakis as standard attire. Only distinguishing identification at high or technical high levels, was epaulette and tie. To avoid being identified and reported to school, they left paraphernalia in desks. Returned to class with excuses, unaware teacher found in their desks, evidence that belied. Excuses rejected, they were subjected to detention. Denied team participation, without knowing their ruses had been exposed. Beatrice Bellanfanti adored him in teenage romance, they got married very young. Much to disappointment of her father, Wembley. He said, aggressive by nature Rory. Would slap his daughter around if she got out of line. Although he was known to habitually knock her mother around, whenever he felt like it. Fearing she would carry out her threat to pour hot coconut oil down his ear when he slept. He abandoned their bedroom and then their home. Slept at his brother's bar, armed with Spanish machete, as watchman against breakers in. Bellanfantis were Mulatto Negroid mix. Dicksons were hard to define, ethnically. That somehow worked to their social access advantage. Rory was formidable and vicious to enemies, or those who threatened his existence. For him, you either got a good natured back slap with words. ***"You is good people, you deserve to live."*** Or you were one of two double worded epithets he uttered, brows tightly knitted and venomous stare. In Jamaica we call him a "Screwface," as in a Bob Marley and Wailers song. Perfect example, movie Scarface. Tony's face just before he shoots Manny, after finding him with Gina at the mansion. One was a four letter word for Rooster or spigot followed by "sucker." Other was mother, paired with word that rhymed with sucker. You can figure them out. Thursday nights, he and a crony went "buying" beef in rural areas. His customers suspected they were only Ones buying meat, but what did they care. No skin off their noses and they dared not raise a whisper of suspicion. Lest source of affordably priced protein was lost. There were tall and short tales of men who went rustling. Put shoes on cattle's hooves, each pair turned to face other. In enclave where ignorance and superstition abounds. Brightest among them will decipher and convince others. Of rolling calves or mighty demons having been involved. Among this group however, are marginally skeptic. Who sometimes muster armed posses and lay waiting in dead of night, with clubs and keen edged machetes. Rustlers usually come prepared for negative possibilities and escape with their skins, sometimes mangled or bruised. Other times, person demised is identified at daylight. Goat thief, caught with five animals. Was drenched with kerosene and bottle torch held to his forced opened mouth. He escaped during process of relighting the torch. Soon sought medical attention and died. Police made token efforts, bringing attackers to justice. Which stymied, they soon abandoned. Now, that village has unsavoury reputation. Gets scratched from list of hunting grounds. See how wrongs have ways righting itself naturally?

Other dimension of island paradise. One never knows how these forays will turn out, but it puts rolling calf myth to rest. On way back home in wee hours near dawn, the truck got a flat. Jasper got ride on market truck with the tire. Rory fell asleep in vehicle's cab. As he tells it, heard putt putt bike go by and stop short distance. Alerted, he sat up in passenger seat, pretended to be asleep. Watching young man stealthily approach. Grabbed the mirror, swung himself up on running board. Began wiping frost from the glass to peer inside. Rory yanked the door open and knocked fellow flat to ground. Jumped on his torso, whacked him with length of three and half core #4 electrical cable repeatedly. Fellow went limp, so did his hand with gun. Rory later found to be toy. I should tell you, both ends of twisted cable. Had a cricket ball sized, node of tightly wrapped retread rubber. Element of surprise and ferocity of onslaught, fellow didn't utter chick's peep. Rory again whacked still form of young man for good measure and settled in, awaiting rider to investigate. It is said, there's no honour among thieves. Less than five minutes, other fellow rode off, abandoning his buddy. Brutal in every respects. **New day cometh:** Dawn was on horizon. Rory was on edge, feared being caught by police. With animal's carcass for which he could not give convincing story. You see fellow citizens, meat without abattoir's inspection stamps. Readily identifies as illicitly slaughtered. Usually of rustled animals. We know, fresh kill emits odour that grabs Ones sense of smell. A stalled vehicle always draws attention of police out on patrol. Be it speed cop on Triumph, or duo in Land Rover. Walking up to vehicle, cop smells opportunity to make a killing from this illicit killing. First is getting to know you phase, where driver's licence is requested. Comparison made and address noted. Aspect of this that worries Rory is, it's never a one shot deal. Oh no. Whatever is agreed on, is down payment followed by surprise pull overs for installments. To rub salt in wound. Cop often sics his buddy onto motorist by giving route and mission. Speed cops are safer bets, being aware of ease with which, there can be accident. Their greed is held in check. And here we are, thinking crime does not pays. It does, but not for those we hurriedly assume. Jasper comes back and Rory fills in events, while they hurriedly put wheel on the truck. Jasper asks Rory. ***"What going happen with him. You think him dead?"*** Rory replies. **"You worried? Roll mother f…er over the banking and come on. Day soon light out."** So they did and went their way. Now before you start assuming murder, trying to justify whether or not. Mere attempt to rob fits felon's demise. Be aware, in this arena where survival depends on wit. Our felon could very well be playing possum. Having felt weight of vinyl coated, ball and chain replica. He's better off playing dead. So, as is often said, put it in your pipe and smoke it. Meantime, housewives came and bought choice cuts for Sunday's feast. And life went on with nary a query about, or anyone reported missing. Felons often lick wounds silently.

Rory and Beatrice had five girls and two boys. Angelina was eldest girl. Eldest boy Clifton, once sauntered past his home in company of a girl, on way from school. On coming home, his father asked about his mission, then cautioned his son. ***"When Ram Goat start follow Ewe go pen. You know what may happen to him? End up in kerosene pan on wood fire over three stone and served, two shillings a plate at dance. Watch how you follow woman go her yard."*** That was his way talking to his children.Which, when their mother decried he told her. ***"Bea, you haffi talk to children so them can understand exactly what you saying and there's no room for misunderstanding. Next thing, them tell you them nevva did*** *know that was what you mean.*" He sometimes looked furtively about, before encouraging children in general not to grow up as boneheads. And girls particularly, not to be fairies or fireflies. Only he knew what fireflies reference meant, but as with children. Most times it goes in one ear and out the other. In quite congenial manner he called Angelina into his study/studio. With a broad smile, asked how she was doing. She gave him wary eyes. Knowing, he was man of surprises. Especially when he made effort to appear unparent. He began. *"You know Angie, we don't rap as we should. There's so many things I could lean on you to make you stronger. Kind of like the brace post against a gate post, but you just hold you corners and....You know what me saying?"* "Not really dad, but I'm listening." *"Awright, this just between you and me."* Her heart went thump, afraid of what would come next. Every dialogue with her father that was prefaced with "This is just between two of us." Has always ended much to her mental discomfort. She braced herself and Rory went on. *"You know, from other day me have to start look at you like one stray puss."* Seeing her recoil, he hastened to calm. *"Hold on now, hear me out. This is not as bad as you begin to think. Listen testimony before you jump to verdict. Between you and me. I would shiver if you was on a jury trying my case. Anyhow, as I was saying. You don't eat this, neither that. What you do eat, you just finicky and pick pick as if...I want tell you, baby bird eat more than you."* He paused. Seeing features relaxed, went on. *"But the thing me can't understand, you putting on weight. You only fourteen, but you behine almost big as you mother's. So the question is. Who feeding you? Which cherry tree you stop on you way home?"* Her lower jaw free fell, she gasped and said. **"Dad, I am not being disrespectful but. Can we continue this when mom is home? I have an assignment that I must**

complete for math class." Not waiting for dismissal, she hied out the door. Rory called out. *"If they feed you they might also breed you. Just want you know. Is nothing for nothing world we live in."* After crying herself calm, told her dad she had to retrieve a workbook from school. He told her. *"If you say so, but make sure you come back before dog fraid of duppy."* Bank closed Saturdays at 14:00 hours. Decorated porter recognized and let her in. Seeing her on brink of tears, mom guided her into an office. Quietly closed the door as Angelina sobbed her heart out. Told mom she's going to run away. Go live with Ma Bell, her maternal grandmother. Couldn't deal with dad's temperament. Calling her a stray puss and negative innuendos. Seemed that was straw to break tolerance psyche. By now you have probably come to think, our Rory is fearless of all. Ready to take on comers from whatever source. This could be fair assessment. Four words that causes him to sweat and narrow his eyes. Are those of his wife, when she once told him. *"We have to talk."* First time she uttered those words, she was on brink leaving him and now his angst level was elevated. Evening came and all three sat to parley. Beatrice repeated what Angelina told her. Gently chided Rory, being insensitive to their daughter's feeling. Angelina's facial glow showed inner satisfaction, short lived by outcome. Rory explained. *"Me never mean nutt'n. Two of we was just talking one and one. If she never did like what me say, she could tell me. And me would give her a nice back rub as usual."* Beatrice continued. **"Coarse as your father's talk might have been. Your eating habits and development, does concern me, Angie. Today, us three are going to get to bottom of, and put all cards on the table."** Rory chimed in. *"Ha! See? Me was on right track."* Went silent as Beatrice glared at and browbeats him, then went on. **"Angie, set of uniforms always last a school**

year and some, except getting bit short. Didn't you notice,
Easter we had to buy new uniforms? I did, because I
wrote the cheque. Now, am going to tell you what I think
happening. You tell me where I am wrong. Your brothers
accusing each other, rifling their pockets small amounts.
Quite often, five or ten comes missing from my purse
which at first I…."** Rory interrupts, with glee. *"Me too, and
me did begin to think….."* He clams up as once again his wife
gives him that look. She resumes. **"At first I thought I was
mistaken, then I figured it could not be coincidence. So
tell me now, Angelina. You not eating junk food. Maybe
binging would be better verb. But tell us if I am wrong.
Because it doesn't end there, that's only first stage."**
Angelina admits, when she spends time at. Ma Bell treats her
to fast food and sends her home with twenty dollars each time
to indulge the habit in secret. Rory exclaims and quickly cuts
short. *"What the ff…..!"* After a long silence, Beatrice softly
says to her daughter. **"Tell us what is cause of your
munchies. You've never lied to us, don't start now. Are
you doing…?"** Unable to restrain himself, Rory puts hands
atop his head and hollers. *"Jesus and mother Mary, fu…in'
crackhead cokehead in my house?"* Bedlam breaks out.
Rory's yelling and swearing. Beatrice yelling him to control
his outburst. Angelina bawling herself into fits. Calm begins
returning when Rory stomps out, yelling more unprintables.
Mother and child continues dialogue quietly. Rory walks
back in, meekly asks. *"So what we in for, going into
tomorrow Beatrice? Me can't live with this. From one of the
bwoy me wouldn't so surprise, but Angie of all…..Me really
don't know what to say."* Beatrice tells him he doesn't have
to say anything. Angelina has sworn she's not now or ever
touched any form of recreational drugs. Has even voluntarily
urged her parents to have her drug tested. Rory stares at both

his wife and daughter in silence, then says. ***"Easy for her to say. She's not paying the bill. Insurance not going cover that. You know how much that kind of blood test cost? It don't come cheap."*** Hypocrisy glares, yet goes unseen by a roaring Rory. Who at this very age his daughter is at. Played hooky, puffing weed bong down gully in secret. Maybe, parents need reflect on their early years before disparaging and demonizing their children. Point out error of their ways, without denigration and low classing. A mom who called her seventeen year old daughter a whore, was reminded she had her at sixteen. Truth angered, mom slapped the kid viciously. That didn't change fact, she gave birth at sixteen. Now for sure, Ma Bell meant well. Never intended any harm could come from indulging her grandchild. Despite which, this was an occasion it could not be said. Saved by the bell with any degree of truth. Came a time, Rory gave up his weekend meat shop, much to disappointment of customers. After Beatrice told him those four words he dreaded. Lectured him. **"You getting old, shortsighted and slow Rory. Consider the family. If you get caught, we all going get daubed with a shit brush. And stench never goes away."** Spectre of prison time and rumors of what went on inside, gave him a chilling realistic view of life. Rory did not yea or nay his wife. If you patronize a certain supermarket and get your beef side carved. Maybe you are being served by Rory. You won't know, and you're not supposed to. After all folks, despite facts detailed and how true to life it seems. This is…. fiction.

Treasure or Trash-15

What do you figure would be useful life of basic motorized lawnmower? You might be surprised to know, it's between eight and twelve years. It could serve far longer, but frequent repair cost soon comes close to price of new one. Hence, in true American tradition. Folks often opt buying, rather than repairing. It's a phenomenon I first saw when I came to these United States, which is this chapter's theme. Told my auto mechanic, who installed new brake master cylinder on fifteen year old Ford Explorer. Back in the island, we bought seals and washers, made self repairs. He agreed, adding. Hourly labour rate, made it cheaper to replace than repair. Regarding lawnmowers, repair tech gave advice, I'm sharing with you. If you own small engined equipment, landscaping machinery, outboard motors, generators, outboard motors. You might want to start powering with ethanol free gasoline. Ethanol blended gasoline is best for internal combustion engines. Having high spark to burn fuel completely. Small engines cannot burn fuel totally, and tar-like residue clogs parts. Plastic fuel lines gets brittle and spring leaks. Not to mention, carburettor jets and nozzles which becomes gummed. Now you begin to see how parts and labour for that repair. Can get close to price of new equipment. You put it in yard sale for ten or fifteen dollars, which no one buys. You put it kerbside, as trash. **Brandon's vintage mower:** When Brandon bought first house in 2004, also bought his first lawnmower. Which with know how and frequent "Gumout" treatment was still serving purpose. Oh it was rusted and very unsightly but that didn't matter. So long as it did what it was supposed to. This Saturday, he first cut rear and sides then took on front. As he began mowing the swale, it sputtered and ran out of gas. He left it there, went in the garage for gas. His wife called out. *"Brandon! Toilet running continuously after flush, again. Whatever you did last time, you need do again."* It had been under two years since he changed flapper valve. Took a spare, made changes and flushed three times. Satisfied with himself, not having to call plumber. Geez, that would need second mortgage. Prices those guys charged for simple fixes like this. As he reached for Red Stripe from the fridge, reminded wife Toni. His father has wooden crate of old Red Stripe beer in vintage long necked bottles. He plans to bring back on his next visit. Sell this rare prize for fortune on EBay. She scoffs at the idea, saying. He'd best sell it in Jamaica. Where it's history would be appreciated. What's more, she doubts customs would allow alcohol content. Transportation cost would be high. He ruminated on this and told her. **"I always say, we make a good couple. I do the talking and you do the thinking."** As he moved towards her, she softly told him. *"I am not in a mood to kiss the gardener today. So go back to your job. Make sure I don't find fault after you're done."* He laughed and guzzled his beer. Found gas container empty. Silently cursed himself, got car keys and hied to gas station. Mid morning May sun was at it's peak. He had set out to get this done before, but what the heck. He walked over to the light post. Stared at void where lawnmower should be. It had simply disappeared. Ken, his across street neighbour, was out trimming trees earlier. Brandon asked if he saw anyone steal his mower. Ken told him, he's been inside for quite some time. Once the sun got overly warm and intensely humid. Ken said, maybe one of those scrap metal scavengers drove by and took it, thinking it had been discarded. Adding cordial insult to injury, Toni remarked to her husband. *"If someone stopped and took that mower, for whatever reason. Things must really be at rock bottom for them. I know, I wouldn't. That's like the man who ate his one ripe banana and tossed the skin. Only to see another man take it up and munch on it. Of our four children, Winthrop is only One older than that mower. Come on Brim, you've had your money's worth and then some."* He reluctantly agreed but asked where she saw the banana incident. Oh, it was one of those tales Nana used, teaching life's lessons. He went to do online search. Son Dunstan, was researching school work. He retired to the den and fell asleep. **The baby pink, mirror:** Newlyweds, Joylaine and Jonas Mullings were excited agog. Moving from small apartment to a three bedroom house. Went shopping for washer/dryer and refrigerator. Hired a Penske truck on site to take them home. After stopping at the apartment and loading items. Wise, well planned, two birds with one stone move. See? They weren't befuddled by love and brimming with joy, still had ability to be sensible. Jonas' brother, Nigel came to lend a hand. Rode in back the truck to steady a baby pink, vanity mirror. It was a short hop really, about four blocks as a hungry crow flies. Lately, recycling and trash trucks began coming, Saturday. Instead of Friday as scheduled. Hence, this mid morning, containers are at kerb waiting to be emptied. Nigel jumps out the truck, stretches his legs then goes back for and leans the mirror against trash bins. Truck is unloaded, Jonas hurries to return in time frame. Much later when rooms are being organized, mirror comes up missing and someone guesses it was left in the truck. Jonas quickly discounts this possibility. Says, having to sweep truck clean before return, debunks that argument. Slowly they come around to recall. Nigel leaning it against trash bins, now empty. Evidencing come and go of both vehicles. Next guess is, maybe the trash contractors took it up. Again, a big no. Those trucks are not equipped loading bulk items. Usually done by another crew in specialized vehicle. So then, who took the baby pink mirror? Someone who saw it and thought. Looky here, this is beautiful discard.**Coconut buds:** In 1994, Cordova relocated from Plainfield, New Jersey to Margate, Florida, to live with cousin Beresford. Whom today was showing him around their community. Driving through different exits, routes and generally a familiarization tour. They turned down a street.

Saw at kerbside, three budding coconuts ready to be planted. They stopped and casually examined their find, put them in their car, continued their reconnaissance. Short time later on way back, two men stood at coconut spot talking animatedly. One had a shovel, was heard saying to other. ***"I am not crazy. I left them, right here."*** Beresford paused to listen. Did not hear what one man said, but other retorted. ***"Yes, I did. But you know how they are. Might not think this important to come out and investigate."*** Cousins drove off and One, feeling remorse, said to other.**"You think we should go back and give them back. Explain to them we thought…..?"** Other, shot it down quickly. ***"You mad? They already called police. We go back with them coconuts, we off to jail. Police don't believe in mistakes. They believe people steal and should be locked up."*** It had been planned to plant nuts in backyard by a pool. Timidity set in and they were tossed over back fence onto FDOT lands beside turnpike. If you see three coconut palms towering above noise walls, you'll know their origin. It should bring closure to the man who went for a shovel to dig holes and came back to find his nuts missing.

Incontinence thwarts Reunion-16

Dickie Fuller and Beverly Turnbull were sweethearts, with which most folks had a problem. Their families lived across from each on a cul-de-sac. There was no keeping them apart, despite efforts by her parents. You see folks, Dickie was nine years her senior and village's face man. Beverly was self styled Cowgirl who avoided boys her age and rousted openly with Dickie. Byron Turnbull once filed police complaint for Dickie's arrest, on charge, carnal abuse of underage Beverly. She denied intimate contact between her and Dickie, making dad's thrust futile. As she made sixteen, legal consent age.

Both were in open relationship. Which Byron Turnbull had sworn, would only event, "over his dead body." In addition to age issues, he openly declared Dickie. A mongrel without pride. His mother not knowing for sure who was his father. Them that knew, said it was case of sour grapes. Others ventured to suggest, indeed. Dickie could be a Turnbull. Based on? Aw! See? Back then there were no DNA testing. *"Mama's baby. Papa's? Maybe."* Settled paternity questions. Without customary fanfare or feast. Turnbull tribe sold their house and surreptitiously migrated to Canada in dead night. That's how things happened, catching everyone, including church parishioners off guard. Took months ere neighbors accepted, they were indeed gone. Old Sourpuss Turnbull was elated, danced merry one legged jig. Thwarting further development in the relationship, not sacrificing his body. Beverly married an older man and had children. It is not known if daddy had objections, based on age disparity. This one was said to be at some point, more than twice her age. Time moved on and hubby died, as did her father. Six years later her mom went home to be with the lord. She did not express any such fate regarding dad. **So much for history. To the present we go:** Beverly joined her adult children and families in the USA. Eventually she hooked up with Dickie. Who had thrice married, was now separated from wife three. Told Beverly, he was lone Cowboy and would she visit his ranch. Get a whoop-di-doo for old time's sake going. She hemmed and hawed, promising to make trips. On dates that never came to be for various inane reasons. He was heard to discuss with friends, possibility bringing her into his circle. She had far fetched, costly, unrealistic demands. He told her, she was no longer prancing filly, nor he no Steed. She should make herself content, where oats bag and stable stall was at her disposal. Each person has sense of value and sees their position as reasonable. He owns Ford Excursion, with which he hauls his boat and trailer as feeling hits. Two years ago he bought new Ford Raptor, a model year older for $10,000 over MSRP. Took pride of ownership to new level when dealer's service technicians. Asked how he was able to retain truck's factory smell, 30,000 miles going into third year. The long awaited, often elusive meet and greet took tangible form. After Dickie went online and bought JetBlue round trip ticket. See pardners? All depends on who wants ham and who gives a dam. As is said, someone, somewhere, sometime, gots to give. Here's our Dickie in airport's cellphone lot awaiting the call. Board shows, flight landed more than forty-five minutes earlier. He is by nature an impatient person and asks the wind. *"A domestic flight. No customs immigration check. What then could be…"* Phone rings. Beverly gives door number, he's off. **Uhhuh:** It was a Jack Walsh, Jimmy Serrano moment as both walked eager, yet tentative towards. Each thinking, other appeared so strikingly different. Folks most times, retains last image of a person. Finds it hard adjusting to new Tom or Pussycat. Despite, they greeted with a hug and long time no see. Then both lied. *"You look good."* I once asked someone. *"How else you expected me to look. Like a guy with a cup?"* But you know, you do laugh to ease the barb. He asked, she pointed to two suitcases. As he moved around her to get them, his eyes caught her rear end. He recoiled and stood erect, slackjawed and mute. Seconds ticked, nothing was happening. She asked in their dialect. **"Ah wha?"** He said. *"Rass! Me don't know how fi tell you. Look like you peepi up youself."* Oh, she panicked. Rapidly craned her neck over shoulders, saying to him. **"Stop chat fart. How you mean, me piss up miself?"** He replied. *"That's what it look like to me. Or maybe, coulda be. Somebody throw away cooking oil on the plane seat."* She huffed at him. **"Then stand up behind me** now, until me can. Jesus have mercy, what a shame and disgrace. People staring at my behine and thinking that me piss up miself." Dickie made situation worse, saying. *"Well, nobody not certain. Could really be oil leak from a place on the plane, like overhead bins and so. If is new plane you fly on, bins work by hydraulic. That's why it raise up so easy cheesy."* She said. **"Stop chat shit and get serious."** There's temptation to see humour in this situation and truth is. Dickie has difficulty keeping staid face. This is so very frighteningly embarrassing for Beverly and her woes has just began. Dickie tells Beverly. *"I will send you home in a taxi. Don't worry, I will pay for the ride. I can just go over the stand. Get a Super Shuttle take you home. Let me talk to this guy with the whistle, him staring at the truck hard."* He's talking to traffic cop, who glances at his wrist. Says something to Dickie who again joins Beverly, kerbside. Poor woman.**The fallout:** She asks Dickie. **"So is why all of a sudden, me is scorned woman and can't drive in you truck?"** He tells her, without hesitation. *"You know, leather is thing hold smell and don't care what me do. It not going get rid of the sti.... smell. Don't worry youself, me going pay for the taxi."* After silent deliberation, she softly told him. **"Alright, if you say so. I don't have no choice. God! I wish the earth would just open and swallow me."** He ran to the shuttle kiosk, chatted briefly with a clerk who accompanied him to where Beverly stood. Trying to disguise her shame behind a round column, from which she would have to move. Handing her a credit card he told Beverly. *"Me going circle the block and come back. Don't worry, me won't leave till me know everything okay with you. Why you looking on me like that. You think me woulda leave you stranded out here, because? Me is not some dibby dibby nigga, you know."* Beverly said not a word. As he drove off it hit him like a missile. She did not have his address. They stayed in touch by WhatsApp so there was no need for addresses. See changes progress brings? Times yore, they would be writing each other by post or pay long distance toll charges to talk. Now he could not find a space close to where he first parked. Saw a blue shuttle bus and dialed number displayed. No, he could not be connected to the kiosk. There was no information as to where Beverly went, or maybe she was still at the airport. He had quandary that beggared a solution. Began having second thoughts about not taking her in the truck. Maybe urine odour could be gotten rid of, but also take, cherished new car odour. He lamented in confusion. Beverly did not tell him or did not have time to. Delay calling him after she landed and retrieved luggage. Was making effort to get phone call as her cellphone battery had gone flat. Now he was calling and texting her without response. Began wondering if this was deliberate. Her being pissed at his not taking her in his truck, because she pissed prior to. He dropped in on friend and guru, Speedy Foster. Who advised he call the credit card company. Ask if and where card had been used. So far, it hadn't been. Speedy told him, Beverly probably could not use the card. Hers not being name on it, merchants might consider it stolen and refuse goods or services. Been two years on three, hasn't heard word from Beverly. He knows she's alive and kicking. Often opens contact on his phone. Gets a message "last seen at time." He keeps texting and calling, not making contact. I say Beverly is again pissed. At him for denying a ride in his truck and also pissing herself. That really was her failure, wearing proper insulation and how this entire pissing affair got started. Did she laugh, sneeze or dribbled unawares? Was she holding and slipping without knowing? Again, I say in empathy. Poor woman. Curious by nature we are caught in a web of uncertainty as to how this all played out, but there's no continuity. We must take what we know and peradventure what came after. Here's my theory which I am sticking to, despite what anyone might throw into the hat. Beverly was mortified by her situation and hating Dickie for not hurriedly ushering her into his truck out of public stares. Yes, there were few who stared but she yearned for mitigation. That was not forthcoming because man feared an odour would linger in his Raptor. Every step she took alongside shuttle agent. Was like final walk of condemned on way to gallows or death chamber. Her ordeal would take on rebirth with every passing stranger. If agent confirmed Dickie having given her the card, she could have been booked for a ride. To where? Good deed was stillborn right there. Methinks she simply paid her way to a hotel, made herself whole and in due course flew home on her return ticket. She seethes and likely scans obituaries for his demise. Oh, she would love to stand over his grave and.... But this time it will not be an accident. I can hear her exult. *"Leather is a thing hold smell. What you smell like now?"* A moment can last a lifetime of pleasure or pain ?

Antiquity and Prejudices-17

Rural, suburban and urban communities can be miles apart, or in known locations, cheek and jowl. Whatever are varied infrastructural developments, giving each their desirability. There's often a thread of commonality. That of strange place names. Some of which are historic to events or characteristics, whilst others have unexplained aberration that confuses. We understand. Ocho Rios is site of eight rivers converging and Germantown is settlement of Germans. How do we explain Animaltown? Where every inhabitant has animal surname such as Bear, Buck, Byrd, Deere, Drake, Finch, Fox, Hawke, Hogg, Lyon, Steer and Wolfe, to name a few. There were no

Smiths, Browns, Jacksons, Jones, or Williams. Let's focus on Germantown, (Seaford Town on the map) with population about six hundred souls. Far cry from heyday of it's existence in Westmoreland parish hinterlands. Some recall thousands, others aver it was much less. One ne'er disputed fact tells, it was settled by German nationals fleeing persecution. Once this haven was found, droves followed and made the old country their home. They weren't known to be hostile, yet kept outsiders at bay. Breeding among themselves and usually that engenders cousin cousin, uncle aunt sister brother relationship, intended or unknown. It's an open acreage in the parish and children attend nearby schools, mixing with the general community to an extent. Beyond which there's taboo that insulates peoples apart. Hard working and industrious agri-farmers, they raise livestock of every kind and specie including Honeybees. Reputation spreading far and wide, folks came in droves to buy German golden honey. Some are gifted in fretwork and joinery, their services sought after. By builders of grandiose homes, churches and restoration of historic great houses. Ornate coffins are an in demand item by those who can squander without inhibitions. You know? Compulsion by guilt or remorse, spare no expense for dearly departed. Village could twin Pennsylvania's Amish lifestyle, but Germans are more integrated in wider community, with limits. They take wares to market and support businesses as their needs dictate. Although theirs is an open village, anyone going there is either by invitation or lost. There is no thruway to other places, which spares invasion by outside criminals. Their own being enough. This one way in and out makes for dangerous escape. Fleeing by unknown terrain thru Cockpit country across six parishes. Known to be festooned with hidden chasms and sinkholes. Germantown natives are sturdy and heavyset. Handy when trampling wet clay in preparation for brick and pottery making. Most houses are made of brick, sun dried then fired in a makeshift kiln. Proven durability to hurricanes and frequent wind swirls. For transportation they rely on vintage model cars and trucks of British makes. Leyland, Bedford, Fargo and Commer trucks. Vauxhall, Austin, Wolseley and Morris cars still zoom city streets. After being rigorously inspected and passed by motor vehicle examiner. Mechanics form a kind of cooperative, occupying large acreage. Littered with numerous old vehicles, which are cannibalized to keep others roadworthy. Next to which is an active Wheelwright and buggy repair lean-to. Visitors are asked to leave cameras in cars before guided tours begins. They can buy curios, tasty, healthy and nutritious baked goods. Washing down with blended fruit juices or nectars, cane juice and sought after crowd pleaser. Honey, wet sugar sweetened, ginger beer. Watch out now, that ginger is a kicker. Definitely not what you've tasted in ginger cookies or tea pouches. If you're willing to plunk down chunk of change for woolen vest or coat. You will be taken to hut where sheep are shorn. Entire process of fleece being made into wool, on antiquated devices solely by hand, unveiled before your eyes. You are being privy to process only, not getting your vest or coat that day. For pleasure of ownership, you're asked to wait three months or more. Locals know, they must bring bowls and jars to purchase any of many fruit preserves. Cane liquor, wines and liqueurs, jams and marmalade from every fruit under the sun. Cashew, Guava, Pineapple, Otaheiti, Jackfruit, Pomegranate, Cactus Prickle Pear to mention a few.

Now, what can One say about Animaltown? Not a lot really. Animaltown lacks history of origin and character of existence, equating it even remotely to Germantown. Animaltonians are all mulattoes in varying shades of white, some bordering on being red. They are said to have come from somewhere in Great Britain, sometimes referred to as The United Kingdom. Meaning England, Scotland, Ireland, Wales and many Isles. Unlike Germantown citizens, they are fully integrated in facets of wider society. Residing in communities far removed from their rural birth enclave. Practiced all professions and branches of industry and commerce. By virtue of skin colour, led privileged existence. Fast eroding in slowly changing era. Spotlighted by political office aspirants, eagerly supported by downtrodden majority. So you might be wanting to uncover thread that ultimately brings these communities into same place mention. It is a young man, named Wolfram Becker. His sweetheart, Victoria Prendergast and other young woman, named Virginia Beecher. I've said it so many times, people are prejudiced as a given. It's never just a racial, economic or status consideration. Whites hate whites, as do blacks who hates blacks and Christians who hate Christians. Although the good book teaches, love one another. Us the unrighteous have an excuse being hatemongers, but what says religious zealots. I say, it's driven by fear that incubates and breeds a mindset which dictates annihilation of other. So that we, us and ours might be guaranteed existence. Therein lies germ that will one day proliferate and engender our self destruction. Until then lets look at these young people. See what's unfolding in their lives. Prendergasts were seen as topping, under wealthy class. Owned only sawmill and lumber yard, serving districts near and far. Five of six children migrated to the big city after high school, pursued training in varied professions. Victoria the youngest, worked in family business before and just after leaving school. Her father hired a young woman and soon an intimate relationship started between them. Victoria watched and took tidings of infidelity to her mother, creating angst at home. Her father reacted by cutting her loose from the business. Wolfram, frequent sawmill visitor in apprentice with an uncle. Met and initiated secret friendship with Victoria. Somehow, this was common knowledge in their village. Unknown to Victoria, Wolfram and Virginia carried straws from school days. Which, once his parents got wind of, met with their disfavour.Victoria had a child, ostensibly for Wolfram. Marriage plans got underway. Village pundits noised abroad, child was spitting image, of boy Fabian Cruz. Which most people concurred, except Wolfram and parents. Wedding and reception was slated to be grand affair, unseen in these neck of woods. Friday evening before Saturday's ceremony and reception, couple attended dress rehearsal of church with reception entry and dry run formalities. Went so far as to practice first dance, which symbolically opened the dance floor. Back then, song of choice for this dance was **"Devoted to you."** Written by Felice and Boudleaux Bryant, sung by Everly brothers, Don and Phil. Backed by RCA's Studio B musicians with Chet Atkins on lead guitar. Renown plucker in class of Duane Eddy and Les Paul then. Taken as too sterile for bumpers and grinders. Rocksteady version by Sensations. Featuring "All Star" musician's ensemble, with Aubrey Adams on organ. From Duke Reid's, Bond Street Studios was preferred. You know, superstition at times lends a hand creating havoc or maybe it's just coincidence. As the saying goes, what is to be, will. However, it was considered bad luck. Couple seeing each, after sunset on eve of nuptials. Separated at rehearsal, not meet again until altar moment. There was no concern in Wolfram's house, he did not come home. Was taken, he went out with friends having last hurrah, before being curfewed by wife's dictates. As sun rose higher in Sabbath sky, Wolfram still no showed. Concern became worry, elevated to alarm by noon. Long story short, there was no wedding. Our groom was nowhere to be found. Didn't take long for it to be made known, by coincidence, Virginia too had disappeared from home. Late Monday, telegraph man rode donkey cubby into village. Brought telegrams sent early Saturday. Telling both families their kith and kin were safe and sound, with rider note. "Do not try to find." We know, as the saying goes. You may run but you can't hide. On an island? After usual nine day talk, dust settled and life went on. Families estranged and silently feuding. Individually, each made amends with his or her kin. Whilst maintaining their independent existence together, as estranged, common law couple. Virginia took to church as she was brought up to do, but parted ways. When elders and pastor, kept hammering about her sinful life as Wolfram's concubine. More than once, she abandoned the union and was sheltered in church. Only to once more harken to Wolfram's yearning for "these arms of mine." He did promise to marry her, when he's able to make their home. Whatever that meant. Skilled in vehicle repairs, he retrofitted engines for Vernamfield racing enthusiasts. Both did vintage auto restoration for a small elite group. Her forte being seats, headliner repair or replacement. Always fashion conscious, they splurged, glowing in lavender lace. But, when summer turns autumn. They are probably unaware not being prepared for winter of their lives. Victoria had two more children for Fabian Cruz. Which, apple to apples confirmed initial rumors. Unable to live down smiling frowns and loud whispers. All five went off to England and has never returned. Hers would be a saga unto itself, but author needs an iota to build on. Absent which, there's not much that can be said. You do understand that? Don't you? Having mentioned "Vernamfield." This was a United States, World War II aerodrome, situated in Clarendon parish. Recent times, rumour had it being used for covert, illicit cargo pickup. Overtly, runway and taxiways were used for auto racing, which has since ended. It is now slated to be developed as Jamaica's fourth international airport. Positively, ambitious contradiction for a country of 4240 sq. Miles. Whose name literally interprets to "Land of Wood and Water."

Coffins and Doctors-18

In previous chapter you read briefly about coffins being made by German artisans for the wealthy. These were type, usually tapered. Crafted from Cedar or Mahogany board, then hand polished. When average Joe or Jane passed. Skilled neighbors got together and made a box, preferably of Pitchpine for good reason. Back then, especially in rural areas. Deceased had to be hurriedly buried or kept on ice. Which item not being readily available and even where it was. Moving ice, was like carrying water in wicker basket. In our tropics, very little if any would reach destination. Hospital morgues catered to them that expired in their care, and other facilities were most times overwhelmed. Quick interment became obvious choice. When odour of death began to swirl. Pitchpine resin blended with and improved air quality. Hospitals were far apart, in towns. Few of those that were seriously ill. Survived arduous journey by draught animals conveyance, over rutted rural paths. Wealthy citizens went by car or buggy, along better parochial roads and city byways. Most significant difference between then and now, was. Doctors came to the ailing when summoned. All males then, they came by buggy or car. With black satchels to diagnose and heal. Firsthand knowledge of deceased's illness, they had onus attesting death certificates. Absent doctor's prior care. Justice of Peace (Notary) attested, knowing person. And further being aware, cause of suffering. From fall, victim of attack by person identified or unknown, or malady of old age. Believe it or not, oft times this was after fact. Given rapid deterioration of body. As an example. Search party bumped into swinging corpse. Cut down and buried from necessity. Justice of Peace attested, deceased was of unsound mind. Common law spouse having fled in company of suitor. Registrar made record, life goes on and. Who's complaining? Let's look at scenario in average rural community. Ritual kept current by traditional lore. At birth, a Mahogany, Cedar, Pine or hardwood sapling is planted by grand or godparent in infant's name. This tree will serve as lumber source for infant's life journey's end. Provided infant survives to where both mature. Let's say, person is gravely ill. Doctor quietly advises, there is no hope. He's sometimes beseeched by family to, and prepares pain tonic with dosage guidelines. Given to patient when discomfort and or pain becomes unbearable. There are those who swear there's arsenic, morphine and other poisons in potion, ease suffering and hasten demise. Remember now, question of postmortem examination does not arise. Doctor will attest death certificate that satisfies Registrar. Stricken One lies abed. Neighbours come to generously lend hands. Making final preparations of the coffin. It must be mentally torturous, for sick and dying. Hearing wood being sawed and hammer pounding, preparing their repository. Akin to western movies, where condemned outlaw hears. In some instances, watches from cell. Whilst gallows for his hanging is being erected and sandbag tested. Maybe, our ailing parishioner's suffering gets worse. He calls for dose of that pain relieving tonic. There have been rare occasions on which, person refuses to die. Miraculously bouncing back to robust health. Such as happened when that coffin was left on display in living room for years. **"Coffin in waiting-The Lucky Bastard."** Whilst preparations are in progress for hurried burial of body. Animals are bought to be slaughtered and food for celebratory feast are being gathered.

This ceremony takes place, ninth night after person dies. At which time the duppy or ghost. Is fed last meal and evicted from place they called lifetime home. Copious amounts of overproof rum are served to celebrants, who sing and chant songs with lyrics conveying message. Telling deceased they're not welcome with the living. Personal items, known to be cherished by deceased are thrown out at midnight. Atop that is platter of ital (sans salt) rice and callaloo.(a kind of spinach, like collard greens) If at daybreak those items are still there. It'll be gathered and taken to the grave by someone strong willed. I can tell you now, there has never been such a person, because before the sun comes up. Some living person will have taken those items and otherwise discarded them. Giving false authenticity to enquirers who come asking. *"Did Frank come for his things before dawn?"* And, reassuring response. *"Every piece mam, not even grain, leaf or thread left behind."* At which everyone agrees, it is certainty, deceased rests in peace. Does this end here? Let's expose a bit of well intended deception and trickery. Supported by beliefs which manifests to our detriment. During deceased's lifetime, there were folks who wronged him/her. Borrowed or stole from, not making restitution or falsely and maliciously accused. Family leaves food and possessions mound intact, which now creates angst in the district. Deceased is believed, carrying sword of vengeance. Will not rest until antagonists are "touched" and made to join him in nether world. Help of village Obeahman, Obeahwoman, Shaman is urgently sought. Beleaguered makes reparations, plus offering to Shaman. Who then visits the mound, leaving monies and messages. It all disappears and folks breathes easy again. Sometimes, Shaman repeats names passed to him by the dead. Of others who are still in default. Of course he repeats names given him by relatives of the deceased, but fear motivates people to act.

Taken a step further are those who decide to tough it out, but soon go crazy from silent worry. Can be seen aimlessly wandering, dishevelled and unkempt. Reminder to others, similar fate awaits. Life in urban and suburban communities are less prone to this kind of trickery. Folks usually scoff at suggestions of. Most times resorting to hilarity and ridicule. As the saying goes. Belief kills and it cures. It goes without being said that city life is more supportive of them that ail from natural causes. In sudden onset of life threatening illness, the local physician is summoned and arrives as he would in a rural setting. Difference being, upon evaluation and if necessary. Recommends immediate transfer to nearest hospital. Taxi cabs are summoned, other times a neighbour obliges. Sick is rushed to place of healing and rehabilitation. Although not a given in all situations, that option existed. Urban folks do at times, come up with tales of supernatural events that are hard to reconcile with truth or fact. Retired physician, Martin Elliot. Raised five girls, after his wife drowned, early in their marriage. Family lived in middle class Mona Heights their entire life. Youngest daughter Giselle, school principal. Always desired, living in more salubrious, Mona Commons. Home to nearby University, academicians professors and gentrified clans. She brought two teenaged children to live with her dad. Pestered continuously, he sell his home. This he put up fierce resistance to, although health was in decline. She had her way and moved into Commons. Doc Elliott, rushed to hospital. Diagnosed to have suffered a stroke. Admitted, he soon had a second. Despite drooling and speech impaired, told Giselle. He would never forgive her selling his home. Call came from hospital, saying he had passed, which they denied making. She called undertakers and was assured of early attention next day. Later that night, Doc called her to confirm he was alive. Accused her starting rumour, upset his chiding her. After failed responses next day, she was found dead in bed. Would you believe, Doc was shortly discharged from hospital. Made arrangements to rent "student's cottage," from new owners of his former home. Lived another eighteen years to ninety-three, marginally senile and cheerful. Siblings silently declared in family chat. "Dad's lost spirit, found and touched Giselle, before retiring to find peace at home. There was no-charge, in home, patient aftercare service to clients. After hospital discharge. HLVNS "Hyacinth Lightbourne Visiting Nursing Service." Trained nurses came to Doc Elliot's home. Gave invaluable nursing care on par with that obtained in a hospital. Feature of being One on One, made it far more comforting and rehabilitative. Methinks this is taking superstition beyond realms of tangible possibilities. So we thumbs up to life in rural enclave, where we breathe clean air. Void of exhaust fumes and industrial smoke stack emissions. But when inevitable maladies, pain and suffering sets in. What would we not do for living in the city and near facilities, bringing relief from discomfort.

Sex and the Citizen-19

Angela Collins at fifteen years old, moved a scale to 130lbs on an empty stomach. Stood 5'7" and harnessed her bouncing nubbies with a 34D bra. Oh, she was a big One of daunting persona. Her and Roger Cummings were peas in pod. Father, Dexter Collins shouted to Roger at kerbside, from his living room couch. ***"Any day, strawn (strand) Angela hair missing, pray me don't find it stuck on you. Because that will be the day you go cow prison, after me finish with you."*** Mortician by profession now retired, he was mighty barker without bite. Intended victims had to come to him. Being immobilized with weeping finger tips, gout and bunions. Roger laughed a laugh, wanting to. Not having chutzpah to tell him. Angela was in unholy rush to begin moulting. Bit his tongue, bided time. Day she turned sixteen, going to town for celebratory goods. She stopped by Roger's house. What a romp they had. On her way up and on her way down. Entering verandah at her house, laden with hampers and bags. Dexter Collins again beckoned Roger. *"Government say, once she turn sixteen she ready fah man. But Angela don't belong to government, she belong to me. Me say, not before she turn twenty-one. So all the work me see you working and sweating with you Rumpelstiltskin grin. You going be holly button work fah nutt'n. Pshaw."* If he only knew, she had sidetracked to the bathroom to sponge. Her Saturday night sweet sixteen party, she was devil in a granny print dress. Roger revelled in fires of devil's cauldron. Peggy Lee sang, 1950's. *"Chicks were born to give you fever, be it Fahrenheit or Centigrade."* Stints were brief, he figured the night was long. Roger was so content in anticipation. Mom, Mrs. Amelia Collins called him and said, in her caring, motherly voice. *"I know you want to stay for last dance and hug with Angela, but son. It's a long way to Tipperary. Is you alone in the dark. So, say goodbye to Piccadilly."* Excerpting lyrics of an English song, sang by maypole dancers and others at cantatas or fairs. Stepping out the front door, Roger's hand securely in hers, she remarked. *"Outside cool eh? You would never know if you stay inside all night. I will tell Angela you said goodnight, walk good now."* See how woman achieves much more with less, or no bluster? Her adult children silently dubbed her "Wise old Owl" She didn't talk much but saw and knew a lot, which made them wary of her, more than their dad. Seething from having fun curtailed, Roger yet found humour in brilliance of her strategy. At first Roger thanked his lucky stars, being happy victim of Angela's intense craving for sexual intimacy.

Most evenings, as she walked by his house on her way home. By ritual, most Saturdays on her way to and from the market. Mom didn't know, Sundays she dashed out of church. As if beset by demons, immediately after the responsory. Came at timid Roger, like snorting Bull at scared matador. Both had in common, an appeal to opposite sex. Angela, more than Roger. She was a graceful young woman, carried herself with poise and strides. Caused heads to turn in admiration and envy. Oh yes, there were schoolmates who whispered, she was a show off. She flirted to get attention and make Roger jealous. Whilst he played to get laid and did, by mostly her friends. They had frequent spats, motivated by mutual mistrust which Roger at times encouraged. Anticipating ensuing makeup. You might be tempted to think there's exaggeration at work here and I would too. Except for fact there exists chronicles that proves factual truth beyond doubt. Six palm sized Collins Handy Diary, made in Glasgow Scotland. Sold for $1.25 to $2.35 through years 1968-1973. When Roger got married. He took these to mother's house, shielded from inquisitive eyes. Last two diaries contained dalliance between number of women, including Angela and future wife. Having given up recording, kept memories alive until faded. Time moved on, Angela had children. Got married and divorced three times to Roger's twice. Through years, they kept in touch. Roger got divorced in 2015 and three years after, his mother passed. Time on his hands, months later decided to rummage mom's possessions. Geez, there was so much treasured garbage to throw out. He never guessed true value of, until stumbling on bandana wrapped bundle. Inside sheaves of 1970's Gleaner, that now heightened curiosity. Can you imagine, lower jaw bouncing off his chest when he opened the bundle to reveal antique diaries? This was almost fifty years of forgotten life's sexploits. Preserved intact as the day they were first written.

He stared at first one, turned cover and musing to himself. *"Dollar twenty-five for a diary back then?"* The currency had just changed from pound sterling to dollars and cents. He began reading, saw names he had encounters with more than once. Yet could not put a face to. Not having first clue who the hell they were. He tried hard recalling places he jotted as having been and drew blank. Mischief being his idle dog worry sheep forte, he messaged Angela. *"Remember when you lost your two five shilling notes and searched for them without success? You didn't lose them. I stole them and bought gas to get us home, or else we would have been stranded in no-man's land"* How she ranted and called him names. Energized anew by contents of his diaries. Roger told Angela he wanted to show her things that would delight. Without reservation, actually. I should say, with reservation on JetBlue by Discover, she made the trip. He let her read selected tomes and they decided to sleep on it. Theirs was a good weekend, she went away happy and reinvigorated. One good turn deserves another. Early next year, Angela repeated the JetBlue Discover match up. Things however did not go as planned. She kinda jumped Roger at landside and he joked. ***"Down Angie down, your treat is at home."*** Which begat a dirty look and snide remark from her. By time they got home, there was full scale war going on. Name calling of B man and chi chi epithets. To which Roger had descended, he spurning female affection. As Alonzo Moseley told Jack Walsh, resign to fate. *"That's way that one went"* Time it is said, heals all wounds. Soon both began cautiously exchanging WhatsApp texts and phone calls. Bringing both to a level of enhanced civility. Having speed read diaries he began nitpicking each page. Wracked his brain to recall facial images, sometimes alarming himself like. ***Vivienne! Yes, Vivienne. She's the policeman's girlfriend who did get pregnant and he was*** *overjoyed becoming a father. Bwoy, hope you know you used to live dangerous."* Musing aloud in chauvinistic, egotistic, self congratulation. Happy to have been close to the flame and not get singed. Roger extends invitation to Angela, which she accepts. On condition he dusts off his Visa and enter sixteen digits online. They went wining and dining, hung out by Bayside Park and reminisced on better times. Morning after, she comes downstairs to breakfast. Accuses him hurrying out of bed, as if her feet had nails. He laughed and told her she probably had a thing going there. They are called toenails for reason. She gave him one of her signature dirty looks then said, she doesn't understand why. But lately, her job induces lots of stress. Clients are more demanding and argumentative, when they can't have their way. Her on other hand, has to suppress reaction and has head throbs. Yes, there are times, women are stressed from work or having to tend children and housework. I waited patiently as a cashier fumbled with items at checkout. Her line which was shortest, now lengthened quickly. Old coot behind, began grumbling at her apparent ineptitude. She glanced at me with a smile, wordlessly asking patience. I smiled back and mouthed. **"I'm okay, take your time."** Her knuckles were red, appeared swollen. Cause of her inability maneuvering items, gondola to bags. I figured her skin was reacting to money or allergy rash. Suggested she should get gloves as many of her fellow cashiers did. She said. *"No, I punched the wall instead of the kid."* Her customer seemed to have run out of debit cards. She waited on supervisor. I asked her. **"Which kid?"** She answered in a soft whisper. *"My kid. I spend all morning tidy the place. I come from shower and place all messed up. So I punched the wall because I not punch the kid. Ooh, the policia they come, and it never ends."* I told her to get ice on it. She said. *"Si pappy, soon my break."* I felt intense empathy for her and wondered what home life was like. Was she alone with kids? Did she have support of their father as family? I can understand her getting home, spurning mate's advances. Yet there will be times she embraces his needs. Some women just say no, for pleasure watching man's hopes dashed. Come to think of it ladies, you sometimes comply with and do workplace chores, just to save your job. Prepare conference room for meeting. Take stock and order stationery as needed. All this, in addition to your defined job description, but you comply. You could do likewise, make a dude happy. Save your marriage or relationship. I do believe in everything I say. Be it right or wrong, you can't explode myth or reality of every situation arising.

Got to Live a Life Plan-20

Wilmot and Laura Sinclair were third generation residents of Leightonia. Already a couple when both graduated Teacher's College. After brief stint in public education system. Unable to forge half decent living for a family, from government budgeted pittance. Rented their local church hall and set up a preparatory school. Quickly overcrowded, given unexpected student growth. Citizens gratified, by children's success and acceptance in high schools. Heaped praises on institution and principals, while clinging miserly to purses. Depriving school of funds to pay salaries and agreed rent to church. A conflict becomes obvious, because. Nonpaying parents were for most part, also church members. Most of whom, being stingy with tithes and offerings. Forced synod seeking income by renting hall for daytime occupancy.When finance committee met behind closed doors. Top agenda topic was school's arrears. Those in discussion were most, hypocritically aware of their responsibility in school's dearth of resources. Their children and grandchildren enrolled. Yet not paying as required. See how dog chases it's tail, not attaining goal? Wilmot joined his father in the US and was trained as electrician. Elated by inner satisfaction, seeing students rise to near stardom under her guidance. Laura stuck with school two more years, before forced to abandon ship. Church elders understood her plight, year's arrears demanded action. Church took over operations, engaged qualified administrator who scoured records. Then prepared debt recovery list. Dissatisfaction immediately set in. Parents fumed, threatened and swore, if children were denied attendance. Installment arrangements for past and current debts had to be made. This was uncharitable grubbing and unexpected of Christians, some denounced. Whilst they so engaged, fame of excellence and status as a preferred place of learning. Motivated others to fill anticipated void. On visit to homeland and being lay preacher. Wilmot Sinclair did take to pulpit and expound to fellow congregants. Success of the school which dogged his and Laura's previous attempts. Is ample proof that though love of money is root of all evil. Without it, good stagnates and dies. He was not booed or amened. You do know that's how Christians cheer. An amen means, ole, right on brother, tell the gospel. Loud silence is their form of booing. Sinclairs went back to their US haven. Five children made good and everyone was content in his or her own way. Teaching was in her veins. Laura joined staff at a school run by her church. Wilmot put in thirty eight years with the county. Coached by financial Advisor to keep his pension and 401k funds in an IRA, taking it incrementally. He said, no. Having worked hard, he wanted to enjoy his money before he died. Live life while he could, instead of dying and leaving wealth to others. Who did not watch clock and fight gridlock for close on forty years. Taking 'the bag' he suffered inertia. Seeing how much beloved uncle grabbed, before it got to him. Felix Underwood could not contain himself. Telling Laura in front her husband. ***"I warned him, but he stuffed cotton balls in his ears."*** Be that as it may, there was money to be spent and time was awasting. Laura had always yearned to own Swedish engineered automobile, the Volvo. Goaded to, Wilmot plunked a chunk of change for a wagon with renown safety features. Yet no longer made in Sweden. Not to be outdone, he acquired flagship of British engineering, Land Rover. Also, not now made in Britain but pedigree stands. With minimum down pay, they qualified for mortgage and moved into home befitting their status. Next, they toured here and there, oohing and aahing at sights that were more magnificent than portrayed in brochures. Dined in cafes at exotic places, although stomachs rebelled. Forcing both to seek pink relief or substitute. But, as Ernie Smith sang. What is life if not for living. Life has a sunrise and eventually a sunset. What we do and how we live from sunrise onward. Determines how we make it to sunset or drop out while our sun is still in it's high. This then is where the chore phase sets in. Youngest son secured management position with same department, Wilmot worked at the county. His wife, also was county employee in library system. Both were known to live frugally, except when came to educating their three children. Someone said. Buying a house is jump rope easy. Keeping it is mountain climbing difficult. I did. Didn't I? This rang true for Wilmot and Laura. When faced with unpaid homeowner association dues and municipal property taxes. They treadled water under their noses until 2008 bust. Their oldest son had thriving professional practice. Laura took to skies and joined him for a short stay. In time, celebrated a year. No sign of her coming back to husband Wilmot. Even when health issues put him in hospital, she did not make appearance. On cusp of losing house. HOA, Bank and County, all fought for dibs.

Youngest son came to rescue. His growing family needed four bedrooms. Family's secure income, made acquisition a shoo in. Wilmot secretly joined forces with a woman, denied she was intimate girlfriend. His existence stabilized. Until the woman came home from part time bowling alley job. Found Wilmot snoring in bed, other woman beside him. Dripping wet like fish hunting Cormorants, both fled the house. Anger not waning, she gathered his clothes and effects. Soaked them in the bath tub, tossed them to kerb in black garbage bag, conveniently untied. One could say she had fetish, inflicting punishment by water. Which makes Wilmot fortunate not to have been water boarded in his sleep. But then she knew, thin line between being roguish and committing murder. It's good for everyone, when common sense prevails. Wilmot now arrives at former residence. Asked son and daughter-in-law for rescue, which they willingly agreed. Morning after night before. Camille Sinclair says to tolerated father-in-law. *"Pa Mutty. Don't smoke in the house or anywhere near. Taking over this house, we spent small fortune fumigating odours, and replacing parts of air condition duct. So please, if you must smoke. Do it away from here and make sure. Smoke doesn't trail back in our house."* He listened quietly, asked. **"Walter know bout this? Is rob me get robbed, why you two get this house for little and nothing. So just go easy on you high horse."** That woman saw red till she went blind. Walked away numb and dumb. Equally vexed, Wilmot called Walter. Demanded he put Camille in her place. Walter, quite amused, told his dad. *"If I come home with slightest smell of smoke on me. I have to undress and leave my clothes at the back fence. Camille not going tolerate smoke in her house. Yes dad, her house. No matter what you believe. Camille's house."* Coming home, he sat with, quietly asked Camille for opportunity. Talking to dad, regarding anything arising to her displeasure in future. To which she agreed. Was not long, something else arose. Camille was horrified, seeing Wilmot walking through the house in a garment. Giving unmistakable outline of his front load. Not only was this offensive to her. But sickening display for her children, boys and girls alike. Walter spoke to Wilmot about this, left for work next day. Camille stopped by Wilmot's door, asked. *"Pa Mutty, you want to eat before it gets cold? I'm leaving shortly."* He emerged from and laid a diatribe on Camille. She listened in abject silence. Walter was rudely taken aback when Camille summoned him to see her at the library, before going home. Failing that, she would not be going home. Would instead take her children and find accommodation elsewhere. He knew what would be ultimate developments. Had unease with his wife from day one, in that she never displayed anger. Although situations dictated, she was. Smiling, she ushered him in an anteroom and to his horror, was told how Wilmot. Advised about breakfast, confronted Camille. Told her in crudest language, with intended defusing grin. Her husband was issue of his front load, something she should remember. Secondly, he's man who cannot wear corsets and girdles as she does. Will dress anyway he feels comfortable. If that's not good enough for her? Wear blinkers like dray mules. There being no question to outcome, Wilmot was homeless. He smooched with friend here and former co-worker there. One of whom having divorced. Children grown and gone raising families, left him with empty house. He thought about renting a part. Hesitated living with people who agreed to rules before coming in and flouted immediately after. Wilmot got wind of, approached Daniel. Sat and dilligently explained his situation. Brought on by cruel uncaring son and his wife, which got him retort. *"Mutty, you and me go way back. You know me is a man not fraid to talk my talk. Me woulda prefer wake up and stare at four walls. Than see ugly copy of Commander Whitehead. Mirror show me enough of that and me not want that shit in stereo."* Wilmot replied with equal frankness. **"Me always know you was stinker than polecat. That's why Beryl left you behine. Stare at you walls and watch them close in and squeeze out you life. If anybody did tell me you was selfish, I would tell them is lie they telling."** Next, he took a trip to Leightonia. Taking tales of woe to church he once prayed at. Initially asked for management position in school, touting previous experience. Was hired as crossing guard. Taking umbrage, he denounced this as belittling of status. Conceding defeat as board refused to budge. Failed authority's mandated qualifications for this position. Now regulates vehicular entry exit traffic on school days. Unanswered question by family and others is. Why did Laura go on visit, from which she is yet to return. Despite being made aware of developments? Only Wilmot and Laura knows and neither are talking. Assumption is, as fortunes waned and existential stress set in. Wilmot got abusive to Laura and she simply flew the coop, aided and abetted by her children. Yet, they're everyday people. What a way to go.

Living in the City-21

Self and I were talking as we often do about matters arising, which tickles inner thoughts. Had just talked with Verne at the insurance company. Asking why my auto premiums kept going up every year, although I had no accidents or tickets. He said rates in the state went up and that's that, but hold my bickering. There's something looming on the horizon, like our seasonal hurricanes. Legislature passed and sent to the governor for signature. Bill that would become law, raising minimum PIP in the state, from $10,000 to $25,000. Told him, that was news to me and does he believe it will be signed into law. He was silent for a minute, before opining. *"Answer is not if, but when. Likely, after midterm elections. Trusting, sting wears off by general election comes around. Politicians, only concerned bout their bottom line. Which means, staying in office as long as they can and moving up the ladder, my friend."* I thought about that briefly, then shifted thoughts to the nurse. Sweet and innocent, young and beautiful. I sent her a gift by mail. Went to YouTube, found and played song of same title by Clyde McPhatter. In other words folks, don't sweat the inevitable or that over which you have no control. If it happens, you have to live with it. If it doesn't, you do the same. Did I mention? Today is Saturday. There's hive of trading activity going on one block North at three houses. Before getting into the story, maybe I should give you wider perspective so you get the picture. City allows certain numbers of yard sales at an address annually, let's say it's four. Homeowner goes online, applies for permit, pays fee and prints placard that must be displayed on site at all times. That's one permit each time a sale is being held. There are four houses on two streets that rotates selling activity among them. Say three or four gets permits and displays goods of all four in grand market style. **Shuffle and bustle:**Neighbour Gerardo let me in on shenanigans when he went and was disappointed, not getting a vase to buy. It had a $20 tag, he offered $25 for vase and two table lamps. Dude told him. *"They're my mother's, let me get her."* A woman came over and told him $30 or nothing, but he figured he could wear them down if he hung on a bit. He kept browsing and soon a petite teenager, too young to be housekeeping. But seemingly at college age, smiled with Rufus and offered $10 for vase, adding. *"I'm trying to get a touch of brightness to my dorm."* He asked which college she attended and she smiled a response which eluded Gerardo. Eyeing Rufus as he stared at and whetted his lips. Gerardo expected Rufus to do back over flips for teenager any second now. Despite his twenty-five stones frame. This was a big fellow, real Beauty and Beast situation that would be worth watching, he mused. Oh, a stone is 14 lbs. Eight makes a hundredweight of 112 lbs. Twenty of these makes a long ton of 2240 lbs. If they come to buy. When they sell, ton is 2000 lbs. Called, short ton. There's metric of 1000 kilos or 2204 lbs. called a tonne. Forgive me, please. I just love getting into these unrelated diversions. Rufus grinned and told Beauty. *"That's funny, because it belongs to my daughter, she just graduated college. Who knows, maybe there's other stuff you might be interested in. Wait right here while I get her."* He came back with an older young woman and introduced her to Beauty with brief overview of what he had learned so far. Gerardo didn't mind not getting the vase but chafed at unnecessary deception employed. **Coming to the City:** Back in 2013 when housing debacle was trying for a comeback, we bought a house here. Not for a song but shy of an album and being newbies went out discovering our immediate surroundings. Internet gave crime statistics, livability and all that, based on zip code. We were out to gather feel of. Wife and I, strolled over to this corner market to see if there were curios or…. As we got to driveway of one house and began browsing tables. I realized, eyes were staring at us and there was a sudden hush. Folks, all white, stopped haggling and just…I paused, restrained my wife's progress and whispered. **"Ni..er alert Peeps. Nape hairs start bristling."** She whispered back. *"Stop being silly, reign in your imagination."* Then upped her voice, greeted. *"Yah hey everyone. We're just looking over your treasures to see…."* Paused mid sentence as a man strode to us with purpose and said. *"Sorry. I don't think* *you'll find anything here of interest. What we have here, are mostly Veterans or wrestling memorabilia."* I said. **"No problem."** We turned to walk away, he hailed and came after us, asked. *"You speak English?"* I said. **"Yes, we do. Why?"** *"Oh, I thought you guys spoke that mix of French and…You know? Where you guys from? If you don't mind my asking."* I said. **"We're Jamaicans by birth, US citizens by naturalization."** Now, he's grinning, rubs back of his head as he says. *"Oh, I thought. You know you can't be too careful these days about…..But youse is all good people. Y'all wanna?"* He began, thumb pointed over his shoulder at the activity. I said. **"No, we'll pass up on the wrestling stuff. But please convey our sincere thanks to your Veterans for their service. Although coming late, we know of sacrifices made and do contribute to rehab support causes."** As he moved closer, I mused. *"God, don't let this dude be hugging me."* He reached out a hand and we shook as he walked away with parting remark. *"Drop in next time. There's always something going on in our little circle. You could find a bargain, makes your eyes go wide."* Self was first to ask. *"Guy thought you spoke French?"* Reading my thoughts, wife asked same question and elaborated. *"Who did he…I mean what's significance speaking French?"* We walked home in silence. I picked up on his prejudice but my wife was slow in certain things. Immersed in my crossword puzzle. I reached for bottle of Red Stripe in cup holder pit on the sofa arm, and found empty space. Causing me to look at and saw my wife taking a swig. I chided. **"Hey, one of us has to stay sober, let it be you."** She laughed and said. *"Black people enjoy wrestling, are players in the sport. Fought and died disproportionately in this country's wars. Why would we not admire and embrace memorabilia of both events? I cannot understand."* Told her, let it be. It was a life's lesson learned without harm. She agrees but now feels uneasy being part of white neighbourhood. Vulnerable to possible harm unless she can quickly tell assailant, she does not speak French. Now watch a husband mislead his wife, as I said. **"It all started with President Bush, when France would not join in the Iraq assault. He changed French fries to freedom fries. Since then, patriotic Americans has had kind of negativity towards people and things French."** She gave me that dubious stare and said. *"Your imagination loose again? I never heard anyone walking into McDonald's and order freedom fries with combo meal."* I replied. **"That's because you went to restaurants owned by Democrats. If you'd have gone to a Republican owned, you would've heard it. Because that was only way you got served fries. Had to ask for it by saying, freedom fries. Ask for French fries and they told you, they're out."** She stared at me long, then said before walking away. *"Who am I living with, do I need to escape?"* Now folks, I'm not saying. French fries thing was responsible, but by mid 2014 we were divorced. Life goes on in neighbourhood. Four corners swap shop convenes quite often. Methinks neighbors called in cops, maybe code enforcement came in and chilled pace a bit. As I said at first, Self and I was ruminating on difference between value and worth and whether or not either had status of reality. Cost has tangibility but value and worth seems derived or shrouded in kind of mysticism. I'm alerted to reckless approach of a hooptie in need of muffler job. Suddenly, rider brakes, before making a left turn. Slowly proceeds to three way intersection. Slows to a crawl by the yard sales. Stops for two minutes then rides off, again in that slow crawl as he scans displays. I watched him go out of sight and thought he had gone his merry way. Self wisely said to me. *"He had better know, there's nothing there that would appeal to him. And he had* *better not start gabbing in French becau…"* Uhuh, here he comes. Squeezing into a parking spot close to the action. Self asks. *"You think he's going to the sale?"* I say. **"Looks that way. This should be interesting."** Dude alights vehicle, crosses the street with long strides. Reaches driveway and begins browsing, even taking up and appraising items. I stand to get a better view, in time to see a young man comes to. Has verbal exchange with browser. He sidesteps young man, advances up driveway, browsing. Young Buck returned with old Bull. I could see an unpleasant discourse afoot. Said to Self. **"Why is that Negro riling them folks without reason? We know he's not welcome there and by now he must be aware."** From where I stood I saw argument getting fat. Bull pointing to street repeatedly as he speaks, not too softly. Although the wind will not carry his words to my ears. It is obvious, the peace, if it ever existed. Has long ago been lost between these two. Dude slowly backs away, arguing and yelling. Straddles his bike, cruises to corner and stops. Seems to be contemplating his next move but rides off in slow mode. His eyes and mine having, as Granny would say. "Made four" He gives a half hearted wave then stops and reverses. *"Can you believe that guy? He's got posters and signs on public streets, advertising his garage sale. Yet has nerve to tell me his yard is private property, and he decides who comes onto it. You ever heard so much prejudiced shit in all your life?"* Self encouraged me to just smile and leave things unsaid. Dude went on. *"You live practically next door to this guy. What do you think of his crappola?"* Ignoring Self, I said. **"Truth be told, it's you I cannot believe. Doesn't matter where event is advertised or signs posted. It is being conducted on private property. I do believe, if you are asked to leave and refuse doing so. It amounts to trespassing. I could be wrong, but I would not stay and** argue the point. Next thing you know, owner gets to standing his ground, and you haven't a leg to stand on." I ended rebuttal with hearty chuckle at unintended pun. Dude said. *"I can't believe, man like you would say what you just said. You talk with kind of accent. Where you come from?"* I smile without further comment, he rides off. I think this guy was searching for trouble. Came darned close finding. Some people wear shoulder chip, eager becoming victim. No use making news, yet missing your minute fame. **Dinner Invite:** Hustle and bustle of Thanksgiving over, friends and relatives all come and gone. Gerardo came down for redemption chat. You see folks, he invited me to family's Thanksgiving dinner. I accepted out of being neighbourly. His wife and daughter both, seemed having sore spot against me. One denounced my barely eating of strange bird, called Turducken. Saying it was Turkey, Duck and Chicken in one. To which I replied, never having heard of. Asked. Is it imported? European or African origin? Sounds like genetic modification at work, and I'm not keen on. When both began lambasting. I said I would not invite them to my house. Expect them to delightfully dine on oxtail, curried goat or jerked pork. They would sample and decide if they want to pass or savour. I am having a salad, stuffing and bit of ham. Come on people, be gracious hosts. **Name calling:** Soon after, wife denounced ongoing hearings to impeach President. Asked, what did I think of it. I said, my father advised never to discuss politics and religion, so mum is the word. Wife insisted, I must have opinion and. *"We all want to hear what it is."* Notice how she speaks for everyone? I began. **"Process leading to impeachment is part of our democratic fabric. Woven by founding fathers to preserve democracy and guard against tyranny. Nixon faced it and resigned. Clinton did and survived. Now it's Trump's turn. Let process go through motions and whatever the** outcome, we respect it and move on. Bear in mind people, this method of checks and balances. Is not common factor in lives of millions, world over. Let's not try repudiating and dispensing with. End result will be utterly chaotic and very un-American." Daughter said. *"You would do well on soap box with saucer at your feet."* Wife said. *"He's another Trump hating Democrat."* I stood to leave, husband tried calming the situation. I told him. **"Where I come from, neighbours do not invite One to sup. Then subject them to hostility."** Wife hollered. *"Yes, because we invite you to sip with us. And first thing you do is criticize what we prepare. You can go to hell."* I leave, knowing I will not ever go back to that house. I think their attitude was fuelled by my not demonizing impeachment process and Democrats. It's been a week since the dust up. Gerardo comes and greets. *"Hey! old man. Older man haven't seen you a while. How you been? Hey! Between you and me. Margaret was high on eggnog but she okay now. Once the eggnog goes down, she recovers and loves you again."* I remain mute, because Self did not prompt me to respond. We chat about this and that, including secret behind main course served at Thanksgiving dinner. It is a factory process, carving choice cuts of each bird. Then stuffing and sewing to be one animal that's cooked, carved and served. Where have I been all this time? Never heard of this delicatessen smorgasbord. Seated in jaw drop ponder of newly gained knowledge. **Proof of the pudding:** Gerardo went to an island restaurant. Saw oxtail on menu for $18.75, bought a sample for $5. Next day on way home, bought two more samples for wife and daughter. Not telling them what it was. Told them to taste and see if they liked. He did that which he had. His wife said at first, it looked like snake steak. Gerardo pointed centre bone that, instead allaying suspicion only served to reinforce. Finally he told them what it was and his wife said. If she was going to eat a cow's tail and enjoy it. May as well pucker up, kiss it's ass. I found it funny beyond boundary. Reminds me, now Andrew is again the news with Epstein thing. Did y'all hear about time back in 1992 when he and his wife Fergie separated? She went on holiday at villa in St. Tropez with Texan millionaire John Bryan. Said to be her financial Advisor. With special lens, a photographer caught John kissing and sucking her toes and foot arch. That photograph first made headlines in "The Daily Mirror" Thursday August 20th, 1992. Story also reveals, it was Lady Diana who messaged Royal writer, Richard Kay of the "Daily Mail" with simple pager message. ***"The redheads are in trouble."*** Proof folks, no matter who we are. *"Everybody plays the fool sometimes, no exception to the rule."*

Bingo, Chess & Dominoes-22

Walls of Sally Thibaulds' house, were adorned with tanned photographs of her and husband Cyrus, in his military regalia. They appeared youthful as teenagers would, yet there were children at varying stages of growth holding poodles, cats and small parakeet. Sally was of Italian lineage and Cyrus was American. Very little of their lives or hers was revealed. Except that Cyrus was part of elite allied force that liberated France from Nazi occupation. There was reference to Charles DeGaulle being part of and Cyrus shared camaraderie with. Who in 1960 became France's president. Cyrus, not now a part of her existence, it has never been disclosed if separation was by death or divorce. For certain her inner circle and adult children knew fact, but curiosity of plebs were left unsated. There was collection of faded photographs showing different angles of properties. One of which had faint inscription. "Cayman Martinique 19??" It was confirmed, family at one time resided in Cayman Islands. But how does Martinique connects to, is anyone's guess. Our story begins, where she lives in a better house on Chaves in Long Mountain district. Housekeeper, Gertrude Bellamy, whom she took pains telling folks. Was not her maid, but her companion. Had been with her family for ages. Starting as nursemaid to Sally's two children. Had now become family member by silent adoption. Her and Sally, two aged women leaning on each for support in their gifted kind. There was mystery and speculation aplenty regarding Miss Sal, as Sally was often called by back fence neighbors. Not necessarily endearing or kind spirited. Location, location at times creates anomalies and this was one such instance. Long Mountain was enclave of upper middle class residents, with paved streets and gas lamps. In bygone years these lamps were lit at dusk and extinguished at dawn by lamplighter on mule back. Never mind, it's been years since they glowed a ray of light. Fixtures have been preserved for ornate design, enhancing visual prestige of the neighbourhood. Chaves, being last street in what is boutique community, abuts the Lanes. Home to less privileged, hard working folks, who find employment within walking distance. Tending babies, gardens and lawns. Hand laundering and house cleaning for wealthy folks. Disparity in status and wealth aside. Mutually beneficial convenience, existed for both. Sally was chauffeured places, always accompanied by Gertrude. Church, doctor, Women's Club, shopping and wherever. They never left home without each other. Folks whispered with unkind intent, seeing Sally and Gertrude board the car. ***"Puh, dress Puss put on dress boots, going to town."*** "Dress boots" refers Sunday's best. Church, funeral or wedding dress shoes of the day. Sally's adult children visited by rotation, each on opposing weekends and at times both, for festivities assumed to be Sally's birthday. However when folks scratched heads and counted fingers. Realized a year had not gone by since previous fete. Oh how they fretted from curiosity. Sally's complexion, shaded white but could not qualify her as white woman. Before coming into Sally's employ. Gertrude reared younger cousin, Pansy Mitchell in Maroon Accompong community of Saint Elizabeth parish. Fourteen year old Pansy gave birth to girl child Muriel. Sired by Rhygin Mitchell her father's top half brother. Effectively, her half uncle. Muriel also bore Mitchell surname as did her mother and grandfather. Rhygin had a wife and sweetheart at the time. Both of whom put animosity aside and tried making life unbearable for child Pansy. Who had to quit school and become literal hermit. Threats of demise by obeah took toll, mental and physical on her. She was One tumbling weed. **A wedding and after:** Two years after giving birth, Pansy migrated to city, leaving Muriel in care of kin. Initially she sat a family's children, in exchange for food and shelter. At eighteen she began domestic work at three shillings a day, and lived a nun's existence until late thirties. Spinster Pansy, met and married twice divorced, late twenties Jessup Willacy. A train conductor who befriended her on frequent trips to rural country, taking goods and greetings to kinfolks. Age imbalance most times creates marital foibles and male is easily distracted. Do you see what I see? No? Let's do it together. When Pansy came to town, she lived with older cousin Gertrude who showed her ropes of city living. While Pansy got by on day's work and later as full time domestic helper. Gertrude had long ago established easy, stable employment with Sally. Living permanently in her household. Before her good fortune however, she leased a Lanes plot. Began start stop construction of two room house with outdoor conveniences. Before house was halfway habitable. Gertrude asked cousin Pansy to take up residence and thwart thieves taking away materials. This Pansy did under canopy of burlap cloth and flour bags, until building slowly took shape over a period gone close on ten years. You know the deal, pound of nails this month, five lengths laths next Easter. At this point, Gertrude and Pansy decided on payment of peppercorn rent. Reinforced when Pansy began bragging about Jessup, the great train conductor. After brief courtship they got married, in what psychic villagers dubbed. "A belly wedding." Bride was thought in early stage of pregnancy. Later confirmed, with birth of son Montieth. Less than two years later her second daughter Vilma was born, and worlds are about to collide. Although no One would dare foresee, albeit on purpose. Our fate is written in our stars and we never know in advance, what good fortune or tragedy awaits. People will seize opportunity to critique sky's hue, so they did regarding Jessup Willacy. Wondering why a young man had been twice divorced. Yet not having children by previous wives. Some thought he lied on this last aspect. Went on to guess, Pansy's haste to marry was drowning man clutching at straw. Pansy now wants place of her own. Fed up with cousin Gertrude's constant probing her personal finances, in effort to increase rent paid. I did not mention. Peppercorn arrangement went South, once Jessup set feet over threshold. Gertrude doesn't mind doing her cousin a favour. Balks at Jessup's benefiting from cheap accommodation. She has never as the saying goes. Liked a bone in his body from day one. Concerting with the villagers. Bar talk over tumblers of over proof rum, was most times centred on Jessup. Twice divorced at so youthful an age. ***"What kind of Cock in farmyard and two Hens have to run from him?"*** They mused amid raucous, gut shaking laughter. Pansy pleads inability to pay increased rent. Forced to admit, Jessup is not supporting the house as expected. Oh, Gertrude puts both hands on her head and calls for heavenly intervention. Chunk of Pansy's income goes to creche for childcare. Finds this unacceptable, suggests to Jessup. She'd be better staying home, caring for their children. He sharply accuses her of being lazy and asks. ***"Whapp'n, because you married, all of a sudden you too good for doing domestic work?"*** You know she was hurt, by unexpected, verbal slap from her husband. Yet, pleaded for understanding. Which not forthcoming, resigned in silence accepting the circumstances. Discussing this with cousin Gertrude, she was comforted with words. ***"Don't worry, God never gives us more than we can bear. He will open doors when we least expect it. If he could deliver Daniel from the Lion's den and Jonas from the belly of the Whale. Think how much he will do for you. Just be patient, pray and trust him."*** Easy for her to say, whilst she exists on easy street with no chick or child. Over the years, daughter Muriel had been silently adopted by Bertha Cousins. Spinster and retired schoolmarm, who ran district's postal agency. Postal agencies sold stamps, accepted or disbursed incoming, outgoing mail and other limited services. Had to be located in contractor's home. Securely boarded from rest of dwelling. Mandated opening hours, were five, Monday thru Friday, three on Saturdays. With little or no supervision, these hours were not observed. Dissent brought reprisal and everyone understood, they grinned and bore it in. "What else to do." Given special tuition by Miss Cousins, Muriel grew to be polished, articulate young woman. Active in the agency, village people were endeared to her good manners and patient demeanour. As opposed to grumpy, sourpuss Bertha. They constantly praised Muriel, saying. It was hoped, she'd take over postmistress' position. When Bertha's arthritis and other ailments rendered her impotent. Muriel, hearing possibility of, echoed in her ears so often. Began anticipating oh happy day, this would materialize. As Bertha's health waned, Muriel's hopes soared. She served village folks with broad grins and apologies, when expected mail did not arrive. Bertha Cousins was admitted to, stayed in hospital over a month. As things are with government business. One expects agency would be closed, but things were different in Accompong backwoods. Call it rural well being or, dog is loose but not being a bother. Declared healed and hale, preparations made for Bertha's homecoming. Discharged from hospital, she was taken to a point by car. Put in carriage for journey's final leg. She should have been home by 13:00 hours, latest. As dusk fell, kerosene Tilly lamps and Home Sweet Home lamps were lit. Folks kept vigil in happy expectation. Near midnight, news came. Wheel fell off carriage, throwing horseman from his perch. Inflicting further injury to frail Bertha Cousins. Who was taken back to hospital from whence discharged hours earlier.**Bertha dies, then:** Mid morning next day news came, Bertha had passed. Member of village church from bi-best days. Open feud existed between administrators and Bertha. Causing her to abandon membership, vilifying elders and pastor. It was even suggested she retaliated, by not promptly handing over mail. This however, could not be confirmed. Feud began after Bertha, ceded headmistress' position at district's elementary school.Took pre-retirement leave, asked to rent church hall for small private school. Common feature of village churches then. However, this was voted down by majority, including pastor. Which Bertha took as deepest cut of all. Having tutored that boy from kinder age to high school entry. Often gave him special after school tutoring, not asking for financial reward. Despite having ceased affiliation with and support of. Church elders opened it's doors to villagers. From whom came support by tithes anyway. Bertha's coffin was laid out for viewing and funeral service. Complete with banjo accompaniment by Jules Pinkney. Bertha was laid to rest and once again good patrons. I have to demonstrate how procedural protocol can escape attention of officialdom, and fall through proverbial cracks. Red vehicles, having crown and ROYAL MAIL painted both sides. In eight inches high black letters, outlined in gold. Still brought incoming, and took outgoing mail. Not to mention, counter sales were reconciled and sale items provided. As contracted on, for five months after Bertha passed. Villagers were happy with beloved Muriel, jumping hoops, bending backwards to surpass expectations. Trained by Bertha, adept at operational functions, she was overjoyed having attained her life's dream in early adult years. Saw herself rising to postmistress, at soon to be built post office. Rumour had bandied before she was born, yet ground would not be broken in her lifetime. Villagers voted one way in every contest. Hence there was no need to bribe them with incentive of new post office. Then came day of incursion. District's constable escorted men who, boarded public's access windows. Further secured section of home used as agency. Posted notices, verbally told curious onlookers, agency was permanently closed. Search was on for alternative location, which was not guaranteed to become reality any time soon. if ever. Until then, villagers should go to town's post office for mail and other services. Our Muriel was not just disappointed, she was devastated and broken hearted. Likened to her first love affair had suddenly soured. **Disappointment and Fear:**You see folks, encouraged by villagers who KNEW government rules for such situation. When papers were shuffled, signed and embossed. Not only would Muriel be confirmed in position. She had acted in past months and before. But, fortune in back pay was forthcoming. Imagine her dismay, arriving at main post office in pursuit of, and being told an audit was underway. If discrepancies were found, she would be jailed to appear in court. Right at that moment, Pansy's firstborn was distressed. Bordering on edge of insanity brought on by Damocles sword, of possible jail and prison time hanging overhead. Not to mention, ridiculing grins, whispers of loving villagers. Who now misguidedly thought her actions responsible. Losing convenience of the postal agency. See how you're hero today, villain tomorrow? Muriel fled the district, sought refuge with her mother, who immediately opened arms of welcome. Got down on chapped knees, thanking God for answering prayers. Now, daughter and mom breathed sigh of relief. Both happy, delivered from life's anxiety today, unaware of tomorrow's possibilities. **"Que Sera, Sera":** Or, as Matthew 6:34 states. *"Sufficient unto the day is evil thereof."* We are both engaged in what is called "table talk," so I ask. "Do you see what I see?" Let's try that in dialect. "Yuh si wha mi si? Yuh nuh seet?" Okay, let's do the math. It is said figures never lie, but liars figure. Maybe then a picture will emerge. We already know Pansy had Muriel at fourteen, she's now mid forties. Muriel just turned or is at best, early thirties. Rolling stone Jessup, is of similar age or close to. Now you are in that frame of mind called denial, chiding somewhat reluctantly. *"Come on now, you're not suggesting? Your imagination is really at a gallop. Running away, more like it."* When it comes to weird sexual encounters. Only one I am yet to hear of, is mother and son. Any combination you can think of, starting with father daughter. Has gone down with mere eyelid's bat. Pansy got pregnant with her third child for Jessup. Did this set village Wiseheads talking? Drunkareddy Benjie, so engrossed with Willacy's affairs. He and domino partner were trounced six love. Engrossed in discussion regarding family's pros and cons. He put forward possibilities, loudly discounted by others. Shouted with finality to concede. ***"All me know is, Rooster in cage with two Hens and one call sit. Hmm, blind*** *can see what's next.*" Pansy decided to keep working, as long as employer allowed. Told adult daughter. *"Sometimes people let money overwhelm senses. Behave idiotic and develop inane prejudices."* Muriel's comfort seat was jolted, world began slowly crumbling with news from old district. Backra were turning stones, searching for her. Backra is a word from slavery, meaning master. In later times it meant government personnel generally. Once again angst set in, her composure disturbed. Thinking only on possibility going to prison. Aware it was only a matter of time before she was found, she decided to flee in hiding. **Seeking refuge:** Big question was. Where to? Solution was near at hand, in person of step daddy Jessup. He could ask co-worker to switch Sundays with him. Take Muriel to kinfolks in parish named that weekend. Parish named was not where his folks lived. But who knew different? Failing co-workers cooperation. Sunday of next week was rostered day off. Escape plan could be effected then. All Muriel had to do was stay indoors and speak to no One. Again, Pansy's knees were bruised giving thanks to God for opening a door. Coworker agreed, not a minute too early. Muriel lost half body weight in twenty-four hours, before Jessup brought good news. Remember, there was no home phone. Jessup getting good news on reaching workplace, had no way communicating this to home. **Perfect escape plan?:** Eve Muriel's departure, mother and daughter had emotional goodbyes. Mother left home at dawn to reach employer's house in time to make family's breakfast. When she and Jessup retired that night, she thanked him coming so willingly to Muriel's aid. He was a good man, whom she was fortunate and happy to have met. Wants him to know, she had always turned deaf ears to people's misgivings, including that of cousin Gertrude. Now she wonders what would her life be without him. Who would have guessed, she's about to find that answer in staid truth. Usually she left work early on Sundays, after serving dinner at 13:30 hours. Their managing to get supper without help as happened weekdays. She rushed home to prepare gratitude dinner for husband. Dressed herself and children in Sunday finery, awaiting his arrival home. When he didn't show at dusk she was not unduly concerned. He had to come home Sunday to be at work 05:00 hours Monday. She awoke with start close to midnight, began worrying something amiss had occurred. Maybe an accident or….No, both were under God's protection. She comforted herself and went back to sleep. When she awoke hours later, told herself. Jessup missed a last bus but would catch first of the day and go directly to work. Monday evening he would be home. Oh what a waste, dinner had soured overnight and tossed to dogs and fowls. Do not start thinking about refrigerator or even an icebox.You ate what you cooked when you cooked. By morning it smelt funny and strands of junju were evident. Some people coached their stomachs over time, to accept and digest such fare. Whilst others attempting this feat, puked until eyes bulged. Pansy was One such. If you take poison in minute amounts, body will develop immunity. Serious thing people, no joke. Just don't shock it all at once. It's like sleeping pills, taken as prescribed is good for you. Taken in excess, you're on way to meet Gabriel. Monday she hurried home but Jessup did not. Neither next day or next week or next..you get the picture. Somewhere in this wishing and hoping, she was hurried to hospital near death and lost her unborn child. Some say it was brought on by Bertram Whyte's bringing news to village bar. Jessup was at his usual post on trains, giving out laughs as if they're going out of style. Others opined, maybe she found herself overwhelmed. Whether from grief of betrayal or uncertainty of Muriel's whereabouts, opting for some kind of suicide. Coming from hospital she seemed prematurely aged.Spirit broken and weak of sinew. Neighbors can be strange lot. Behind her back, gloated at misfortune with comments such as. *"Me did know, serve her right. Young bwoy she want. Break stick put in her ears. Turn round and malice people, who only trying to help."* Yet they came empathizing and. *"Don't worry Miss Pansy, everything happen for good. You can't see now but one day truth will be revealed. Just put you trust in him."* This, as finger was raised skyward. Her children were fed and cared for in her absence. Although Vilma told, how old man Trenton rubbed her "dukkus"When she sat on his lap sucking on a lollipop, which he denied. A common feature of life then was, girls of single digit years did not wear panties as a rule. Except when going to day classes or Sunday school. Pansy went with time, withdrawn from those around her. Doing her best surviving and caring for her children. Got them enrolled in school. Whether or not they attended punctually or at all, she could not be certain. Her leaving home before dawn and coming home after dusk. It could be truthfully said, children were raising themselves. Boy Montieth, was terror in the Lanes. Throwing stones at animals, fruit trees and neighbors who dared speak to him about mending ways. He did not live in a glass house or one with, but Sally Thibaulds did. When he broke her second window pane, she learned well kept secret for first time. Gertrude and Pansy were cousins. Was briefed at length on cousin's fortunes and misfortunes. Her finding solace in everyone's prayer. **Invited to Supper:** Sally Thibaulds told Gertrude, Pansy's daughter and husband could be located, easy as snap of a finger. Which she was willing to initiate if asked. Told Gertrude to invite Pansy's family to Sunday supper. Top wooden step tread had aperture that fitted door mat. Under this was lever that reacted to weight of a visitor and clanged alert inside. Mechanical, but ingenious for the times. Wouldn't you agree? Gertrude verified by peephole and opened the door. Warned Pansy and children. *"Don't forget, show broughtupsy. Make sure bow when Madam come out."* Sally emerged and greeted, extending arm and hand simultaneously with verbal welcome. Was taken aback and asked. *"My dear lady! Whatever are you doing? Unless you are suffering a seizure of some kind. Please stand as you would when meeting another person."* Formalities done, Sally mirthfully pressed. *"Wherever did you get idea, you had to bow when meeting me? I am not queen of England."* Pansy hastily replied, avoiding cousin's eyes. **"Beg pardon mam, cousin Gertrude say that's what we must do. Or else, we can't come back a next time."** After a hearty laugh, Sally chided. *"Gert, oh Gert, tut tut. How mischievous of you to so inflict on your family."* Five sat down to supper. Children gobbled voraciously in wild abandon. Granny called this being niggerish or niggardly. Pansy gave up browbeating, which was ignored. Called them to stop being gravalicious. Sally gently intervened, saying. Kids will be kids, learning as they grow. Having experienced similar behaviour whilst raising hers. Time came getting to business at hand. Sally told Montieth, quoted cost fixing her windows. Asked if he regretted breaking them and intended paying to replace them. Boy said he was sorry. Would pay to fix them when he started working, or his father came home. Promised, he would ask him to. Both children were twelve and ten years old each. Asked why he regretted breaking the window panes. Montieth said, because he now knew she was a nicer lady than what "them" say. Fearing that boy would name names, Pansy told her son. **"Bwoy, stop making up stories."** Bad move, she shoulda kept quiet. Boy obviously miffed at his mother, quickly shot back. *"Me not tell no lie mam. Mr. Tomas and Brer…"* Sally intervened and shushed him, saying. *"You should never raise voice or talk back to an adult, even if you think they are wrong. Now tell your mother, you are truly sorry for sassing and I will tell you something to your good. Come on son, don't keep adults in wait."* Montieth hung his head and grumbled incoherently. Sally was not going to let him off that easy. *"Look at me."* She coaxed. When he did, she told him. *"Now look at your mother, way you're looking at me, and tell her you are sorry so we can all hear you."* End of which, she asked. *"Doesn't that feel much better? Your mother does and be sure to never again do anything like this. You understand?"* Boy replied. **"Yes, mam."** Sally asked. *"Would you like to go to a very good, new school?"* **Irresistible Offer:**.Seeing him about to jump from the chair in eagerness, she warned. *"Now you have to think about this before saying yes or no. It's a newly built school. Classrooms are airy with overhead fans and each student has chair and desk. There's canteen where delicious meals are served. You get to play games you like and learn new ones. On the other hand, it is far away and you would not come home evenings as you do now. You would probably get very homesick, missing your mother."* Last syllable had barely left her lips when Montieth said. **"If is a nice school and food nice, me wouldn't miss mama."** Sounds ungrateful but it's naked truth, without tact or diplomacy. Pansy stifled physical cringe, eyes betrayed her thoughts. Although she tried smiling away disappointment. Kids are such ingrates at times, especially when times are lean and prospects of nice food gets dangled. Give the boy a break, you would too. Sally next turned to quietly shy Vilma. Told her, she could attend same school if she wanted to and her brother would always be there. She merely whispered. **"Yes, mam."** Then withdrew into herself. Sally actioned adults to join her in living room, telling children stay where they were. Asked as afterthought if there was anything else they would love to have, whilst adults went to talk amongst themselves. Ice cream, cookies, fruit drink, soda, she ran off a list of options. At end of which, Montieth eagerly replied. **"Yes, mam."** ***"Yes, to which?"*** Sally asked. Boy beamed and echoed. **"Yes, mam."** She gave up, told Gertrude. ***"Gert, see to the kids and join us when you can."*** Seemed, Gert joined the two, quicker than expected. Sally told her. ***"Gert, please go back, make sure children are occupied and not get into mischief."*** Her way saying. Stuff their guts, immobilizing as snakes swallowing large prey. Pansy sought offer conditions, regarding her children being away. She welcomed assistance. Father's whereabouts was a mystery, she could not give them needed financial support or otherwise. Notwithstanding, she wants it made clear **"Whoa!. Not so fast":**She would not under any circumstance give up her children for any kind of adoption. Sally assured both cousins, no One wanted to adopt the children. But in Pansy's position as birth parent, she had to sign admission documents before her children could be enrolled. Others also had to sign in respect of tuition payment, that burden would not be theirs to bear. However, evening was far gone and this little get together is at an end. Consider and let her know what's decided. Abruptness at which Sally considers evening far gone and ends discussion, tells us she's miffed somewhat. Trying to do kind deed for plebs. What makes Pansy think, she would want to adopt those urchins. Hmph. As visitors were accompanied towards outdoor. Sally made it known. ***"Only benefit accruing to me from my proposal. Is satisfaction seeing children achieving all they can be, with a little help and guidance."*** As Sally smiled her goodbyes to each and walked away. Gertrude ushered Pansy and children outside, asked her cousin. ***"You is idiot. What you have to think bout? You have better plan for them two***

Moffeena pickney?" Gertrude knew Sally was a bit angry at Pansy's concern. Saw once in a lifetime opportunity for these children slipping away. Pansy softly replied. *"Tell her, yes. Me agree with everything."* **Transformation??:** "Moffeena" is slang describing single parent child, existing under near destitute conditions. Breath away from an orphan. Matter of fact, there are better cared orphans, than some Moffeenas. Children wrote mom in timely fashion. Girl Vilma, more so than boy Montieth. Nevertheless it was three school years before they came home to visit. As word spread of their pending arrival. Good neighbours anxiously waited chance to indulge favourite pastime. Scrutinize and critique. Sally's chauffeur, Mr. Gideon parked the car and walked children up lane to their mother's home. Followed by village entourage, reminiscent of Sicilian wedding that grew as it progressed. Pansy saw her children and almost didn't recognize them. She stared at them in jaw drop surprise before hugging each and shedding joyful tears, asking each in turn. *"Vilma, is really you? Montieth, good God you almost favour man and dead stamp ah you dawdy."* Then she stopped, as if jolted by electricity. Took both children by hand and trotted down the Lane around to Chaves, where she stomped the door mat repeatedly. Cousin Gertrude opened the door and whispered a reprimand. *"Good God woman. Is why you stomping the door mat like you is ole Nayga?"* Her employer called form inner recesses. *"What's the racket about. Is there invasion of some sort, Gert?"* Before Gertrude could respond. Pansy, unable to contain herself, shouted. **"Is me and the Pickney them Miss Sal. If you ever see how them grow big, you would never believe is them same one."** She could not know, that which surprised her. Was common knowledge to children's benefactor, who got periodic reports on both. After greeting everyone present, Sally asked if anyone wanted refreshments, to which all accepted. *"Thanks, very much."* Coming from children. If a day makes a difference, as Dinah sang. Three years makes for a transformation. Sally then said, she would not be speaking. Was all ears. Boy Montieth asked his sister if she wanted to speak first, he would yield to her. Girl Vilma replied. *"Yes, thanks."* Went on thanking her mother and Miss Sal, making her tuition possible. She cannot find words to express depth of her gratitude but what few she does, comes from the heart. Cousins lower jaws hung agape. Whilst Sally beamed in silent pleasure at what she had wrought. Now we find out real reason, boy Montieth yielded to his sister. Couldn't come up with text of his own. Merely echoed sister's sentiments, adding. *"I'm making every effort to achieve success, so I can repay for fixing your window panes."* Oh how adults laughed. Pansy chirped, asking why there were no photographs sent in letters she received. Vilma replied. Photographs were only taken at start of school year. However, she has few in her valise. Last word threw Pansy into a tizzy, she blurted. **"Say which part that now child?"** Gertrude elbow nudged cousin to be quiet. She sat back in her chair, concern still etched on her brow. Perhaps the rude awakening, that brought home to Pansy, extent of children's development. Was Vilma's saying to her mom. Montieth could not share sleeping quarters with her. Not quite getting gist of, she yelled. **"Well, if you did expect me gwine take you Myrtle Bank, you can forget it."** Child calmly replied. *"I do not want to go to Myrtle Bank or any hotel, mom. I am certain Aunt Sal has spare room at her house. I would much rather be here with you. It's been a long time and there's much we have to talk about. It's just not proper for children of different genders at any age, to share sleeping quarters, mom. Very, very improper."* So, Pansy told Mr. Fiedler, he could not share space at her house. Nights whilst her children were home on holiday. **Mr. Fiedler?:** Oh, I forgot you weren't told about him. He was a church brother, who by coincidence. Played bow fiddle, previously owned by brother Cyril. Who died after twenty years accompanying worship at church. His wife gifted it in his memory. Brother Fiedler began dropping in, to give a hand with things manly. Husband having gone awol without trace. Sleepovers began during rebuilding phase of her house. Inquisitive church elders sought assurance. Both respected sanctity of marriage and need to observe Christian teachings. Yeah, right. They rolled together in ecstasy, like hogs in a mud pond. Holiday over, children went back to school and life was good. Happy faces all round for everyone. Children became adults and both held executive positions in law practice, where Sally and her older children had controlling interest. So that's where the money came from? Pansy bought her cousin's two room house and made it into a comfortable bungalow. About seven years after her disappearance. Muriel wrote mom from England, expressing sincere regret. Begged forgiveness for having allowed Jessup to inveigle her in wrong doing. When they came to England, she found he had a wife in waiting. Jezebel of a woman who found them and beat Muriel into hospital. Jessup went to her house retaliating. Bloodied her and is still in prison serving time. As mother and daughter exchanged letters and tension eased. Muriel sent photographs of children born in England. Two were coloured and two were white. It is said. '*A picture tells a thousand words*' Does these pictures? I would say, it probably shows Muriel had two children for Jessup. He being gaoled, her having financial issues. Found herself white bloke and started family with him. Genealogy puzzle is, trying to figure out each person's place on family tree. Some are both of and neither One or other. Now we come to the "what if" of our journey.

If Jessup hadn't eloped with his step daughter. His two children, possibly three. Would have had benefit of guidance by both parents. Boy Montieth would not be run about recalcitrant. In which situation, they would not come to Sally's attention and gifted opportunity provided by her. Which we have to admit, would have been out of reach of their parents. How far then, would they have been able to qualify themselves towards facing life. Beyond that of their scrounging parents? Sally Thibaulds died, willed her house to Gertrude. Dray carts made four month procession, as Gert sold pins to anchors. Each time, stowing returns in her bosom. How it grew, and then there was only the house left. Firm of Auctioneers came. Gert sold the house and retired on family acres at Accompong. Do not fault her selling the house. What else could she do? Probably got a purse also but maintenance of that house and municipal taxes would have drained it in an eye's wink. It would be mere postponement of inevitable. We could be gifted yacht or private plane and have to do same. Being unable to maintain and use our gift. Unschooled and illiterate, Gertrude "made her mark" on pages of documents. When ink dried, she hollered "fraud" Claiming to have been given less return, than went to Auctioneers in fees. Niece and nephew, ignored pleas for help. What a journey….

Sex and marriage-23

Goes together like horse and carriage. Actually, spin on song by Frank Sinatra, recorded August 1955, titled "Love and marriage" Lyrics by Sammy Cahn, composed by Jimmy VanHeusen and music by Nelson Riddle orchestra. It's adage reinforcing sacrosanct melding and inseparable bond between love and marriage. It's like feet and walking, tongue and talking. I venture to say, "Sex and marriage" shares equal if not elevated profundity. There have always been instances of marriage without love, driven by pursuit of wealth, prestige, or arranged by tradition and social dictate. Most if not every known animal or life form, pursues some kind of sexual intimacy. Spawning as directed by nature to reproduce and ensure proliferation of the specie. I think it fair to say, people pursue sexual intimacy for emotional gratification, more than facilitating specie reproduction. Hence, multiple prevention devices for both genders. Naming a few, intrauterine sponges, condoms and pills. At other end of spectrum there is rarely used vasectomy and controversial abortion for those who do not want to conceive. In Vitro Fertilization for those who are having difficulty doing so. I have no statistic to support my belief. More sexual encounters take place between unmarried rather than married couples. So, sex is emotional experience most people hanker to enjoy and be ecstatically gratified. There are women who do not want to have sex with men. Men who do not want to have sex with women and men who cannot have sex, period. My daughter reminded me of this, when I posted. Women should stick their nipples in baby's mouth, eliminating formula crisis. She made comparison, not all women can lactate. Just as some men cannot get a rise. She is testament, that does not include me. Men who cannot get an erection are out of contention. When a woman abstains from sex, that's by choice. There is no physical impediment that would prevent her, if she so desired. Unless there arises rare profound situations as with. **Sheila Cameron:**At age twenty-seven, Sheila had tried having sex once when she was seventeen, and swore she would never again do so. Now she was in love with Marcus. Yearned with all her being to make love with him, as he equally yearned doing with her. She told him of excruciating pain on first attempt and fear of a repeat. He consoled her, saying. Once he very gently broke through hymen, sex would be painless and fulfilling, beyond anything she could experience. Trembling, muscles taut from fear, did not make event any easier. When she screamed in agony, pounding his head to sponge repeatedly with both fists. Marcus almost lost consciousness. Crouched on wobbly knees, stared in vacuum of disbelief at Sheila as she cried and writhed in acute pain. It would seem, this young woman was afflicted by Vaginismus. Left untreated, this would severely restrict chances having intimate male relationship, marriage and child bearing. Marcus would not be denied glory of virgin sex, so he kept wooing and curry combing as old folks are wont to say. Curry combing refers, monkeys preening in expectation of intimacy. Frustrated by her constant refusals to endure another go at penetration. His visits got farther apart and eventually stopped. "Love's labors lost" One might say. For her part, Sheila was relieved. Her heart exulted in good riddance, she found different solace in church. **Richard Denton:** Without debate, an exceptionally attractive young woman, and despite spurning advances for more than a year. Richard Denton came to church quite often in her company. Wasn't long ere he received the holy ghost, was baptized and asked her to marry him. She told him, there had to be conference with both and Bishop. Before accepting offer and arrangements going forward. To which he willingly agreed. **The conference:** Without preamble, with surprise, she upped and said. ***"Bishop, I want Dicky to know I cannot have children."*** Both men seemed momentarily stunned, Bishop ventured. **"Well, that is common situation affecting lots of people. But in most cases I have heard of, there are remedies including minor surgery."** She blew them away once more with her retort. ***"I know that, Bishop. But, truth is I cannot have sex. The pain is unbearable. I paid nearly four hundred dollars to a doctor who examined me and said***

the operation would cost ton load of money." Dicky pledged his love and averred, her revelation was no damper of his fervour. But Bishop knew better. Asked if he was aware of consequences that could develop in marriage without sexual intercourse. Went on to opine. Indeed, such a marriage would not be legally binding, without consummation. Irrefutable recognition here folks, sex and marriage does goes together. Brother Dicky quickly latched on to sister Evadney. When she showed early signs of pregnancy, church attendance became less frequent. Both backslid, abandoning their faith in holy ghost, church and Bishop. Dicky only wanted to swim in that enchanted pool that beckoned. Once it was determined a no go, he was gone. Holy ghost notwithstanding. I had a girlfriend who refused to embrace long diatribes. Like her, you are probably asking. ***"So you're saying all this to say what?"*** Well, it's all about Ethel Deere and her daughters seven. Specifically Melissa who met and married Milton, but did not live happily ever after, as told by story books. It also raises a poignant, divisive, emotional and contentious issue of husbands. Gently, stridently coercing wives who are reluctant to engage sexual intercourse. Not occasioned by discomfort, exhaustion, mental ennui or lack of privacy, but as a rule. Let's explore this relationship for it's worth. It began in that era referred to as roaring twenties.There's a village hidden deep in the valley among billowing Pines, where little Ethel Deere was born. Kind of mirroring life and times of Little Jimmy Brown. Whose life was chronicled in song by The Browns' hit in 1959. During her mother's pregnancy, villagers whispered she would have twins. Others scoffed and took wagers on her having triplets instead. Ethel made solo entry over eleven pounds and straightway created hubbub of identification. Predominantly Negroid, there were Mulatto and Indian traits. Questions were raised as to father's identity, not being her mother's husband. Precocious at an early age, she recited verses and acted in school/church concert skits to thunderous ovation. **Little Ethel Deere:** Quickly became a regular Shirley Temple sans television exposure. Next, she was trained to be graceful. Sought after as petite flower girl at weddings, graduating to bridesmaid. Alluring teenager, she often eclipsed brides. Her preferred complexion and naturally curled tresses. Knocking everyone over with a feather. At seventeen she gave birth to her first child. Wagging tongues, drew resemblance of baby and newly wed husband. In which ceremony she participated. At twenty-one she was mother of three, as some folks said. "Had lost her shine." James Newby helped financially with her children, but her daughter and his. Could pass for twins, except their hair. Willy Faulkner's son also, had striking resemblance to her second daughter. As did Joseph Beckett to her first born. People refused to take this as coincidences. Her having played role in weddings of all three. Wives felt jilted, anger intensified. She became as is called, scorned woman, village Pariah. Who fled to city, leaving her children in care of near relatives. **Starting all over anew:**Not caring or fearing repercussions, adamantly named children's fathers, confirming suspicion. Further made it known. If they did not give financial support for offspring's welfare. She'd seek Family Court's enforcement. Shame and embarrassment of all and sundry. Being that era, when young women were brought up to be wives. Expecting and accepting husband's infidelity as part of the game. There were silent voices behind sealed lips, but faces were long and reflected misery. One wife went back to parents, was encouraged by family's pastor to return. In time all was forgiven, although not forgotten. Wounds, ever memorized by children's presence. In the big city, Ethel Deere found employment as domestic with families of means. Had four children for different heads of households. Whom although in position to give financial help, did not always do so willingly. Trying to hide dalliances. Rambunctious and confrontational, she went rattling gates. Making purpose of her visit known. At one residence she got into physical altercation with equally rebellious wife. Whose husband calmed waters, by gifting her sewing machine from inventory. On condition she stayed away from his home and family. She found ready clientele among church parishioners, making work clothes and school uniforms. Children growing to adults, despised her for what they took as abandonment during infancy. This did not phase her in any way. She was woman with don't care attitude, ready to step in anyone's face. Was heard to declare, no hesitation putting her Bible aside. Beat the devil out of a church sister. Who would not pay up for services as promised. This phase supposes circa 60's thru 70's. Now in her mid sixties, is juncture at which Milton Cowan walked into her orbit as daughter Greta's lover. He was young man reputed to be a "Joegrine" Who in pursuit of sexcapades. Had been confronted by boyfriends, husbands and father. Toting force issued service revolver. He had so far been a lucky fellow. Keen of hearing, smooth talker and fleet of feet. Unvollendete, that's Schubert's N°. 8, best known as "The Unfinished Symphony" This then is "Unfinished saga N°. 23. Paused to create new input, retaining fictionalization

How Tommy met Martha-24

We will now examine another couple's union with premarital dictates, see how this goes. Martha Vendryes was employed as accountant/relieving day manager at Twin Gables Guest House. Was thirty-four years old and thrice divorced when she met twice divorced Tommy Bolton, US short stay visitor. In town to oversee late mother's funeral. Dispose of family's real estate and assets, before returning to US. Martha cooed to, upgraded his room to rear, away from street noises. She got boyfriend Seymour, to act as chaperone and tour guide. Taking Tommy wherever business took him. Although native to this land, had been twenty years since his last visit and everything changed dramatically. Local roads and shortcuts had given way to highways. Motorists seemed crazier than recalled. Traffic signs and signals were no longer regarded, resulting in close calls. Avoided only when One backed down from other's mad dare. Practiced in figure eight track racing. Not only was this alien to experience but also nerve wracking, even when chauffeured. There's way someone can fleece you if you're not a coot. It pays then, to have second nature yen for skullduggery. Day's end, Tommy asked Seymour how much he owed. He smiled sheepishly and replied. ***"Me leave that to you, boss. See how things run, how much ground we cover. So me going leave you to you conscience."*** Tommy proffered hundred and twenty dollars. Asked if that was enough. Seymour said. ***"Well, me not going cry but me not smiling either. So, as me say, up to you, boss."*** Tommy did rough exchange conversion and added thirty dollars. Eliciting satisfied grin from Seymour. They left early next morning and drove to rural areas, returning midnight. Tommy gave Seymour two hundred dollars, uncaring whether or not he was satisfied. Appears there was disgruntling, as Martha took vacation time. Ferried Tommy here and there during rest of his stay. During which, both developed mutual attraction. Back in the US, Tommy sent Martha instructions to liaise with banks and attorneys. Ensuring his business transactions were accomplished in timely, satisfactory manner. She hinted, he offered a paid trip to spend time with him, whenever she had opportunity to. She came, saw and was awed. Six months and three visits later, marriage was being debated. He made it known. This would require a pre-nuptial agreement. Martha vigorously queried reason for. Tommy with equal vigour told her, he had put assets in trust and divvied between children and grandchildren. Without intent to alter what was done. Which could not be sustained if he re-married without a pre-nuptial in place. It was nothing personal, but a business dictate, he assured her. Also, Martha had to give assurance she would take steps not get pregnant as he did not want to sire any more children. Having done so eight times. Again, onus on the woman, although it takes two. Only Tommy could know mindset or expectations regarding this marriage. Martha's focus was, US green card and eventual citizenship. She had plans and as saying goes, clock was ticking. Knew, once she got green card, citizenship was five years away. Six months prior, process could be initiated. Time slowly moved on and Martha was sworn in as legal citizen of the United States of America. Shortly after, despite having given verbal commitment not to. She got pregnant and resulting rift was born, threatening to end this marriage. Tommy accused, she did this on purpose. Martha countered, he did. Not taking preventive action. Hence, both at fault, should embrace expected outcome. **Things swiftly downhill:**This pregnancy, if successfully brought to term, gave Martha. Eighteen years umbilical attachment to Tommy, even if he divorced her. Her child would be entitled to share legacy Tommy touted having painstakingly tried safeguarding for himself and eight. Their union became cantankerous, involving police, court dates and next thing we know. Tommy is ordered to stay away from his wife and matrimonial home. While paying spousal, child support and property upkeep. What a sordid situation this has turned out to be.You see, my dear hearts and gentle people. Martha convinced herself and powers that be. Tommy was intent on hers and child's demise. Diabolically focussed, keeping intact, planned succession hierarchy. Hence his legal ostracism. Time did not heal wounds, Martha refused to be divorced from Tommy. Son Atlee, made strides in basketball skills and Martha was never more content with life. But then, tragedy awaited, some blamed karma. One could guess, our Martha planned going home in triumph. Popping out of a cake and pirouetting for friends and family in. "Hey look at me now" happily festive song and dance occasion. **Martha goes home:** It was no secret. hometown was beset with unchecked crime spree of unsolved murders, kidnapping and rife home invasions. Not to mention, contract assassinations by suspected unemployable deportees and other criminal elements. In this atmosphere. Martha unwisely made plans to pay family surprise visit, turning up unannounced. Arriving at home airport, she avoided regulated taxis. Opting instead for discounted ride with unregulated hacks. Stripped, robbed of effects and murdered, she ended up Jane Doe for months. Until folks there, them here put pieces together. Someone ventured to make identification. It is sobering, blood chilling realization. Within our civilized places of existence. There are jungle instincts that motivates behaviour, where humans hunts and demises another. To ensure his or her survival, as if it were natural thing to do. Surprise visits are never good, especially One coming from abroad. Recently, a son-in-law flew from Norway to surprise his father-in-law in Florida for his 61st birthday. Son-in-law knocked on door and hid in bushes. Poised to yell "peek-a-boo." Father-in-law opened the door. Son-in-law jumped out to surprise father-in-law, who shot him through the heart, instantly killed him. Lesson is, don't travel from abroad to surprise anyone. Let them know you are coming and take steps to guarantee your safety. You don't know if, how neighbourhood's character has changed since you were there. Regarding Tommy and Martha.

Some are convinced he had something to do with her demise. Had she taken regulated taxi. Without doubt she would have arrived at intended destination safe and sound. It would seem therefore. There's no fact to support whispers and conjectures, of Tommy's plotting to have her done in. Although he might have experienced relief at her death. Who wouldn't? Normal human reaction to what he saw as betrayal and vindictive behaviour. It hurts, paying upkeep and being barred from your house and home. Let us now analyze and hypothesize to see human psyche at work. How deviousness can lurk behind facade of seemingly good, honest intentions. First we look at Jack in the bush shooting. There were ten or more men in barbershop forum, between twenties to sixties. Young men outnumbering older. Old guys agreed they would have reacted as father-in-law did. Said, son-in-law was stupid to have tried such a prank. *"Not so fast y'all, better stop and check this out. First of all, we don't know there wasn't some kind of family trouble between them two. Maybe wifey wasn't happy with sonny boy, we don't know. But one thing is certain. This guy could not have left Norway, flying to Florida and his wife not know. Think of it. His daughter stays put, whilst her husband comes to surprise her father on his birthday? What! She doesn't want to hug her dad on his birthday too? So the guy takes off on a long flight to surprise his wife's dad. What! Did he vow her to secrecy? You know, like she in on the joke? Or did she maybe, call her dad and give him a heads up? So the question arises. Did she innocently tip off her dad about her husband's intention. Totally unaware of what would unfold, and dad decided to settle a long held score with his son-in-law? Or was there conspiracy in which, she prodded her husband to proceed into a carefully laid trap? Y'all need to dig deeper and find out about the insurance money that's coming to her and all that. We could be looking at the perfect crime and not even realize it. Things aren't always what they appear to be."* Youngblood ended his oratory. Silence descended as minds pondered and heads slowly bobbed in acceptance. One older male was first to respond. *"If you were my son, or worse yet my son-in-law. I wouldn't want you living in same house as me. If it's my house you would be out on your ass, and if it's your house. I would rather set up condo under next overpass. Your way of thinking is very dangerous, sinister and evil. Making me shiver."* Younger men unanimously agreed. Youngblood had raised interesting and debatable scenarios. They were certain law enforcement would also pursue. If there was minute whiff of anything fishy, rest assured it would be brought to light. Law enforcement hate being made fools of. If person commits and gets away with crime, that's exactly what's been done. Pride and ego are compelling forces, why cold case files are often reopened and re-examined. Using up-to-date forensics and investigative techniques by police, to solve forgotten crimes. I think, if barbershop minority can agree with this possibility. There's certainty the vox-po-pu-li would concur if petitioned on the subject. Next we look at Martha's about face on pregnancy issue. I find it absurd on part of a male who says to a woman. He does not want to have children, yet covers not the mighty cod. If and when woman decides she doesn't want children. She will take steps to prevent her getting pregnant. Believe that as you believe you are you. No Goalie, however skilled. Shoots through her net, and triumphantly yells, "Goal." I am led to assume Martha did just that, during years she waited to get citizenship with Tommy's support. Which he most likely would have withheld or stymie had she become pregnant prior to. It was with much reluctance, she agreed to pre-nuptial. Knowing in absence of, Tommy would not proceed to altar. So with stratagem and female cunning she bided. Decides to renege on promises made and sidetrack this marriage to her selfish benefit. Even at expense, it being derailed. She had reaped much more than sown and her life could only be further enriched from this point forward. Her fears of being demised, along with her child was not without basis. She knew, in her country. That could be achieved for a few dollars more. But she was now in USofA and knew. Tommy knew, even contemplating such a move. His chances pursuing with ultimate success, was slim to zero. Would be deterrent to his making an effort. To add layer of insulation, she noised it abroad, those were his intentions. Making him a suspect, before crime was committed. Oh so brilliant and effective, but see. She did not plan on meeting vicious, cold blooded stranger. And being a known talkative and braggart. Probably sealed her fate by blabbing, she's making a surprise visit home and kin being unaware of her visit. Our world is filled with cruel, evil people who often prey on unsuspecting others. Before eventually falling as prey themselves. Mercy.

Born that way-you think?-25

You have heard of or seen, families who creates identical initials among members. Like four "BMW's", five "M&M's" and six "MD's" Latter being Manzie Delfosse and his five children with wife Betsy. Claiming his children were born "titled," quite certain. Their initials were precursor to their excelling in medical and allied professions. He lambasted their failure to meet his grand expectations. Often called them underachievers. To which Betsy took strong exception and made point. He being first "MD" had onus to excel, which had he attained goals. His children would naturally have swam in his stream, as young crabs did the old. Their eldest daughter Mitzie, and youngest sister Mandy, were closer than peas in a pod. Pretty, vivacious Mitzie was in love with Delroy Strachan from junior high school. Both drifted apart after graduation. His not attaining final exam grades or skilled to qualify for better than mediocre jobs. It has never been divulged how they met, but one rainy evening. Porter Adams brought her home in his new Toyota Pajero and soon became frequent visitor. Acclaimed virtuoso percussionist, having a day job as licensed real estate broker. Porter Adams asked for Mitzie's hand in marriage. Manzie opposed but sanctioned when Betsy whispered in his ear. ***"Your daughter is a chip off the old block. She will walk out of this house and marry that man whether you like it or not. In similar fashion as you did with your father. Who has only in recent years come to accept me as worthy daughter-in-law."*** Mitzie was nineteen, beau Porter was thirty-three. Roadie with band on gigs, she studied and qualified as underwriter. Landed executive position with preferred firm. Seventeen years old sister Mandy, had bridesmaid role. See how she shone, new diamond paled under her halo. It was only natural she maintained close bond with big sister. Naturally warmed to brother-in-law, Porter. Couple's professions made for healthy combined income and ultra lifestyle. Manzie's opposition to Porter, evaporated, after the marriage. He finagled a yet to be repaid loan, to repair his roof and windows. Now he gushed with pride, whilst imbibing at local bar. On his son-in-law's mastery of musical instruments. When his and Betsy Delfosse's milestone anniversary came around. Both were given a cruise, compliments of the Adams. Manzie compared Porter to supreme being. His wife cautioned him against blasphemy. Her being a proper God fearing churchgoer who knew. All good things around us are sent from heaven above. Despite whom the bearer might be, it is ordained from on high. Manzie shrugged her beliefs off as inconsequential. The Adams lived a comfortable existence in a well furnished and equipped home, in better residential area. Travelled often to exotic places and were seemingly content. Folks looked at the happy couple and wondered why they did not yet have a child or children. Grandma Betsy dared comment. *"They need start having children, to will the threadbag."* Manzie was noticeably silent on that theme. Possibly seeing himself as worthiest heir. It was rumored but no One could say for sure. On one of their trips overseas. Couple sought medical help and soon Mitzie was pregnant with her first child, aged mid thirties. There was celebration and old kinfolk as well as strangers averred. Given shape of her belly. Mitzie would give birth to a boy. A prediction that found favour with Porter but not Mitzie. Yet both were overjoyed becoming parents, despite gender. Talk about child who was going to be born with true gold spoon in it's mouth. No expense was spared outfitting nursery with furnishings and accoutrements. With professional input, theme was struck that would complement child of either gender. The wait was on. By what stretch of imagination, could anyone think this period of anticipating joy, would usher turmoil and rancour in this perfect union. **Daddy goes visiting at maternity suite:**Masked, gloved and disposable suited, before cleared into sterile recovery suite. Nurse held out the newborn female child to daddy, Porter. He stared in silence without reaching for the child then stuttered. *"No, nuh me, me um, me can't. I mean, I can't hold them when they so small. Is like they would slip out of my hand. You know what I mean, nurse? I mean, if you really look on her you will see....Mitzie. I come back later or tomorrow. Maybe by that time my head will more settle and....."* By which time he was shoulder pushing one half of the double door on his way out. In the hallway, Mitzie's sister, Mandy.

Seeing Porter all suited up. Asked if he held the baby. He told her he did not, because he's wondering if a swap had taken place. Awed, she asked her brother-in-law what he meant by that and why did he feel that way. Porter hemmed and hawed, searching for words to explain his mindset. Finally he began, after taking her shoulder and walking her farther from other family members. *"I'm telling you, Mandy, just between me and you. Way how the nurse bring up the baby and I look down around the blanket thing. All I see is her face squinge up between her jaw like two Michelin ready to roll. Jesus, I so frighten. I, I, I was speechless for a minute in there. I know they think me weird but you would have to see it to believe it. Anyhow remember now, this just between us."* Mandy all this while, stood silently staring at Porter, finally asked. **"What you saying Peter, the baby ugly? How you mean her jaw like….what is Mick…who you know name this Mickale that the baby would resemble?"** Now he regretted having said to her, as enormity of his blunder began sinking in. Knew this would not be kept between them. He desperately pleaded. *"Mandy, forget I said anything about the baby. Please, I beg you."* Seems he was only adding fuel to flame. Mandy stared him both eyes and asked in whispered rage.**"Peter, you are saying my sister was having an affair with this Mickie or whoever. And expect me to swallow and pretend you didn't say that? You know that's big fat lie you telling yourself. Mitzie would never two time you with any man. But, you know what? Maybe I should tell her how you massaged my breasts on way to my prom and then bought my silence with the laptop. Yes, Peter! maybe I should out you for what you are."** Porter stood speechless in deep thought, then once again held her shoulder and steered her down ramped walkway towards the parking lot. Unaware, attracting quizzed passerby stares. It was

Mandy who told him. **"If you're not going back in the hospital, ditch the astronaut suit."** Out in the parking lot, it seemed Porter couldn't say anything in his redemption that didn't draw Mandy's intense ire as he began. *"Mandy, let's be sensible and loo…"* She cut him off. **"So now, I am an idiot?"** Porter sighed, long and deep then went on. *"Mandy, what did I ever do to you why you secrete so much bile to vomit on me? Tell me."* Both remained silent and Porter went on, slowly choosing words. *"Mandy, I have always been there for you and we are special. Prom thing was a big mistake and I told you ten times how sorry I am. You have to understand, they were more out than in. I was only joking when I said. Let's tuck these babies into bed. You slapped my hand and punched my face, which I deserved. When I asked, how I could make it up to you. You said you would think about it and that's when you told me to buy the computer. That incident has nothing to do with today and…and what I might have said to you. Which by the way is one big misunderstanding on your part. Michelin is not an actual person, but never mind about that. Raking up the past, taking it to Mitzie and eventually the entire family will put me knee deep in shit. But a little bit of stink going cling to your shoes. No matter how hard you try it just won't go away. That's what I was trying to tell you, when I said be sensible. I was not implying or calling you idiot."* Both stood silently as Porter awaited Mandy's response with guarded resolve. You would not have seen this wind coming, neither did Porter. Taken aback when she asked him. **"So you gonna talk to your buddy about the engine?"** Then sucked her cheeks in as she waited on him to say yeah or nay. Caught off guard, he stared at her and pondered in silence before finally asking. *"I thought you said Papa Manzie had that under control? You looking at a two bills job. The car* *not worth more than two and a half at best. Left to me, I would scrap it and move on. Let's face it Mandy. Mitzie and I bought that car and put it on our insurance. All you had to do was pay for service. You ignored oil change light for over one year before the car breakdown and now it need the engine….."* She again truncated his speech. **"Thought you just said there's no point raking up the past as it can't do anyone any good. So why am I hearing a sermon about what I already know. I asked a simple question that needs very simple, yes or no. Spare the lecture, come to the point."** Porter quietly asked. *"Didn't Papa Manzie promise to take care of the car for you. Because he had money to give towards the purchase before knowing Mitzie and I would pay for it? That's all I am asking, Mandy."* She replied. **"Papa probably spend that money at the bar and on Miss Guthrie, long time and forgotten."** Porter thought on this, then said. *"Well, Mandy. All I can tell you is, when Mitzie comes home and settle herself, I will discuss it with her. Don't bother say anything, you know I can't lead a cow out pasture without her seeing hoof prints. Computer was a goat that went out with the sheep but cow is a different animal."* Again, silence prevailed which Porter ended with a question. *"You hungry? Me coulda eat a horse like Pacino in that movie. That guy is number one in my book, him can't do anything wrong. You did see the movie "Scent of a woman?" Man gave a speech to his young armour bearer on virtues of a woman. I tell you, it's a killer. You must check it out on YouTube one of the time."* She said to him. **"Why not tell me what he said about women that's so earthshaking?"** *"Oh, no. This you gots to hear with your own two ears. Next thing, I get in trouble again."* He ended with a hearty laugh as they waited for the car to cool. **Naming a Baby:** They went to eat and we would say all was well that ended well for that day. I guess harmony going forward will depend on whether or not Mandy or if Mitzie and Porter agrees to fund repair of Mandy's car. But this saga has only just begun. Events so far are iceberg's tip. Mitzie and baby comes home. She reprimands Porter for hospital snafu with a disarming smile, life goes on. It's been quoted from Shakespeare's Romeo and Juliet. "What's in a name? A rose by any other name would smell just as sweet." Porter and Mitzie each chose a name for their baby, Porter sees to formalities. For reason not yet known or fully explained. He tells probing Mitzie, the certificate is not in hand. He has chosen an exotic name, pronounced N'Lou. Family asks, where he got the name from and he ignores their query, but tells his wife. It's an original Afro-Italian-French made up by him. You know how things not pertinent to present, can get shifted to back burner. Off stove top and eventually out the kitchen, without anyone taking notice? So it was with baby N'Lou's exotic monicker. She was taken to daycare nursery and Paediatrician as need arose. There was no evidentiary paperwork required. Mitzie's job being more confining as opposed to her husband's. Who worked in office and outfield. Most times dictated road chores to him. Time came to enroll N'Lou at preparatory school. Registrar read birth certificate, gave an eye popping glance at Porter before completing the process. Shortly after, a note is sent home seeking parents' consent for child's taking part in yard games. There might be soft or hard students contact, occasional fall with possible bruising. Play area is carpeted with artificial grass but still, there could be welts or abrasions. Mitzie read, reread the form, then called Porter's attention to child's name, spelled. "Inlieu" He laughed out loud and asked her, between chuckle spasms. *You soon give birth a second time and is just now you asking bout first child's name? Remember? Everyone said she would be a boy. But she born in lieu of him. So, the name is original. Guarantee you won't find it anywhere else. No matter where we travel, and you know we've travelled a lot."* To say Mitzie was furious would be putting it way too mild. She immediately sought legal advice, effecting change by deed poll.This created quite an imbroglio in their marriage for first time, as Porter threatened seeking legal advice in pursuit of divorce. See how big issue that should have prompted legal consultation, got committed to secrecy vault. But this issue of child's name created a tornado that loomed with destructive capability. Lawyer took fees and advised. Since child had been called N'Lou from birth and not suffer distress, spelling was not immediate negative issue. She would recommend, name be kept and if in adulthood or at marriage. Child wants name change then, let the decision be hers. Both parents embraced wisdom of that advice and tension was relaxed, but life was never the same. As N'Lou grew, she began making changes long before she made adulthood. Most of which dismayed both parents and rankled Papa Manzie's last nerve. Unhinging his undiplomatic tongue and already loose lips. I should mention, Porter and Mitzie had four girls as Porter desperately tried for a son. The quest was abandoned, when fourth girl born had developmental issues. Making her, lifetime care reliant. Papa Manzie said to Porter at christening. ***"Bwoy, you back weak early."*** There was light titter, Porter's brow twisted in repressed anger. Other girls thrived without concern but N'Lou sidetracked. One might say, veered contrary to expectations, alarming family, friends and neighbours. Became subject of intense focus and angst. Pampered and overindulged from birth, she was enrolled in exclusive doll's registry or boutique. Said to upscale with dolls of all sizes. Designer clothes and furniture, including beauty salons and all that jazz. Taken to venues by her mom. N'Lou discarded dolls and trappings, showing preference for skateboards, archery sets and guns. After initial games introduction at prep school. She took on every sport with determined fervour. Excelling to surprise of folks who whispered, *"What's next?"* She tinkered and discarded training wheels on her bicycle soon after getting it. Outdoors recess play time, fearlessly roughhoused with boys. In any game considered male's domain. She was growing to be a man's girl, or maybe a girl's man. Watch out now for tongue in cheek. At double digit age, her mother took closer interest in her physical development as she progressed into puberty, seeing signs that gave cause for concern. First, she discovered N'Lou wearing chest girdles. Compliments of grandma Dell, unknown to either parent. Asked for an explanation, grandma Dell said. N'Lou complained severe breasts discomfort with brassieres, that went away when kept rigid against her chest. Grandma Dell had not mentioned to either parent because. N'Lou brought the issue to her, purportedly from Mitzie for guidance as older woman. Confronted with her lie, N'Lou told her mom. Students harassed at school, because of breasts size. Story she quickly changed, when Porter began searching for his war vest, on mission confronting tormentors. Mother and child sat reasoning, One on One. Child disclosed being uncomfortable as girl. Her voice was deep as a male's should. Hairline came down in sideburns and horror of horrors. She had shadow on upper lip. Although she plucked hairs from her chin, they quickly regrew. Family business soon got to Papa Manzie's ears. His assertions and epithets were like brine in un-bandaged war wounds. **Mandy's pregnancy:**

Lets pause to bring another aspect of this saga to fore. It is not clear as to whether or not, Manzie discussed question of a loan to Mandy with his wife. However, her being pregnant.

Coincidentally, when her boyfriend went visiting his mother in Canada. With parting promise of "Soon come" and yet to do so. Mandy was anxious to once again have wheels, and made this known to her brother-in-law. He found her a three year old Ford Fusion. Had very low mileage, was in excellent shape and price was right. She wanted model of her first car. Porter pointed out, oil change on that make car of any model is six times cost of similar service on most other cars. To drive home his point he suggested. Maybe, that was reason she did not change oil when auto prompted. Ignored instead and kept driving, whilst saving funds to do so. Papa Manzie again had something unsavoury to vent on, saying Mandy was last and worst of his daughters. Allowing a man to breed her, and gallop back to his village before daylight. Porter took Mandy to hospital, kept vigil with her and baby. Came home and proposed a plan to his wife. **The adoption?:** Without much ado the family sat down to discuss Mandy's plan. Giving up her son to big sister and husband for adoption. This had Porter already sprinting to Registrar's office. At that point, Mitzie had two girls and advanced in pregnancy with her third. Seemed Mitzie said yes, reluctantly. After parents decried losing their grandchild, if adopted by strangers. This was wisest move, Porter being overjoyed having a male child in the house at last. In all this hesitance and elation, no One saw next twist coming, until late following year. **Daddy's home to stay?:**Garfield Parchment returned from Canada and straightway came to see his girlfriend. He had heard rumours, wanted to know if it's true she got pregnant while he was gone. And if so, who was son-of-a-bitch she allowed to defile her. Vowed virginal innocence to him on his leaving, pledged to stay that way until their wedding night. So. *"Who put the bomp in the bomp bomp bomp, who put the ram in the rama lama ding dong?"* Garfield would not recite verse, saying.

"Who was that man, I'd like to shake his hand" Oh no, he was in a fighting mood. She reminded him. Every time he wrote, saying he would be home month end. Month ended without him showing. After one and half years, she figured he bailed on her. No, not so. His mom was sick and he could not leave her alone. Had to take her to and from various doctors and specialists. Recuperation after surgery was slow, ere she regained stability and skills. Eventually admitted into assisted senior living home. Had to visit her at least once a month. But was home to get his, rather their life back on track. He still wants to know who is the man. Is that like the British nursery rhyme question *"Who killed Cock Robin?"* In that instance, someone fessed up. *"I"* Said the brave Sparrow. *"With my bow and arrow."* Prevailing silence on Mandy's son and his adoption will soon become a deafening roar. Web's weave got more tangled when Garfield kept enquiring to whereabouts of Mandy's baby. **It's in hiding-Why?:** You see, patient readers. He loved this woman and despite being angry at deception. Papa Manzie imbibed and got Garfield to admit his shortcoming, leading to situation. Musing wisdom of, Garfield sipped and admitted. Willing to forgive, marry and start his family. We three going on to bigger and better things. Despite dangling carrot of happily ever after, Mandy would not divulge son's father's identity. At family gathering, Garfield silently asked Papa Manzie's help, finding solution to this riddle and was assured. ***"Don't worry, foot soldier. When time ripe, is either confession or crucifixion."*** True to word, when he was all liquored up. Called Mandy to his table and hollered at everyone. ***"Stop run y'all mouths and listen what Mandy have to tell us. Go on child, tell us who's be father of our Lilliputian."*** Mandy was mute, stared at her father defiantly. He said. ***"If is won't you won't tell, that's bad and bad enough. But if is can't you can't tell, may as***

well bury you head and not look anyone in them face again. So, tell us now. We all love you. Who him be. From where him hail?" Poor child, overcome with embarrassment began crying. At which Papa Manzie turned to Garfield and said. *"You can't say me don't earn the prize, you see how hard me try."* Garfield embraced his girlfriend, who shoved him hard before running away. Betsy in comforting pursuit. Meanwhile Porter whispered reservations to close friends, as first daughter was going off to college. Disturbed by Mitzie telling him. Their daughter did not want to be girl or woman any longer. Wanting instead to become male. Planned doing sex change surgery once she began working and had financial resources to support the procedure. He doubted this could be accomplished. Was convinced by his wife, this could be set in motion with hormone injections that ultimately retards menstrual cycles, breasts development and possibly other negative side effects. He voiced belief, there was possibility of cancerous growths, incurring unaffordable medical bills. Surprised everyone when he averred. *"God don't like nobody tamper with what him take one whole day to make. Step back, look at it and holler. Whoa Man! See? Y'all never know, that's how woman get her title."* There followed thunderous laughter and table thumping. So how is this reconstituted family getting along, you ask. Garfield married his lady love. Phillip Adams spends some holidays with his mom, Mandy. Brother and sister born to her and Garfield. He called both fathers "Daddy P" and "Daddy G" in their own right. At a family gathering, Papa Manzie opened up and said, regarding twelve year old Phillip. *"You know Porter, the longer this child live in your house, is more him resemble you. Seems like is really true, when people live together too long, them begin to resemble One another."* Guffawed and went on. *"Betsy, you is a pretty woman. But I pray to God, I*

don't start looking like you." Now, Porter loudly decried Phillip having resemblance to him and Papa Manzie quickly cautioned his son-in-law. ***"Careful how you doth protest now. Old time people say, when you throw stone in hog pen. One that squeal loudest, is him the stone hit. So cover you mouth and make people think you yawning."*** This was tongue in cheek comment. There's a saying "People will talk" and they did, not necessarily in whispers. Regarding, who fathered Mandy's first child. Only two persons in family and wider circle, who myopically did not see Porter as culprit. Were his wife, and her sister's husband, Garfield. It is a certainty, had Mitzie known about breasts massage and computer gifting. She would have had, different perspective on her husband and sister. She would definitely revisit his fast tracking, adoption of her sister's child. And sister's willingness giving unconditional support. There wasn't one iota of reluctance, feigned, real or second thought. I would think, their being closer than peas in pod. Mitzie must have coerced little sister, (in vain) to share secret of her child's father. What with they be tight and together. No such information was forthcoming. As Porter asked Mandy. What good could come of these revelations. Secrets get taken to the grave. As for Mandy, she seemed willing to rain on sister's parade. Pursuing financial gain from Porter. First a laptop computer and then asking, if he's going to repair her car in exchange for silence. See folks. Those closer to you, are them that needs to be watched more than them that are distant. I say "For shame" For benefit of those not in the know. Lilliput, is island in Gulliver's Travels, whose inhabitants are mere six inches tall. Hence, people short in stature are often referred to as Lilliputians. Definitely not in a complimentary way. We can however assume, Mandy's son must have been wee at birth. Hence, Manzie's tag.

The Fools Game?-26

We have heard of social event, pajama party. Sometimes called slumber party, of pre-puberty girls dubbed "tweens" Event smacks of contradiction because, if one act is engaged, other becomes redundant. Either you're at slumber or in gaiety. Made that point, first time an event was mentioned at home by my daughter. Was covertly chastened by my wife, with a cold, demeaning stare. Browbeating, my grandmother Louise would say. So, I left well alone. But seriously folks, just between us two, look at it. Slumber is sleeping, partying is gaiety and hoopla. How can both be in progress at same time? That's another cliche, like folks who sample food and comment. "This is good shit" Since this was not a decision in which I was asked or expected to arbitrate. I walked away without comment. Lydia and Darnelle Gresham were couple, having intense marital issues. He entered a home through back door, was warmly greeted. Made himself at home for the day while Lydia chased false leads trying to find him. Their daughter tumbled and was unable to stand. Possibly from fracture of one or all three ankle bones. Lydia went by his workplace to get health care card, on her way to hospital. Alas, he was on one day vacation, although leaving home for work. At ER, you either have care provider information or sign commitment to pay, which Lydia did, reluctantly. There was a monkey on the lam. Initial mindset, was concern for her child's discomfort. Fact that her husband took a day off but left home dressed for work, made her suspect he was up to his usual womanizing pursuit. So it was sweet revenge to burden him with medical bills for their daughter's treatment. On other side of town, Darnelle was in jail. After trying to leave the home he was visiting, by backdoor and fence. Got trapped behind a fowl coop, by three snarling mongrels.

Woman of the house tried desperately to pacify canines, without success. She fed, watered, lured and played with them. But those animals when riled, responded only to their handler, who was also a cop. There is a common conception, some men train dogs to only obey their command. To thwart girlfriend or wife, accommodating Joe Grine with impunity. This and unusually swift police response, suggested there was forward planning by someone. Darnelle knew, girlfriend Patrice had been friendly with a police detective. Convinced him they had parted amicably, after dust up with his wife. True, landlord served notice to quit and she had hastily found sanctuary at this efficiency unit across town. Yet, she lied to Darnelle about an amicable breakup with the cop, as he was footing rent for place she now lived at. Lydia hurried to the jail and asked to see her husband. Whose elation at seeing his wife was shattered when she told him. *"Wipe the shit eating grin off your face. I'm only here to get the health plan card. See ya later."* She explained her situation repeatedly to law enforcement officers at different ranks but got basically same response. *"Prisoner's property can only be accessed by prisoner upon discharge, after posting bail. Which could not be considered until Monday."* Who knew? Yet, it made sense. Accused has to attend court where charges are read and application made for bail, which could be denied. Could be granted subject to monetary parameters. Average Joe never focuses on this aspect of living. Never expecting to find himself in this predicament. Until he does and once this is known, he sometimes frets and loses all hope of redemption. **One good lie deserves another?:** Truth told, Patrice lied to Darnelle regarding her relationship with the detective. They were very much an item, despite. She had bills to pay, an image to burnish and neither One could be her sole provider. Two could, if each tried harder as did Avis. Would rather be with Darnelle as he was a lover who showed caring and tenderness. Helped with niece's support, whilst sister was in prison for stabbing boyfriend. Patrice did not have aggressive temperament and ability to defend physical assault. Detective slapped her around, on suspicion her two timing him. This was fairly often. Knew when he was coming upside her head. Rolled sleeves up. Laid his gun on a table or someplace, after emptying ammo and grabbing her tresses. Poor unwitting girl strategized and deliberately fell on the bed. Evaded an open hand slap to grab the weapon. Pointed it at and dared him hit her once more. Which he did with impunity, then showed her clips with cartridges from his pocket. Wasn't she paying attention? Already knew she could not admit knowing or having Darnelle as visitor to her home. Had to support police report of possible home invasion. Found on enclosed property without lawful excuse and or burglary attempt. Darnelle in jail, did not have access to and his wife Lydia was in no hurry to help. Request for bail in his own recognizance was denied and so he stayed in the Tijuana jail. Not really Tijuana. That's title of a 1959 song by the Kingston Trio. You remember 'em? In 1958, sang the true saga of "Tom Dooley" Calvin Gresham travelled miles to see only son in jail. Called daughter-in-law. Pleaded with her to facilitate her husband's release from jail. She told him, her daughter was in hospital. She could only cope one situation at a time. Darnelle had to wait his turn. However, in another day or two he was out of jail, thanks to co-workers and their Union. Which now prompted him to become dues paying member. Hitherto he always maintained position. Union had to bargain for and represent all workers, whether or not they were dues paying members. A fact which did not find favour with Stewards and those who paid dues. Leading to Darnelle and like minded, being called Leeches. When Daniel Parsons went in for emergency surgery and call went out for volunteer blood donors. Not one Brotherhood member responded. See how enmity thrives in a friendly brotherhood, work environment and no One knows, until? **Who done it?:** Employee's parking lot at Lydia's workplace was secured by card swiped automatic gate. Open from 06:00 to 08:00 hours. For crews ending 23:00 to 07:00 shift and those starting 07:00 to 15:00 hours. Surveillance cameras caught female motorcycle rider, entering and exiting car park. Neither her mission, during seven minutes stay or image could be clearly defined. Yet, Lydia's car had two flat tyres. Pierced through sidewalls, all four would need being replaced. What was taken to be hat, was Beekeeper's helmet and veil. Despite, facial recognition eluded. Question was, who had it out for Lydia? Which female was known, riding motorcycle? Then, someone asked. Why everyone thinks figure is female? Could be male disguised. Another incident on her street, which although there was no viable connection. Made her decide to leave her home and live with her parents. Until she decided on her marriage, that now hung by a thread. A young white male was seen cruising the neighbourhood. Slowing at times to peer inside open garages. Police were notified. Although cars approached suspect from opposite directions. He bailed and fled on foot before being apprehended. Drunk and semi nude he was taken to jail and that should be end of that. Mid morning next day, two young men parked their truck in an open lot and approached neighbours. Asking if they had seen wallet dropped by young man, taken to jail previous night. All asked, said, no. Noon they returned, asking one neighbour. If he thought folks across from him, were Ones who called police. Neighbour said he would not know about that. One of remarked. ***"You know black people love calling police. They'd rather call police than swat a fly buzzing them."*** Neighbour again denied knowing anything about who called. Two hours later, duo were back. This time rapping at suspects' door. Asking more questions about apprehension of previous evening, and whether they knew who could have called. Pollsters became agitated when questions were asked and adults responded in Creole. Eased when younger family members answered in English. Feeling threatened by these two. Now regarded as fiends. Friends or acquaintances of jailed suspect. Lydia took wings to. **The Big House:** Two storey home on acre plus lot in Horse Country. Takes a bundle for upkeep, taxes and mortgage. All of which, the Greshams found difficult to maintain. Added to which, property was upside down and could not be sold for rising liabilities. Darnelle had a plan and lost no time putting it in action. Rented three on site storage containers. Advised, the county might not approve, he replied. It would take time for code breach coming to light, and time allowed for correction, before enforcement. This redounded to money in his pocket. County would be coming down on him for more far reaching breaches, but let us not jump ahead. His ideas found favour with two others and three wise men put their plan into action. Having stored household items, they brought in amusement and gaming equipment. Such as billiard tables and coin chance devices. His buddy, with casino gaming knowledge set up systems and safeguards. Stag joint, offering pre-sold adult entertainment. Hence no money collected on entry. Depending on level of cover paid, decal was stuck on a guest. Designed to "time out" at which guest was asked to leave. Cellphones were quarantined and other restrictions in place. So far, we are talking about ground floor, before venturing up stairway to heaven. Each step asked elevated "contributions" Ultimate jackpots were for "Braves" Patrice fled to brother's house in Tampa. He got her seasonal employment at the Post Office. Life was half way good, she yearned for Darnelle's emotional support. Wanting to spend Christmas with him, but that was his busy period. They planned for weekend after Christmas, before New Year's. Brother Justin, drove her to Fort Myers. Asked to stay, making three. He and girlfriend were on outs. Darnelle voiced opposition but relented after Patrice voiced support. Who wants a big brother in house, whilst sister and her lover whooping it up down corridor? Very idea chilled Darnelle's ardour. Justin decided going back to Tampa and Darnelle would take Patrice home. Justin drove to Tampa and unexpectedly found his girlfriend in his house. She attacked him verbally and physically, suspicion he had been out with a woman. Called the police and reported his beating her. Police agreed, Justin showed bruises and signs of battering, compared to girlfriend. Whose lipstick and makeup was still in place. Yet, they had to take him to jail, let a judge decide. Darnelle was out of his happy zone and kept silent all way from Fort Myers to Tampa. Some silence that was. Both were pissed having their planned funscapade cut short. There were places to go and things to get done before taking her home on Sunday. Comes New Year's Eve night, fun was on in Horse Country and there was great anticipation on who would win lotteries to go upstairs. Quoting Marconi "Momento clou della notte" or Enrico "lumine noctis" In plain English. Evening's, highlight arrived with Cinderella fiat. Time was not on players' side. First, you got in upstairs pool by bidding. Highest bidders entered the draw to select three who would go upstairs. Once upstairs, there was another bidding for chance to enter which room and be surprised, depending on your fantasies. One thing was certain, some level of sexual gratification awaited behind those doors. If male's price bid wasn't exceeded. **Prize winner lucks in?:** Enzo Cardena won "Eden" and entered room with diffused Fresnel lighting and soft music. She had on bikini top and two very short aprons with rounded bottoms. She met him at the door, walked back to small table and twirled to create uplift apron's hems. Showing there was nothing under aprons but her. How his blood boiled as he dragged a palm across his mouth. Ran it over his pate from back to front, then clasped both tightly. Found his voice and beckoned her softly. To which she shook her head side to side in denial. Gave him a drink and told him house rules of the game. Sometimes a problem can cause over thinking, when solution seems overly simple but overlooked. In other words, we see obvious but tell ourselves it could not be that simple. There's got to be more mind boggling facet to. Enzo probably told himself. *"Aut viam inveniam aut faciam" "I will either find a way or make one."* He had won three chances to pull string of the front apron, failing which he would be asked to. Or removed from the room if he failed to leave. Each time he failed to untie correct apron, she went back and retied before giving him another go. Sounds simple enough, you would think, not having engaged in this game before. Look at the big picture if you will. You know it can't be as simple as it seems, there's got to be an unknown facet which you have very little time to study and get hang of. Your mental resources get confused between knowledge that even finding the correct string, your go at the prize is severely limited by the clock. All fun and games ends at midnight, when patrons are hurried out. That is, those who had not already left, frustrated and disappointed. After midnight, sound of car engines being revved all at once and horns being honked at one guy who's stopping to chit chat his loser buddy. Neighbours take note, cops are called to investigate events next door or across street. That's one per chance Darnelle and his stakeholders want to avoid. I am quite certain pulling a correct string is far more challenging than could be imagined, but the concept is not new. At first he coaxed and pleaded. Had he been student of US Merchant Marine Academy, he would have been familiar with motto. *"Acte Non Verba" "Actions not words"* Yet, he proposed. Even as clock ticked, closing window of opportunity. ***"Hey, give a little something. I'm out big bucks with nothing to feel for it. Make the evening worthwhile. Come on, I know you can do it, if you really want to. This is between you and me, there's no camer...."*** He stopped, scanned walls and ceiling for telltale signs of equipment. Then his demeanour suddenly changed to aggression without warning. At which she yanked parlour rip cord. Two men stepped out from the aperture she went to retie her streamers. Took hold of Enzo and asked him to accompany them. Headed out of the building to his car and be escorted off premises. He was not going without a fight and hell broke loose. Somebody was pushed or thrown downstairs and a Jack came tumbling after. Both stood and fists flew, faces were pummelled and teeth knocked out as friends dashed here and there. This fray was barely underway ten minutes. When blue lights arrived and called for reinforcements. Exit points were blockaded and folks interviewed as to what was going on and reason for this hullabaloo. With best of intentions, this aprons party had serious miscalculations. Denying this novel form of adult entertainment becoming viable investment. Enzo aside, I was at first curious as to nature of other prizes. Later learned there were male, female and "whatever is your delight." Still, I am trying to visualize games played how, and were outcomes more rewarding? Gonna keep snooping around and I promise you, fictional truth will outrun factual lies..

Two blind Mice-One Cheese-27

It's possibly oldest vice, goes hand in hand with the oldest profession. Simply put, men who patronize prostitutes, are very often in committed relationships with partners. Married or otherwise. Prostitution is often defined as act or practice of engaging in sexual intercourse for money. We have to agree, this definition has been broadened to encompass scenarios, where there's no monetary exchange. Woman goes on job interview and is told, position is almost hers. But there are finer points to be discussed, in more leisurely setting. Maybe, lunch or dinner at venue conducive to mutual understanding. Depending on her upbringing, values and home life situation. She has reservations and says, no thanks. Or jumps at offer. After all, what's worse that can happen. It's not as if anything is going down that hasn't before, with less tangible reward. They meet and after song and dance, get down to a bout of pleasurable fun. Maybe not quite so for her, being inwardly reluctant. But definitely for him, who is probably making another coded entry on his calendar, ala Milton. Now, the job is hers but watch out. She has to keep the kettle boiling, lest it runs out of steam. Boss man goes out hiring again. Other times, it's getting coveted promotion. Women encounter level of overt and covert perverse discrimination at workplaces. That's never mentioned or talked about, and in rebutting your argument. Yes, there might be men who face similar situation. Yet, it's definitely not on scale faced by women. Definition of rape is "to force a woman into having sexual intercourse." Once again, it is borne out without doubt. Men cannot be forced to have sexual intercourse. Anatomy isn't structured to facilitate. But let's talk about the woman. This is consensual rape, akin to when felon holds knife at her throat. She then disrobes and engages intercourse. Not induced by pleasant emotions, but from fear being hurt or demised. This article is not about prostitution or rape. It's about people playing games, running here and there with another man's woman or woman's man. Tragedies that sometimes emanate from, or is avoided, until next time. Most jealous man you can ever find, is One playing around with another man's woman. Why? There are women who probes and finds irrefutable evidence of her man playing the field. She doesn't make a fuss, keeps her cool. Finds her own hairdresser and life goes on. If dude gets slightest whiff of another man coming around his woman. Oh, he's ready to take them out and confess to cops. Again. Why? Life is give and take, live and let live. Joy and pleasure of sex for male. Lasts only as long as he's able to maintain an erection. After which, shrinkage sets in and he snores in deep slumber. Any woman can tell you. Sunday's romp can last her all week. Through to next Sunday and beyond. Glance across to where she sits at her desk. See her pause and look far away with that glow of content on her face. Memory of yesterday and anticipation of tomorrow. Has just erupted and filled her to indescribable thrill of orgasm. She's harnessing mental and physical willpower to not yell *"Yyyyeeeesssss."* A good hairdresser does that for women, but can't help himself from mediocrity. William McLaren was late thirties, married with a wife and four children. One of which was born two years after his marriage, by another woman. Julian McIntosh was late forties, married with a wife and five children. Two of which were born before he met his wife. Felicia Fisher was twenty-two, single and did she turn heads wherever she went. Signals changed, motorists stood still and gazed. She is kind of creature that convinces, there is a God or supreme being. Who makes all things bright and beautiful, all creatures great and small. I dread not day I die, but tremble at thought mine eyes might one day lose sight. Borderline glaucoma should get best of me. And I should dwell in darkness, losing sight of God's creations as they mature to prominence. For this continuous joy of life, I beseech and pray. William was called Billy, by young women who surrounded him. After all, his father had ministerial portfolio in governing party and he lived off his father's fame. Held out promises, being able to get jobs for some. Promotions for others and was go to guy for getting ahead. Julian was in business with company Felicia had recently been hired, he made his introduction. She smiled her pleasure. He said he was filled with warmth of, causing her to blush. Went about his business and on leaving, told her to take care of herself. Then walked towards the door. Paused, came back and told her. **"I am not implying you are incapable, but just in case you need a hand. I am your handyman."** She blushed again with that innocent schoolgirl head and shoulder movement, then told him. ***"You scare me with your know how to toast and get women eating out of your hands. But I just might call on you."*** Midweek, he was back at the office and asked her to lunch. In course of which a date was set for that weekend. They partied at an uptown discotheque and on strolls through the gardens. She briefly mentioned boyfriend. Not having heard from him, nearly one month.Went on describing him as "Girl's rush" of pedigreed lineage. Figured, she had simply fell off his top twenty chart. Julian could have mentioned seeing Billy's name, bandied frequently in newscasts. Detailing his involvement with boy's high school cricket teams. Vying in annual competition for prestigious Mulgrave shield and DaCosta cup championships. But why shed positive light on erstwhile nemesis. Seizing metaphor, Julian replied. She was number one on his chart of two. She stared him, brow forming frown that morphed to broad smile when he said, number two was himself. Adding. **"You do know, it takes two?"** Her family lived in rural district on city's edge. In an area with waterfalls and hiking trails. Tour vehicles brought foreigners on excursions. Locals also enjoyed ambience, frolicked in mineral springs. Felicia once did ticket office stints on holidays from high school. Her parents sold refreshments and souvenirs at mom and pop shop, fronting main thoroughfare. Area was rugged hills with lush vegetation, springs and abundant flora fauna specie. Soothing escape from drudgery, five minutes walk from parked vehicles. **Julian goes to meet the Fishers:** Julian was being taken to meet Felicia's parents for first time. The shop was setback from the road, a good twelve or more feet, which allowed for customer parking. Still used as, although there were no longer any customers. Her parents tried once to collect parking fees. Area councillor told them, the level was not part of their holding. If they continued doing so, they would be taken to court, so they stopped. Main house was about thirty feet horizontal and vertical eastward of the shop. Steep descent of steps carved in hillside clay, led partway down. Then gave way to terraced walkway in an endless Z pattern to sloped flat on which the house was built. Steps and terraced Z's were always slippery from rain or late night dew, except during droughts. Sand was mined from stream behind the house. Brought by buckets and sprinkled on pathways for feet traction. The house of concrete nog was big and airy with large windows, semi wrap verandah and high ceilings. In case you're asking what is nog house. It is first framed with wood for support pillars and load bearing walls. Galvanized mesh or strips are attached to supports. Next, concrete mortar is flashed onto and smoothed to create finished walls. An elevated tank provided water for a shower and other domestic use. There was usual outhouse or latrine built over a hole in the ground. Came upon a Sunday when Barbara Fisher came from church. Julian wended his way down the precarious pathway and was introduced to Festus Fisher and his wife. He refused taking Julian's hand in greeting. Saying he did not shake empty hands. More so a man's. *"If you really want me to take you hand in greeting. You woulda bring a Q *flask in other hand, with a pack or two of Buccaneers. Other than that. Why take you hand and we not going dance?"* Barbara Fisher scolded. *"Festus Obadiah Fisher. You need to get up off you backside and come church with me. Instead of sitting down worshipping things that going end you life before long. You need to be showered with blessings of the faithful and be redeemed before it's too late."* Festus simply brushed Barbara off with flash wave of both hands. Simultaneously, Felicia whispered to Julian. *"Pay him no mind. He's an old curmudgeon who barks without bite."* Okay, time to enlighten supporters. A Q *flask is quarter of quart, or half pint of over proof rum. Tradesmen, Artisans, Farmers on daily trek to places of occupation by feet, bicycle, donkey or mule would have a Q *flask firmly wedged in a back pocket. When the feeling arose they sipped a sip and got energized to continue their task. Of course there were others who took a bag of weed and rolled spliffs to give them that get up and go kick. See? There was a time when living was carefree and easy. One could consume alcohol or smoke weed on the job, without getting drug tested and/or fired. Buccaneers were cheap cigarettes, made from unrefined leaf tobacco by Jamaican Cuban family, B&JB Machado Tobacco Company Limited. Packet of ten sold for seven pence, compared to ten pack "Craven A." More than twice the price. Barbara was busy, setting tray with glass tumblers and frilled serviettes on saucers. From eared brown and cream stoneware flagon, she poured liquid. Brought slivers of fruitcake from her pantry. Everyone sat and taken by surprise, Julian was asked to say grace. He did, brief and to the point. Barbara explained, fare on table was fruitcake and grapefruit wine with tamarind and honey. Festus felt under his wicker basket chair. Came up with a flask of rum. He tipped copiously in his tumbler, finger stirred and licked. Held it out, still finger licking, said to Julian. *"Barbara good at what she does, but any drink taste better with a little kick."* Julian declined with a smile. Festus stared at him and said. *"Me don't know who raise you, but make me tell you supp'n. Is bad manners, you come smaddy house and refuse them hospitality. Bad, bad manners for a young man. If you was up top, I would throw you out. But from down here, me can't throw you far enough. So thank God, you get away this time."* Felicia pinched Julian, whispered. *"Remind me to tell you something about my father. Why he hasn't been to church longest time."* Repast over, Julian again complimented Barbara on her brewing and baking skills, before led off to nearby stream. Eagerly, Felicia began. *"Years ago when my parents got married. It was customary for newlyweds to attend their first communion service as turn thanks. My father sipped wine from the noggin, smacked his lips then said to pastor. "This is not blood of Christ, this is watered down grape juice. What kind of sham you pulling on these people and calling youself...."* He paused and laughed hard before continuing. *"Oh, I just get it. The Bible did mention it. This is part where wine did done and them bring out real stuff. Where you hide it, parson?"* Pastor said, communion was a holy rite, not to be trivialized with comedy and blasphemy. By then, my father walked away, leaving mother ashamed and so embarrassed. From that day he has never gone back to church. Can you believe that man?"* Felicia should know, she would not hear a syllable of condemnation or comment from Julian, regarding her father. He remained stoically silent. They necked and fooled around, headed back to the house.

Which Felicia steered him by, wending their way uphill. She went offtrack, headed under the shop to rickety wooden stair that went from ground to floor. Julian stopped at ground and watched in amused curiosity. Felicia ascended, stopped half way up and pushed on floor above. Then turned around and came back down, saying. *"It's locked from inside."* She walked towards the sanded path. Julian paused to examine floor above the stair. Saw a large hasp and staple pair in place on the floor. On closer examination he saw outline of a large door or hatch. Outside, it was weather beaten and decrepit. When Felicia opened one side of a heavy, triple panelled, double door, inviting him in. He was awed at shop's interior. Former display shelves now had clay and porcelain figurines, vases and stuffed toys on show. Wallpaper of varying designs, covered wood seams shrinkage, allowing for draft invasion. Cedar floor was polished, brilliant auburn gleam. Who would believe, there was this cozy inviting nest. Inside what seemed, a ramshackle hovel from outside. Felicia walked to one end of the room, asked Julian to help shift the bed. Locked trap door was revealed and held his gaze. She told him, during it's trading post era. Parents used trap door after locking up at day's end. Two chimmies on floor caught his eyes, he asked her, jokingly. **"What have we here. His and hers piss pots?"** Not finding humour, she icily replied. *"No, sir. They do multi-purpose, catching raindrops. Dad usually fix the roof but hasn't gone up there in a long time. He says, since I don't pay rent, least I can do is pay someone to fix. Which I think is fair. But everyone that comes, wants arm and leg to do the work. By time I gather enough money, they ask for an internal organ in addition to limbs. My older sister used to share with me. She moved to "chateau" in Orange Grove with her boyfriend. Chateau? Give me a freakin' break."* Felicia, love shack, river below and overall aura of this place.

Julian had found all-inclusive paradise, spent as much time as he could. Perched as it was on wood stilts. Shop vibrated when vehicles rumbled along the road, at first startling Julian. Like most things of similar nature, he soon adjusted mentally and ceased to notice. Two weeks on, he thought Felicia was in tight, he could tell her he was married. She casually replied. *"Oh, I knew. Wondered when you were going to tell me. Billy is too, but he has never told me. Once, when I asked, he kind of lied."* **"What do you mean, kind of lied? It's quite simple. One either lies, or One doesn't."** Julian tried demonizing Billy and Felicia replied. *"I first asked him if he loved children. Did he look forward to being a father, how many and was he married. His frightened response was. "Of course I love children. Me look forward to be a father, hope you not pregnant. Where this question about me being married comes from?" He could have said, yes he's married and already has children. Yet chose to lie in backhanded way, and poorly so. Sweating like a Boar who sees Butcher coming. Men!"* Julian pressed her. How she knew his status and that of her boyfriend, if she had never been told. With a smile she replied. *"A girl has to know what kind of animal she takes to her bosom for a pet. There are pleasures not worth the grief they bring. Don't look at me like that. I am not older and wiser, as you are. Neither am I young and naive. Come on let's play Jose Feliciano. I needs soothing."* Curious as to what that means, aren't you? Comfortable with each other, she led him to city Crafts Market some Saturdays. Where he bought curios and collectibles for her shelves. First kink in their armour, came quite innocently and unexpected. She called his office, he answered and said. **"I'm in middle of something. Call you back in thirty minutes."** Later he returned her call, was shocked into silence as she asked in clipped tone. *"So! You are one boss, who also screws your* *secretaries. Haven't you heard popular slogan, two is better than too many?"* He figured she was surely jesting. Abrupt disconnect of the call, told him she was not. Not wanting to take this serious, he stalled midpoint re-dialling her number. One head told him, call it a day, be done with the relationship. Other head recalled pleasures of their encounter. Mulling this mental imbroglio. She called back, saying, in tone betraying earlier stance. *"I wanted to do lunch today but missed out. Can you put it on your list tomorrow? There's something very important I have to discuss with you."* He told her he would make reservation at "Boca Chica" and asked her meal preference. Management vowed, if a reserved meal was not served within five minutes of guest being seated. Meal was free. It was mere PR stunt, as on entering. You waited whilst a table was being readied, before you were seated. By then they had shared the meal and all that remained was a waiter bringing with smile of achievement. Julian once challenged Babu, who reminded. It was not five minutes after walking in. Clock began ticking after he was seated, big difference. Felicia began her tale of woe. Company secretary, Leland had stepped up game. Inviting her to weekend soirees which she kept saying, no. Leading to his bypassing office manager, Gwen Andrade. Assigning her work in accounting, outside her job description. Which, when she failed to meet time and accuracy earmarks. He threatened termination, on grounds of incompetence. She was at loss to understand why, accounts receivables had been taken from. Three person accounts department, and given to her, a legal secretary. Went on to tell her, he could see her boyfriend didn't visit the office so frequently, or at all. Julian told her, not to worry, he would explore avenues on her behalf. Called a senior female partner at legal firm he retained. Felicia went for an interview and skills evaluation. Was offered, starting salary exceeding her present, with better benefits and Jewish holidays observed. In addition to those on calendar. Went two Saturdays on paid training to familiarize with switchboard. Which she would relieve on rotation, at operator's lunch break. Telex machine and IBM Selectric typewriter. In place of Smith-Corona manual she was accustomed to and proficient at. End of which, two weeks notice of resignation had been met. And her making formal complaint to management about Leland's behaviour that he vehemently denied. Not being first such accusation levied. He did not come out smelling as sweet as hoped. So there, problems do have solutions at times. Depends on who knows whom. Street life had gradually taken air of insecurity at night, more so than at daytime. Person to person crime had risen. Without signs of abatement or law enforcement containment. Folks took to preemptively arming themselves. With this spike in applications for firearm licenses, a rumour swirled to effect. Names of those approved for licenses, were sold or somehow dispersed to criminal elements. This was supported by coincidence of licensed folks, being waylaid and robbed of newly acquired firearms. In most instances, killed when resisting. Goaded by mistrust and coincidence. Julian bypassed legal process, got a firearm. This was not foolproof. Using unlicensed firearm, even in self defence. Resulted in prosecution and prison sentence. So, what's a citizen to do? He came for, among other things. A Ford C6 transmission, rebuilt by Fred Jones. Now armed, Julian thought it couldn't have happened a better time. Rural Eden was slowly losing charm and sought after chiqueness. Word spread of visitors being robbed at gunpoint. Folks who resisted paying, to have cars watched in absence, returned to find tires flat. It was only a matter of time this would escalate to tragedy. Visitors stayed away until they stopped coming. Once thriving facilities, suffered from disuse, misuse and ruin.

Julian however experienced no sense of fear or trepidation, having two fellas by his side. Ultimate interpretation of the phrase "Cold Comfort." Felicia had mouth on her, not unlike her dad. Julian at times brought Festus Fisher, a Q flask of rum and packets of Buccaneer cigarettes, sorta keeping the peace. Seeing items on seat one evening, she opened up and told Julian. ***"You shouldn't pacify my father by taking him gifts. Comforts you enjoy from a Fisher comes from me, not him. Furthermore, he's been told by doctor over and over, to give up smoking and alcohol."*** Julian stared her in silence before replying. **"Leeshi, you could have began message at furthermore without preamble. You know, I don't yearn for male comforting so why…"** She cut his speech, saying. ***"You could have stopped at preamble, instead of telling me what I know."*** **Billy comes calling:** They ogled each other intensely, then laughed out loud and hugged, aborting the angst. It came upon a weekend night about 23:00 hours. Loud banging of the door. Boisterous male voice calling Felicia's name. She asked no One in particular. ***"What the hell him want now! Him just realize me still alive?"*** Then said to Julian. ***"Is Billy the idiot."*** He was yelling as loud as he ever could. ***"Open the door. Open the f…in' door let me see the man you have in there. Open the door, or I burn this place down right now. I draw gas from truck out here and ready to smoke everyone out."*** Felicia opened a side window and hollered. ***"Mama, mama, beg you come talk to Billy for me. He's out here in one of his mad spells."*** Julian thought. *"One of his mad spells? He does this shit routinely?"* Turning to Julian, lying on his stomach. Amused smile on his face. She at first stared, then asked. ***"How you lie down so calm. You realize there's a mad man out there who will really set fire to the place."*** That was frightening situation to contemplate, in rural enclave without telephone, hydrants or fast method summoning fire brigade. Nearest station being eighteen miles away. For sure the structure would burn and tumble down the hillside, before firefighters arrived. Strange how Julian did not surmise such possibilities as he laid on his stomach. Falsely comforted by press of blue steel onto his rib cage. Felicia yelled for mama until she began going hoarse, while Billy's voice got louder and more frenzied. Soon Barbara Fisher's voice was heard saying. *"Billy, a decent boy like you from a decent family. You think your parents would be proud of your carrying on? Coming to my gate with no respect for my family. With filthy expressions coming from your mouth? When Felicia brought you here, we thought you were a good boy. Of good parentage, who sent you to a good school and you graduated. Ready to take your place among upright folks of society. I never would have believed, you were capable of this kind of behaviour. But a little will show what great will be. I don't know if you and my daughter are still friends. I tremble to think if you two were married and misunderstanding arose. You would butcher her in uncontrolled rage. And say you're sorry, when faced with the gallows."* Then came the deafening sound of silence. Julian wondered if Billy had walked away, there was nothing being said. Finally Billy uttered in subdued voice. *"Ma Fisher, is some clothes Felicia have for me I come for. I never want to make ruption or disturb you. And cause you to come out of you bed this time of night. If you just ask Felicia pass out my clothes for me, I would..."* Her mother called out to Felicia. *"What you have for Billy? Hand them to me down the cellar."* A tee shirt with word "C O A C H" stencilled in large letters on back and front was handed to her mom who asked. *"This is it?! You certain?! Make sure, because I don't want come back up here."* She went up and gave the tee to Billy. Who, again expressed apology before driving off. Barbara Fisher who did not want to come back down there, did come back and rap hard on floor door. The bed had been re-positioned and Julian again shifted it aside. Felicia held it ajar and began. *"Mama, I never…"* Her mom cut her speech and began her own. *"I have to say something and it can't wait, in case I die tonight. Let me say it from now. Billy's carrying on was loud and disgraceful. Yours is just as disgraceful, in it's silence. It doesn't always have to take two, situation do alter cases. Good night, young man."* Julian decided he was not going to leave in middle of night. Billy might be lying in wait. Although equipped to defend himself against attack, doing so would be start of his life changing woes. He did expect to see tires flat in the morning. Now was the time for everyone to come clean, although they did not know this. Julian asked. **"What me want know is. What breeze blow him up here all of a sudden, after all this time you heard not a word from him?"** Then, Felicia slowly said. *"Actually, a girl who used to be my friend, before she and him started a thing. Saw me in my uniform one day, and told him where I worked. He called me but I told him I was busy. He came one evening, began talking bout how he missed me and wanted us to get back together. I told him that was not going to happen, no matter how much he pleaded. Then he really scared me when he said. It will either be him or nobody, and I should think about that. So I walked over to see Mr. Millings and told him what Billy said. Mr. Millings said he would talk to Billy's father and make sure he understood seriousness of his threat. Apart from that, I was really surprised to hear him out there tonight. He scared the daylights out of me. I never knew that side of him. You were so calm. What if he had really set the shop afire?"* Julian thought about it and replied. **"Our only chance of escape would have been the trap door."** To which Felicia replied. *"Billy knows about that door. He could easily waylay us as we emerged and do something to harm me, you or both of us."* "Don't worry your pretty little head. That is possibility, for which I planned and was well prepared. If Billy made a move to inflict hurt on either of us, he would not even live to regret it." So said Julian, taking the gun from his waist. Ejected magazine from the grip, and released one bullet from the chamber. Felicia stared with eyes wide open and mouth agape unable to speak. Let herself fall back onto the bed, where she laid staring at the ceiling. He sat with a cartridge and gun in one hand, magazine in other. Silence reigned as each deciphered their thoughts. She reached up and gently touched him, then patted space beside her. He laid down, she turned to, hugged him. Both fell asleep, just like that. Awoke to sound of slight drizzle making symphony on the zinc roof. It was then she spoke for first time in many hours. Said to him earnestly. **Start of the end?:** *"I want you to know, I love you. Would hate to lose you by any means. Don't do anything to make my worst fears a reality. I know why you think you need a gun. But you must know, the moment you use it will be.....What you planned telling police last night if Billy had attacked us and you retaliated?"* She did not want an answer. Immediately kissed his lips into silence. From that night on, things were just never the same, magic was lost. For one, he had problem looking Mrs. Fisher in the eye. Aware she put blame on him for night's fiasco. Not to mention, telling her daughter. How she disgraced herself by seemingly having relationship with two men at same time. He never could enjoy emotional contentment, not knowing if Billy would come back or lie in wait. That boy was going to be a long time getting over Felicia, if indeed he could. Unable or unwilling to overnight at her house, us time between them were curtailed and emotions waned. A year and some after the incident. Felicia introduced Julian to a young man doing internship at the firm. Born in Cayman, schooled in England. Was now doing apprenticeship before exams, to be qualified as attorney. They went here and there as friends, but she resolutely made it known. He would not be ringing her bell unless they both had same surnames.Told Julian with a grin. *"Next birthday, I'll be twenty-four. Too dam old, screwing for fun. It's time, life and living had a purpose. Ain't that right, Danke Schoen?"* He asked her. **"Danke Schoen?" "What's that mean?"** Felicia told him. *"Haven't a clue, but my British Caymanian chaperone uses it quite often with a smile. So it must have positive meaning with complimentary echoes. Come on, take it for it's intent. You don't have to know everything."* She said and followed with a tight hug. Ended with admiring stare. *"You really are last of greatest and best, a man without limits or boundaries. Remember what I said? I will always love you. No matter where I am, who I am with. Come here."* With that their long last kiss began. Isn't that a storybook ending? If only real life could be. Who knows? Times it probably is. So how did it all work out? There are some stories if told to end, strays from fiction to fact and we never want that to happen. Now we get a glimpse into what happens when people play the love triangle game. Julian and Billy both had wives and families, yet sought and found emotional comfort in Felicia's arms. She knew there could not be permanence with Julian, even as she accepted. Billy had lost interest in her. Having roster of women at his disposal from which to choose. So why did he come storming her door in dead of night? Would be content if no One showed interest in her. When someone did, suddenly, she shines like a new diamond.*Flask-214 There are two most common types of flasks in use presently. Vacuum flasks, best known by trade name "Thermos" for keeping liquids hot or cold. Flask referred to by Festus Fisher is commonly called **"Hip Flask"** Modern version was designed in 1920 by Osmond Jamouneau. Used solely for conveying liquor, it aids concealment and portability. Some are designed with vertical curve, allowing it to comfortably hug, person's leg or arm. Average bottles are bulbous, tall and cumbersome. Distillers, notably whiskey producers. Saw hip flask as unmistakable method, increasing sales. Wayfarer walks into a bar and gulps quick shot or two, quenching his parch. Moves on with eye on next town. With hip flask or two tucked in his boots, snug against his leg. Hits the dusty road, content in knowledge. Whenever he feels parch coming on, salvation lies in boots on leg or up sleeves on arm. Brings to fore, oft repeated phrase. "Necessity is the mother of invention"

Friends with Benefits?-28

Is a phrase we hear bandied about these days by people who would rather call the shovel a spatula. We know both are far removed from other, but allow folks to indulge their escapade. After all, it's no skin off anyone else's teeth. Things have changed in the oldest profession over time. Today it's hardly recognized for what it is. Couched in pseudo euphemisms and phrases, with tacit nods of acceptance or nonchalance. As a boy, there were two sisters who went "to work" every evening. Dressed nattily and skimpy, rouged and perfumed. Guardians commented on their way of life quite frequently, referring to them as H-O-R-E-S. That was their way speaking in codes to shield children's delicate ears. Those sisters stood on corners and hailed prospective clients. Once a price was settled, both went off to a dive and engaged. Each trying to make double or triple score for the night, if only she could be so lucky.What a life. Next, there were "call girls" who went when called. Usually by men, a notch above ordinary Joes. Methinks the phrase "kept woman" is more descriptive of the "friends with benefits" tag and yet not quite. A "kept woman" is like car kept in garage, should designated vehicle breaks down. Or when there's urge to go from sedan to roadster. Car is serviced and maintained but not available to other users. A girlfriend I know, has a "friend" who pays her rent, car note and gets accommodated when he signals intent to drop in. Other "friend" pays utility, food and personal maintenance bills. He sometimes has to settle for excuses. As to why she's not available, sometimes there's none. Both men know of other and accept, that over which neither has control. At slightest hint of jealousy or pet peeve disgruntlement. She gives either One the "finger" and says. ***"All it takes is a band of gold and two witnesses. I'm not fussy about church, maids and train. So long as you make me an honourable woman."*** Of course, both have already made their wives honourable and have no intention of ever dishonouring. This game will play on until someone quits. Few men can grip without gripe. Knowledge his woman sweats in another's embrace. When he's probably sweating in his wife's embrace. Leads to old standard. "I wonder who's kissing her now." So the naive might very well ask, how does this coming together of persons begin. Where is stage set and what are nuances of appeal and ensnaring. It's the age old hunting instinct.**This Game Begins:**With the "hunt." Both parties are out stalking the other. Each has to exhibit traits that makes him/her attractive. For a male, it depends on quality of woman he's trying to get. There's a saying, "The catch has to be worthy of the bait." Or "The prey has to be worth the hunt." Most men win by simply driving a model car with expensive price tag. If he's dressed cheap, or raggedy assed. He could be mistaken for detailer taking it for a spin or contraband dealer. He could also be the latter if he's appropriately dressed, but this is game of chance. Guided by instinct and sheer gut feeling. For a woman, looks most times makes her winner without effort. Attractive figure and face, she's past winning post. Has ability to pick, choose and refuse. He sees her go by and takes note of her manicure, pedicure, coif and quaffs at dining venues. Because those hands never prepare food in kitchen. Then he's overheard saying to a friend. He likes her, but she's high maintenance. As the saying goes back in the old country. "Every hoe that's made has stick growing in the bush." Two meet and greet. Watch them trying to find chink in armour. Giving an edge to outsmart each other. Wanting something for nothing or very little. He wants maximum benefits with least payout. She's trying to dangle a carrot, keeps him meeting her needs, eye on the prize. Always seemingly, ever so close at hand. At some point in this game, there will be verbal fights and vexation initiated by both. Just when he's about to close in on the prize and there's no more reasons to deny him. She accuses him of trivia and sends him packing. Fully aware, he is loathe to walk away from all he has invested. She knows he will come back bearing all good gifts. Penitent for the wrong, although he's not sure what it is. Now she gets to milk the Bull a bit longer. On his part, he's probably not satisfied with level of pleasure or somehow it's not working for him. He starts a fight, usually accuses her of having someone else. She throws him out or he leaves, with a contented smile. I hope nary a One of past girlfriends sees this, but as a teenager. Our clique had mantra to quarrel with our girlfriends, when birthdays or Christmas came around. That way we avoided buying gifts. Tried making up after season's end or next birthday remote. Truth be told we didn't have much to spend, and sometimes our girl found a lad who could. Moved on by time we came around to make up. Life was rough. Lester and Jethro are work buddies, both now retired. Lester is married to a younger Brazilian woman who swears at him often in Portuguese. He replies in Jamaican patois, which makes them evenly dumbfounded. Jethro is divorced and pinch hitting here and there, women he meets. Before each becomes disinterested in the other. Both are tight, one in fist and other in legs. He's with Brianna at doctor's office and needs her to send records to a specialist by email. She asks him the name, he tells her. She asks him to repeat then tells him. ***"Spell it".*** He toyed with spelling "IT", but didn't want to yank her chain. So he told her with a big grin. **"Moo like the cow and Young as you are."** She goes. ***"Ooh, you smoother than my silk pajamas."*** Jethro began his witty response but she says. ***"Uh-huh. Don't even go there…Dam. You slippery too. Put you in the basket and you be wiggling in my pocket."*** You can see she's making him out to be a coot. But she it was, who started this trip when she went to pajamas. Could have said he's smooth as silk, and stop. I guess she inadvertently opened a door. And quickly slammed it shut when realization hit. Let's credit her with good mental reflex. Lester tells Jethro he knows a nice looking woman. She divorced her husband when he was caught in a federal sting operation, and deported after serving time. Their children are adults out of college and pursuing respective family lives. He suggests waiting until after Christmas to go look for her. That way he's not caught up with door buster sales crowd and black Friday hustle.Worst of all, having to show intent by gifting. First week of new year, Lester asks Jethro to come by for his lawnmower from Sheena Pinto's home and get words in. That way it doesn't appear planned. They arrive and Jethro is introduced to Sheena, a fifty-ish woman who could pass for early forties. Talk about sex appeal. Jethro dribbled at the lips as Sheena asked, where in the ole country he came from. Jethro is taking time drinking her in and smiling his slow responses. Lester pushes the mower out to the truck. Then comes back, joins the two and says. **"Whapp'n Jeff, you making headway? Sheena have plus, big time. Unlike many other women. She born February 29ᵗʰ So you only buy birthday gift every four years."** Both men laughed up a riot and caught themselves, upon realizing Sheena was not sharing the joke. She said to Lester. *"You did not tell you friend the truth, the whole truth and nothing but the truth. You left out the best part. Should have told him I only f*** on my birthday. Know what else you should have told him? How you couldn't wait for it to snow. So you could scoop yellow snow into your sippy cup, no matter how many times your mom slapped you blue in the face."* She turned to Jethro and went on.*"Know how she finally cured his thirst for yellow snow? Took him by his feet and shook him upside down, while yelling. It's not pineapple syrup Lester, it's friggin' dog peepi. Try that shit today, they take the kid from you and send you up the freakin' river for life."* With that she turned on her heels and went inside. Lester told Jethro. **"She just thin skinned, can't take a joke."** Now, that fight got started from git go, ended before it's begun. Yellow snow makes second round? I'm thinking if a Donkey was nearby. Would Lester pick up droppings, thinking they're Granola Chunks? Kids needs constant watching for their well being. Yellow snow? The very thought chilllls. It's been said. *"Women are brainy. Men are brawny."*When both qualities coincide, it's foregone which will inundate other. Lester should have made comment to his friend, sotto voce. Giving advantage to use at discretion. That's how woman would have done, given similar situation. Men enjoy jokes that often, surprisingly boomerangs.

Days of the Week···?.

Reluctantly handing Jamie my credit card, I said. **"Your bosses should wear mask, holding gun in hand. That way, customers would know they're dealing with bandits. All costs paid by insurance. Charged $30 to send glasses to workshop?"** Silence prevailed, she gave me the card, said. *"Glasses ready, second week in June. Which day you want to come?"* Poring calendar. **"Lemme see. This Saturday."** *"We're closed, Saturdays."* **"What you talking bout? On your doors. "Open Weekdays 8:30-4:30 pm."** *"That's right, weekdays only. Monday to Friday."* **"Yeah! So what's Saturday and Sunday, if not weekdays?"** She thinks, I prod. **"Tell me! Ma Cherie. Gently as you can."** She says. *"You know? You're right. But, I don't make signs or rules. Hold on."* Takes up phone. *"Karl! Customer face time."* Man comes out in sleeveless tee, chest partly exposed. Would female customer appreciate? **"Yes, Sir. How can I...?"** *"He says the door sign is wrong. We should open Saturday and Sunday, because they're weekdays too."* Karl thinks, then says. *"What can I say? Customer is never wrong, always right. Get Antonio over here to change that sign. He needs to take out "Weekdays" and put "Monday to Friday."* Takes two steps, pauses at inner door. *"Oh! Give our customer a lollipop."* His chuckle rings as he disappears. I says to Jamie. **"I have a friend, whom if he was here, would tell your boss "The sarcastic is churlish and wasn't necessary."** She too chuckles and asks. *"Would your friend have meant to say "sarcasm" instead? Looks like everyone is having problem, saying what they mean. Which day for pickup?"* I was just feeling cantankerous at being fleeced. Wha yuh tink?

Meet the Winners:29

When thoughts are not fettered and enslaved by life's daily grind. Some of us indulge emotional luxury, reminiscing to ourselves or with partners and friends. The untold, forgotten saga of "How Mary met John" It's mostly an aah moment with quirky missteps. Now, inner being revels in delightful history. It was sports day and renewed rivalry between two high schools that were once one. Started out, coed institution, then became girls only and boys only. One kept original name, other adopted new monicker. Traditionally they played together, but in separation. Sports day reignited camaraderie in friendly, yet focused competitive environment. End of competition, both students with most points from variety of games, proudly stood on dais. Follow closely folks, because this is where it all begins. Acorn that's going to settle and become a shady Oak, if not mighty. He was Winston, she was Winsome. Everyone cheered the winning coincidence. *"Just look at them. He, manly handsome and her, so virginally appealing. So Antony and Cleopatra."* Gushed Mrs. Webb, a music teacher. Caught her errant musing with a shy smile and apologized. *"Pay me no mind. Moments such as these, I get carried away."* Well, both students probably felt way Mrs. Webb did as they exited stage, hand in hand. Loathed letting go of each from that day on. Wore each other to graduation festivities and soon became. Unmistakably a couple, although there were no formal. "Hear ye, hear ye." Most folks in his community, tended to be wary of Neville Gardner. Given his rambunctious temperament. Met at airport by the Winners. Oh, I didn't tell you. That's how Winston and Winsome were introduced to friends. Pa Gardner asks Winston, his intended son-in-law, with furied eyes and knitted brows. *"Whapp'n! You couldn't wait till after the wedding before you breed me daughter?"* Turned to Winsome, expressing disapproval. *"If me did know is belly wedding me coming to. Me would just send some money and stay on me job. Might as well give back the photographer money. Because me not going have any photo out there, with me walking belly woman down aisle."* Winsome piously began timid retort. **"Dad."** She got no farther as he went on. *"You might think it not showing, but a blind can see, you breeding. Is four woman besides your mother me breed. And me could tell everyone, them was breeding, long before them even know. Anyhow, as you granny always say. What gone bad in morning, can't come good by evening. Don't make sense try close gate, after the horse done bolt and running wild. Come Sam, grab the two heavy piece, and make we find a JUTA."* Winston figured his balls were big as Neville's. Respectfully set him straight. **"Winston, Mr. Gardner. Not Sam, sir."** Next he motioned to a hustler, had luggage taken to his Toyota Coaster. Neville Gardner did not take kindly being reprimanded, however respectfully done. Stepping into the vehicle he guffawed and said to Winston. *"Rass! Oonu did expect me pack America and bring with me. Why Oonu hire this helluva bus to come meet me."* A kerfuffle began, Winston said. **"Winsy! Talk to you father."** Neville retorted. *"No! You talk to me and say what you want say. You is man, don't shelter behind woman skirt tail."* You all can see this building into something ugly, and mark you. This was first time both men were seeing each other. Let's explore more. On all his trips home, Winsome's mother avoided mentioning any amorous affiliation between her daughter and any male. Knowing, Neville had openly stated intention to vet and approve or not. Any man coming forward to be with his daughters. Winsome was fourth to escape this process. Neville was far from the happy camper. Ignoring Neville's taunt, Winston went to and got the vehicle amoving. Winsome steered her dad to back of the bus and began. **"Dad, I respect and love you as my father. But you must recognize I am now all of twenty-four, and should be allowed to make my own decisions and mistakes. From which I will learn, as you did. Don't forget your mistakes that put you in jail four times. Yes, Nana told me and no. I haven't told anyone else, and don't intend to. Not even the man I marry. I say this to you, to say. Do not judge people, first time meeting them, without trying to find out what they're made of. When we get home I am going to show you. A full Yellow Page advertisement for company named "Winner's Coaches" Dad, look at me, relax your face. That's our company, we have four more like this one we are being driven in. Winston drives this one because it is brand new. You smell it? I'll tell you something else, you would never guess in a million years. You both took dangerous paths to better life. He made one big stride and came out winner. Before anyone even figured he was in the race. Relax dad and remember what Bob Marley said. Every little thing, gonna be awright."** By time trio arrived home, all jolly good fellows. Not anyone could guess airport scene and if told, would deem it a bold faced lie. Neville proudly held Winsome's hand and walked her down aisle, belly and all, despite earlier misgivings. Discounting his keen eyes, photographs and video shoot of event. Did not give hint to pregnancy. It could be assumed, peace on earth had been established, with goodwill among Winston and Neville. Alas, nothing could be farther from truth. Winsome vowed to her dad, not divulging what Nana related to her, regarding him. Yet, Winston's father, seeing him ham it up with Winsome, did sit his son down and relate.What he knew, assumed and suspected, relative to Neville's past. Back in day, undercover detectives went buying weed at the jerk pit. They paid and arrested twelve year old Neville, who was released in care of his parents. Two weeks later he was again arrested, taken to juvenile court, got probation. Lull in errant behaviour ensued until late teens, as he matured into bucking Bronco on his new Honda Dream motorcycle. Cavorting round town with females, he openly took to fun jug cat houses. Parked that bike out front to advertise his presence, whilst young women dodged in alleys. Fame went ahead of him until he took a soldier's wife pillion riding. A sting arrest was made and his herb stock confiscated. After four of five arrests followed by juvenile probation. Eighteen month sentence halved, another eighteen month sentence fully served. Neville went, prison to airport. Without anyone outside his circle, aware he had been set free. That embellished history, related by Winston's dad. Made Winsome's father a reprobate individual. Ended his narrative with bit of lore. ***"Memba now, young crabby swim behind old crabby."*** I should mention, Winston's father was Devonaire Kirlew. Retired cop at sergeant's rank on miserly pension, after forty-eight years service in constabulary. Still having to work as store watchman, to make ends meet. Self promoted to store detective, craving status. His wife, Miss Myrtle. Plied her trade as seamstress to church members and wider community. From whom, payments were slow coming to hand, if ever. This to say, there was no family wealth being passed down to seed Winston's enterprise. Having grown to present level of success. Call it envy or knowing the ropes, Neville looked at his daughter's and her husband's wealth. Knew something was amiss, to say. Not kosher. In life there are those who think small and most times get caught doing something they shouldn't. There's also those who think big and don't get caught in short run. Because wheels that would otherwise squeak are well greased. Speaking metaphorically now folks, please stay on track. There's this comparison of men passed down by other men, who see life's panacea in a bit of well planned skulduggery. Objective being to think big. Man caught shoplifting, gets five years hard labour in prison. Whilst man caught embezzling thousands, gets six months keeping commissary ledger and auditing shackles that will never be used on him. Indeed there are no peers in prison. Neville sat his daughter down for a serious talk and began.

"You know Winny, Sam is a smart bwoy…." She cut her dad short and stressed. **"Winston!! Dad, Winston. Where you get Sam from?"** Neville laughed out loud and said. *"Is really, Samfie me out to call him. But me going easy on him because you married to him. Don't stop me in middle of me talk when me chatting, show respect. No matter how old you be, you is still child and me is dawdy. Me was saying, with all smart him smart, me hope him also fair. Because very few man can see pile of money and decide to go fair and square with it. Next thing you know, danger hang over them head and also them family. When hataclaps come, it don't respect who is who. It come like when gully come down. Wash away whole village and drown them. So watch what Oonu doing. Me know at least three man, who did prosper quick and big for short time, before hataclaps drop on them. One did have big furniture store and when a bwoy come out of prison. And try reason with him bout promises, he failed to keep in respect of bwoy's youths and baby mother. Him have security guard chase bwoy out and threaten lock him up. Well, bwoy wait over theatre one morning when him come open store. Hail him with big grin, walk up to him and shot him dead pon sidewalk like stray dawg. Next One did set up mine with bulldozers and huge trucks working. Him two storey house did all have in elevator. Can you believe that? Down in bush there, house have in elevator.*

Same thing, bwoy come from prison and shot him dead." **"So, dad. Why tell me all this about those people. What they have to do with me and my husband?"** *"Well, Sam is him own man but you is my flesh and blood. So me just telling you make sure. Peter give Luke and John whatever them agree on, and don't try nyam wholea hog by himself. Craven choke puppy, him don't live to turn dawg. That's all me have to say for now."* Neville's parents both migrated in his youth. Left him in care of grandparents. It is not known if parents were married. One went to motherland whilst other went Dominion of Canada. It is understandable then, why he was coerced into petty crimes at an early age. Reputed to have sired seventeen children, he claimed some of those were "jackets" Meaning he was not their father but there was no way telling, back then. Released from prison he flew to England and joined armed forces. Parachuting mishap during training, left him with physical impediment and life pension. He moved to Canada, worked at a motorcycle assembly plant. Before moving to Bahamas, then United States. Rekindled love affair with Vilma, who bore his third child when both were fifteen years old, now an adult. They got married and he became stepfather to her four children, who did not conceal their loathing for him. Young adults and teenaged children will not find compatibility with brusque stepfather. There was always aura of low keyed tension that stymied harmonious existence. Despite angst, shortly after, he got green card and life was good. Never let it be said, he ignored his children's welfare. Doing everything to make sure they were cared for financially in every respect. He worked tirelessly in pursuit of that goal. Skilled in motorbike repairs, he joined partnership with a French born Vietnam veteran. Gained skill in small aircraft and helicopter engines maintenance. Poised for great advances, veteran retired and sold business shares to Neville.

It goes without being said, he now basked in that good life, resulting from wealth and prosperity. Telling his wife he had to pay homage to departed grandparents. Visited home once or twice a year. Prompting remark to daughter Winsome once. ***"Every time me come home, me find you breeding. Oonu trying to raise driver for each bus?"*** She wisely ignored his comment, concentrating on peak hour traffic. Generous and free handed when he came home, trouble was brewing for him unawares. Lawyer advised, he could start filing process for citizenship before expiry of his green card. Seems he misunderstood, and took list of qualified children. Which the lawyer perused and mailed back to their home. Wife Vilma, found two children, born after they had been married. He denied paternity, again claiming them to be jackets. But yielding to avoid negative clamour. However, rummaging through Western Union and bank statements. Found evidence of financial support to mothers of jackets, promptly divorced our Romeo. Of course, this created major setback in his pursuit of citizenship. His woes were short lived, as Mabel who had two children for him. Made proposal that called for payment of generous sum and employment at his business. Mabel does not mind rumours she hears, Neville still fathers children on frequent visits home. Theirs is marriage of agreed convenience. Having aged parents and siblings back home, she travels frequently also. Found her latest visit, conditional on being quarantined for a period. Winners' fleet has grown to ten coaches. Three units are operating from airport today. One of which will take Mabel, after contract passengers are bused to respective hotel. Flight delay pushes eta an hour ahead. Mabel gets huffy and sour pussy. Driver radios base. Complimentary fare, cantankerous. Cannot be accommodated with visitors. Grumpy Granny will detract from visitor's first impression of paradise. To hear them relate ordeal to friends.

"Oh, the bus crew that met us at the airport were a bit surly. Especially One woman who was probably a guide but kept silent with a long face the entire trip. We felt unwelcome as to be threatened." Couldn't have that perception given one minute of life. Base instructs driver to advise Mabel, delay has been extended two hours or possibly more. Hence, she had best reserve JUTA vehicle for her ride. Someone didn't think this sleight of hand through. Because, JUTA ride to Mabel's rural location would have been quite a purse. She did take a taxi, but to Winsome's house and the angst began in earnest. She called her husband, who declared he would take Mabel home later when he got home. Oh no, that would not happen, as unknown to Winners. Mabel gave their address as quarantine location during her stay. With arranged trips to visit parents and other family members. Folks were vexed stiff but smiled nevertheless. Tried to reason things amicably. After all, Mabel was Neville's wife, dad and father in law. So Winners had best tread softly, but yet asked. How could she do what she did without consulting and getting okay. As things are, there's no room to put her up and naked truth is. Winners don't want to be quarantined among someone they hardly know. Possibly putting their household at health risk. Well, Mabel did discuss this with Neville. He assured her he would talk to Winners. Mabel made it known, they were being extremely unreasonable. Expecting her to spend time in rural setting, without basic necessity of running and hot water for a shower. Had been years since she showered in leanto of posts and burlap sacks. Thought of again doing so, made her shiver involuntarily. Mabel was not up to fish for supper. Asked maid Merle, if there was chicken or other meat. Winsome, stiff lipped, reprimanded Mabel. ***"Please, whilst you are here, do not give instructions to our housekeeper. If something needs doing, speak to me. I will decide if it can***

be done or not. Remember, this is not Sheraton or Pegasus. Despite what my father might lead you to believe. Conduct yourself as any guest should. The way you would expect someone to conduct themselves, whilst a guest in your home." Two teen girls bunked, a bedroom was made available to Mabel with shower, toilet and basin. Closet was stocked with linen and towels. Lady of the house pointedly told guest. Who paid scant attention, if any. *"Whatever soiled towels, changed linen or clothes to be washed. Please take them downstairs to the laundry hamper. Woman to woman, I am sure you know better than, including underwear."* This would be typical cat fight, except that home cat had fangs at the ready. Alley cat was docile whilst seething. It cannot be taken as stealing, there's got to be other rational explanation. Methinks it was a way of One person deciding to exhibit a fu@& you attitude, but that's a guess. You know the passive aggressive psyche we often employ? Among toiletries placed at guest's disposal, Winsome pointedly included, packet of "Mr Clean" scrub sponges. Her way of conveying a message. *"You use the bathroom for two weeks, leave it the way you found it and here's what to do it with."* Not only did Mabel not clean anywhere, sponge pack was nowhere to be found when she left. I think she looked at that package with scorn and loathing. Fully aware of message being conveyed. Took and dumped it in trash, first chance she got. Reveling in covert aggressive retaliation. Methinks it's unnecessary overreach to ask, suggest or expect guest to clean bathroom before leaving. It reeks of pettiness and can only create ill will and reflect negatively on hostess. But then, what do I know about these things, and protocol of visitors and guests?

Making Safe Investments?-30

There's a fallacy, if ever there was one. Financial wizards can sense money making opportunities with remote chances of failure. Every investment is a gamble, in and of itself. Some have lower risk and others gravitate higher but none are safe. There is no ironclad guarantee of success, as we will see from this tale. Folks with high hopes, point to Amazon, Apple and other technology giants. Wish they had jumped in on ground floor and be basking in wealth today. Amazon is one out of millions that soared, yet hasn't paid a dividend. Remember banks that were too big to fail? Some did and had to be bailed out by federal funds. Amazon can fail, but there'll be no bailout. That scenario a focus, I'd rather be getting periodic dividends in dribs and drabs. I could at least see something coming in with the tide. Instead of knowing, my wealth rides the waves somewhere out there. Other endeavours sank so fast there was nary a murmur. Except when pledged assets were changing hands. Robert Morgan's first boy had walking impediment, some folks dubbed "knock knees" This was false diagnosis as seen by symptoms. Knock knees should result in wide space between ankles but this was not situation with Donald Morgan. His ankles bumped each other, causing him to fall quite often as a child. Not to mention skinning that made for frequent dabs of blue lotion and mercurochrome. Wisdom of lore frighted Roberta into seeking help from Beth Jacobs Family Planning Clinic. Them that were worldly wised, said. Donald's knees knocked, being their first born. Others following, would have feet plaited in deformity like vines hanging from guanghou trees. They had seen it before. Called names to verify, bystanders nodded in confirmation. Talk about, "Village Idiots" Doctors said his was a kind of polio and young Donald spent eight years at Rehab facility.

Parents, Robert and Roberta, were gardener and housemaid of pastor Huckerbancey. American charismatic leader whose church had large membership in, and community support. Back then, American citizen simply gave nod and an alien was allowed entry to US, temporary or permanent. Morgan's were set up where adults continued working with the church and Donald had access to "better" recuperative treatment. His issues were resolved by shoes being outfitted with ankle pads. Aided by forced habit, walking hippy cocky wide. Parents on other hand, still young in their thirties and ever ailing from frigid weather that courted pneumonia. Took up and relocated to sunny Florida, where too little too late, Roberta passed. Robert took her body home for interment in Gimme-me-bit family plot, and returned to face life as Portia did. Who is Portia? Grace-Gibson creation. Who is Grace-Gibson? Go Google. Robert gets hired by Pacifick Energy and Gas, where he meets Rosalind and soon after they get married. With two girls of her own, she cannot understand Robert's reluctance. Sealing their union with one, preferably two, children. Citing lore and uncertainty who carries bad genes. This not having been pursued before Roberta passed. Rosalind laughed that man to shame, went on to have two girls and a boy. Years rolled on and Donald was called up for military service, then excused as disabled. Shortly after, he went to be interviewed at PE&G. Was told to register at union hall and return with his card. Confirmed as member of the Brotherhood, he was hired on at PE&G as helper. Robert told his son he was bushwhacked into joining the union. This not mandated condition for employment. Nevertheless, deed already done, cautioned his son 'Let sleeping dogs lie.' One or two dogs are easier avoided, than a thousand fleas. Time marched on, life was good for everyone, barring expected challenges and those unexpected. Donald is now groundsman, working with two crew linemen on a pole. One asked for a baler, other a Kleins. Instead of sending equipment aloft by lanyard, he threw both items up. Kleins ricocheted off transformer base. Opened nasty gash over Donald's eye. He was given stitches and bill for services, which he questioned. Company had medical coverage and insurance for employees. He sought explanation from union steward who agreed. Taking matter to supervision, and HR if needs be. After work appointment with supervisor who explained. He did try getting a one time reimbursement at highest level. However, after review of facts, HR denied request. One, he should have used lanyard and two. There's doubt he wore a hard hat. Had he done so, tool would have been deflected by hat flange without hitting his face. Still seeking justice, Donald spoke with a co-worker who told him. He could get fired for doing so. Referred him to young woman at Claims, where incidents were revised under different rules. A midweek evening, Janice Hornsy met Donald Morgan outside her church. He immediately mused. *"This could be start of something big."* Janice told Donald, then tried explaining. His inability to grasp meaning, not yet a verified employee. Three years without reprimands in his file, were required. Before he could be verified. After which he would be eligible, for health and other benefits. Including enrolment in pension fund with company match, and all that good stuff. Both became thick as thieves. It was no surprise, their engagement was quietly announced. Quickly followed by marriage. Vainly trying to convince whisperers of obeying christian principles. But as is customary, no One was fooled. One month baby bumps are always visible to trained eyes. As years passed, so did Robert. Rosalind and two children from brood of five. Donald thought his father stayed on the job too long, until barely able to swing a shovel. Instead of retiring whilst able to live good, enjoying accumulated pension and

401. He planned stepping down at fifty years, before turning seventy. Realizing twin ambitions. Coveted fifty year plaque and cash canopy to weather storms. Janice felt debilitated, after three C sections, fibroids and heart valve surgery. She thought age sixty would be good time to abandon daily grind. Breathe easier before St. Peter came calling. Preparing for later years, both agreed it was time they acquired a home.

Indeed, counting rent paid over years, they could have paid for and owned a house of their own. Hoping to pay their children through college, savings were being accumulated for that grand purpose. Decision was taken to detour funds for down payment on their new home. Wisdom dictated, a bigger deposit for better interest rate and less recurring financing expenses, such as mortgage insurance. Both were agreed on this venture, until they went model viewing. Janice wanted kitchen and bath upgrades in place. Donald said, let's move in as sold and upgrade at leisurely pace later. We know, when it comes to matter of home and decor. Woman is going to have her way, by subtle or bustle. In after fact, thumb-finger snap. Someone suggested, they should have had attorney or at very least. Realtor representation at closing table. Financial difficulties arose, and by time legal services were secured. Shouting was over, participants gone home. They lost their deposit, irreversibly. Was a bad day in Eden as Adam blamed Eve, but they survived. Rancour quickly ebbed, then died. Woman, having Ace in hole. Picked selves up, dusted off and faced life with vigour. Borrowing from 401, they bought smaller townhouse and realized Exocet rise in value. Sold it after six years, moved into two storey, five bedroom house. Singing "Oh happy day" Of their three children, One is Pharmacist, other is Veterinarian and boy is into auto racing. His father complains to coworkers and relatives. **"That boy**

been going round track in circles all his life, like fu..in' mongrel with flea hive on it's tail." Janice feels differently, makes excuses for her son who lives at home. She retires at fifty-eight and nudges Donald to take short term guests in spare bedrooms. Tells him. *"There's good money in this BB thing, if you stop to think about it. We could pay off the mortgage, refund 401 sooner. Have money to splurge, do whatever we want."* Donald agreed with all that but balked, having strangers in his house. Reminded his wife. **"Jan! BB supposed to be. You have place you fix up. And people come there and stay by themself. All you do is furnish and put in house stuff. This is not like Peace Corps, or foreign student come live with you. And next thing you come down with Ebola."** Despite which, prospect of wealth from this endeavour lingers and grows. Possibilities appealing, he consults Realtor. She looks around, advises. There's a four three foreclosure nearby that would be ideal. A flip investor is bidding this property. Keeps outbidding her, she retreats, or appears to. One minute before bid closes, she shrewdly ups bid by one dollar. Gets property for her client. See what can be accomplished, having professional by your side, in your corner? Having secured the property, next comes refinancing their home. Maybe, another dip into 401 but BB property is ready for grand opening. Management company has occupied round clock, folks start thinking. *"We should have done this years ago. Imagine how much better off we would be? If only we had thought of this earlier."* That's where people say. *"I could have beaten myself."* Donald trained and went from groundsman to lineman over years. Climbed and belted off on pole, he didn't know was severely rotted, until top quarter sheared off. Surrounding him with three phases of thirteen kv and neutral wires. Inches from sweating, breath held body. Spoiled his flameproof britches repeatedly. Switches opened and closed, redirecting load, allowing for safe rescue. Recalling ordeal, seemingly eons long. Told, attempting to sidle round to other side of pole, not certain spurs and weight would be supported. Gave up the idea because, if he slipped. He'd fall and be filleted on zinc fence. Put his spurs in storage and trained as a splicer, which is by no means less dangerous. Underground vaults will erupt in hell flames that traps workers without warning, or escape avenue. Maiming and killing moreso than overhead lines. Let me say this, folks. Every time you enjoy comforts and convenience of electricity. Take a moment to consider and appreciate. Men and women who "work it hot" so as not to interrupt your service. Know that it is not a job for the faint hearted. Perils are numerous and come from most unexpected sources. Most times from hidden generic devices, by people trying to bilk free service. And someone doesn't go home to a family. Wife, children and wider family, solemnly gather in sorrow because of you. Poachers too, have been scarred and baconed in this illegal act. Think about that, next time you're prompted to attach device to steal electricity. Now, Donald is back where he started, in position called "Hustler" Basically it's a motorized gofer who takes equipment to field crews. Or shops for stationery, provisions, runs errands generally. Donald stacked vacation hours and benefits as he slowly progressed to retirement goal. Janice expressed anger, having retired at disadvantage to husband's benefits accrual. This, by her position being non-bargaining, and husband's in bargaining. Turned out he had no regrets, railroaded into the union. Although he would still benefit from negotiations and awards, without being dues paying member. On other hand, them that paid dues would see him as renegade Leech. Make life miserable for him. Some say, accidents could easily happen to people who didn't pay union dues, freeloaded instead. It would seem Morgans are swimming in wealth. New RV was acquired to go touring. Enjoying brochure sights unseen, of American landscape. They took to seas on massive liners and on one such voyage, dream began evolving into nightmare. Their ship denied docking. COVID had made it's worldwide debut and spreading unchecked like bubonic plague of 1800's. Sure, they were disappointed their fun trip had been curtailed. Yet, had no inkling of what was in making as a result of this potent virus. Reality of, soon hit them hard and unrelenting. Hospitality industry was at a standstill, by government order. Lockdown of commerce and some industries are order of the day, duration uncertain. As things now stands, it appears this state of affairs could prolong for quite some time. Now, that last minute one dollar bid has lost appeal and reason to exult. First casualty was RV, mere fourteen hundred miles driven, yet to be broken in. With all that's owed and can't be recouped, one thing becomes clear. Like his dad, Donald will be working for as long as it takes him to make an appearance, just as his father did. Quite contrary to his plans, but then. What choice does he conceivably have? Janice sulks and seems poorly, devoid of mental or physical will to carry on. Children encourage, rotate her for extended periods between them and families. Grandchildren delights, gives incentive to proudly watch them excel academically. Developing, tot to teen. Shows her phone screen to church members and ask. *"Would you believe, this is the first One? Not yet fifteen and look at her, could pass for grown woman. Hold on until you see her sister. Look, this One just turned twelve and…"* She gushes with grand parental delight as she kneels and prays for deliverance from above. Sometimes our life's endeavours can abound with missed fortunes or misfortunes. But how are we to know, what's among pearls before jumping in. See how "sure thing" gets derailed? Because, we never know. Here's a fictional item, mirroring fact of today. 1950's movie titled "Blondie's Hero" depicts scammers selling family's home, without their knowledge. Hardly a day passes without news item of someone renting a house that doesn't belong to them. Homeowners returned from visiting relatives in another state. Saw locksmith changing locks, at behest of realtor, whose name he could not produce. Yesteryear's fiction is today's fact of life. Indeed, fact is stranger than fiction

"In flagrante delicto"-31

Latin for "Caught in sexual or criminal act" Question arises. Have you ever been caught in similar situations? I have, repeatedly. Sprinted to safety, often. Caught and pummeled, just as often. But, here I stand again, looking around me. How about your catching someone in this position and either blabbed or kept your secret? Well now. Patrice's parents were both teachers at different schools, when she was four years old. Mom usually left home much earlier than dad, as she had to catch two buses. Whilst dad walked to work, when it didn't rain. Sometimes, Mr. Hogg gave him a ride. Both on staff at nearby school. Seeing the car approach their gate. Patrice rushed in daddy's room to hug and kiss him goodbye, as was her school morning ritual. This time, exuberance was dampened. She quietly backed out the door. Frightened by leer Miss Bertha flashed her, from supine position under her dad. Mr. Hogg was ever impatient. Honked once whilst creeping. If his coworker did not appear, he sped off and was gone. Needless to say, that's just what he did this morning. You see folks, Patrice's dad was having "one for the road." Simultaneous with dad's departure, Miss Bertha emerged and took Patrice's hand, unusually firmer than ever. On way to Mrs. Nesbeth's nursery school, quarter mile North on their street. On the way, Miss Bertha again glared at Patrice and told her. *"If you ever tell you mother anything. I make the boogeyman take you away and cut out you tongue. "You hear me?"* Patrice kept silent, grew, knowing there was no boogeyman. Adult, at Bertha's funeral. She whispered to, vowing a first met brother to secrecy also. But here is the catch. Neither knew, other existed before then. They stared and marveled, how each resembled Mr. Mack. It quickly got better as four more children came out from the woodwork. As is colloquially said. Without DNA test, not available anyhow. A blind could see they were all siblings of same father. Mr. McGregor in player role, stood out in this Caribbean isle. Syrian, Mulatto, Oriental mix, his kind tended grocery or haberdashery stores. Sometimes, hiring help from among blacks. But, never went prey hunting in the wider community. Preferring instead to let prey come knocking at their door. Player status was realm of Negroes, traditionally. It was not unusual, black children attending school with surnames that often identified with Syrian and Chinese population. Lue, HoChoy and Wongsam, naming few. Came about because Orientals hijacked mothers, whilst she was wrapping flour and chopping saltfish for next day's trade. This was secret that everybody guessed. Wife Madam, could hear husband's wooden slippers, clogging rhythmic taps on the palletized or concrete floor, as he pursued his nightcap. He was a wily One too. Never more than half filled provision barrels and each time the help bent down to scoop. Puff the magic dragon was "Fire in the hole" and mutual happiness existed. There was an embracing of peaceful coexistence as Madam did not fuss or cuss. Knowing there was no alternative, safeguarding her well being and future. Bertha's man would not get rankled, because family's larder would be adequately stocked. Children with elite or oriental name, had running start in life's marathon. Y'all recall when I came to Miami and was advised to get an easy name if I wanted to be favourably considered for employment. Thought my name was easy, until it was revealed. Name ending "EZ" was what my mentor had in mind. Martinez, Suarez, Hernandez. You get the picture. It's not racist, just a thing. I always encourage people with whom I relate, including my adult children. Discuss events of the living years, so there's no undisclosed, unresolved rancour. Sometimes I say, I'm sorry. Other times, tell them it was good, responsible parenting with their welfare in mind. Reminds them of fore parents lore which dictates."What doesn't kill, makes you stronger." So there, you are more resilient to Covid than others, who did not eat secret meat. Patrice wrestles with inner self, whether or not she should discuss her four year old experience with daddy. Brother prods and goads. *"Let him know he shattered your innocence at so tender an age."* I say for sure, jump at it whilst he's lucid and only in his nineties. Who knows if dementia won't set in tomorrow and he has no idea what you are talking about. Tell him whilst he can relive moment and realize, his shenanigans were well known. And being a good child, never breathed word to mom, who died not knowing. So to reinforce, I went YouTube and played Ronnie Dyson's "I think I'll tell her." Theme is in the title although lyrics doesn't coincide with situation. Mike and the Mechanics has more aptly titled song. "In the living years." What about you? Got anything to unload? This could be theme for fireside chat. Participants usually repair to den, back area or picnic ground at agreed intervals. For sole purpose, discussing subjects that nags at harmonious existence. Everyone comes clean, clears air and then comes copious quantities of vittles. Indulging to heart's delight, next season of goodwill and tranquility gets underway. Until…Four guys sat playing draughts or checkers, as some prefer. Fifth stood observing, all recalled boyhood days in their neighbourhood. Observer confessed how he walked atop brick wall to Mabel's house, where they romped in her backyard. Rejjie sought confirmation, before slugging him hard. Had he forgot, Mabel was now Rejjie's baby mother? Both having hooked up when she was fifteen? Her rendezvous with Mr. Happy was much later at her eighteen.

Customer Service-32

With a wry amusing twist, was how Al Parson's Home Depot visit ended recently. His house came new in 2004 with under sink disposable machine. You know, gadget that grinds food waste and sends them down drain. But they oxidize when not in use, soon seizes all together. After installing number three in July 2016 that has now froze. Said, he's decided it's time to discard and make straight drain connection. Handy in numerous trades, he figures out what's needed. Keeps pacing aisles, guided by signage but there's a piece missing. Pacing that aisle, tells himself it's got to be here. Section is plumbing, although choice seems limited. Female clerk comes, middle aged and looking so good all over. He slowly appraises her with a satisfied smile. She asks. *"Can I help you, Pops?"* He said. **"Yeeeeessss."** Still ogling her. She presses him, asks. *"What you looking for?"* He tells her project and what's missing. She says. *"Put those back and come with me."* Two aisles over, she gets pro lesson going. *"First, you need this to reconnect outflow from dishwasher. Then you need one of this and…..Is there separate drainpipes for each sink or are they connected?"* He tells her there's only one outlet to the wall, she moves farther along the aisle. *"You'll need this and one of this. Put back can of cement. These are all twist and connect fittings."* His attention is divided, hearing her but can't help, as said, 'drinking her in.' Wanting to prolong this brief engagement. Says to her. **"I have to admit, your knowledge surprises me, for a woman. I'll bet you are a Jill of all trades, fix it at your home."** She says. *"Sure am."* Then with a coy smile goes on to ask. *"You got anything you would like me to come and fix?"* She just opened the gate ajar, now watch this fella jump enthusiastically at the query and responds. **"Oh yes, lots of things and then you could stay for breakfast."** She goes. *"Whoa Pops, you sharp. I thought you were harmless. Where you from?"* He tells her. **"I'm from Jamaica, but don't let that spoil what could be good, mutually satisfying fun and games."** Now she's giving him that wary eye and says. *"You got all you need for your job? I gotta help that gentleman. He's been standing there for a long time. Okay?"* She kinda sidles off with both eyes on him in that amazed stare. Al figure she's early forties and knows for sure. She would not make invite to male, her age or younger. She looked at Pops with white hair on pate and face. Thought he was an invalid to whom she could holler "Get set" Not only did Pops spring up from his kneel, but sprinted down track before the gun. You know, Al will be frequent customer at that store. No, it's not stalking. Al will be subtly aloof and slowly, slowly, catch monkey. See how people play at work? Know how times arise you are in someone's presence, electing to engage that person in what is called "small talk?" Ostensibly to fill silence, or for no reason at all. It's like being asked. "How have you been?" Without expectation you will begin relating recent or past misfortunes. There being surprise if you should have fortunate encounters to relate. We are inclined to most times, dwell on and relate negatives, ignoring positives and blessings in our lives. Stephanie is young and appealing to the eye, especially so to grandpa Johnathon. He is in quest of big bucks as advertised on radio and television, resulting from a not to blame auto accident. She is legal secretary at attorney's office and coyly effusive when interacting with Johnathon. He looks forward to visiting her office. Johnathon is from out-of-town, residing in the 33033 district. Travelling to his attorney in the 33990 zone. Today, he seems bit off colour. Stephanie offers, then brings him a bottle of water. He sips and silence reigns as she goes through evidence files and statements. Looks at him and turns on that glowing smile, intended to offset blah. Says *"I'm certain should have a January calendar somewhere here. You never can lay a finger on what you need, except when you don't need them."* Continues rummaging. Looks up again and says to our Johnathon. *"So, you live in Miami and drive over here every now and then. Where do you stay?"* He perks up and replies. **"Oh, someplace. Why, you got somewhere else more comfortable?"** She goes. *"Hawwww, and here's a 2022."* Small talk got too big.

Having second thoughts-33

Charlie Shakespeare was neighbourhood patriarch in early nineties. Everyone respected his persona and knowledge of things past, present and future. Credited longevity to not ever been seen by medical doctor. Except when forced to do so, as enlisted member of British armed forces. Coaxed by a grand daughter to do chest X-ray. He agreed, with one stipulation. *"If them see anything, me rather it kill me slowly. Than go under knife and dead, poof."* Rationale being, death by malady is certain in time frame. Opting for cure by surgery. Can have immediate results of which patient is not aware, or prepared. Post office clerk told me recently*. "I would rather endure years of arthritic pain, than Rest in Peace forever."* So, it's taking advantage of guaranteed existence, go out in contented state of mind. A position I would embrace at age ninety but not at seventy going backward. There's always that yearning for long, happy life that gives surgery an appeal. If only it could always be done successfully, without surprising complications and finality. Sam Gooden was fifty-five in 2010. PCP recommended colonoscopy, endoscopy. Having been treated for stomach ulcer in previous years. Discussing this with workplace Brotherhood, Ned Bligh said. *"Shiiiiit, Man! Me had uncle by distant relative who they did that. He never made it back. You know they put camera on a stick and slide it up you ass all the way to you mouth and do slide show. When they draw it back out, some people can't deal with that. Remember now, if that camera get caught on anything up there?"* He left rest unsaid, but meaning was crystal clear. Sam sought assurances from his doctor, who told him the procedure was safe. Had performed countless surgeries without negative outcome. But, every medical procedure is risky. There's rare occasions, outcome can be unexpected. After that blunt slap, doc smiled. Touched Sam's hands, entwined in contemplative clasp on edge of the desk and said. *"Don't worry about a thing. I will take care of you. That much, I promise."* Didn't help assuring at appointment, accompanied by wife Myrna. He was given sheaves of pages to sign. All stating he was aware of and accepted risks. Will pay as billed if insurance doesn't. And absolves facility and staff from responsibility for negative outcome. His eyelids fluttered open, blinking rapidly. Stared into Antoinette Lue's eyes, who said. *"Hi, Mr Gooden. How you feeling?"* Sam looked around, rubbed his pate and replied. **"Feel awright doctor. It done now?"** She smiled. *"See? Promised I would take care of you. Didn't I? You're ready to go home within the hour."* Confidence established, Sam called her office for every malady arising. Only to be referred to specialists in their fields. Fifteen years after first, he mailed, home test kit provided by primary care physician. It was again suggested, there be repeat of the procedure, but alas. His trusted doctor was not on insurance provider's list. She could not or would not recommend someone from list he had. By contrast, wife Myrna had had both upper and lower scoping. Since Sam had his first, which convinced Sam to go ahead. You're reading a book that looks at "Everyday People at Work and Play." Sometimes they are doing neither, just being themselves, observing others at work and play. Myrna chided Sam's route, approaching the facility. Pointing out, he could not make left turn from avenue to street entrance. He told her, there had to be avenue access and followed a panel van. Signal changed and Sam ruminated on the van as it continued unhurried down avenue. It was grey-brown metallic with factory tinted windows. He knew those kind of vans, saw them often at three facilities on SW 117 avenue. Still stopped at signal, he watched the van turn into a place. Anxiety grew as he now hurried, on getting green. Confirmed his suspicion when he saw said van backed up at a service entrance. Stopped and said. **"Myrna! See that van? You know is somebody who kick, it come for?"** She looked at her husband with perplexed countenance. ***"Kick?! What you talking bout kick? Who kick who and what…..?"*** He slowly explained.**"Them work on somebody here and the person kick. Van you see there, only carry dead people to funeral home. Me know that for sure."** She told him. ***"That's a staff bus massa. Stop chat foolishness bout kick and funeral home. Turn in and find a spot before the place full up."*** Registration done, they waited for the call. Sam sat where he had partial view of the van, and focused eyes on. Hoping to confirm loading process. Myrna tried calming his anxiety, telling him to mind raising his pressure. Soon the van drove out, made a right turn going

North and stopped to chat briefly with driver of similar van entering. First van continued North and second van turned into courtyard, parking where other had. Suddenly warm he swiped a sleeve across his forehead. That was it for Sam, he blurted. **"Rassclawt Myrna! You see that? One run out and another run in."** She scolded. *"Sam, you is big man. Behave yourself. What wrong with you?. See people looking on we, like we drop from sky and…."* Receptionist called Sam's name. He walked to the window. Looked at the van, long and fixedly, then told her. **"Give me a five, me have to go use bathroom."** Off he went, after pausing by Myrna to whisper. **"Come, me going home right now. Today is not my day. Me going home go pray for deliverance or a sign."** Sam never went back to have his procedure done. It's been eight years since he ran out of the building a Thursday morning. He has herbs plot in back his yard. Growing Guinea Hen weed, Leaf of life, Fever Grass, Vervain, Sinkle Bible (Aloes) and Ram Goat roses to name a few. Two fences are overgrown with Cerasee and his Soursop tree gives leaves and fruits. All of which he consumes, guided by lore. Primary care doctor recommends, plethora of shots to ward off illnesses. Starting with flu, to bubonic plague. All of which he declines with reply. **"Doctor, me prefer dead from myself than from something you going put in me. Can't give away certain for uncertain these days."** We all will die one day. How long will Sam go on? What with onset of Covid 19 and…? Sam now boasts superhuman powers and indestructibility. Doesn't obey mask mandate and claims not to have taken any of available Covid shots. Now finds he's odd man out, because he's denied access most places without wearing face mask.Told family at gathering. He's happy not to catch anything from them, being all masked. One retorts, they're happy not being infected by him. Ah well.

Who is Lola?..-34

That's not question to Jeopardy quiz answer. It is start of a mental odyssey on which people embarked. Not knowing how it got started, or how and when it would end. Because that's life's essence of "Everyday people at work and play." Sometimes we jest, resulting in serious, unexpected, negative outcomes and if One were to stop and think of every outcome arising from spoken word or phrase. We would never get around to saying a lot about very little. Felicita at ten years old, was fourth of six children, and last girl born to family Delgado. It went without being said, she was daddy's pet although he denied it. Mom, an ICI had gone shopping for a week in Miami. Getting wares to stock her "Bend Down Plaza" store for upcoming independence week celebrations. Felicita's class was going on educational trip to Denbigh agricultural fair, for which funds covering transport and lunch had already been paid. She came home a Monday and said to her father, Richmond. *"Daddy, Miss say that we don't have to wear school shoes to the fair. Can wear sneakers if we want."* He replied. **"Well, you mother in Miami where she can get a nice pair sneakers for five dollars or less. But there's no way to reach her and me not going buy one for arm and leg from higgler."** Next day she revived the subject with glee, saying. *"Dad, Melanie mother say she'll sell you a sneakers for three hundred dollars. Only because is me."* Knowing, wife Sandra and Melanie's mother, Petula were friends. He yet maintained opposition to the bargain. Felicita intensified her moping, until Thursday she came home and found a box with sneakers on her bed. She kissed and hugged her dad, squeezing him in gratitude. He bantered. **"Child, is what we feeding you make you get so strong overnight?"** They both laughed, she was taken aback by a final comment.

"Now you going start thinking you name Lola." She asked. *"Who is Lola?"* He told her. **"That's a long story and older than you."** She went to fair Friday. Did essay on event, for submission Monday. Mental focus was taken, figuring who was Lola. Didn't help any, when she sweetly asked dad again and he laughed, before telling her. **"Bwoy, you born name woman areddy. Once one woman hear another woman name. Every strand of hair on her head start jook like macka and the scratching begin. You too young for start going bald."** And he laughed again. Let me interpret that last comment so you get a clear picture. *"Even in youth, she is already showing woman's curiosity on hearing another woman's name. To extent, her hair becomes prickles and thorns. Itching her scalp, causing her to scratch incessantly."* You can see where this light hearted exchange, initiated by dad to his ten year old. Potentially, is going to snowball down a hillside, although he hasn't a clue it will. Sandra comes home, her friend who is a Customs Broker clears her goods. She's businesswoman with purpose. Came upon a calm night. Richmond and Sandra in bed, she says to him. *"Richie! Is which One of you concubine name Lola, and why you have to introduce her to my child?"* Shocked into silence, he was at loss for words. She side elbowed him, none too gently. *"Answer me, is a question I ask you. Whapp'n, you dumb all of a sudden?"* He slid off the bed sideways, hitting the floor hard. Switched a lamp on and stared her in the face, asking. **"You going break few ribs me have left. You can't satisfy with one you get already? Me don't know which Lola you talking bout. I hope is not the little joke I run with Ceeta. She take and swell up you head. Make you going on like when Baboon want wife."** He was jovial and laughing but she was riled, now seeing red. Rising from the bed and near berserk. Ruckus soon woke mother-in-law, who entered the bedroom, asked. *"What ah gwone?"* Richmond responded. **"Ma Phil, you daughter getting mad. Go to her bed and dream me have woman name Lola. Is that make she jump up and start boco."** Sandra adamantly declared there would be neither peace or piece in the house. Until she knew who the hell was Lola and how long has this been going on. Deprived of that night's piece and frightened by threat of no more. He sat his dubious wife down and explained as best he could. **"You never used to listen to Rediffusion? Them did have a long time song, bout girl name Lola. Whatever she want, she always get. That's what me was joking with Ceeta and tell her, she going on like Lola. Nuh real Lola not exist and that is truth what God and Devil love. That's one thing, two of them agree on. Have to get truth, or else."** Her still angry, asked him. *"You think this is a joking matter you dealing with. Talking bout God and Devil love truth? I going get to bottom of this and find out bout this ready fashion."* **"Psst! Rediffusion. Nothing not name ready fashion. Dressmaker business you gone into."** He guffawed. She had last word, saying. *"Me going walk you out. Might do something I regret."* Life went on, subdued and muted as tension thrived. One could not get piece and other, not satisfied with Lola explanation could find no mental peace. Sunday came and so did friend, Glen the Broker. To collect for services rendered, two weeks hence. Sandra was an exceptional client of his company. Worked exclusively for corporate clients and did not work for informal importers. She was only client he extended credit for services rendered, because this has to be kept fictionalized. He stepped in the house and hugged his god-daughter, who ran to hug uncle Glen. He said out loud. **"Rawtid Sandy, smell you pot two miles up the road. As a youth round Backbush, you would need me to watch it. Once you stop** smell it, you know it gone." She replied. *"You time it right. Five more minutes and it ready. Have some soup meantime. Janine, come set the table."* She called a daughter. Glen yelled out. **"Richie!! Man in you house. Come out and make sure him behave himself."** Richie appears, begins a gabfest with Glen. Sandra interrupts, says. *"Sit down and have soup."* Glen says to Sandra. **"Business before pleasure, because that's why I am here. If I start eat and my gut full. I might forget my real mission. So, let's get that out the way."** Sandra tells him. *"Me not going run away for little monkey money I owe you. Sit down, have you soup."* Now, Glen goes biblical. **"A feast is made for laughter and wine maketh merry, but money answereth all things. Amen. Thus endeth reading from good book."** Quashing disbelief before it's aired, quickly adds. **"Ecclesiastes 10 verse 19."** There was a hush, as Sandra went off and returned with a cheque that she handed to Glen. He let it flutter to the floor and settle, before taking it up. Looked at the couple and said. **"You know how much of these I drop. And them jump up into my hand, all pass over my head. But Oonu is good people, let us eat."** Sandra lifted a hand to the ceiling, saying. *"Lord. You see liberties me have to put up with, just because me poor? Send me a dream with magic numbers, I pray you."* There was gaiety as those present sat down to eat. Ceeta told godfather Glen, she got B+ for essay. He rewarded her with a hug and promise to get her the bicycle she's been asking for. It will be stuffed in her stocking. Sandra scolds her daughter. Watch this, folks. *"How much times I tell you, no talking at dinner table?"* It is written. "Example is better than precept." We shouldn't say or convey to a child. I can do or say it, but you can't because you're child. *"Sorry, mama."* A chastened, contrite Felicita whispered. Silence reigned fifteen seconds. Sandra cleared her throat and began. *"Glen,* *you is a man big into music, with you disco and know whole heap of songs by heart. What is this Lola song?"* He furrowed brows in concentration before asking. **"Lola song. What Lola song? Me nuh know no….You mean, song bout woman name Lola? Mind you tawkin bout, Layla."** Sandra, now energized, remarked. *"See? If Glen don't know bout the Lola song, that means it don't exist."* Richmond put his fork down and said with stridency. *"Glen! You not senile yet. There's song use to sing on radio. And it say, whatever Lola want….."* Glen jumped in with recognition. **"Oh! You mean, Sarah Vaughn's from the fifties? Between 1956 and 1958 I think. That Oonu talking bout?"** Richmond nodded enthusiastically. Sandra looked warily at Glen, dared him to. *"Sing the song make me hear."* So he stood and assumed a sultry, cabaret pose. Began singing in suggestive voice and poise. *"Whatever Low-la wants, moimama Low-la gets, moimama and little man little Lola wants you."* Went on amid laughter. **"I can't recall the words, it was years ago I used to hear music like that on Rediffusion."** Sandra was laughing hardest and between gasps for air, told Glen. *"Massa, we never did have Rediffusion up in Lawrence Tavern back in them times. Matter of fact we never even have electric. But is one thing me can tell you. If business get bad, you can go turn Go-go and dance on pole. Make woman stick money in you brief waist."* She was still laughing herself to tears. When hilarity ended, dinner resumed. Sandra asked children seated at table. *"Is what Oonu laughing for, who give Oonu joke?"* Quickly told Felicita. *"See Ceeta? You father was telling you joke from a song. Because you wanti wanti and always geti geti. You better pray you find a man in life, who can live up to that. Man with letters behind him name."* Richmond jumped in, adding. **"Instead of numbers on him chest, robed in white or stripes."** And the laughs began anew. Sandra hugged her husband and kissed top of his pate telling him. *"You lucky, Glen come here today. Save you skin and bring peace with him and piece for you."* Glen looked stumped and Sandra added. *"It's an inside story that have to stay inside."* Like ship at sea, this joke created waves that crested and rocked the boat. Eventually, all was calm again, until next joke gets told by **"Everyday People at Work and Play."** We are by nature, complex animals. Because we were given skill of and ability to reason. Like other animals, we are designed with levels of intelligence. Ability to rationalize is our inherent Achilles heel. Whether by divine design or evolution, this element of our being. Will ultimately serve purpose, annihilating our specie from planet earth. Be comforted, you won't be here. Know why?

Criminal Confessions:-35

Here is one more Vox Populi email from a Reader: *"Your novels "People at Play" and "People at Work and Play" states, contents are fictional. But in some instances, seem so poignantly factual they take on wings of reality and fact. Question arises. Is it fictionalized fact, designed to disguise places, people and truth or what?"* Giving an informed response. Author would point out, fiction is essentially lies in print. A lie or truth begins with a subject, then goes on to elucidate on said subject. In manner that's totally or partially one or other. Hence, truth or lie, must have a genesis to take on existence. Neither can materialize independently in and of itself. If response seems ambiguous, that too is a trite element of fiction. Having cleared that up, let's get on with next episode which although fictional, could be deemed factual.

Every person of double digit years through to centenarians. Will engage in some kind of criminal act in their lifetime, yet swearing to contrary. Seeking absolution by claiming deeds as "petty," "borrowing" and "those little things don't count." But, they do. Of course there are Kleptomaniacs. Proven impulse control disorder, occurring mostly in females. Career criminals whose crimes does not always involve objects per se. Pursue criminal activity across wider gamut from fraud to murder. Let me allay raised eyebrows by stating. There was no murder involved in what's related here. Gilbert Oakley was called Gill, reported to his fifth job since leaving high school. On his twenty-first birthday, 1966 with a company in John Crook Group. One-man band, handling clearance of company's imports. He was well versed in aspects of this undertaking. Enjoyed camaraderie with staff at government agencies, steamship and airline offices. Made for easy access thru doors and across red tapes. Roxy Reid was office Friday who among other duties. Cleared mail box, when Morrie messenger went awol. From one or more of many age related maladies he suffered. Roxy too ran errands for managers and secretaries. Collected cheques from clients and was almost given task, taking lodgement to nearby, Barclay's Bank DCO. Cashier, Mrs. Decaprio looked long and hard at Roxy, then told him. ***"You too young to walk with so much money. I will take it, on my lunch time. Tell Mr. Betton I said so, and if he has questions, he's to come and speak with me."*** Roxy made his signature retort ***"But how that now."*** Followed by amused cackle. Quite often, items had to be taken to head office for signature. Gill was signing officer for incoming drafts and import documents, provided a director also signed. Came one day, Roxy brought unsigned drafts. Directors were in emergency meeting. Said to Gill. ***"Me can draw Webster fist and nobody woulda know difference, not even Webster himself."*** Gill told Roxy, he was tired. Welcomed absence of signature, giving him alibi taking respite. Yet he took note of

Roxy's offer . Wondered at thought process of an elementary school dropout, with skill to accurately forge. Yearning for a chance to prove he could. Roxy was epitome of oft quoted phrase. Marginally educated but brilliantly smart. Type of fellow who could sell you a Bull, point to it's extended gut and promise it will calve in two months. We know, light only glow where there's dark, so it takes two to tango and lots more. When management crowned Roxy with hat of being Gill's right hand aide in addition to. Gill hesitated burdening him with chores. Although needing help, Roxy's basket overflowed. He in turn told Gill. *"Use me, man. Me want learn what you do. So me can seat behind desk like you and pay what go with it. But how that now?"* He followed with signature cackle of a laugh. Let's pause Roxy's story for awhile, as his mother enters the picture and stays put.

Mrs. Decaprio buzzed Gill, saying. Marilyn Oliphant waits in the lobby for Roxy, but will speak with Gill. At sea for a minute, recognizing surname and asked she sends visitor in. She sternly reminded, company policy does not allow visitors who are not customers and Gill should know bett...." He interrupted. **"Mrs. Decaprio. I am midstream something here. Please send the lady in. I will be brief and not make habit of it. Please? Thanks much, you're ever so kind, understanding and accommodating."** She replied. *"Don't lay it down so thick you might slip in it."* Young woman walked briskly to Gill's desk, spoke muffled. *"Morning Mr. Gill, me is Roxy mother. You can step outside little bit so me can spit?"* Both walked out. Her, fast paced ahead to the Lignum Vitae tree mound where she unloaded a glob. *"Ptui."* All this time, Gill's head is trying to reconcile her being Roxy's mother. He just made twenty-one and her seeming to be a big sister, began. *"Me wake with a toothache and go to* *the dentist up Peters Lane. Him say the teeth have to come out and is ten and six. If me want him use cocaine, is going be twelve and six.(shillings and pence) Pardon me, sir. Ptui. Yes, beg pardon, sir. As me was saying just now. The teeth hurting me all the way down to me..."* **"How much more you need?"** He asked as she's doing the math and not coming to grips. So he offers. **"Will five shillings do?"** *"Oh yes, sir. More than. Me did never want bother you. But the lady did tell me Roxy not here. Me will make sure him give you back. Pardon me, sir. Ptui. Alright Mr. Gill, God bless you sir. Roxy tell me you is a good boss and it look like is true. You must make we meet again, when me jaw not be like Constant Spring."* Monday came and Gill asked Roxy how his mom was doing, if the dentist visit eased her distress. He replied not going to see her over the weekend. Opted spending time with his girlfriend, who did not get along with his mother. Friday evening, Gill visited Marilyn to see how she was doing. She assumed he was there to collect on a loan. Preempting, she began. *"Me sorry you have to beat track come for the money, after you was kind to help me out. But Roxy don't come look for me, going over two weeks now. Him be with a girl who have two fatherless twin, and they be like termite in board house."* He told her he was calling to see how her dentist visit went and if she's okay. Ventured to say with a titter. **"I guess you're better, as your mouth not like Constant Spring."** She joined the titter with a laugh, asked as he made to leave. *"So is really doctor visit you making. What kind of hurry you into so? You have fish spwoiling?"* So, they sat for a getting to know you gab, she went first. *"If I was to tell you..... I not happy how my life turn out, you would want to know why. So, I is going tell you. Because me have to tell somebody. And although you much younger than me, you have big position with big* *business. So you must be well smart. Me is poorest of my mother's children. Because me never did get good school opportunity like others. Who don't have government job, flying up and down on plane as stewarder. Every minute them keep birthday or Christmas party and invite me. But as usual, me end up servant in kitchen. Last time me tell them, me done with Cinderella shit. Them can no bother invite me to no more party. Unless me can dress up, come sit down as guest and enjoy meself. From that them not into me but me not care. Me tell them, kiss my wawty behine."* A friendship began. Gill warmed to Marilyn, admiring rounded full bodied frame. Lusting, wondering how he could get with her as more than friends, given age difference. Wasn't an issue for him. He had scaled higher fences. Thought it might be for her. Time marched on, she began visiting his ranch. Evening they settled in, after stuffing guts with curried goat and plain rice. Washed down with Peardrax, she was enjoying very first time. Refilled her tumbler twice. Making Gill guardedly elated at possibilities. She was curious, how in youth he came to have position with the company. Did he go to which high school. Did he have a full time woman. He told her what he could, she resumed her story. Frequently pausing to suck food remnants through her teeth. Swirling tongue around gum line before swallowing. Stuck a finger back to molar in deft concentration. Emerged with fragment on fingernail, admired, picked it off with incisor. Nibbled and swallowed, after sigh of content, before going on. Ugh, ugh. *"Is really Pantry me name. Me mother husband sign paper, name me Oliphant when me almost eight and them married. Me was a chubby child and right away. Melvin did love lift me up and play with me, and me always laugh. But when him start play.... down there, the joke stop. Me did know that was not no playing, but.... me blame meself. Because me never say anything to him or anyone. Thirteen year old, me start breed same time with me mother. Roxy born February, Dawn born April. So me have two baby to mind same time, wash nappy and everything. See here, sir. When me mother find out me breeding. That woman cut me ass one whole week straight. Night and day, couldn't siddung straight. Haffi tilt me batty pon one side, like when yabbaw broken.* (Yabbaw is Arawak domestic bowl of fired clay) *That's how me behine get to look like toad back. So me run way to me Granny, tell her is Melvin breed me. Me mother come there, say is lie me telling on her husband. Because she know, is him brother, Raymond breed me. Me and Raymond was like sister and brother, although him four or five years older. Me know them want pull shame. So, them going swear on cross that Raymond is Roxy father. Him believe him father in England and Melvin is him uncle. Well now, me was young and very foolish. Tell truth, shame brush daub me too and me did galong with the play. That's how me get Evadney when me fifteen, and there is where the mystery lies. Because by that time now, both of them. Married man and single brother, took turns with me. Sawka me front, like them ah shave ice for snowball. Lawd!! Me tell you. Is not for want of tongue, why cow don't talk…..So, who knows who is who, done what? Joanna father was going make me wife. But people whisper into him people them ears. All of a sudden, Clive drop me like hot blue drawz. From that, me keep meself to meself and don't bother with man. After me breed with Roxy and stop from school. Is like me never get to really go back full. Because me was mother for all my mother's children. She only push them out, like how fowl push out egg from him batty. Me had to be there to catch them, wash them and take care of them. Never see a lazier woman in me life, all day long she have headache. At the time me did glad to don't go school. Not knowing it was going stunted me future. But me have to tell you, school was living hell with a name like that. And as me tell you, me was a chubby child. So it was easy for Oliphant to change and called something else living in jungle. Me mother always tell me, pray me find a man and married early so me name can change. Only change is, me have three pickneys and just turn thirty-five. Which man in him right mind going take up woman with three pickneys already? So when them come showing teeth and promising uptown and downtown. Me just smile and lap me skirt between me foots."* Seeing an opening, he casually asked. **"It really have warts?"** She retorted. *"What?! You nuh believe me?"* He shrugged, flippantly serious, said.**"Make me seet".** She stood, hoisted her skirt, eased her drawers down. **"Oh! You have Keloid skin? Is batty, so nobody not interested how it look. Me think is a good "B" side. Make me see hit side and the pasture."** She spun round and there it was. After a satisfied stare and long silence, she asked. *"Well?"* He said. **"Nice little punny, me mean, Pony. Him crop grass round where him tie. So One don't have to look for him. Open the gate and is him that. Me can see him well cared for, plump and round. Ready for laps round the....You wouldn't believe, but me always have saddle, just in case."** Stoically silent all this time, she finally reacted, hissing teeth and said. *"You have plenty lyrics as if you can stand up for youself. At any rate, you know Roxy older than you. Him call you boss, but him older than you. If is even a day, him still older than you."* Gill chuckled and replied. **"First of all, me ride Mac before me coulda even siddung steady. When it come to Roxy now, we in different category. Him pass through once in him lifetime and can't go back. But man like me, can come and go as much as we like so long as gate open."**

She tittered and. *"Well, when you come. Make sure you bring enough grass to keep Pony happy. Or else next thing, one backfoot reach you head and you stunted."* She laughed loud and long, suddenly got serious. Beckoned him closer with a finger and said. *"Me rent due month end and me owe ten shillings in the back. If you can take on the burden, it will make me happy. If me happy, that mean you ten time happy. Come and go as you like, not even haffi rap pon door. Just walk in like man a yawd. Not a soul to ask who you, or wha you want. So, what you have to say now?"* There was no need for verbal response, his smile told all there was to say. He dove in as is said, headlong. Seizing the opportunity to revel and romp to heart's content and beyond. That's where bit of discontent arose. Gill found it hard to maintain pace with Marilyn's fervour. She had pent emotions, having abstained since having third child. Gill, in youthful prime. Made multiple forays in weeds. Coming away bruised and chapped. Began making excuses to pass up rendezvous. Came home one evening, told by landlady. *"One woman was here asking for you. She was out the gate standing for a good while. If you don't see her, she probably catch a bus and gone."* Folklore would say, Gill bit off more than he could chew or "Greedy choke puppy." Way he saw things, she was enjoying privilege, double dipping. Having rent paid, not to mention loans that never got repaid plus thrill of being sexually sated. Way things turned out, I would say Marilyn was twice a winner. Gill was not losing out on this deal. It comes down to oft told tale, of the king. Hearing contented purr of his cat as he stroked her. Paused to question, who was being comforted by whom. Not giving himself rational answer, tossed Pussy over parapet inwardly gloating. *"Let's see you land on all fours as reputed."* Hoping she didn't. We just always want to be absolute winners in life's games, and that's sometimes called being selfish. If you think Gill is carping, distancing himself from Marilyn, you are mistaken. She's ever at his pad and always heads first to refrigerator. Where she takes and slowly sips, no less than three bottles, often more. Either "Babycham" "Peardrax or "Cydrax." Most times preferring variety of what's called. "Creeping liquors." Comes up on you slowly, then feather touch, knocks you over. Seems when somewhat inebriated, she loses inhibitions.

Now let's get back to Roxy's and Gill's story as it develops over years. Roxy was quick to grasp methods and procedures. Which, once he got hang of would volunteer taking steps to fruition. This played to Gill's benefit as he had more time to be less occupied. Saw that? Access limited as an itinerant, Roxy suggested. Gill file documents with authorities making him, associate clerk. Again, this to Gill's benefit, but moreso to Roxy's. He now began hustling or as is said, moonlighting. That is, helping people with personal business and getting paid for doing so. Time was, Mrs. Decaprio would buzz Gill and ask if Roxy is late again. Making a habit of being tardy. Her cage being out front, she saw everyone coming and going. No One died and appointed her timekeeper, but she zealously took on task. Gill covered for Roxy, saying. He told Roxy to stop at a department, get things done before that office got crowded. Hence his seemingly late arrival in office. Roxy turned up one morning. Straddling a gleaming new 50cc bike and was never again late to work. Watch this young fellow now, capitalizing on his bike. Convinced Gill it was in company's interest, using his bike on round town errands. Tween various government departments, including far flung places such as airport. Suggestion taken to management and rate set for using bike on company business. Roxy was not done. Went to office attendant, Miss Rachel. Who shopped for goods, making morning snacks, cooked lunches and hot or cold beverages for staff. Usually she took taxi to and from market and wholesalers. On such occasions, Roxy was taxi and his fortunes soared. Wherever he went hustling he was not averse, sharing earnings with facilitators. Creating doors of preferential accommodation and passage. One coworker named the bike, Mrs. Roxy. Given time spent polishing and preening the machine by him. He told the man with a big grin. He had to keep the bike new to get best price, when he sold it to buy a car, which would be very soon. Second year of his employment, Roxy told Gill. He would take the test to be qualified and licensed in their profession. Gill told him, he was confident he would pass. Congratulated him on coming so far so soon, urged him to keep on pushing. As expected, Roxy passed required tests and was rewarded with licence to practice. Soon after, landed first client and unfamiliar product, asking Gill's guidance. It was then, Roxy confidentially said to Gill. *"Hey boss, me have a book, you know."* **"What kind of book?"** Gill asked. *"Book, what can get anything and don't cost nothing."* Roxy replied with self composed grin. That evening they went by Moby Dick's lounge. Roxy took Gill into sworn confidence. He had purchase order book, and had used it to get goods from various places. **"What kind of goods?"** Gill asked. *"You know? Things for set up business. Typewriter, Marchant calculator. Pitney Bowes machine and a nice two tone, Chubb filing safe."* Jaws agape, Gill told him. **"Roxy! Them things have serial number and will send you go jail. What you need postage machine for. You doing mass mailing? Let me tell you what you don't know. When you carry machine go post office to pay for stamps. Right away, serial number going tell is bandoolu."** Roxy countered. *"Watch me boss. When bill them come, them get lost right away. Hey! Hey! Hey!. If a bill get through to* *accounts, them haffi find which department charge it to and that take time. Memba now, boss. Company don't write cheque and pay one another. Them do thing name reconcile, that's what Claudia upstairs tell me. She have file thick so with bills that she still trying to charge out to departments."* Gill thought a minute, said. **"Roxy, look at me mouth. This company sell Diebold, Sankey Sheldon, Monroe. Question arising will be. Why we buying something from Geddes Grant, we sell? Think bout that, it not no way foolproof. Me Granny say, tell it to dead Jackass, him get up and kick you."** Wouldn't you think, Gill would have no part of this thievery? You sure would, but you would be so wrong. Roxy went on, as Gill listened. *"Me get oil, tyre and things for my bike. You know how long? All now nobody not ask question bout anything. Your car coulda use set of tyre you know, boss. If you wait till mosquito season. You won't able go anywhere without get plenty puncture tyre."* Roxy urged. Gill was hesitant taking advantage, although tempted. As was custom, Roxy asked to borrow Gill's car, taking his woman or children to doctor. Again urged Gill to have tyres changed. **"You sure this thing can work?"** Dubious Gill asked Roxy, who confidently replied. *"Sure as spider that ate the fly."* Came evening, Gill walked out. Saw his car at the kerb with new tyres and balancing weights, including spare. He was apprehensive but what the hell, deed was already done. Noticed also, petrol goose neck gate resting on bumper. Surmised Roxy had syphoned gas from his tank. Dash gauge confirming, Gill went to nearby Shell station. Began chatting up classy, smiling female attendant. During and after she filled the tank, then hung the hose. Impatient motorist began honking. Gill hurriedly began exiting onto Harbour street. Braked, yielding to passing traffic. At same time a motorist braked and yielded to Gill, he drove out. Only to be flagged by a speedcop who was riding behind motorist that yielded to Gill. Accused Gill, driving careless, dangerous and reckless. Forcing yielding motorist to brake, avoiding collision and speedcop closely in tow. Almost collided with car ahead when forced to stop by Gill's action. Cop checked licence and papers, peered windshield disc. Began slow vehicle walk round, asked. *"Why the rear licence plate being disguised?"* Simultaneously, raised gate with booted foot then letting it fall back in place. Pounced on Gill. *"What's your licence plate number?"* Gill without hesitation, replied. **"Y3758."** Cop asked. *"So, why is AR790 plate on your car, different from plate on front and what in the book? Don't bother try answer, we going Elletson Road. Just follow me."* Gill's mind raced, he quickly figured out what took place. AR790 was company's plate. Roxy switched it when taking Gill's car to tyre dealer.. Ensuring, plate would appear on invoice. Therefore, escape intense scrutiny. Cop kick started his Triumph motorcycle, shut it down, walked back to Gill and said. *"You know what? I will follow. You know where we going, lead the way."* Elletson Road was regional compound on vast acreage that headquartered constabulary's motorized division. Station and jail facilities. Serious as things seemed, soon became evident, cop was not in pursuit of upholding law. Gill's response to exchange of plates, surmised. Vehicles having had repairs at same garage, somehow plates were removed and misplaced. Allowed phone call to Roxy who eventually came and compounded issue. Driving company car to the station without one plate. Cop saw his fortunes grow as he assailed Roxy. Quickly set bailment at two pounds each. Gill did not have cash but could get a cheque cashed at the Shell. Cop kept Gill's licence and paperwork, telling him to go and hurry back. Arriving at base, Roxy found a manager had been enquiring after the car so he had to give up keys. Gill was not going to ride pillion on a bike if his life depended on it and. Dusk fell by time he exited a bus and walked into station compound. Cop told him. *"See how you make me drive leave me? You have to carry me home now to Pembroke Hall."* Gill headed South going shorter route. Cop asked his intentions, then told him. *"No! no! You must learn always to ask questions. Don't just jump and do what you feel, like you in charge all the time. Turn round and drive through Cross Roads, so me can stop Hi-Lo and get groceries."* Not one word was exchanged between both men, during nearly two hours. Caught in snail traffic until nearing end, cop told Gill. *"One church round the corner, drive in there. Me wife and daughter in there and will help carry the bag them. Bring them in and rest them on the bench at the back. Thank you, sir."* It was then, cop handed over Gilly's licence and papers, told him. *"You is good bwoy, but you must learn to ask question and don't gwone like you know everything. That way you keep out of trouble. Else, you going wet you foot sooner or later."* How was he to know, Gill's feet already been wet and would later wade into deeper waters. Now, a truth of human nature becomes clear. As time went by and there was no question about tyres. Gill became emboldened, getting batteries and accessories from Roxy without fear of being caught or having to pay. It's human psyche with anything forbidden. First time out, there's timidity, waryness and fear being caught. With every successful escapade, these deterrents decrease until replaced by boldness. That's invisible force that drives serial killers or repeat embezzlers. Most times, therein lies the Waterloo.

Here's where we begin another phase of Gill, Roxy adventure and fortunes take wings. In case it was not clear, alliance began early 1960's and lasted well into mid 2000's with ups and downs. Gill sassed a big wig and was fired a year later, at which time Roxy filled the slot. Straightway expressed deep reservation and disappointment, not being paid Gill's salary. Management told him, it was take or leave it situation. He took it for a year and some before quitting, to join a firm run by two retirees. One a former upper level civil servant, other of equal status in private sector. We are now in mid seventies, a decade since this saga began. Lots of things have changed. Roxy is banking on both aged retirees, either dying or having to stay home. Ceding business ownership to him. Truth be told, his is persona that clients came to be acquainted with. Making deliveries, collecting documents, arranging rigging, crane equipment as required. Old guys seen as figureheads, consulted out of respect. As each waned in health, ultimately passing. Roxy took over and expanded the business. Can you believe that? Gill too had set up business in same field, enjoying tremendous success. Acquired real estate, vehicles, got married and started a family. Met quite often with Roxy, reminiscing unashamedly on good old days. Both expressed surprise the caper had gone unnoticed and nary a sound heard about this period of thievery. Roxy smugly told Gill. *"Me did tell you but you never believe. Know how much more things you coulda get if you never fraid of you shadow? Me have house full of stuff me don't know what to do with. Can't sell them and not going give them to nobody. Because you know how black people stay. Them tell you thanks, then go blab to them friend and next thing you know. Is either them friend come rob you. Or police come to find out where you get things from."* So it was, Gill went to Roxy's house by invite to a party, was led into private room. Took interest in Chubb fire resistant cabinet and two hanging scales. One, thirty pound Detecto and twenty pound/kilo calibrated Chatillon. There was talk in mercantile circles of government's pending introduction in trade. Decimalized system of weights and measures. A weekend, Gill went to his gate for choice Butterfish from fishmonger and took his scale. Told her to use it weighing his fish buy, going forward. They got into debate, she offered to buy it. He agreed for twenty pounds of fish over four weeks. Deal was struck at fourteen pounds over three weeks using Gill's scale each time. In show of good faith, Gill decided to highlight self inflicted disadvantage to monger, saying. **"You know, me watch how you do you thing. Customer pick out fish, you clean and gut them before you put them in the scale and weigh them. Know how much you lose in gut and scale? You should weigh fish first and clean them after."** Oh, Miss Ivy had a good long stare and loud laugh before replying. *"Stop it Massa, my scale not hang up like Chineeman. Fish go in before my scale go up. If you selling anything at all, whatever it is. If you don't have tricks in trade, you can't make profit."* She looked at Gill and laughed again. To think, he thought she was stupid. Because she didn't attend college or graduate from, as he did. She didn't say as much, but her laugh conveyed sneer. Other scale he kept and can't recall, how or why it's no longer in his possession. Maybe it went way it came, having appeal to someone else. Chubb filing cabinet was a safe, with combination lock and fire resistant insulation, Gill used to secure documents at working day's end. Of course over time, people make acquaintances and friends anew. One of whom for Gill was Leonard, a young flashy talk-to-be-seen-and-heard lawyer. He was in some circles cloaked with flamboyant title, worn with pride. Befitting familial connect to Liberian president, William Tolbert. As told by him, his father was cousin or some kin, making Leonard somewhere in lineage of greatness. He was going on safari and invited Gill to grand national affair. Bestowing honours and countrywide celebrations. Tad short being knighted or sainted in ritual and pomp. Cousin and party would be official guests, accorded privileges befitting. Gill always wanted to do Africa, yet as might be recalled. Jamaica was at politically unstable juncture, early seventies forward. Gill took trips to Miami and New York quite often, yet Africa seemed light years away. There was always news of coups and counter coups. Gill feared, no guarantee One could catch next flight if need arose. So it was, he passed on grand Africa junket, seeing lions and elephants close hand.. Well, what do you know folks? Leonard was living it up at family estate in Liberia. Filling numerous rolls of film, depicting pageantry and safari sights to bring home. Day of April 12th, 1980 kinfolks set out on trip to somewhere and soon sniffed trouble in the air. Coup led by Master Sergeant Samuel Doe, raided compound Leonard and kin had just left. Slaughtered every living soul, including President Tolbert. As Leonard tells, news caused instant breakdown of sinew and physical well being. Bedlam reigned, upheavals ran amok. Never had he seen so many machetes, wielded aloft and glinting in sunlight as natives rampaged. There was no knowing who was law or outlaw, as money was demanded for safe passage. Enemies among them that offered escape, for a price. Massacred or captured, some of his party, took them away, fate unknown. Resigning to fate he somehow got on a 747 bound for America. Didn't matter where, any place out of Liberia was a haven. He swears that plane flew nonstop for more than twenty-four hours. Us listeners told him. What did he know? He fell asleep, was unaware of plane landing for refuelling before taking off again. He avers differently. Saying he slept and awoke to hear silent scream of jet engines in his ears. Fell asleep and awoke twice again to same low pitched wheee ringing in his ears. Of course, not having papers got him confined to semi jail until diplomatic pursuits unravelled situation. People looked on in wonder as he laid prostrate and kissed tarmac at Kingston's Norman Manley International. Bobby Lee was joker of the pack, saying. Tony Bennett left his heart in San Francisco. Leonard could have done same in Africa, the ancestral motherland. Came mid nineties Gill had an office building, choice real estate with retail showroom and offices on ground floor. First floor had three tenants, One of whom was a trucker. Came looking for space to set up a despatch and accounting office. Building in rear was leased to an appliance repair and sales company. Then trouble began with trucker. Second month going forward, he paid no rent. Lawyer Leonard, began collection proceedings, morphing into eviction pursuit. Trucker began coming to office in hunting fatigues, toting shotguns that appeared authentic. Although laws there were against this. He began bringing trucks to office for minor repairs. Blocking access and egress to other occupants. Appliance company was first to move and trucker simply took over the workshop and began servicing vehicles. Lawyer Leonard served court injunctions, writs, estoppel and all necessary legal rigmarole. Without tangible abatement of distress to property owner, including payment of rent. Adding insult to injury, people from trucker's side frequently stressed doors. Gaining access to client's effects in safe storage. Stole paintings, stereo equipment, phonograph records and memorabilia among other valuables. Gill and Leonard sat down to deliberate what could be done. Courts weren't working in their favour. Creeping at snail's pace, whilst situation deteriorated from worst to unbearable. Lawyer Leonard had a solution. ***"Burn down the place and grab insurance."*** That plan did not find favour with Gill, who knew there was no perfect crime. Prison was not on to-do list. Roxy was certain, deed could be pursued with easy chances of success. Took on role of mastermind. In preparation for, he moved office furniture and equipment. Desks, chairs, typewriters, photocopier and prized Chubb cabinet. Trucked in, decrepit wooden pieces bought from Queen's Warehouse auction. Exhibiting genius, he told Gill. *"Steel furniture can't burn, they only singe and distort. Old wood is like dry hay in barn fire."* Gill yet had reservations, but gallows was already built. Noose around a neck, waiting for trap door swinging loose. Friday, plan was put in motion and both retired to Roxy's house in the hills with panoramic city view. They could accurately identify general area of building's location. Eyed area for billowing flames and smoke all night to early morning without success. Saturday morning they went down and everything was same as night before. Roxy knows where plan failed, urged. Let's do this again, outcome guaranteed. Gill took it as an omen of good tidings the plan failed. Told Roxy, bring back the furniture and equipment. Was astounded when Roxy told him in surprised stance. *"Rassclawt!! Gill? Me sell them things before me come get them. Me couldn't have them things anywhere round me. You have to just call that a loss and move on. I mean, look at you. Not like you going hungry or shelterless. Hug it up and move on, you name man."* That was it, end of an adventure and an era. I am certain people will cite karma at work. Roxy and Marilyn both passed from respiratory issues. He from apnea in 2008, years after his mother, from asthma. On entering the church, Roxy's hands were by his side. During the service, one began rising until it was visible. Leonard asided Gill saying. *"They better hurry before he start sitting up."* Both are old men, still friends. Talk about Roxy's funeral, but never talk about the failed arson or lost furniture. If you take you have to be prepared to give in like manner. If ever there's one thing certain about our existence, it's uncertainty of it. So we embark on Play and Work until…… Whew, what a litany of peoples, places, skulduggery and their crapola..as you yawn, open mouthed and blink bleary eyed. Yes, go sip a sip. There's more.

Mother & Daughter-36

Felix Rattigan walked into the ethnic store, greeted Guyanese proprietor Akbar and said to him. **"See? I brought my cheque book today. No more fussin' and fightin' now."** Akbar told him. *"I is not much for like cheque, because people does have lots paper, but no money. For where this shop stay I much prefer card, debit or credit. That way they come to steal, I show till very much empty."* Felix replied. **"First thing you should know, Akbar. If the man come for to get money and you show he empty till, he likely shoot you or something bad. You see, Akbar. He be vex, very very much vex. So, it's good have something for robbers. Next point I want making is. You charge fee for I pay with credit card and…."** *"No! No no, you very wrong. Not I charge. People who take money and give me, they take that charge. It not make Akbar rich, he still barely poor. See? I lose weight last year and not get back."* Felix continues. **"No matter how much weight you lose. When I go the Publix, the Bravo or the Walmart. I not pay extra charge. They sell one dollar, they too pay guy to collect."** Akbar insists on being right, he avers. *"Those name you call, they make millions every day. So what is few hundreds to them? We is small people, and we gots to support each…..Good morning mam. I see you for first time and say very special welcome. Come boy, make way for customer."* Felix asks. **"So what me be, beggar from Salvation Army. Me ringing bell. Where the kettle?"** As he looks the lady over and is pleased with what he sees. She is a handsome, mature lady. Maybe late sixties. Has matured gracefully with that school teacher or nurse persona about her. Offering a hand, he introduces. **"Felix Rattigan, at your service mam. I see a list and since this your first visit. I would be obliged if you allowed me to be your guide."** Turns out she was shopping for "Miss Birdie" Easter bun and "Tastee" cheese. Both quickly recognized they were Jamaicans and as is common. She asked, where in Jamaica he's from. He named various places in Kingston and St Andrew. She was from Tombstone, St Elizabeth parish. Held a finger up as her phone rang. Answered and stepped outdoors for privacy or best reception. Felix thought *"Dam, she might not come back and I didn't get her name or anything."* Twenty minutes later she came back and said. ***"My last daughter. She works at a medical facility and thinks she has to update me on every patient she sees. I'm her last hope. Her husband and children all have things to do when she wants their ears. I would too but what else do I have to do? So, I listen and say. Hmm, hmm and, Oh no, I hope not. It is parade of empty chairs in a playhouse. I just remembered, I never told you my name. I am Felicia."*** Agog with excitement, he told her. **"Can you believe that? Felix and Felicia."** She smiled and replied. *"Isn't that a coincidence?"* She focussed scanning shelves and finally asked Felix. *"You remember "Castile" bath soap?"* He told her. **"Yes, but I think Akbar don't sell it. You have to go Jamaican shop, like one at SW 160 Street. You know where me talking?"** Just then her phone rang and she hurried outside again. Soon forced to curtail her call as light drizzle began. Was now steady downpour with bright sunlight overhead. Felix took his cheque book out and Akbar told him. ***"I not take charge, this time only. Because you help lady with buy stuff."*** He knew what Akbar meant but pretended not to. **"Oh, thanks Akbar. If I knew you were going to reward me with free fish, I would have taken more."** Akbar and Felicia simultaneously asked. *"Free fish?"* Akbar sneered and went on. *"Something happen in you head that not good. Grab it before it spreads rest of you. Listen boy, my wife don't take nothing out this shop and not pay."* That settled, Felix and Felicia stood aside watching the rain, making small talk. She retired from Matron's position at Black River Hospital. Waxed warm how she enjoyed the job despite workload. Built facing, nearly touching the Caribbean Sea. Gave calming allure to facility, not found elsewhere. Rain not showing signs abating, she asked Felix how he came to the store. Having come by bus, the bay was a walk away. Could he give her a ride to the bus bay. He offered taking her home, quickly pointing out. He could not drive on Busway. Restricted to buses and authorized vehicles. She eyed him reproachfully and asked. *"Who says I want you to know where I live? My husband would not appreciate my being brought home by a man I met two hours ago."* Felix told her, he would get her close to Busway as he could. Resumed chatting about this and that. Belting herself in the seat, she said. *"If it's not too much trouble, I am on 187 Terrace near to 122 Avenue."* Gave him a mischievous eyelid flutter. At the address, she told him. *"Come inside, let me reward you with jar of wonderful fruit preserves for your troubles."* He chuckled and said. **"I have to tell you, my running days are done. So where's your husband?"** She told him. *"I'm only One you have to fear, there's no reason you should want to run from me. So stop being silly and come on."* Top of steps she told him. *"Park your truck in the driveway. This street is generic racetrack, that's why houses lost fences."* Entering, he stood awkwardly until she said. *"You can sit anywhere. This is not a theatre, so don't wait to be seated.*

Let me open a window or two. I use air-condition sparingly in effort to stretch pennies. So, tell me about yourself. How young are you?" Felix told her he was seventy-four. She said she was right behind him at seventy-two, but he looked mid sixties. He returned the compliment, telling her she doesn't look day older than sixty-two. **"You know Felicia, turning on central air only at certain times. Uses more or same amount electricity, as running it full time?"** *"Yes, how you arrive at that?"* **"Okay. Your thermostat is showing 85 right now. If you set it at say, 76 and leave it running. Once it cools to 76, it only comes on for five minutes each cycle to stay at 76. Where it really burns current, is coming from 85 to 76 every time it's turned on. It's like in Jamaica, where car climbing uphill. But once it gets to the crest it can coast down other side on fumes."** All this time she's looking at him with a wry smile, then says. *"If I turn it on and go talk with my neighbour at the fence. It keep me cooler out there, than if I stay inside the house."* Felix simply said **"Oh, I see."** She went on. *"My husband took a loan to work on this house, when we bought it eleven years ago. We migrated here. Our adult children in England, Spain, Canada but none in Jamaica. Him couldn't stand him heel, like sprig pop up through the leather. Kept going back to Jamaica to tie up loose ends. Sometimes three, four times for one year. I asked myself but couldn't understand. What kind of ends this man could be tying up. I never knew, it was a rope to hang himself. Was at the point, I don't ask questions because I don't want hear lies. Since I couldn't follow him to help hold the cord, I just let him be. It's poetic, but you know people say. Give him rope to hang himself. Money he borrowed to fix our house, he used to build a house in Spaldings for woman. Much younger woman than himself, she had three children. I don't know if the children* *or any are his. Anyhow, five years ago he was there and to what I hear. The woman's man and Cyril knocked heads, and people part them. But days later they found his body. It is mystery unsolved, nobody knows. Well, children wanted me to go make funeral arrangements. They love their father, but don't understand pain he caused their mother. I prayed about the matter, was relieved of a guilty conscience. I don't know how that story ended. I don't qualify for assistance in this country. Although I pay into social security, since I began working at the nursing home, right after I came up. Other than that, my children are sole source of support. I can't ask them to remodel a house. While I have to be scrimping, to pay back loan my husband squandered. Is either that or let them take it from over my head. Put my things out on sidewalk, like I see so many places. God forbid, I hope and pray. Or go kotch with one of my children and their family. I don't want to do that. Because your children will love and do anything for you. However, spouses can be fly in sore at times. That's why some canker never heal, they only get worse with time. You want something to drink? I only have sodas. I don't drink them, but I quickly offer them to visitors."* Felix told her he didn't do sodas either, because of sugar and caffeine content. There was silence, she said. *"So, what happen? I want to hear bout your family. You married? I want to know, because I don't want to harbour a married man round me. My conscience is not allow it."* Felix thought. *"This lady very conscientious."* Went to his life story that was not dramatic as hers. It was close to eleven when he bid her goodbye that night. During which she paused conversation twice to take calls from her daughter. Can you believe that? He was a happy man making progress. Called Saturday, asked her to Sunday breakfast at Island Restaurant, she accepted. After eating, took her to his house where she was taken aback. ***"This is a big house for you alone. Two storey and brand new."*** Felix told her it was over fifteen years old, to which she scoffed. ***"Fifteen? If my house was even forty years old, I would feel good. I think it was built in sixties or early seventies. So you can see why it falling apart."*** Her daughter called, Felix drove themselves to the park. They relaxed and gabbed some more. Months into their friendship, she told him. ***"If you want my company, I will stay at your house sometimes. I know what's going on in your mind, because you done born name man. But to tell you the truth, it's been so long. I cleanse my system of those feelings. Don't expect a change anytime soon. So, I will use your guest room if you agree. I just telling you, so you don't start walking round with…..excuse me. Rochelle calling. Lord help that child."*** If you ever knew Felix, you would know things are not going as he expected. First weekend she spent, the house was too cold at 76. He raised it to 78 and it was a bit warm. He told her to turn on and gauge overhead fans. He's watching Perry Mason 00:20 hours and she's on phone with her daughter. Felix is thinking, if that's how it would be if they were in bed together. Finds the thought distressing. Already warned to not expect such a situation any time soon. You know the more remote his prospects seem, Felicia loses shine and appeal. Felix thinks if it ever gets off the ground, this could be start of something big. Felicia is a mature desirable woman. She's kept herself pristine and flawless, firm handful with ever pleasant smile. He mentally mutters in brief incoherence. You remember the Italian wedding in that movie.Was either Godfather or Goodfellas. Guest sees bridal purse envelopes with cash lying in a room and exults in Italian. How happy he would be and wanting to get his hands on the stash. So much, so near, yet so far. Another day, finds Felix at Akbar's shop. He heads to the freezer and Akbar calls him. *"Boy, you just walk in the shop. You not even say, bless you Akbar. Come here, I is want to say you something."* "Boy" is term used by some Caribbean people in lieu of sir. It does not convey disrespect, as among some African Americans. Akbar goes on. *"I does got some ladies coming today for to get Butterfish. I know you is love the Butterfish. Let me show you right here, what you not see. Banga Mary, Snapper, Sea Wiskers, Pink Parrot. They all nice fish. So, I is appreciate you good business. I is also appreciate housewifes too. Happy if you mix you fish. That's all I say. Two this, and more two that keep everybody happy."* Felix let's out long sigh, begins. **"Akbar, me buy only what me like. All them fish you showing, not what me like. Again, we come back to Winn Dixie and Publix and Sedano's, where me buy what me want and nobody don't…."** Akbar puts a hand on Felix's shoulder and pleads. *"My friend, my brother. I is happy you come my store and not Publix, but see my condition. The fish guy in Orlando. Eighty pounds Butterfish? He asks. What else? I say, only. Because I have much other fish not yet sell. He say, no. You want eighty pound Butterfish? You buy twenty pound this. Twenty pound that and twenty pound other. So tell me, you in my position. What you say to customer, who only buy Butterfish?"* Felix responds. **"Akbar, that's why me don't sell fish, me only buy fish."** Then laughs at his genius. Akbar makes final thrust. *"You mix this time, I not make you pay card charge."* He stares Felix for acceptance that's not coming, so he adds in a whisper. *"Also, I take fifty cents every pound. Make special price, only for you. Because you good man, good customer too."* Assuming all's well, he changes subject and. *"How nice lady and you doing? I be look through glass. See you hold paper over she head, and rain does near drown you. I say to me. Look that boy. He* *hardly can walk. Water does full he boot and heavy down he dam feet. All for looking what he not got and not going get. I tell you boy, that lady not be no come and go. She be class, because she gots big glass in she bedroom. And every morning, she does looks in there and says to she self. I is still class, just like yesterday. I go tell you boy…. That be thirteen dollar, twenty two cents, mam. Very much happy you have coins, if not I try..Thank you again, very good. Glad to see you. Tell you sister, I get Iguana."* He glances about and resumes in low whisper.*"Yes boy, I is tell you how you get class woman in you bed. First, you is got to marry she. Take she home, feed she, clothe she, give everything. And always be smile, when put up with she shit and the all family too. She does tell you, lend she brother money and you say "How many." I does know, because me been there, boy. That way, when she does come bed at night. She is drop pyjama outside door."* Felix asks. **"Pajama? Woman not wear pajama, them wear nightie or negligee. Man wear pajama."** *"No boy, you never not see Guyanese woman, when she coming bed for she man. She never do them nightgown and neglijeans you talking bout. She does have on pyjama. I tell you now. I is see my wife and me daughters, they all put on the pyjama."* Felix says. **"So what the man wear?"** *"He not wear nothing…Thank you mam. Always happy, see you in the store and you bring good luck too. Lady came last week, she say you tell she we here. Thank you much, tell more and God bless. Look boy is like animals, all kinds. Dog, hog, cow, goat you look at all them there. Woman animal got tail cover the behine. You not see the, the, you know what. But now, man animal he just there with bells swing. And the, the, right under the belly."* Felix laughs loud and long, during which Akbar checks one more customer then tells Felix. *"You gots to talk inside you shut.*

(shirt*). Me not want customer think, they in shop with two man whore."* Felix goes on. **"But Akbar, them animals you talk bout. Man kind have tail cover him behine too. You got two sons in you house. They walk round with they bells flopping and….."** *"Ah my friend, that too protect him from sodomy. You watch, man animal fight over woman. One who know him lose already. Watch what him do. Lap tail tight over he behine till it reach under belly. Because he fraid winner jump him, just like what man in prison. Adam offspring is only kind, do him own kind. And later now, Eve offspring start do she kind too. But I tell you, if my son be walk with in my house, the bells for me to see. I cut and put them in he mouth to swallow. I swear."* Felix paid for mix of fish and went home in happy wider frame of mind than when he awoke. Stops by Felicia, gabs a bit before saying goodbye. She tells him, hang on a second while she consults her brain. Seems deep in thought, says she will get ready and come with him. Today being Friday instead of usual Saturday, but *"The house feel heavy sometimes."* Oh, sorry I haven't been keeping you abreast of happenings. It's been a while since Felix and Felicia connected. She's been coming to spend some weekends with him, albeit always in guest room. He's biding time, assuaged by adage "Patient man ride donkey." When she spends weekends, he often takes her to church. Ever resisting invitation to come inside. She breaks silence and they open up a gab. *"You know, is one year we know each other? I never did realize it till last night was thinking. Maybe that's what people mean when they say "Time flies when you having fun."* Felix glanced at her with a wry smile, thinks.*"You having fun, not me. It's time you spread the joy."* Tittered when he replaced "joy" with body limbs. Dared not verbalize thoughts, she asks. *"You never realize it?"* **"Not really, is like you said "Time flies when you having fun."**

Reaching home, Felicia got uncharacteristically industrious in domestic sense. Cleaned his bathroom, whereas usually. She now and then, cleaned that in guest room. Next she changed his bed linen and towels. Felix asked. **"Working up a sweat? There are other ways to burn energy."** She leered at him. *"Don't spoil the moment, it's start of good times."* He clammed up, went his way. Dusk came, she showered in his bathroom. Firmly closed doors, saying. *"You're not allowed to peek at your present until day begins. When I get out, we going have a talk."* He went in to brush, began humming old Terror Fabulous, Nadine Sutherland reggae. "Action-Not a bag a mouth." Quite certain that was outside her repertoire, he came back in the room and she asked. *"Is what have you chirping so, like Canary find feeding tree and calling other birds?"* He let it pass without comment. Feeling peckish he chomped raw cashews and grapes as she enjoyed strawberries. Seems each was waiting on other to make a move and what do you know, both fell asleep. His phones were on silent, hers rang loud and jarring. She got up and headed out as she began talking. He turned TV on and caught second episode "Two and a half Men," then two "Seinfeld" episodes. Switched channel 10-2 for second half of "Perry Mason," then "Twilight Zone." "Alfred Hitchcock Presents" was halfway through, when he realized. She had stopped talking. Walked quietly to and saw her prostrate with phone under her chest, trailing a line back to a wall receptacle. Went back to bed thinking. *"What's with this daughter who calls whenever, and mom just answers and goes off gabbing? If we were getting a groove on, would I have to endure interruptions? This is bulls."* But he slept on it. Greeted Felicia with a smile, when she walked downstairs mid morning and said. *"Middle next week. I am asking for a ride to FLL, to pick up my daughter. They're coming for a few days, to recharge mind* *and body."* It's an early flight. Felix is at cellphone lot, where Felicia scans arrival screen. He watches never ending freight trains with assortment of cars. Go back and forth until three engines come in sight. Two are smoking so he reasons, other must be spare, being piggy backed to….Gazes skyward and is surprised at amount of "Spirit" planes taking off to places far. They soar three in a row, then three other airlines take off and here comes Spirit again, one two three four. Wow, this is the day when Spirit takes flight and soars. He smiles at his inane attempt at philosophizing and notices. Felicia wears a frown. Nearly an hour after flight's arrival. Her phone rings and she says, among other things. *"I don't know why he didn't answer."* Then says to Felix. *"Rochelle calling you hours ago and you didn't answer. Why?"* He, taken aback remains silent, then tells her. **"Why and how could Rochelle be calling me? I didn't give her my number. I don't know hers, we have never…"** Felicia snaps. *"Never mind all that, she's been out there for God knows how long and Julian is driving her up a wall."* In an afterthought, she went on. *"I give her your number, because you driving. Anything wrong with that?"* He explained. **"First of all, my phone is still on "silent" from last night. Even if it wasn't. I never, ever answer unrecognized numbers, period."** She resettles her rump, does neck head realign. Sign of silent discontent. Both women stare at Felix and luggage with quick head jerks. He says. **"Don't look at me. I have compromised range of motion and aches when strained."** He was silently pissed at phone presumption debacle.Young woman has to be early twenties. Child about three years old. Math seems off, when merged with grandma at seventy-two. A lively debate gets underway when Felix asks. **"Where is child's seat? Driver is One who gets ticketed."** Rochelle says, at four years old. Julian doesn't need child seat, so long as he's securely strapped in back seat. Felix has doubts but rests his case. Instant Julian sits, he reaches for buttons and switches. Felix says. **"Give him toys to distract him, please. Switches are not joysticks and they're all disabled from driver's side."** Rochelle restrains his arms and he begins to kick. Felix never liked boys. This one was shaping up to be a Phantom Imp. A Punchinella, Felicia switches seats with Rochelle. So she can take charge of Julian, who is now screaming, feet kicking and arms flailing. Felix says. **"Will someone give him a touch of brandy, white rum or something stout in the mouth. I can't drive like this."** Rochelle finds it funny, Felicia explodes. *"What kind of nonsense is that?! Give the child, brandy or rum. To do what? He's been awake from early morning and is just being cranky. My God, rum or brandy. It's a good thing you weren't in the village that was raising children. They would all turn drunkards. Rum or brandy?"* Rochelle reached across to mollify Felix. Patted bared knee beyond his Dungaree cargo pant. *"I am very sorry, just remembered we weren't even introduced. I am Rochelle DeLeon."* Felix introduced himself, adding. **"Can't honestly say "it's a pleasure" but maybe the tide will turn and seas will be calmer."** She withdrew her hand and turned face forward in her seat. What did she expect? There was a fight going on in back. Felicia had long ago said to Rochelle. *"Put these (eyeglasses) in your pocketbook for me, this child is a handful and then some. Felix, we are going to your place."* Time for another debate, as he replies. **"Why? My place is not set up for children. There's heavy art pieces on slender pedestals that can tumble on. Or dragged down by an active child, crushing limbs. That earthenware jar with dried arrangement atop the Torchiere is about thirty pounds. There's stairs to tumble down. I don't carry insurance for that sort of thing."** Felicia told him. *"Stop it,*

Rochelle just wants to see your house. She's heard so much about it, be a sport. Stop somewhere so we get something to eat." Rochelle asks. *"Any U-Hops nearby?"* Felix asked the server, as she passed out menus. **"Got any of them really fat sausages. You know, kind that can really fill a mouth?"** He gave away his plot by laughing out loud. Felicia told the server. *"Pay him no mind, he hasn't had his medication."* Rochelle is looking at both, trying to get gist of things and Felix laughs again, getting visual of huge sausage in Julian's mouth. Queried, he tells server. **"Oh, nothing for me. I get filled just watching other people eat."** Checked himself from saying. *"You should too."* Her being obese in a bad way. As she walked away he thought. *"Maybe I shoulda riled her, she couldn't spit on my food."* Julian is now all grins as he pinches and tosses food at Rochelle and Felicia. You think a four year old understands certain things? Well, watch this. First morsel he tosses at Felix, he tells the child. **"Don't you dare do that. I've got brandy in my back pocket."** Another morsel never came his way. Felicia said. *"Felix, get the bill squared away whilst we go to the ladies room."* He says. **"What you talking bout? I didn't eat."** Rochelle said. *"I've got money, I'll pay."* Felicia declared. *"Nonsense, put your money away. Do not make a scene Felix, meet us at the car."* He signals Baby Fats, she walks over and says. *"I am sorry you didn't see anything on our menu that you like."* He tells her. **"I am ackee and saltfish person, it's not your fault."** Thinking she would be at sea with ackee and saltfish, she promptly told him. *"I could make that for you, but not here."* Followed by eye dance that wowed him. He laughed and added tip to tab. Which when she saw, said an emphatic *"Thank you very much, sir."* Felicia asked, why he kept windows rolled up, umpteenth time. Felix told her for equal times. **"I hate inhaling stripped rubber particles, asphalt**

and exhaust fumes." Rochelle is second behind Felix entering the house. Exhales long, contented, relieved sigh as cool air swathes her face and body, saying. *"This feels so good, I could undress and go to sleep right here."* Felicia scolds. *"Stop it, don't let Felix paint a picture. His creativity has limitless boundaries."* He keeps quiet as he's thinking her reason coming his house, instead….Rochelle is admiring paintings and art objects until.*"Oh my! That's mannequin. Isn't it? So vividly descriptive, it borders hideous. Breasts are life like and just look at the vagina, it's as if you could stick a finge…Why don't you put a shroud over it? You know, a kind of light fabric drape that allows the image to come through without finer crevices and….Ooh! My God. This is not right for a child to see. It's bound to arouse his curiosity in negative way. Come Julian, let's go around here."* Felix grins smugly, says. **"That's why it's important, he shoulda look where he's going on way out. Now, it's gonna scare crap outta him."** Felicia adds two bits. *"Felix has it for inspiration, before, during and after."* Felix is quietly musing the situation. Knows sometime soon the real he is going to debut. These people forget they're in his house as guests. Felicia tells Rochelle to bring suitcase in through the garage. Satisfied there's enough detergent, she suggests to Felix. *"Why not take them down to Park for a bit of sea breeze, while I get things shipshape here."* Felix has taken to browbeating that child, every time their eyes meet. Child reacts by averting stare and cringing. Felix tells himself. *"I've got you under my skin."* Rochelle corrals frisky, agitated Julian between thighs and bollard of coin operated viewer. Which gives panoramic views of sea and nearby vistas. Boy Julian now restrained, looks lethargic. Sagging at knees and soon falls asleep across Rochelle's lap. Felix is anxious to, does ask. **"How old are you? I hope you don't consider me**

forward, or. But you and your mother seems....." She replies. *"That's okay, but Aunt Phil isn't my mother, she's more my stepmother. My mother, Rachel, is from Honduras and lived with my father. Aunt Phil's husband, when he used to come and stay. My mom says, she never knew he was married in Jamaica. Because he always told her he would marry her, when his papers came through. Anyhow, she found out he was working and took him to court for child support. It was then she found out he had a home here. Few years back, my mom, brother and me were going home to Honduras for Christmas. You remember the mosquito disease going round? Anyhow, they say I couldn't travel. Mom didn't want to lose the airfare so she left me with her brother. Before the plane even took off he began making moves on me, and I got the biggest surprise of my life. Mom gave me Aunt Phil's name and phone number to call. Ask her to let me stay with them until she comes back, because her husband is our father. She said, yes. Was nice to me, my father wasn't. Hardly spoke ten words a month to me and he was rarely home. I don't really know. Get the feeling they weren't married, but what did I care. I finished school, began studying for associate degree in radiography. Hoping to go on to my bachelors. I was going to school and doing clinical sessions at the hospital. It was there I met this young intern. We got it going and someone yelled "Bingo" Julian."* Two things happened, impacting my life for life, emotionally and physically. Things have never been right since. Mom kept saying, she would be back month end, but each month came and went. I asked her which month and year she really planned coming back. It was then she said, there was something amiss. Embassy in Tegucigalpa would not give her a visa. Now, it was up to me to sponsor her, but I still don't have resources to do that. So she is there with *my brother and I am here. When he gets older he can come, because just like me, he was born here. Leandro finished internship and went to work at….. at a big military Fort in Virginia. He said he would be there for three years. We planned getting married, so Julian can have parents in a family setting. Overnight, he says he's being sent overseas and he will contact me when he's settled. After months not hearing from him. I contacted the place, even went there with Julian seeking information. They claimed, because I am not his wife they can't give me information. I didn't even get to know anything about his parents or where they are. It's just me, myself and Julian struggling to stay afloat. So Aunt Phil says to come down. She will look after him and I can see what I can get with my half qualifications. I'm too young to be having life so freakin hard."* She pauses and stares off at the gently roiling sea in silence. Notice? She hasn't divulged her age. Figures she talked the question out of existence. Felix is One who will smile and resurrect it. But decides, give her a pass. She's got stripes upon her shoulders and chains around her feet. When she breaks silence, it is with a big grin as she asks. *"So seriously now. You and Aunt Phil play in and out the window?"* Giving her taste of her medicine he begins. **"You know, first time I saw your Aunt Phil was at Akbar's Grocery and…"** Went on to tell her about Akbar, fish and other things. How horse died and cow got fat, although others say it's crow got fat and in the end. She didn't know if he played with Aunt Phil and he didn't know how old she was. Let each be content in own ignorance. Getting back, Felicia said it was dinner time. Rummaging refrigerator, freezer and pantry. Damn her. Felix said, he has stuff cooked, to warm up for himself. Why doesn't Felicia wait till she gets home and prepare their meals. She said to him. *"Come here, because you not talking anything that* *makes sense."* That got him more than a bit itched, but listened as Felicia led him upstairs and went on. *"See, I push the bed against the wall so Julian won't drop off. Him and Rochelle will use the guest room, and we get comfortable in your room."* He stared at her hard in silence, she went on. *"It will only be for a….Why you shaking you head like bobble head? You suppose to shake up and down, not sideways like you having St. Vitus dance."* "Felicia!" Felix almost yelled. Got her attention and said. **"You carrying on as if I am invisible. Not asking, only telling. Gave my phone number to Rochelle without asking whether or not I minded. Now you're re-arranging my house, to make your people comfortable. Ussipu ejerpleh not going make it right. So start folding them laundry. Or throw them in suitcases and let's get out of here. Ask yourself if you would put up with someone walking in and taking over your existence, the way you're trying to take over mine. Not going work Felicia."** She asked. *"Well, I don't know what you saying when you go into unknown tongues. But I suspect it's not something pleasant. Since it's almost six, they could stay the night. Tonight we talk about it and see what we can come up with. What you say?"* Felix sensed the party was over, but hungered for pleasure of even one slow waltz. Told Felicia. **"I'll carry y'all to your place, you show Rochelle what's where. Then you come back with me and we talk it over without interruptions after….."** She did a quick eye squint question, he added. **"After we drop asleep and wake up."** She stares him long and hard then asks. *"Why me would carry me daughter and grandchild to my house. Leave them in a strange place. Then come back to your house for talk and drop asleep. Me look like me born big?"* Done being nice, he says. **"Well you know what old time people say. If you want good you nose have to run."** She replies. *"Massa,* *what you talking bout, is nose bleed. Thanks for the drive home. If you still feel up to it."* Comes hell or high water, Felix was not going to capitulate on this. He figured he could taste of the fruit and talk Felicia in circles till her head spun. In the short and long run. Neither had their way and friends became acquaintances and then "Use to knows." Months after, Felix stops by Akbar, who greets and begins. *"You not come my shop, but the lady, she comes. I ask where you at, she says you not nice man. Very uncute, talk strange cuss words and no manners as you should. I tell her, I tell you to marry she and make she happy but she not…."* Felix asks Akbar. **"What she say uncute. How she means uncute? Oh, you mean uncouth? Come on Akbar, get it right. Anyhow that ship done sail."** **Ussipu ejerpleh?…..**Pussy pleasure

Gratuity and Service charge-37

Are reasons, or I should say, one of. Why I no longer dine out. Others have to do with my retiring, losing access to overtime trough at job site and dearth of funds for occasional splurge. Most compelling is uncertainty of food source and quality of. I think it fair to assume that restaurateurs, faced with rising overheads and pursuit of profit. Will of necessity, source food and ingredients from cheapest purveyors. That's where 'farm raised' takes place of 'wild caught' seafood. Recent eye opener revealed, 'certified organic' can be so dubious, as to be 'lost in translation.' Let me then begin by exploring theme of this chapter. Gratuity, should not be imposed, but earned and amount or absence of, left to discretion of Servee. Some places show scale of percentages and dollar amount, for customer to decide. There's also a 'No Tip' button, and I do declare, that should be industry standard. Forced tipping, leaves no reason for server to excel at his trade. We train animals by rewarding obedience to commands. It's an incentive to try harder and attain positivism, instead of indulging lacklustre. In my eat out heyday, venue of choice was "Tony Roma's." Food was top par, service was excellent. Servers were all young people, earning their way to greater life careers. Service began when you left your vehicle and ended when you walked out the door. They did impromptu entertainment for your celebrated occasion. A Chef came to our table once, asked if the meal was done to our satisfaction. Now, here's the funny part of that. Telling my experience at workplace, co-worker snickered and said. ***"Chef" was, busboy under five gallon hat, kept on a nail for PR skit."*** Contrived or not, customer care creates invaluable goodwill for any business. You recall Al and Francine went dining, and the lad fawned on her while being indifferent to Al. Forgot he would want a drink, even as he rattled off choices to Francine. Well, Al mentally declared. *"There goes your tip, buddy."* What's with some men? They get into a pandering frenzy, soon as they're close to a woman. They don't realize, women are not impressed by. Women are impressed by their cute babies and later, grandchildren. Did you see this video doing rounds on every social media channel? It's funny as melting ice cream. Captioned on UTube "Lion bites off man's finger." Victim is zoo worker and he's amid female visitors. He's One who gives details about the animal, but decides to entertain the women. Begins reaching through the wire, petting Leo who responds roaring and snarling. Leo gets hold of a finger and tries yanking hand and arm into his mouth. So much so, he braces two paws and gets leverage to haul the man in. Man also gets feet against cage wall, bracing back from Leo's pull. All this time, women are filming and recording man, who keeps repeating. ***"Fu..! Fu..! Fu..!*** Having chomped the finger, Leo lost hold and man tumbles to ground on his behine. Leo stood firm and kept roaring. Says lots for four wheel traction, against two wheels or feet. Man didn't have a leg to stand on, whilst Leo had all four. Now, we know he can't tend that lion ever again. Having sampled and savoured a bit of him, that's stored in Leo's sensual memory or what it's called. First chance Leo gets, he's gonna tear into that fella and roar a burp. Note well, not any of women filming, paused to help him or empathize. They were focussed getting a Kodak moment, highlighting their Jamaica zoo visit. Hear them laugh when they replay and retell. Wouldn't put it beyond them to castigate him as an idiot. Everyone else who has seen the video, does. Having deviated from our theme, let's pick up on our thread anew. Friends visiting from Curacao, were after-the-fact, comparing eatery tab. Asked me to explain, gratuity plus service charge amounts. We figured,'gratuity' was what we knew as 'cover charge.' After numerous phone calls and extended holds, came response. Gratuity is staff incentive, service charge goes to help defray overheads such as health insurance and training. Our existence is similar to last man in the trench. It begins further up and is told to next, ending. "Pass it on." We have no One to pass it to. We exist under strenuous burden until done in. What a travesty. Ask patronage of your shop then gouge to recover 'cost of doing business.' That's what profit was meant for, but as Babu asked. ***I is got gun you head, boy?*** Easter tradition, we do fried fish, bun and cheese. Fifteen Snappers at $30 each were ordered, paid for and given to me by proprietor, whose wide grin mirrored pleased as punch satisfaction with sale. Each fish was average 24 ounces at $5.99 a lb retail. He buys much cheaper, do the math and get estimate of his profit. He could, should have used fresh oil to fry, instead of re-used oil. First telltale sign was, dark flesh inside instead of white. Fish tasted like washing soap. Left tar-like stain presence on the tongue. We bought Snappers at Sedano's, tipped el vendedor de pescado to clean them pot ready. He expressed, "Mucho gracias Papito." Fried to golden tan, Easter was saved. Business owners should stop and recognize, in pursuing profits. They also should make effort to nurture and ensure customer's satisfaction. That is cheap, priceless advertisement. This then is one basic aspect of quality uncertainty. Finding cheap, low grade foods to stock the cauldron and dish out at exorbitant price to unsuspecting customers. Adding insult to injury, are service charge and gratuity. What a scam. So, you ask what is the. 'Feeding trough, epitomizes barnyard, animals fodder layout. Having it's genesis at unionized work sites, references access to extra hours worked at time and half or double rate. Regulated by seniority of tenure, rather than of age. Although, age can be a factor. Let's say, worker joins company out of school at age nineteen or twenty. With attrition, he will at some point be most senior employee in the company. Applicable only to his work location. Before attaining top cat status, he will be underdog to them that hired on before him. If he goes to work site, manned by later enrollees, he's king of the heap there. Low seniority of tenure is two edged sword, putting those so classified at double disadvantage. Having higher seniority gets One, first access to trough. Also gives option, refusing what's served. Forcing low seniority with no option, but to take and get the job done. There's shift no One wants to work and will refuse, until it comes down to low man who has no choice. Nobody wants to work that area? Holiday eve? Cold rainy night? Who's going to make best of situation? Low man, of course. Who else? Which brings focus on another scourge. That of high gas prices and efforts to tame upward spiral. Tapping into emergency reserves, tax holidays at federal and state levels. None of this is filtering down to motorists. It's all going to enrich the wealthy. Whilst some boards show price fluctuations, others only move up. Uppers are stuck at \$4.89, one added "cash price." Board on SW 128 street, displays \$4.67. They'll get my support, in and out of good or bad times. One station's board "broke down" after customer asked. How come their prices never trend down, similar to other retailers. When good deed goes up against greed, we know who will be winner and loser. It is said, living is a matter of give and take. We know there are them that taketh and durst not giveth. Purveyors of greed and gluttony, other deadly sins are in their armoury. Woe is we.

Epilogue

Did you know? Is it happening to you, or anyone you know? Like all things of like nature, people wants to avoid talking about it. Why? Because they shiver at consequences. We, some of us have a mindset which dictates. If we close our eyes and mind to a problem. No matter how dire, it will go away. In reality it never does. Covid is stark testament to that, after 1,000,850 deaths and counting. We now have and are ever developing new and more potent vaccines to treat and hopefully eradicate this scourge from our environment. Until next plague comes knocking at our doors. Covid and it's trauma are very much on everyone's discussion board. One most shunned subject takes origin from our 2020 general election and economic burden, dumped on those who were already marginally existing. Some ascribe blame solely on present administration, while some say this was crafted by leaders prior to present coming to office. Others say the war in Ukraine is to blame, but all these assumed factors to our misery and stagnating quality of life. Are remote from our ability to effectively confront and demand salvation from. So, where do we turn? You ask. I'll tell you where. On friends and neighbours, that's where. Recently, I was out and saw gas being sold twenty four cents below average price. Texted my friend, stone's throw from source with the good news, I thought. He texted back. ***"Guess you're f...in' proud of what you voted for."*** I have always heeded my late father's advice, and never discuss politics or religion with anyone, not even family. My neighbour's position is. Republicans and former president, can and have done nothing wrong ever. Democrats and president in office, are bane of our existence in every way imaginable. They expound at length, often in fury. Then ask my opinion, to which I smile and say. "I'm listening to you." Ours is a democracy, but I do fear, not for long. When neighbours collectively, begin seeing others whom they suspect of voting a particular party. As origin of their ills, be it high gas, food or prices in general. Hatred is being festered, and let me say this. I have lived through such situations, and tremble at thought of what that would be like in these United States of America. Our country is slowly being caught in an aura of hatred and intolerance for others who are not like us. Use to be colour, race or religion. Now expanded to include dissimilar or suspected thought process. Those with power to effect changes, blaze new paths in voter disenfranchisement. Often encouraged by warped legal system that acquiesces in this sorry state of affairs. Failure of democracy in our country, will be followed by that of the empire. There are those who sees writing on the wall, or as the song is titled. "Bad moon rising." Instead of collectively adhering to procedures and tenets of sane deliberations, archived over the years. Solution on the table is. Enact laws to stifle dissent, never mind these could be ultra vires the constitution. Strength in numbers is deciding factor, consensus has been executed. Next, build newer, larger prisons to house the marginally dispossessed. e.

Arm others with weapons of devastating firepower, and observe the conflagration from our citadels. January 6th, 2020 demonstrates, these are not bulwarks or bastions as originally assumed or intended. Question is. Can this change? Answer is found in adage which reads. Where there's a will, there's a way. Once "will" is found, "way" comes natural as rain. We know how humans react in an existence of helplessness. Fear sets in and disposes fortitude to defend. Throngs with helmets and sabres will be quickly embraced. Hoping they bring mercy and relief to our bane. Alas, expect the unexpected.

F o o t n o t e s:

Diction of dialogue depicts quoted speaker's verbatim comfort vocabulary. Folks, rural and urban between parishes, have diverse parochial English adaptations. This quite often excludes proper parsing and grammar usage. Some words and commentary are dialect, slang, adage and patois in standard usage of times past. Still maintained in perpetuity by tradition. Editing to scholastic standards would emasculate and divest events of inherent, natural harmonic syntax. In other words, grammatical imperfections lends authenticity to the story. Author welcomes comments. Please see contact information. Publishers joins the author expressing sincere appreciation for your purchase of this book and trusts you found literary satisfaction. Would introduce you to other books by Colleen G. Lowe. These are available at Amazon/Kindle or. www.theglenwoodcollection.com. Where there are special pricing that includes shipping to US zip codes as well as excerpts and full chapters of selected books.

Map to our website. www.theglenwoodcollection.com
Click: Introduction Lucky Bastard. Navigate pages and
themes of choice. View all books on sale. Click "Island Art
Sale" to view art by thumbnail or collectively.

"People At Play" and "Everyday People at work and Play."
Are short story, fiction novels. First and second in a series
of three that observes behaviours and life pursuits of
people within a plethora of adjectives to describe and or
put in a perspective that serves human fundamentals..

"The Lucky Bastard" is a non-fiction autobiographical trilogy

on "Life and Times of Lenny Kingston"

"Everyday People at Work & Play" Fourth edition. Revised
and printed July 2022.

Coming in Autumn "People Working thru Life's Challenges"

Colleen G. Lowe.

The End

Colleen G. Lowe

www.ingramcontent.com/pod-product-compliance
Lightning Source LLC
Chambersburg PA
CBHW072123020726
47501CB00003B/948